since her teens. She is very
, to an understanding husband who
has learned to cook since she started to write! Her five children keep her on her toes. She has a very large dog, which knocks everything over, a very small terrier, which barks a lot, and two cats. When time allows, Lynne is a keen gardener.

Joss Wood loves books and travelling—especially to the wild places of Southern Africa and, well…anywhere! She's a wife, mum to two teenagers, and slave to two cats. After a career in local economic development she now writes full-time. Joss is a member of Romance Writers of America and Romance Writers of South Africa.

Also by Lynne Graham

The Ring the Spaniard Gave Her
The Greek's Convenient Cinderella

Heirs for Royal Brothers miniseries

Cinderella's Desert Baby Bombshell
Her Best Kept Royal Secret

The Stefanos Legacy miniseries

Promoted to the Greek's Wife

Also by Joss Wood

The Rules of Their Red-Hot Reunion

South Africa's Scandalous Billionaires miniseries

How to Undo the Proud Billionaire
How to Win the Wild Billionaire
How to Tempt the Off-Limits Billionaire

Other books by Joss Wood
for Mills & Boon Desire

Lost and Found Heir
The Secret Heir Returns

THE HEIRS HIS HOUSEKEEPER CARRIED

LYNNE GRAHAM

THE BILLIONAIRE'S ONE-NIGHT BABY

JOSS WOOD

MILLS & BOON

First Published in Great Britain 2022
by Mills & Boon, an imprint of HarperCollins*Publishers* Ltd,
1 London Bridge Street, London, SE1 9GF

www.harpercollins.co.uk

HarperCollins*Publishers*
1st Floor, Watermarque Building,
Ringsend Road, Dublin 4, Ireland

ISBN: 978-0-263-30083-3

05/22

MIX
Paper from
responsible sources
FSC™ C007454

This book is produced from independently certified FSC™ paper to ensure responsible forest management.
For more information visit www.harpercollins.co.uk/green.

Printed and Bound in Spain using 100% Renewable Electricity at CPI Black Print, Barcelona

THE HEIRS HIS HOUSEKEEPER CARRIED

LYNNE GRAHAM

MILLS & BOON

CHAPTER ONE

'THANK YOU...IT'S amazing,' Zoe purred with satisfaction, having chosen the flashiest bracelet on offer and holding it up to catch the sunshine filtering through the limo window. 'I *so* deserve this. Diamonds truly are the perfect foil for my beauty.'

A famous supermodel, Zoe had locked her avid and triumphant gaze to the sparkling gems as if she had won the lottery. As Gio had yet to see Zoe show that much appreciation for anything else, that glimpse of entitled avarice and unashamed vanity made his shapely mouth compress. He was glad that their affair was over, the diamonds his final gift.

Greed was a turn-off, a major turn-off for Giovanni Zanetti, and yet the richer he became, the more cunning rapacity he recognised in the women he met. For the very first time in his life he wondered what it would be like to be Mr Nobody from Nowhere, rather than the billionaire owner of a technology empire with a much-envied lifestyle. Until that moment he hadn't known that he could even picture such a fanciful and absurd possibility because he had not appreciated that he had that much imagination. Would women even want him without the diamonds and all the other extravagant trappings he provided? It was an interesting question.

Gio was, first and foremost, a self-made man, who had grown up in dire poverty and deprivation with a violent drug-dealing father and a beaten, uninterested mother. His meteoric rise to phenomenal success had been marred by only one mistake: at twenty-one: he had been conned into marriage by a gold-digger. Aside of that damaging error of judgement, he had, eight years later, already attained almost everything he wanted in life.

Only one major goal had so far eluded him, he acknowledged wryly, and that was the acquisition of his late mother's former familial home, the Castello Zanetti. When his unfortunate *mamma* had shamed her snobbish family by falling pregnant by the local bad boy, they had thrown her out and sold up, moving away to escape the humiliation of the resulting scandal. Although his mama had been a decidedly imperfect parent, alongside his papa, something visceral in Gio had always longed for a connection that rooted him in another world. And the world of history and ancestors that his mother had run from, a family tree that he could proudly claim a connection to as opposed to the shameful one he had been born into with his parents, had enormous pull with him. That house, that family property, meant a great deal to him.

As Zoe trailed a sensual hand of promise down over Gio's lean muscular thigh, he tensed with distaste at the inevitable suspicion that his generous gift had *bought* her sexual enthusiasm. Revulsion gripped him. Shifting away, he was relieved that their association was at an end. Exposed as the vain and mercenary woman she was, the model had lost much of her appeal.

At the same time, Gio was, however, uneasily accustomed to the keen interest that his spectacular good looks invariably invoked. He had not a shred of vanity on that score. Indeed, he actively despised the familiar image that met him in the mirror because it reminded him sickeningly of his brutal, toxic father. The lustrous black hair, the hard chiselled jawline, the classic nose and exotic high cheekbones teamed with unusual ice-blue eyes turned the heads of both men and women in the street.

That same night at a Manhattan party, when he was literally ringed by a circle of beautiful women vying for his attention, Fabian, one of Gio's friends, rolled his eyes to say, 'You have got it made. Any woman you want whenever, however. I don't think you appreciate just how lucky you are.'

'If I weren't rich and single, I wouldn't be half as appealing,' Gio retorted with innate cynicism and an acute sense of boredom.

He thought instead of the magnificent freedom of walking the beach at his rarely used house in Norfolk, England, of the cool refreshing breeze and the isolation there. He needed a break. That awareness in mind, he checked the time in the UK before calling the caretaker to instruct her to set the house up for his arrival the coming weekend.

In an anxious tone of apology and audible dismay at his unforeseen request, Miss Jenkins confided that she had broken her ankle and would need to find someone else to ensure that the coastal mansion was prepared for his occupation. Apologising for the short notice he was giving her, Gio voiced his sympathy and immediately offered a substantial amount of extra cash that the older woman could use to persuade someone trustworthy to take on that necessary task and get it done in time.

As always, he mowed down any hint of opposition like a steamroller that simply refused to be redirected. Life since adulthood had made Gio highly unfamiliar with disappointment, and even a disturbing hint of that possibility was sufficient to make him more determined than ever to leave the business world and designing women behind for a few days and enjoy that energising breeze…

Leah tempted Spike out from behind the chair. 'Come on…the vet's gone home. You don't need to be nervous because you've had all your treatment now,' she murmured soothingly.

A scruffy three-legged Yorkshire terrier with an incongruous purple bow on top of his tufty head crept into view. He was exceedingly small and very scared. He was terrified of all men, even of the kindly vet, but that didn't stop him from trying to sneak up behind unsuspecting males and nip them in the back of the leg. Luckily for his victims, Spike had few remaining teeth after years of neglect. As he surged into her arms, she lifted him to pet him while she absently listened to the conversation her former foster mother, Sally, was having on the phone with her sister, Pam Jenkins.

'Absolutely *silly* money,' Sally was proclaiming, her round good-natured face below her halo of grey curls full of incredulity. 'Clearly, the man has more money than sense, but Leah can do it, of course she can. A bit of shopping, a bit of cleaning, a few beds to make up…

not a problem, Pam. Will you *please* stop worrying about it now? Of course, the man's not going to sack you just because you broke your ankle!'

Sally came off the phone. 'The Gazillionaire is coming...'

Leah grinned at the announcement, sitting back on her heels, a cascade of glossy dark ringlets framing her oval face and then tumbling back across her shoulders, her big brown eyes dancing. 'So I gathered...and I assume that I'm going to carry out Pam's usual work for her—'

'Yes, she's got a shopping list that he forwarded to her, says it's the usual fancy stuff you'll have to go into town to find. My goodness, do you realise what this means?' Sally carolled in excitement. 'You will actually get to *see* inside Shore House!'

The buyer of the imposing building had been christened 'the Gazillionaire' once word of the wildly expensive restoration and improvements he had ordered had filtered out into the nearby village. Curiosity had raged about the new owner and the house but, over the three years that the Italian had owned it, he had made very infrequent visits and neither he nor any of his guests had ever ventured into the village and even Pam had never actually met him in the flesh. Apparently, he travelled with his own personal household staff. A landscape firm in Norwich looked after the grounds and the indoor pool. Sally's sister, Pam, was the caretaker and cleaner, but she had never dared to bring anyone with her on her visits because the house was full of cameras and she didn't want to break the rules and lose her job. For the same reason she had been afraid to take any photos of the property.

'I'll go and get changed,' Leah proffered, because she was still in her pyjamas. 'When do you need me to go over there?'

'Asap. So, Pam's lawn and *her* shopping will wait,' Sally told her because, with Sally busy running her small animal shelter, Leah had been looking after Pam while she recuperated from her fall. The two older women were close but, even though there was space in Sally's old farmhouse, her younger, single sister had preferred to remain in her village home, pointing out cheerfully that she and Sally squabbled when they got under each other's feet.

'My goodness, I just said that you would take care of the Gazillionaire's house for Pam without even first asking you if you would!' Sally suddenly exclaimed in belated apology. 'What on earth was I thinking of? With your fancy degree, cleaning would be far too much of a comedown for you—'

'Of course, I'll do it...aren't I living here free of charge? And don't talk nonsense. I'll do virtually anything to earn cash right now,' Leah admitted without embarrassment. 'I hope it *is* absolutely silly money I'll be paid too. You could do with some of it for the shelter. That last vet bill was steep.'

'I don't want the money!' Sally informed her sternly. 'Look at all the help you've given Pam. You've kept her garden, taken her to the hospital and done her shopping when I've been too busy—'

'You took me in when I had nowhere else to go and I'm grateful, so let's not hear any more about cleaning being beneath me,' Leah urged, thinking that cleaning was no more humble than stacking shelves in the village supermarket, which she had also done. Unfortunately, there were few local employment opportunities. Her business degree was no more use where she lived than it had proven to be in London where, only two years earlier, she had embarked on what she initially hoped would eventually become a successful career. As her mind threatened to linger on everything that had gone so terribly wrong in the city, she buried the thought, because there was nothing attractive about bitterness.

Leah had learned very young that life could contain many bad moments, a great deal of loss and frequent disappointments, but she had taught herself not to dwell too long on the negatives. There had been Oliver, who had broken her heart, but before he came along she had lost her father, then her mother and her two siblings, and whenever she thought about her missing family a terrible wave of sadness would threaten to engulf her. Her mother was dead, and it was hard to care about whether or not her father was dead or alive because he had chosen his *other* family over his family with her mother, making it clear that she and her siblings were second best.

Eventually, however, Leah hoped to trace and get back in touch with her twin brother and younger sister, but that was likely to take both patience and money. She had seen her brother several times over the years, but their relationship had been strained by his drug addiction and his willingness to steal from her to fund it.

Sadly, she had left London with nothing but credit-card debt, which she had only recently contrived to pay off. Before she could move out of Sally's home and return to urban living, she would have to have a nest egg saved up to cover accommodation and at least the chance of a proper job.

An hour later, Leah was scouring the supermarket and eventually a delicatessen for the more unusual ingredients on the shopping list. Wakame seaweed and Thai basil were not easily found in a small rural town. Equivalents or total substitutes purchased with the credit card Pam had entrusted her with, Leah drove to Shore House.

A long winding driveway led to the grey stone house, bookmarked with a substantial round tower at either end and embellished with a forest of tall elaborate chimneys and equally tall mullioned windows. Built in the style of Victorian Gothic, it was a white elephant of a house, which had been fortunate to find a buyer. Its biggest selling point, though, was its multiple views of the sea and the long sandy shoreline that lay only yards below the edge of the gardens. Parking in the cobbled courtyard and gathering up the shopping, Leah let herself in the back door, punched in the code for the alarm and headed inside.

Cameras high up the walls silently swivelled as she moved, making her inordinately conscious of their presence. She put the shopping away first in the vast kitchen with its huge central island, granite worktops and top-of-the-range fancy stove. Pam had written down explicit instructions about where to find everything she needed. Armed with the comprehensive cleaning box stored in the pantry, Leah went upstairs to start her work. The foyer was a breathtaking space, the very centre of which was the split staircase, which went up one flight and then divided imposingly into two. All that ornately carved wood would be a challenge to dust, she acknowledged ruefully as Spike scampered at her heels.

According to Pam, the six principal bedrooms were

routinely prepared for guests and that was where Leah began, dusting and vacuuming as she went before shaking out the expensive linens and deftly making up the beds. The property might be Victorian, but the furnishings were light and contemporary, using the elaborate carving and fancy plasterwork as an ornamental backdrop, rather than allowing it to dictate the whole mood. Surprisingly, that decorative approach worked, and Leah was eager to explore the whole house. Unfortunately, she knew she would have her work cut out just to cover the basics of cleaning such a large property and she didn't have time to dawdle. Despite regular sips from her water bottle, Leah got steadily warmer even though she was only wearing denim shorts and a tee.

Having completed the bedrooms and ignored the dusty staircase altogether because it looked as though it would take hours, Leah explored the ground floor, choosing where she would concentrate her energies next while reminding herself that she would be able to return to clean again the next day. Hopefully nobody would arrive before the following evening, or her goose would be cooked because no way was she likely to get around the whole house before then! It was simply too big.

Closing the door firmly on a library that was a tremendous temptation to a book lover, Leah embarked on the vast sitting room instead, relieved that the house was gloriously empty of the kind of knick-knacks that her foster mother and her sister adored. There was art on the walls and occasional elegant sculptures but no clutter to lift or work around.

She was contemplating cleaning the kitchen when she saw a door at the end of the ground-floor corridor that had previously escaped her notice. She sighed, already tired and hot as she was and wincing at the awareness that she would be returning at the crack of dawn the next morning to complete the cleaning. She had been cutting corners, she conceded guiltily, the undusted stairs looming like a monster in the back of her brain as she cleaned the cloakroom. And what about the dining room, the smaller sitting room, the library and the room with the giant snooker table?

Before she tackled the kitchen she decided to explore through that closed door, lest it was concealing a whole host of other rooms that would require her attention. The door took her into a tiled hall and she crossed it to move through glass double doors into the indoor pool area, which she had totally forgotten about. Off to one side and entirely separate there was a gym, and on the other side there was a very fancy Victorian circular conservatory area packed with towering tropical plants kept healthy by a temperature-controlled environment.

In front of her, however, stealing centre stage, was a curved, arched and tiled wall that housed an extraordinary lotus-shaped fountain fanning water down into the swimming pool. High above, an ornate cupola and a ring of gorgeous stained-glass windows cast a rainbow of light down onto the shimmering surface. Mermaids were entwined in a huge, tiled panel above the fountain. It was very Victorian and very exotic, and it had been so beautifully restored that it might have been built the day before. Presumably the feature was listed and protected by law, Leah assumed, finding it hard to credit that the Gazillionaire might have conserved the mermaids and the ornate pool out of the goodness of his heart.

Hot and sticky, Leah looked down at the cool water

lapping the edge of the tiled steps and sighed with longing. She would strip off and have a sneaky swim *after* she had finished the kitchen, she promised herself. She had no swimsuit, but she could use the clean T-shirt in her bag…or she could swim naked. After all, there was nobody around to see her…

Shaking her head at that amusing thought, Leah walked back out of the pool area and got stuck in the kitchen, which, all credit to Pam's efforts, required little attention. The pale floor, however, was a different story and she began returning it to pristine perfection. In the aftermath, hot and sweaty from her efforts, she raced upstairs to the cavernous hot press, extracted a big towel from one of the towering fleecy piles and headed straight back down to the pool. It was the work of a moment to undress and walk naked into the water, and that wonderful coolness on her overheated skin was an immediate reward that made her sigh in blissful relief.

Gio walked through the hall, noting the abandoned cleaning box, and he suppressed a sigh as he strode upstairs. The cleaner was still here, which was hardly surprising when he had arrived earlier than he had expected. He, however, wanted the house to himself. He would tell the cleaner to come back tomorrow to finish. He peeled off his jacket, removed his tie and was about to embark on his trousers when he thought he felt something nip at the back of his leg. He swung round but there was nothing there, only a faint suspicion of movement from the throw draped across the foot of the bed. Gio bent down and peered under the bed.

A small, frightened yelp sounded and something brown shot out from below and pelted full speed for the door. It was the size of a rat, but rats didn't have purple bows in their hair so it had to be a dog. The cleaner had brought a dog in with her. Gio frowned, thinking that his dogs in Italy would have made a snack of the wretched little creature. He cast aside his jacket and started back down the stairs again. For the first time he noticed that the door to the pool complex was ajar and he strode down the corridor towards it.

From the doorway he was able to see that he had a naked mermaid in his pool. A mermaid with a topknot of cascading black curls and a pale pink bottom as ripe as a peach showing through the water as she swam. Gio grinned, amused but annoyed because, instead of reacting with the humour he was struggling to restrain, the onus was now on him to play the censorious boss and lay down the law, spelling out what she had done wrong and why she shouldn't be doing it.

'Hi…' Gio murmured quietly, staying well back from the side of the pool, not wishing to make the naked intruder feel threatened.

'Oh, for crying out loud!' the mermaid exclaimed, throwing her hands high in dismay and then lurching across the water to grip the rail at the side to anchor herself. He caught a wickedly alluring flash of full perky breasts adorned with taut brown nipples. 'Who are you? What are you doing here?'

'I think those are my questions to ask,' Gio countered lazily.

Leah tilted her chin. 'I'm here because I'm cleaning the house—'

Gio elevated an ebony brow in measured challenge. 'From the pool?'

An angry flush mantled Leah's cheeks. 'I've been

working here all day and I got really hot. The only person that has the right to question me is the owner of this place…and I know that's not you—'

Gio could not help grinning because she kept on coming back at him, refusing to be quelled or cooled. 'And how do you know that? Are you acquainted with the owner?'

'The Gazillionaire?' Leah quipped. 'Are you joking? Of course, I'm not! But I *do* know that you're not him. He looks like a wild mountain man—'

'The Gazillionaire?' Gio queried with raised brows as he repeated that description. 'How…a wild mountain man?'

'I saw a picture of him in a newspaper and he has long hair and a full beard,' Leah informed him with a rather smug look. 'So, what are you doing here in his house? Are you the gardener?'

'Do I look like a gardener?' Gio asked with interest.

Leah appraised him, which took time because he was very tall and powerfully built. He had cropped black hair and exceptionally light eyes of an unknown hue that were very obvious in his lean bronzed face. He was quite staggeringly good-looking, an acknowledgement that severely unnerved and surprised her and made her wonder why she was still hanging around naked in the water with him present.

'No, you don't look like a gardener,' she admitted uneasily, noting the sunglasses stylishly hooked in the pocket of his red shirt, which was open at the neck. His trousers looked as though they might have been part of a suit, because they were narrow and very fashionable and almost indecently well fitted to his narrow hips and long powerful thighs. He emanated casual sophistication and a distinct urban edginess. 'Not a gardener… you work for the pool company?'

'No,' Gio said quietly.

'Do you work for the mountain man in some other capacity?'

His light eyes danced. 'I might…'

'Well, while you're thinking about that could you move away and turn your back so that I can get out of the water and back into my clothes?'

'I could if I were a gentleman,' Gio told her and shrugged with easy grace. 'I'm not.'

Temper flashed into Leah's caramel-brown eyes. She let go of the rail and swam over to the steps in an attempt to reach for the towel lying at the edge. 'Don't be a pig!' she urged.

Gio laughed with genuine appreciation and scooped up the towel, turning his back and extending it behind him.

The water rippled and shifted noisily, and he imagined her climbing out, close enough to be touched, that pale luscious wet body gleaming with water. She plucked the towel from his grasp and stepped up past him, wrapped from shoulder to calf in the largest towel he had ever seen.

'So, you work for Mr Zanetti,' Leah recapped, dabbing at her damp face with the loose end of the towel. 'Are you a member of his household staff?'

'What do you know about his household staff?' Gio asked with a frown, wondering what had sparked that incorrect rumour.

'Only that they travel with him, presumably doing his cooking and driving and whatnot—'

'This Gazillionaire sounds pretty helpless,' Gio commented, watching her scoop up her clothes. She was petite rather than tall, but that magnificent head of glossy black curls was spectacular. Add in huge brown eyes, creamy skin, delightful curves and slender shapely legs and she was a remarkably tempting package. Too short for him, of course, because, being six feet five, he preferred taller women and she was a good foot shorter than he was. Only that conviction did not explain why he had got as hard as a rock just looking at her in the towel. She might be small, he conceded, but she was all woman and incredibly sexy.

'He's probably too busy concentrating on the tech stuff that makes the money to waste time doing the ordinary stuff for himself,' Leah contended as she bent to gather up her clothes while wishing that her faded blue undies had not been sitting on top of the pile. 'And maybe he *can't* cook or drive. Not everyone can. I'm a demon behind a steering wheel but I can't cook for peanuts…'

'I'm an excellent cook,' Gio told her, crossing the floor to yank open a door almost concealed by the tiles. 'Changing facilities in here…'

'Thank you.' Leah gave him a mischievous smile. 'You're more of a gentleman than you think you are.'

'No, I'm not, but being politically correct around women is safer these days,' Gio fired back without hesitation.

Leah vanished into a cubicle where the lights fired up automatically and shed the towel, shivering as she climbed back into her clothes, her bra sticking to her damp flesh as she hurried, thrusting her feet into her battered trainers with a sense of relief. Being naked around a strange man in an empty house was unwise.

Who on earth was he? Obviously, he worked for the Gazillionaire in some capacity.

'Are you his cook?' she asked inquisitively as she emerged from the changing area, breathless and flushed.

On the cusp of announcing his true identity, Gio decided on a whim that was seductively playful in comparison to his usual deadly serious state of mind that he didn't want to be a cook any more than he wanted to be himself. 'No, office staff. I'm an executive PA—'

'I was a PA once.'

'How did you end up doing this job?'

'I was a PA for a guy who was hauled away by the police for defrauding thousands of people of their savings. He set up one of those pyramid schemes. He's in prison—'

'Patrick Lundsworth?' Gio incised, mentioning a name that had become a byword for dishonesty and that had been on everybody's lips only months earlier. 'How come you aren't doing time as well?'

'The police questioned me for two days, but I wasn't much use to them. It was my first job out of university and I was the office junior. I made coffee, answered phone calls, checked emails.' Leah grimaced. 'I wasn't in on anything to do with his con. I didn't even meet any of his investors. I was lucky…or so I thought at the time—'

'But you've still ended up cleaning,' Gio reminded her drily, thinking that she was very innocent and confiding for a woman with a stranger.

'Lundsworth has proved to be a very serious blight on my CV. I couldn't get another job in London, so I moved up here to try and get my life sorted,' Leah explained. 'And hopefully memories will eventually fade and I'll be able to get my feet back on the career ladder again.

'Would you like some coffee?' she asked as she walked away from him. 'I'm taking a break before I get back to work.'

'Not right now. I'm going upstairs to change before I go for a walk on the beach,' Gio responded.

'I'll finish here about six but I'm going to have to come back tomorrow to finish the job,' Leah advanced uncomfortably. 'I hope that will be all right. Is anyone else due to arrive before six tomorrow?'

'No,' Gio confirmed as he headed towards the stairs.

'I'm Leah,' she said quietly. 'What's your name?'

Her easy friendliness made his mouth twist. It had been so long since he had had that from a woman. Women always posed with him and played for a certain effect. It was false and it was fake but, in his world, it was a tried and tested female route to popularity with wealthy men. If he told Leah who he was, she would be aghast, apologising all over the place and out of the house within minutes. And, really, what harm had she done? A dip in his pool? A damp towel?

'I'm Gianni,' Gio told her truthfully, although it was not a diminutive he had used since his mother's death. She had named her son for his father, Giovanni, because she had still been in the first fine flush of love back then and she had called her son Gianni to distinguish between them.

'Have a lovely walk on the beach!' she urged. 'I've got the staircase to tackle.'

Gio smiled. 'Sounds like a challenge.'

'Have you seen how many nooks and crannies are hidden in those carvings?' Leah asked very seriously. 'It's a nightmare.'

Walking along the deserted strand in jeans and a sweater, Gio recalled that conversation and laughed out loud. She would never have acted so normally with him had she known who he really was. 'A wild mountain man'? Could it be that she had seen a photo of him on his return from his charitable trust's trek in Borneo? Afterwards, he had cut his hair shorter and dispensed with the beard he had worn for years. And what was with the Gazillionaire tag? But, *Madre di Cristo*, she was outrageously pretty…*and* currently engaged in cleaning his stairs, he reminded himself wryly.

By the time he returned, she might be gone…although not without the little rat sneakily trailing him along the shore, Gio reckoned, casting a quick eye over his shoulder just in time to see the little dog duck behind a rock to hide. It wasn't the brightest dog he had ever met. It was low to the ground and thought itself invisible behind the rock but, being so tall, Gio could see it clearly, cowering at the risk of being caught. He ignored it. Had it bitten him or tried to bite him earlier in the bedroom? There was no mark on his leg. He smiled, thinking it wasn't much of an attack dog.

An hour later, Gio strode back into the house and found Leah still down on her knees on the stairs, wielding a brush and wiping the woodwork with a cloth. His breath hissed between his even white teeth as he took in the jut of her luscious behind shaped in skin-tight faded denim and he averted his attention, reminding himself that he did not perve over employees…*ever*! Although, strictly speaking, she wasn't working for him, he reflected with a jab of satisfaction. It was stretching a point but when she glanced up at him, her vivid little face framed by that glorious mass of black curly hair and dominated by those huge dark sparkling eyes, whose employee she might be was the very last thing on Gio's mind.

'Stay and join me for dinner,' Gio heard himself urge without any awareness that he had even considered that idea before he spoke. The immediacy of that random prompting sharply disconcerted him.

Leah flung a startled glance at him and then dropped her head to concentrate on her task. Of course, she would say no, because she had decided six months ago that she was done with men after having wasted a year on a male who had ditched her without a pang. Oliver had been an education and no mistake. He had taught her a lot, hard lessons that had hurt. But didn't cutting herself off from the opposite sex merely hand Oliver yet another victory? A shot of defiance flared inside her at that suspicion.

'OK,' she said casually, as though agreement had not cost her a single moment of consideration. 'I've nothing to rush home for… I assume you're offering to cook?'

A wicked grin slanted Gio's mobile lips as he read her dismay at the prospect that he could be expecting her to whip out the pans. *'Sì...'*

'Oh, you're Italian like your boss…that's where your name comes from.' Leah stumbled over that awkward little speech as his pale eyes, the colour of glacier ice, glittered with unhidden amusement. 'Sorry, not very travelled or cosmopolitan here.'

'That has an appeal all of its own,' Gio informed

her truthfully, watching her blush, wondering when he had last seen a woman blush around him and quite entranced by it, any doubts he had had about his invitation draining away. He was in the mood for company, he told himself. It was harmless.

In something of a daze, Leah gazed back at him, hopelessly captivated by his looks and charm. She didn't think she had ever come across a more handsome guy unless he had been on a movie screen and even then, in her humble opinion, Gianni could have knocked spots off all competition. He was drop-dead gorgeous and when he smiled, she got butterflies in her tummy as though she were a teenager again. For goodness' sake, she castigated herself, start thinking like a grown-up for once…

CHAPTER TWO

'Do you want a hand?' Leah asked uncertainly from the kitchen doorway.

'You could chop up some of the vegetables if you like,' Gio suggested.

Leah didn't like but Sally had raised her to have manners. Striving not to stare at the male efficiently working with the salmon she had bought at the island unit, she scrubbed her hands at the sink and returned gingerly to the centre of the kitchen. 'Knives over there in the block,' he advised, lifting out another cutting board and settling it on the other side of the unit. 'Could you dice them?'

Leah was sure she could have done had she known what 'dicing' entailed.

Minutes later, Gio watched in silent wonderment as Leah wielded a knife much as though she were sawing up a log for the first time. 'Watch your fingers,' he heard himself say as he strove not to wince or be critical.

'I'm not a child,' she told him drily with an upward glance of her glorious dark eyes just as the knife sliced into a finger, causing her to drop it and yelp in startled pain.

For a split second, Gio said nothing because he was

stunned by that level of cooking incompetence, and then he dropped his own knife and went to her rescue. He picked her up like a package and settled her down on one of the bar stools while blood dripped from her and she whimpered, white with shock. 'Let me have a look…no, it won't need stitches,' he informed her soothingly, swiftly registering that she was one of those people terrified by the sight of blood.

White as a sheet, Leah sat shivering on the stool, fighting back the urge to throw up while Gio wrapped the bleeding finger in kitchen towelling to cover it from her gaze. He was incredibly competent in an emergency, she realised dimly as he broke out a first-aid kit and speedily cleaned her up and affixed a plaster to the offending digit.

'There,' Gio completed, pausing only to lift Leah and the stool back to the island unit. 'Now you can watch me cook.'

'I can't possibly—' she began, her throat tight with embarrassment at the show she had made of herself.

'You can't do anything with your hand out of commission,' Gio countered gently, recognising the glassy sheen of tears in her eyes. 'What's wrong?'

'I was such an idiot. I freaked out at the blood,' she mumbled sickly.

'It affects some people that way,' Gio responded lightly, keen to lighten her mood.

Leah breathed in deep and swallowed so hard that she hurt her throat. 'I was with my mother when she was in an accident and died,' she told him jerkily. 'It's been a problem for me ever since.'

Disconcerted not only by that admission but also by an unfamiliar urge to demand further details about an event that had had such long-lasting consequences for her, Gio pulled a bottle of wine out of the wine cabinet and uncorked it. Such intense curiosity was unlike him, because he didn't tend to get personal with other people lest it encourage them to assume that they could do the same with him. Yet Leah confided in him so easily and he definitely wasn't accustomed to that trait. Was it because he was a stranger? Or was she like that with everybody? Or, even less likely, was she feeling the same weird relaxation in his company that he felt in hers?

'That's not surprising. Don't worry about it,' Gio urged softly, resisting a far too personal prompting to pat her slight shoulder in a comforting motion, utterly unsure whether he liked or disliked the first protective urge any woman since his mother had fired in him.

'But a little cut and suddenly I'm behaving as though I cut my whole hand off…like a drama queen,' Leah framed in severe mortification at that image, which offended her practical soul. 'Sorry about that.'

'It doesn't matter,' Gio dismissed, slotting a glass of red wine into her hand. 'Have a drink and relax.'

Leah breathed again, thinking he was really quite kind and the absolute opposite of her selfish and critical ex-boyfriend, who had been utterly indifferent when her life had fallen apart. Of course, that had likely been because he had neither wanted her nor loved her and she had simply been a useful adjunct to the image he'd chosen to put out in the world. What a gullible, trusting fool she had been with Oliver!

That one glass of wine went to her head a little and she gulped down the water he handed her because she had been getting a bit giggly. 'I'm a cheap date when it comes to alcohol,' she muttered, wondering why on earth she felt that she should always be apologising to him as if she were failing to live up to some perfect ideal.

'I noticed,' Gio murmured, disconcerting her with that piece of frankness. 'I don't want you drinking too much.'

Leah flushed and drank more water in embarrassment rather than inform him that she already knew that one glass of wine was pretty much her limit because Oliver had often mocked her for that weakness.

Gio slid a plate across to her, a plate perfectly adorned with salmon and crisp, colourful vegetables, and she blinked. 'This looks amazing,' she said truthfully. 'When did you start cooking?'

'When I was a student. I like good fresh food and if I wanted to eat it, I had to learn how to make it,' Gio admitted, sinking fluidly down on the stool across from hers and lifting a knife and fork.

'I continued living with my former foster mother while I was a student,' Leah responded. 'And Sally rules her kitchen and would be offended if you tried to cook for yourself, so I was lazy—'

'*Foster* mother?' Gio queried.

'I was in care from the age of eleven. Mum was dead and my father disappeared from our lives when I was a toddler.' Leah lifted and dropped her narrow shoulders. 'Sally became much more than just a foster parent to me. I was lucky.'

'Most people would say you had it tough, rather than lucky,' Gio remarked softly. 'But I know where you're coming from. I didn't have a conventional secure childhood either.'

Her dark eyes widened on his when she thought for a

split second that she had glimpsed a world of hurt shadowing his lean strong face and his pale gaze. *'Oh...?'*

But he deflected her curiosity by turning his handsome dark head in the direction of the small dog nervously peering round the edge of the door. 'What's *his* story?'

'Sally runs a small animal sanctuary. Spike was brought in last year. From what we were told he was an older woman's much adored pet until she died in the same accident that lost him his leg. Her partner tied him up in a yard afterwards and neglected him. I think the man beat him as well, maybe for barking or something,' Leah told him in a pained undertone. 'So now he's terrified of men, which is why he won't come in here.'

Gio watched those huge caramel eyes gloss over with compassion and regret on the little animal's behalf and that softness in her, that gentleness he wasn't at all used to seeing in women, seemed to fill him with the most extraordinary lust. As his jeans tightened and his arousal pulsed against his zip, he marvelled at the sheer novelty of her effect on him. It was because she was different, that was all, he reasoned impatiently, an unsurprising reaction when he had clearly become bored with the predictability of the women in his life.

'That's strange, because he followed me all the way along the beach and back. Perhaps I remind him of someone from happier times,' he murmured huskily. 'Would you like coffee?'

That enquiry flustered Leah. Here she was, supposedly cleaning his employer's house, and now *he* seemed to be somehow waiting on her hand and foot and that could only strike her as an uncomfortable development. In haste she slid off the stool to help in some way while he reached for the percolator. For a split second she veered closer to him than she had intended and she froze, her dark gaze utterly entrapped by the pale icy brilliance of his.

His hand settled on her shoulder to steady her as she lurched a little off balance while their eyes kindled and white volcanic heat fired in her pelvis. He lowered his dark head and she waited, full of anticipation, yearning for that connection with every fibre of her being. His wide sculpted mouth brushed hers and she trembled, engulfed in screaming awareness of his proximity. It truly felt like the most exciting thing that had ever happened to her. Her hands lifted of their own volition and closed into his forearms to hold him there and then he kissed her.

And it was every kiss she had never had but always dreamt about: a slow burn of sensation teaching her that her lips and her mouth were a much more sensitive and sensual vehicle than she had ever guessed. The circling caress of his full soft lips on her own made her knees wobble and her heart thump ridiculously fast and when he slid the tip of his tongue into the moist interior of her mouth, she ignited like a burning torch thrown on a bale of hay. She was stunned when every inch of her body responded to that unexpectedly powerful stimulus.

Gio kissed her, her breasts swelled and her nipples snapped taut and her pelvis clenched down deep inside, ensuring that she flushed and shifted her hips in heated awareness like a teenager who had never been kissed before, she acknowledged in mortification. She was shocked by his influence over her, struggling to handle it even while she was mesmerised by the physical feelings engulfing her in pleasure.

Gio lifted his head, so aroused that he almost gritted his teeth at the exuberance of his libido. He didn't know what had come over him, but it was just sex on his terms and therefore an acceptable urge that should not require any greater examination. He stared down at her vibrant little face with intense appreciation gripping him. 'You're beautiful,' he murmured quietly. 'Will you stay here tonight with me?'

A sliver of surprise snaked through Leah at those blunt words, because she had yet to spend the night with *any* man. It galled her to still be untouched at twenty-two years of age, but only a couple of years earlier she had truly believed in saving that ultimate intimacy for a more meaningful relationship. And, most ironically, she had been saving herself for the likes of Oliver, she thought sickly, a man who had never desired her in the first place, although he had tried to pretend otherwise to keep her keen in the girlfriend stakes. Crushingly, that gambit had only worked for him with her *because* she had been naïve and inexperienced with men, and ever since that betrayal she had despised that ignorance of hers, which had left her open and vulnerable to hurt and humiliation.

'Leah…?' Gio prompted in the bottomless silence, wondering what was amiss when her wonderful expressive eyes lowered below her feathery lashes and she evaded his gaze.

'I thought you were making coffee,' Leah reminded him daringly, playing for time, struggling to get her frantic thoughts and those unwelcome memories of her ex under control. 'I'm thinking about your invitation… You're very er…frank—'

'How else would I be? You are single, *aren't* you?'

His ebony brows pleated at the sudden realisation that she might not be, that he was in a different place with her than he normally was with women. She hadn't offered herself to him first, hadn't sought his attention, and a bare ring finger meant nothing these days when she might already have children and a partner.

'Yes, free as a bird,' Leah confirmed in a rather brittle response, because Oliver's deception had cruelly wounded her self-respect.

Gio was slightly disconcerted by the surge of relief that immediately assailed him.

Leah tilted her chin up as she slid back up onto the bar stool, deeming herself safer from being stupid with him at that distance because she still didn't know how she had ended up in his arms, only that the temptation to get closer to him had been irresistible and incredibly strong. That she had never felt that way before had impressed her. Life was short, she told herself, and she planned to make the most of it without falling for any more males of Oliver's ilk. 'I'm very loyal,' she told him with quiet pride. 'I wouldn't have kissed you had there been someone else in my life.'

Gio was almost amused by that pointed and pure declaration of loyalty and honesty, which only accentuated the gulf between them. After all, he had never been able to trust a woman to that extent, not even when he was a teenager. Even the mother he'd adored had lied to him as and when it had suited her to do so. His mother's first loyalty had always been to his father, no matter how badly the older man had treated either her or her son.

'Is that so?'

'Yes, that is so!' Leah proclaimed with spirit as she slid upright again, restless as a cat on hot bricks, to make the coffee he had forgotten about again. She might not be much of a cook, but she could manage coffee, couldn't she? She was shaken to see that her hands were trembling as she flipped through cupboards in search of china. Yes, there was a much bigger question looming over her blitzed brain. Would she or wouldn't she spend the night with the most sexually enthralling and gorgeous guy she had ever met?

In her restricted circle, when would such an opportunity ever present again? She didn't want to be an old and grey virgin, did she? And that *was* a distinct possibility, given the way she now felt about relationships, wasn't it? No man was ever going to get the chance to make a fool of her a second time!

'This proposal of yours…'

Brows pleating at that very word, Gio turned to look at her, surprised to see the now shuttered aspect of her vivid little face. 'Yes?'

Leah strengthened her backbone. She had been Oliver's doormat, silently swallowing his criticisms of her weight, her clothing choices, her accent and lack of culture. That would not be the blueprint for her future. From now on, intimacy of any kind would only happen on *her* terms and right now she could only contemplate the most superficial of bonds. 'If I agree,' she said tightly, 'it would be an agreement that it's a one-night stand and nothing more. I won't consider anything else.'

Gio laughed out loud in delight and astonishment combined, for no woman had ever offered him only one night without the potential for the connection to turn into something more. In that instant he decided that being Mr Nobody from Nowhere was sheer magic. Leah didn't want him for his money, his social position or his business influence because she was not aware of his true status, and while in other circumstances he might have considered it wrong not to admit who he was, when it came to one casual night he believed that nobody would be harmed by his decision to remain silent on that score.

'You think that what I said was funny?' Leah pressed tautly, taken aback by his amusement.

'Not in the sense that you suspect,' Gio told her confidently. 'Women can sometimes be a little clingy with me, so I was pleasantly surprised by your attitude and your directness.'

Leah could perfectly understand women getting clingy with a male as drop-dead beautiful as he was, but she was still encased in the protective armour that Oliver's deeply hurtful deception had inflicted on her. Her heart was now as frozen as any cartoon princess might wish for and, with it, any desire to *cling* to any man. To stay strong and safe, she reasoned, she needed to stand alone and control her own destiny, not allow either foolish romantic dreams or, worse, some self-serving male authority to influence her intelligence and her judgement again.

'Let me do that,' Gio interposed as she searched the entire kitchen, it seemed, for a teaspoon. 'Sit down—'

'Watch it. You're a bit too bossy for me,' Leah told him, a warning gleam in her caramel eyes.

Gio sent her a wolfish grin, thoroughly enjoying himself with a woman for the first time in a long time. All the size of her and trying to look tough, he acknowledged, impressed once again by that hint of an irrepressible spirit. He showed her the food he had put in a bowl for her dog and watched her attend to the little animal, before making the coffee and extending hers.

Leah was nonplussed by the level of his control, having dimly expected to be urged straight towards the nearest horizontal surface or whatever. She scolded herself for that naïve assumption. He wasn't an unpolished teenager keen to score at speed with the first available girl, he was rather more sophisticated.

Gio had never been so tempted to abandon all cool with a woman. Arousal was humming through every inch of his big powerful body. It was years since he had experienced anything like that level of desire in female company and he was determined to figure out what it was about Leah that revved him up to such an extent. A *ridiculous* extent, he told himself impatiently, when one conceded that he had never in his entire adult life been desperate for sex. So, what was it about her?

The vibrance of her expression? That amazing glossy mane of curls? The big dark eyes, whose expression she veiled when uncomfortable…like now? What the hell was she uncomfortable about? Telling him that the most he could expect from her was a one-night stand had been a pretty feisty move, not the behaviour of a shy or naïve woman, so why had that feisty assurance somehow struck a vaguely bogus note to his ears? *Dio*, was she one of those old-fashioned women, who still thought she had to play hard to get even as she surrendered to the same hunger that infused him?

Gio smiled and Leah was entrapped, instantly, irrevocably, watching the way that shift of his wide sculpted lips threw his exotic cheekbones into prominence and allowed those stunning eyes of his to narrow and glitter. Pale grey, she had thought at first, then she had tagged them as the palest possible blue with a near Mediterranean hint of turquoise when passion flared. A tiny shiver curled low in her pelvis and her whole body lit up like a firework display, forcing her to shift uneasily in her seat.

'I'm usually very good at restraint,' Gio told her truthfully. 'But right now, right here with you… I'm not feeling it, *cara*.'

His boldness made her feel outrageously shy, and she could feel her skin heating and tightening over her bones.

'You blush,' he said in apparent wonderment.

'Occasionally—'

'Will you blush if I ask you to come upstairs with me?'

'P-probably,' Leah muttered as he pushed away his untouched coffee and stood up to extend a hand to her. She tugged out her phone and sent a quick text to Sally, telling her that she wouldn't be home.

Her heart began to pound inside her as she too got up and reached for that hand, feeling rather like a drowning swimmer while fighting all those insecure feelings to the last ditch. So, this raw, powerful sense of connection was something new and different for her, but she would get used to it, being very adaptable as she had had to be throughout her life, she told herself firmly.

CHAPTER THREE

GIO PAUSED TO kiss Leah on the first landing because he, literally, couldn't keep his hands off her any longer. Passion flared like lightning, shooting through Leah like a jet-propelled rocket, both stunning and seducing, urging her arms round his neck without her realising how they had got there.

She was breathless and flushed as he walked her on up the next flight of steps, anticipation provoking a dull tugging ache at her feminine core. But for all that, she was disconcerted when he led her into what she had assumed was the master bedroom. 'Isn't this Mr Zanetti's room?' she exclaimed in surprise.

The faintest edge of colour scored Gio's cheekbones, because it was not a moment when he wished to be reminded of his whimsical impulse earlier to deny his true identity. 'He doesn't use this one,' he asserted, reaching for her again, determined to distract her from awkward questions while remaining unusually aware that he had just told an actual lie, which was not something he was in the habit of doing under any circumstances. *Harmless,* he reminded himself stubbornly as he collided with those wide dark eyes of hers with something weirdly similar to wonderment because *she* was making *him* act out of character. He didn't want to give her any excuse to walk away, but even less did he wish to see greed and ambition spark in her beautiful eyes.

But, usually, sex wasn't really that important to him, bearing in mind that it was always available to him no matter where he was because beautiful, willing potential partners were plentiful. As a rule, he didn't do one-night stands; he would stay with one woman for a couple of weeks and then move on before it got stale. It never lasted any longer than that, never got any deeper than that. He didn't offer commitment—indeed, since his short-lived marriage he had not surrendered or shared control in any element of his life. Sex was a trivial pursuit on the periphery of a driven life he devoted to technological research and business.

'Gianni…' she said, her soft voice purring along the syllables, and it was sufficient to spring him back out of that rare instant of introspection.

He kissed her again and the worry about whose room they were occupying melted away in a fresh tide of longing. Her T-shirt fell to the floor in the midst of a frantic bout of kissing, the zip of her shorts sliding down, the garment dropping to her ankles as he lifted her clear. She lay back on the bed where he placed her in a fevered daze, watching him dispense with sweater and jeans and toe off his boots to reveal an incredibly powerful physique, all lean, muscular strength and bronzed masculinity. He simply took her breath away. He was beautiful in a way she had never known a man could be, beautiful from his wide shoulders to his corrugated abdomen and long, strong legs.

As for the rest of him, she glossed her eyes over in haste because really there was rather more than she had dimly expected, but nature had made men and women to fit, so she wasn't going to stress about that aspect. He came back to her with a wolfish smile that blitzed her thoughts as much as his kisses because she was just enthralled, all her inexperience and insecurities overwhelmed by his breathtaking appeal.

'You are so beautiful,' Gio told her and, for Leah, it seemed as though she had been waiting all her life for such words. She didn't believe it was true but on such an occasion he was allowed to exaggerate, she thought forgivingly.

Having released her hair from its topknot, Gio was watching that fabulous mane of black ringlets spill across the pillows, taking in the shining brilliance of her dark honey eyes, the reddened allure of her luscious mouth, and hunger took him by storm as he came down over her and ravished her lips again.

A little bit later, Leah discovered that her undergarments had magically disappeared, and the smoothness with which those items had been removed bothered her a little because it warned her that he was much more experienced than she was. And she didn't want to think about that for some reason she couldn't explain. She didn't like to think of the *other* women he had learned such skills from. And she knew that such a thought was ridiculous in a woman who had declared upfront that she was willing only to consider a one-night stand but there it was, denying her own feelings was beyond her: she was jealous as hell of any woman who had ever touched him.

'You're so quiet,' Gio purred, gazing down at her with smouldering eyes semi-screened by lush black lashes.

'Do you know that you have lashes longer than the

average girl's? No?' Leah went beet-red. 'That's *why* I should keep quiet—'

'I don't mind quirky,' Gio broke in with a surprised laugh of appreciation, big hands curving to the full firm curves of her breasts, thumbs gently skimming her prominent nipples. 'In fact quirky is refreshing.'

Rather belatedly, because everything had seemed to move so fast to her, Leah registered that she was naked for the very first time with a guy, and she could feel a wash of heat blossoming on her entire skin surface, but his touch on her sensitive peaks was sending an arrowing flame to the very heart of her, making her shift her hips under his weight. And then she could feel him against her, long and hard and urgent, and that ache between her thighs intensified.

Gio ran his lips down the side of her neck to where it met her shoulder and she gasped, because inexplicably that touch *there* seemed to light up her every nerve ending. She smelled like sunshine and fresh laundry, and he inhaled deeply, amazed by how evocative such natural scents could be. She panted as he lingered at her throat and tipped back as he glided lean fingers down over her quivering tummy, skated through the landing strip of curls below and circled the most sensitive spot on her whole body. Her spine arched, her teeth gritting on a powerful wave of response. He shimmied down the length of her and found the same place with his mouth and his fingers and his tongue.

'Oh…' Leah gasped, utterly awash in more sensation than she had ever known. It was as if a fierce pulse was beating through her while her heart thumped even faster, and she was so overpowered that she just closed her eyes tight and let the intoxicating wave of climbing pleasure take over.

Her reaction excited Gio as much as though he were with his very first woman and he was way too involved in that urgency to even consider what was so different. He raised himself to grab a condom from the nightstand by the bed and tore the foil open with his teeth, dimly acknowledging that he was struggling to stay in control while revelling in the excitement of that unique experience. Even the taste of her mouth drove him wild, he conceded, stealing another kiss with driven insistence, already knowing that no one-night stand was likely to sate him...but she'd change her mind about that, *of course* she would.

Leah felt him push past her tender entrance, even lifted herself a little as he canted up her hips and then he was driving into her, giving her what her entire being was keyed up to demand.

'You're so tight,' he proclaimed at almost the same moment as the burning stretch of his invasion became uncomfortable for her. A second later he withdrew to gain greater traction and drove back into her hard and fast. It hurt and she jerked just as he repeated the movement. The next time was less painful and, indeed, her breath caught in her throat in surprise when a renewed wave of hunger mixed with pleasure turned her pelvis into a cauldron of hot, melting liquidity.

His urgent rhythm ramped up her growing excitement. Her heart was thumping so hard it left her breathless. She wanted more, in fact her whole body was primed to a peak of burning need, so that every thrust of his body into hers felt agonisingly good and necessary. The surge of exhilaration engulfing her carried her to a dizzy high and then her body convulsed and broke into a million pieces and in the same instant she soared in an ecstasy of pleasure.

'Extraordinary,' Gio husked in her ear, dragging in a shuddering breath that shifted his broad chest against her, muscles rippling below his hair-roughened golden skin. He was bemused by the unexpected discovery that simple sex could be *that* good and a slashing smile at his own surprise lightened his lean, dark, serious features.

Leah looked up at him in a daze of satiation, struggling to hide a surprise even stronger than his because until that moment she truly hadn't thought she had missed out on much by not experimenting more. He eased back from her to spring out of the bed and then registered that for the first time ever his precautions had failed him.

'Are you using contraception?' he asked tautly.

Leah blinked in consternation. She had taken the pill the whole time she was with Oliver on the assumption that eventually their relationship would become more physical, only it hadn't done and in frustration at that lowering truth she had dumped her pills after he ditched her. 'Er…no,' she muttered awkwardly.

'Unluckily for us, the condom broke,' Gio told her as he slid out of the bed, only then seeing the smear of blood on his thigh. He froze and lifted pale glittering eyes to her mortified face. 'Would it be crazy of me to ask if you were a virgin?'

As the ramifications of what he had told her set in, Leah cringed in sharp dismay. Nobody knew more about unplanned pregnancies and their unwelcome consequences than Leah, who had grown up virtually without a father. 'We don't have to talk about that,' she murmured flatly. 'And we may have had an accident, but I doubt that anything will come of it…my system's irregular.'

'Right,' Gio breathed between gritted teeth, already blaming himself for not having discussed contraception beforehand with her. Checking that his partner was additionally protected was an extra precaution he had practised for years after his divorce. Unhappily he had stopped being that careful because no such accident had ever occurred to him before. But what were the odds of conception? he asked himself with sudden impatience. One mishap, one chance, pretty good odds in his favour, he decided, repressing any further concern.

Without further ado, Gio disappeared into the bathroom and Leah flopped back weakly against the pillows, trying not to recall her mother, who had once joked that she was fertile enough to fall pregnant just by looking at the wrong man. Oh, why, oh, why had she stopped taking the pill? But she knew *why*. At the time she hadn't envisaged ever being with a man and certainly not on a casual basis. Regret and insecurity threatened and, in the midst of that attack, Leah leapt out of bed and began to scrabble for her clothes at speed.

'What are you doing?' Gio asked from the doorway.

'I thought I'd take a shower downstairs and then go home—'

Gio reached for the hands she had filled with her clothes and she fumbled to continue holding them, but they fell to the polished floor. 'I don't want you to leave… I want you to stay.'

Disconcerted, Leah clashed with the silvered glitter of eyes bright as diamonds in his lean, darkly handsome face. Her heart performed a somersault and her tummy shimmied with butterflies. His tousled dark head lowered to hers and her hands went up into his hair to tug him down to her. The need to touch him again was frighteningly instinctive and it had nothing at all to do with the defensive 'let's escape' urge that had been controlling her only seconds earlier. His mouth claimed and captured hers and her head swam and her knees wobbled as an intoxicating rush of hunger awakened every nerve ending afresh…

Dawn was the merest hint beyond the blinds when Leah woke up. Her lashes fluttered with confusion until she remembered and then she almost groaned out loud at the embarrassing prospect of having to rise and finish cleaning the house while the male beside her was still in residence. She eased out of bed with all the nimble quietness of a cat burglar, gathered up the clothes she had dropped and crept downstairs. Spike was waiting at the foot of the stairs for her.

Dressed after a lick and promise of a brief wash in the cloakroom, she registered the time and decided to try and finish the outstanding work before departing. Once she had one of the solid mahogany doors closed, the noise she made would not carry far, she reasoned, heading quickly into the nearest room with her implements. No, she wasn't going to have regrets, she told herself. What was done was done. She wasn't about to slut-shame herself for doing something that most women had done long before her. She had made a decision and she stood by it.

Having dusted at speed, she winced as she had to stretch to vacuum a corner. She ached all over; she ached as though she had run a marathon overnight. Her face burned. He had proved to be sexually demanding but he had made the whole experience a positive one. He had been respectful and considerate, and she was grateful for that. That aside, however, the passion, the wild intensity of their encounter had shocked her.

Gio sat up in the empty bed and glanced at his watch with a frown. He had slept in and that was most unlike him. He studied the space where Leah had been and his frown grew even darker. Where was she? He rarely spent the whole night with a woman and, since he had chosen to do so with her, her absence irked him. A faint noise from the ground floor, however, followed by a low wuffly little bark, released his tension and made him smile. Vaulting out of bed, he went for a shower. He would tell Leah the truth, he conceded as the water pounded him. Being Mr Nobody from Nowhere had been entertaining, but it was a lie and he could not continue lying to her, at least not if he intended to spend more time with her. An empty weekend loomed ahead of him and he could see no reason why he should not spend it with Leah. True, it had not seemed empty before he had met her, he conceded; indeed he *had* been looking forward to his own company.

Leah reeled in the vacuum cord with a sigh of relief. Her back was sore, her mouth dry, her tummy running on empty because she had not dared to stop to eat or drink. She was exhausted after working at top speed following a night during which she had only enjoyed snatches of sleep. The reward, however, was that she had pretty much completed the basic clean Pam had requested and now she could go home.

The door opened just as she lifted the vacuum cleaner and she froze, before noisily setting it down again, her oval face flushing from the intensity of Gio's scrutiny. In casual cargo pants and an open-necked black shirt, he somehow contrived to look ridiculously sophisticated… and gorgeous. His lean bronzed features were classic from his high cheekbones, narrow masculine nose and sculpted mouth. He was undeniably sheer masculine perfection. And just that one look and she felt giddy.

'I've fed Spike and made coffee,' he informed her with a faint smile that turned his handsome mouth up at the corners and exuded an incredible amount of bare-faced charm.

'Thanks for Spike…but I'd already fed him. He's a trickster. He always acts like he's starving,' she gabbled, her hand tightening on the cleaning box she still held. 'Unfortunately, I was just about to go home—'

'Give me ten minutes,' Gio bargained. 'There's something I have to tell you.'

What on earth could he have to tell her? Oh, my goodness, was he about to confess that he had a girlfriend? Even worse, a wife? Her empty tummy hollowed out sickly. Was it weak of her to feel like telling him that she really didn't want to know now that it was too late to change anything? Conscious of him on her heels, she stowed the cleaning box in the pantry and went back to retrieve the vacuum. She put away the vacuum, knowing that she just wanted to run but that that would be gauche, and she wasn't still that immature, was she? Perspiration had broken out on her short upper lip as she returned to the kitchen, her car keys jangling in her pocket.

'What's the problem?' Leah prompted stiffly.

Gio studied her, entranced by her beautiful eyes, the tumble of black curls surrounding her eloquent little face and the very bossy, purposeful bustle of her movements when she was working. Nothing was studied, nothing faked for glossy presentation or sex appeal. Everything about Leah was so *real*, from the shadows below her eyes to her curvy, wondrous shape. There was nothing gym-honed about the softness of her against him either. A surge of intense lust hit him, disconcerting him with the speed of that renewal.

'I don't see why it should be a problem,' Gio told her truthfully, for he had never heard a woman lament the discovery that her lover was a billionaire, 'but, unfortunately, I wasn't entirely frank with you when we first met last night.'

'Frank?' Leah queried the word uncertainly.

'I didn't want things to be awkward, so I said that I worked for Gio Zanetti when, in fact, I *am* Giovanni Zanetti,' Gio spelled out.

Leah's tummy was churning, her skin turning clammy with shock. 'You said your name was Gianni...'

'That was true. Both Gio and Gianni are diminutives of Giovanni, although the latter name was only ever used by family,' he conceded.

Leah had turned pale as death because she really couldn't credit that this was happening to her again: a man lying to her about who and what he was. What was it about her? Did she have stupid, trusting fool stamped on her forehead?

'You're saying that you're the... Gazillionaire?' she almost whispered.

Gio was struggling to work out why Leah was looking at him in horror. It wasn't embarrassment or annoyance. It was more like the response he might have expected had he announced that he was a serial killer.

'Yes, but telling you that yesterday when I surprised you in the pool would have been more upsetting for you—'

'No,' Leah framed. 'It would have been the truth.'

'The truth isn't always welcome,' Gio countered without apology. 'I would have had to read the Riot Act about you being in the pool.'

Leah parted bloodless lips. 'Better that than lying to me. You let me think you were someone else and then you slept with me. That is unforgivable.'

'I hope that you don't mean that,' Gio commented smoothly. 'Once I had claimed to be an employee I was stuck with that story.'

'Otherwise, I might not have slept with you,' Leah suggested.

Pale eyes as bright as diamonds below a lush curtain of black lashes inspected her. 'I don't think that would have been an issue.'

'I don't like liars,' Leah almost whispered, stepping past him to scoop up Spike from his position in the hallway. 'I would never have spent the night with you if I had known you had lied to me.'

Gio frowned. 'You're making far too much of this. I saved us from an awkward moment with a harmless lie. At that stage I had no idea that we were going to end up in bed together and now I've come clean—'

Leah shot him a furious glance from her dark eyes. 'It wasn't harmless. You're not the man I thought you were. There's a huge chasm between who you are and who you pretended to be. I wouldn't have got into bed with the Gazillionaire—'

'I'm apologising!' Gio broke in, his dark drawl raw-edged. 'I am truly sorry that I misled you and I promise that I will not tell the smallest untruth from this minute forward.'

Spike tucked under her arm, her bag over her shoulder, Leah tugged open the back door. 'It doesn't matter anyway. It was a one-night thing—'

'I don't *want* it to be.'

Leah spun back to him, volatile sparks in her angry gaze. 'You accepted it last night…so you *lied* about that as well?'

'Most women aren't offended when a man wants to spend more time in their company—'

'I'm not *most* women!' Leah hissed and turned on her heel again to march out into the courtyard.

'You're telling me,' Gio muttered in gritty agreement under his breath.

Pausing at the side of the shabby old hatchback parked nearby, Leah stared back at him. 'I don't want to see you or hear from you ever again!' she declared as she stowed her bag and carefully installed the dog in the carrier box in the back seat.

As she drove off, grinding through the gears and executing a noisy handbrake turn, Gio swallowed back an astonished laugh. She was a hellish rough driver and she had an even more hellish temper. How many years was it since a woman had censured him? Refused him? Turned her nose up at an apology? Acted difficult? He couldn't remember. In fact, he couldn't remember that *ever* happening to him, even during his divorce. Gabriella had been sweet as sugar throughout the negotiations while she'd robbed him blind after only a few short months of matrimony. He had been hung out to dry by the gold-digger he had married without ever putting a foot wrong…

CHAPTER FOUR

The nerve of him! Leah thought furiously as she drove away from Shore House. Gio/Gianni/Giovanni Zanetti had run rings around her. She had not suspected a thing. And there he had been, cool as ice and full of lies and deception just like Oliver! Never again would she even contemplate a guy who told her anything but the truth because she had learned the hard way that lies cut her deep. Left her with scars she couldn't shake, rubbished her pride and filled her with insecurity and self-doubt.

Sally's eyes were bright with curiosity as Leah walked in the back door.

'Least said, soonest mended,' Leah quipped ruefully.

'A mistake?' her foster mother prompted.

'Partially,' Leah agreed after a reflective pause. 'But not important in the scheme of things.'

Sally winced and then smiled. 'Well, I'm not about to pry.'

Relief swept Leah. She had called in with Pam on her way home and had reported back on the state of Shore House without mentioning Gio's early arrival there. Then she had collected Pam's prescription and promised to return the next day to cut the lawn. Changing into her oldest clothes, she went out to the rackety collection of old buildings that housed the rescue animals and helped one of Sally's keen volunteers to clean out inmates that ranged from goats and rabbits to cats and dogs.

When she came back indoors for lunch, Sally sent her a veiled appraisal and murmured, 'Pam phoned. Mr Zanetti will be calling here this afternoon.'

Leah flushed to the roots of her hair. 'Yes. It was him and he's…persistent—'

'Oh, dear,' Sally said without turning a hair. 'Do you want me to deal with him?'

'No, thanks. I can handle him,' Leah breathed, more embarrassed than ever.

'You should get changed,' her former foster mother remarked, eying Leah's ancient jeans and tatty T-shirt with a frown.

'No. I'll do fine as I am,' Leah declared, lifting her chin.

Gio Zanetti drew up in a Bugatti Centodieci, a long, ridiculously sleek white sports car that looked as though it would be far more at home on a racetrack than a narrow country lane. It was Sally, who had an interest in cars, who excitedly told her what it was and what it was likely worth.

'What a show-off he is!' Leah commented, determined not to be impressed.

She walked stiff-backed to the front door and opened it, watching as Gio swung gracefully out of his phenomenally expensive vehicle. Sunlight gleamed over his black hair and bronzed skin, accentuating his classic bone structure and the piercing brilliance of light eyes set below level ebony brows. His physical impact was intense, she acknowledged, her tummy clenching with nerves and her heart hammering. She breathed in slow and deep. 'Mr Zanetti…' she said.

'Really?' Gio hitched a satirical brow. 'Is that how we're playing it?'

'I don't know what you're doing here,' Leah admitted tightly.

Gio strolled towards her. 'Evidently, my interest in you is less fleeting than yours in me…or so you would have me believe—'

'So, vanity brought you here,' Leah contended waspishly.

'No, the way you look at me even now brought me here and keeps me here,' Gio countered with a slashing confident smile. '*Dio mio*…what is the problem?'

In receipt of that smile her mouth ran dry and something in her pelvis heated, tightened and clenched in the most intimate way. 'I didn't say there was one, only that one night was as much as I could contemplate—'

'*Please* change your mind,' Gio urged, staring down at her with those extraordinary eyes that made her head swim. He lifted a hand to trace the outline of her mouth with a caressing finger and instant heat flooded her as she stood there, her physical response a screaming denial of everything she had told him.

'I can't,' she whispered unevenly.

And he bent his head and the pulse at the heart of her kicked up, flaring in anticipation. His mouth came down on her slowly, touching, brushing, tasting, and her hand came up to rest on his chest, feeling the fast beat of his heart. Hunger flooded her in an intoxicating wave as his tongue dallied with hers and she felt him, hard and ready against her, his long, lean, strong body as taut as her own. She wanted, *needed*…

Gio stepped back. 'Leah?' he breathed roughly.

'You lied and I couldn't forgive that,' Leah admitted tightly.

'You're a vengeful little soul, aren't you?' Gio murmured with grim amusement as he extended something to her.

'What's this?' Leah muttered, staring down at the black and gold business card he had handed her, her body still quivering from that kiss that had liquefied her bones and filled her with an almost unbearable craving.

'My phone number. In case you change your mind... *Buongiorno*, Spike, better luck next time,' Gio said in an aside as the little dog tried and failed to get his mouth into the back of his denim-clad calf, and then turned back to her to add, 'Or should there be consequences for the little mishap we had.'

Leah was struggling to understand how he could be so hot and sexy and yet make her want to slap him at the same time, but at that reminder she lost colour and dug the card into her pocket. 'Unlikely,' she replied flatly.

'That's some powerful chemistry,' Sally commented, coming up behind her as Gio drove off. 'Takes some backbone to say no to that.'

'No...it only takes common sense,' Leah contradicted tautly.

In the aftermath of the sickness, Leah freshened up, grimacing at her watering eyes and her pallor in the mirror. She looked awful, felt worse, if that were possible. And she was only twenty weeks pregnant. Her fond belief that what had happened to her mother wouldn't happen to her had been foolish. She had conceived and now she had to deal with her plight. For the past month after the doctor had confirmed her suspicions and outlined her options, Leah had been lost inside her own head, making and discarding unrealistic plans.

From an early stage she had known that she would keep her baby and raise it. She had lost her entire family growing up but now she felt as though she was receiving a second chance at having a family and nobody was going to take that opportunity away from her. True, the way she was having her first child, alone and without support, was far from being ideal. But, sometimes, life threw up the unexpected and it had to be handled. She was excited about her baby and didn't feel that she could freely express that truth because becoming a young single mother put her into a category that some liked to mock and deride.

Sally, predictably, wanted her to stay with her to have the baby but Leah was determined that the older woman should not pay for *her* carelessness. And a young child in the household would definitely be an added burden. Rediscovering her independence, Leah reflected, was a necessity.

For that reason she was moving back to London to take up a live-in job as a companion/carer for an elderly woman. Sally had argued vehemently about that decision, but Leah knew that it was time to stand on her own feet again. She had no idea as yet what she would do to support herself after her baby was born but thought that, with her business degree, she might be able to find paid employment that allowed her to work remotely. If she was able to support herself, she would be willing to move back in with Sally then.

It was also time that she informed Gio Zanetti that in a few months' time he would be a father. She had no idea how he would feel about that, but she acknowledged his right to know. Keep it impersonal, she urged herself, that being the attitude she had sworn to take. He was unlikely to be pleased at her news but then she wasn't that pleased either that the father of her child was a liar.

Recalling that truth, she lifted her chin and reached for her phone because she had been putting off contacting Gio for long enough.

'It's Leah,' she announced when he answered. 'Leah Ramsay. We met at Shore House.'

'I haven't forgotten,' he intoned, his dark deep drawl shimmying down her spine and up again, sending a ridiculous little shiver of awareness through her.

'I need to see you to discuss something—'

'Something?' a faint chilling note laced his intonation.

'I won't take up much of your time. Ten minutes at most,' Leah asserted tightly. 'I'll be in London in two weeks.'

'I'll text you an address and a time,' Gio responded flatly and rang off.

Well, that was short and sweet, Leah conceded ruefully. Had he guessed? She supposed it was better allround if he had, at least, an inkling. Thirty minutes later, her phone buzzed with the address of an apartment building and a time that suited her.

It was a very fancy apartment block with that sleek elegant air that just screamed expense. Fresh from moving into her damp bedsit in a basement, Leah was less well groomed than she had planned to be. Since her return to London she had been very busy completing a long list of tasks for her new employer. Mrs Evans was a kind woman, independent and pleasant, but her reluctance to bother her daughter with constant requests had ensured that many of her needs went unmet until Leah's arrival.

Leah wore jeans, a jazzy long-sleeved top and ankle boots, a practical outfit she had donned for a shopping trip, and she carried a bag crammed with the craft supplies she had collected for her elderly charge. Gio occupied the penthouse suite and an older man dressed like an old-fashioned manservant answered the door and ushered her through an opulent foyer into a large lounge area, decorated in tranquil greys with flashes of turquoise. The luxury was quiet and understated but she was very much aware of feeling that she did not belong in such a rarefied milieu. There Gio awaited her, spinning round from a tall window overlooking a leafy roof garden to study her with narrowed mercury-bright eyes.

Her heart began to hammer inside her chest, her mouth drying, her tummy tightening. It had only been a few months, but she had still contrived to forget the intensity of his physical impact and the spectacular good looks that literally stopped her in her tracks. Every honed and chiselled inch of him commanded her attention. There was nothing laid-back about either his appearance or his stance, not the smallest hint of informality or relaxation. He was sheathed in a beautifully cut charcoal suit that fitted him to perfection, outlining broad shoulders, lean hips and long, strong legs. A dark blue shirt was set off by a grey tie. Tension was etched into the hard cast of his lean, darkly handsome features, his bronzed skin taut over his slashing cheekbones and strong sculpted jaw. He had guessed, she registered, he had guessed what she was coming to tell him. But even that knowledge could not prevent the demeaning tightening at the heart of her or the prickling of her nipples, the soaring shameless surge of sexual awareness that she could not suppress.

Gio scrutinised her with innate concentration. She was paler than he remembered, smaller too, but the tumbled black curls, the beautiful eyes and clear creamy skin were unchanged, and hunger sparked in him at unnerving speed, intimate recollections teasing at the edges of his usually disciplined mind. He hadn't forgotten her, no, he certainly hadn't forgotten her in spite of every effort to do so.

He shifted position, irritated by the warning throb at his groin, inwardly talking himself down from that sexual edge while questioning what it was about her that so easily revved his engine. She had walked away from him and he wasn't used to rejection, at least not since he was a child. Back then he had met with rejection at every corner. Rejection from neighbours, classmates, teachers, from all those people who could see him only as the loser son of a vicious drug dealer, guaranteed to follow in his papa's footsteps. He had learned early to fight rejection and simply accepting it was still a challenge for him. But he had not chased Leah, he had respected her decision, which made the current situation all the more infuriating. Gio preferred to be in charge when trouble kicked off…and if she was about to tell him what he assumed, it *was* trouble.

'Obviously you're here to tell me that you're pregnant,' Gio murmured coolly, his silvery gaze tough and penetrating as steel. 'But that's not a discussion I'm willing to have with you yet—'

Taken aback by that blunt opening speech, Leah paled. 'It's...*not*?' she heard herself say in confusion.

'No, it would be pointless for us to discuss anything without proof—'

'Proof that I'm pregnant?' Leah queried. 'You know, it would have been nice if you had at least greeted me, asked me how I am and invited me to take a seat—'

'I don't do nice in these circumstances, but you are, of course, welcome to sit down,' Gio breathed tautly. 'My apologies, if my businesslike approach has offended you.'

'It hasn't,' Leah hastened to assure him, although she could feel the heat of mortification rising over her skin in betrayal of that brave claim and she felt too uncomfortable to take a seat.

'To answer your question,' Gio continued smoothly, 'no, I didn't mean proof that you're pregnant, I meant proof that any child you may be carrying is *my* child—something which can easily be established by a simple DNA test. We each give a blood sample at a laboratory and paternity can be established right now.'

Her eyes widened with bewilderment. 'Why would paternity have to be established?'

'Let's not be naïve,' Gio urged very drily. 'You've waited a long time to tell me that you're pregnant. You could be pregnant by some other man you met *after* you were with me.'

All the heat in Leah's skin retreated, leaving her very pale. She blinked rapidly, biting back an angry response. Not since she had broken up with Oliver had she felt so insulted or humiliated. Gio seemed to be insinuating that her very first sexual experience had set her on some immediate path of loose living in which she moved on very quickly from him to sample other men. 'I haven't been with anyone else. I've only been with you—'

'Surely you understand that I can't just take your word for that?' Gio shot back at her arrogantly.

'No. I'm afraid I don't accept that,' Leah countered stiffly. 'Not at this stage anyway. After all, I require nothing from you while I'm pregnant. I only contacted you now and came to tell you that I was pregnant because I felt that you had the right to know. Now that I've done that, I'll leave again.'

Gio stared at her in growing frustration. He was being realistic, totally realistic in his request that she take a DNA test to prove that her pregnancy was *his* responsibility. 'Are you saying that you refuse to take that test?'

'Right at this moment, I think it is humiliating for you to expect me to take a test when the only reason I'm here is to tell you that I'm pregnant,' Leah countered tightly. 'It's unnecessary and I won't agree to it. When the baby is born I will agree to a DNA test, not before. For the present you can keep your nasty suspicions that I could be trying to con you in some way to yourself.'

'I didn't make such an accusation,' Gio parried curtly, a hint of colour highlighting his exotic cheekbones. 'Women have been known to make an honest mistake in that line and I think it is wiser to establish the truth from the outset.'

Leah shrugged a slight shoulder, not prepared to concede that she was at fault because she could tell from his reaction that in some way she had drawn blood with her words, just as he had done with his. She supposed that made them even and each of them knew where the other stood, even if it was on opposing sides. Even if it had taken her a long time, she had done her duty in telling him about their baby. It was up to him if he chose not to believe her. 'We can agree to differ,' she murmured flatly and began to turn on her heel.

'Are you still living with your foster mother?'

Leah glanced back at him. 'No. I'm back in London.'

'I'd like to have your address.'

Grudgingly, she gave it and he put it into his phone.

Leah returned to her bedsit with the lowering sense that she had the weight of the world on her shoulders. She didn't know what she had expected from Gio but it had not occurred to her that he would question that any child she had conceived was his. She had been naïve, she told herself ruefully. He was a very wealthy man, probably used to people trying to take advantage of him. But no matter how much she tried to make excuses for him, she could only think of how alone she felt in her current predicament and how small and somehow soiled his attitude had made her feel. For that reason it was wonderful that evening to receive a phone call from Sally, asking if it was all right to pass on her contact details to a solicitor, who was keen to get in touch with Leah, concerning 'a confidential family matter'.

Leah's heart leapt with hope at that information, and she urged her foster mother to give her address and phone number to the solicitor. Was it possible that after all this time her twin brother or her kid sister could be trying to find her?

A busy two weeks passed as Leah settled into her job. She missed Spike terribly, but she had not been able to bring him with her. Towards the end of the second week she received a call from the solicitor offering her an appointment at an office in central London. Infused with curiosity, Leah attended, only to immediately recognise by the older woman's grave demeanour that she might be about to receive bad news. And so it proved.

Leah learned that her father had passed away several years earlier. As she had barely a blurred memory of the man, the discovery suffused her with only bemused sadness, more regret for what might have been than true grief. The announcement that her half-brother, Ari Stefanos, wished to meet her had a much more powerful effect on her. She was stunned by that idea, having always assumed that her father's legitimate son would want nothing to do with his children by another woman.

She was even more pleased to learn that Ari had been trying to trace her siblings as well and indeed that he had already had some success in that field. Finding out that her twin brother, Lucas, had died from a drug overdose was a crushing blow and a wrenching disappointment for her, however. She had last seen Lucas when she was a student, by which time his substance abuse had made him almost unrecognisable. He had stolen their mother's jewellery from her, presumably to sell the items and buy drugs. Leah had been devastated to lose those keepsakes, particularly as nothing in that small collection had been valuable. Even then she had suspected that her twin's addiction would eventually kill him and had felt hammered with guilt that she could not get through to him and change his outlook and habits.

By the time she had expressed keen interest in meeting her half-brother, Ari, Leah was in a daze and increasingly upset by the discovery that she had lost her twin for ever. The little boy she remembered playing with so innocently was no more and it broke her heart that her twin had been unable to cope with the world he found himself in to the extent that he had tried to block it out with his addiction.

When the solicitor went on to inform her that she had been left a large sum of money by her late father, she was very much taken aback. Discovering that the man she had barely known and whose name she had no longer recalled because it was not on her birth certificate had left her several million pounds bereft her of breath and she struggled to accept the concept of her sudden wealth, because she had lived her entire life stressing about money. She signed the document extended to her in a state of astonishment. Only as she travelled back home did she process the idea of having inherited sufficient money to have choices that she had never had before.

And thanks to that inheritance, her child would never know the insecurity that had been Leah's lot from an early age. Sudden intense relief assailed her, piercing and lightening the veil of grief that had consumed her. Perhaps she would buy a house somewhere near Sally or some sort of small business that would provide her with an income. She felt wonderfully liberated by the truth that she would not need Gio Zanetti's financial help to survive.

When the doorbell rang early that evening, she was surprised because her employer already had a friend visiting with her. It was a shock to open the door to Gio. Leah froze in the doorway, her lips parting in surprise, her heart hammering as if she were engaged in a race and rushing to the finishing line.

'What are you doing here?' she asked helplessly, intimidated by the sheer size of him that close. In the dusk light, his stunning eyes were pure silver, enhanced by lush black lashes as effective as eyeliner. He was gorgeous, particularly with a dark shadow of stubble outlining his stubborn mouth and jaw, arrestingly masculine, shockingly sexy. As always, that lean bronzed face momentarily froze her to the spot. A lot of good that sexiness had done her, Leah scolded herself impatiently.

'I wanted to check that you were OK,' Gio advanced with precision, connecting with eyes as intriguing as tiger's eye gemstones, brown streaked with warm gold and honey, striking in their colour and intensity. The passion she couldn't hide drew him like a burning flame on a cold day. He was learning that it didn't matter that she wore no make-up, that her hair was tousled and her clothing unflattering. None of those facts mattered when it came to the fierce sexual blaze she lit inside him.

'Why wouldn't I be?' she asked defensively.

'May I come in?'

Leah wanted to say no but reckoned that would be pointlessly provocative and there was no advantage to being on bad terms with the father of her child. 'I suppose so…'

While wishing for a little more enthusiasm on her part, Gio lifted his proud dark head high and moved past her into the confined hallway. He had obeyed a random prompting to visit her unannounced and was unusually uncertain of his motives. 'I was concerned. I need to know you're all right and that you have everything you need. This is not a good area for you to be living in—'

'I don't go out much at night, so that's not a concern.

You'd better come downstairs,' she sighed, leading the way down the twisting steep stairs into the basement area, which smelt of damp and disuse.

She opened the door reluctantly into her scrupulously tidy bedroom. Gio skimmed his gaze over the drab little room, taking in the signs of damp in one corner and grimacing. 'You shouldn't be living like this while you're pregnant. It's not healthy.'

'I'm fine. I shan't be staying much longer anyway. In fact, I'm about to hand in my notice.'

Gio frowned. 'Why? You've only been here a week or so, haven't you?'

'My circumstances are changing,' Leah stated grudgingly. 'It was unexpected.'

'How?' Gio asked bluntly.

'I don't think you're entitled to ask me personal questions,' Leah told him thinly.

'If you are carrying my baby, I am naturally going to feel responsible for your welfare,' Gio imparted curtly.

'But it positively shines out of you that you don't *want* this to be your baby or to feel responsible!' Leah snapped back at him, her voice rising slightly in volume.

'Does any single man really want to become a father after one fleeting encounter with a woman who wants nothing more to do with him?' Gio enquired very drily.

Colour stung her cheeks. 'It wasn't that I wanted nothing more to do with you—'

'It was,' Gio incised. 'Don't try to wrap it up. Best to be honest in our current circumstances.'

'Look, it wasn't like that,' Leah protested, feeling unexpectedly guilty when he described their brief connection in such terms. 'It was the fact that you concealed your identity and lied. I had had a recent bad experience with someone who had lied to me throughout our relationship and what you did reminded me of that and that unnerved me.'

'I am very sorry that I pretended to be an ordinary working guy. I lied on impulse without thinking it through. I didn't think I'd ever see you again at that point,' Gio imparted with decided sincerity.

Leah nodded as though she understood and accepted his explanation when in truth she was neither so understanding nor so forgiving after Oliver's deception. Oliver had destroyed her faith in her own judgement. Even before Oliver, her trust in the male sex had been seriously damaged by her father's irresponsibility as a parent and her brother's many broken promises and lies. She had once been so infatuated with Oliver and his status as a high-flying lawyer that she had swallowed his every word as though it were gospel. And the very memory of that weakness, that lack of judgement, still shamed Leah in her own eyes.

'I wasn't ready for another relationship anyway,' Leah summarised, keen to drop the subject since she did not want to argue with him and create bad feeling for no good reason.

'I've been there,' Gio breathed, with sudden darkness shadowing his handsome features. 'What happened to you?'

'I once fell for someone who was lying to me from the day that we met,' she muttered uncomfortably, not wishing to explain how blind she had been to Oliver's unscrupulous character and behaviour.

It was not as though she were stupid and yet how else could she interpret her failure to spot Oliver as the cheat, liar and master manipulator that he had been? Oliver's moral compass had been non-existent.

The suspicion that he was virtually paying for some other man's mistreatment of her could only infuriate Gio and he gritted his teeth on the temptation to tell her so. A phone rang out a noisy rocky tune and she dug it out of her pocket to answer it.

'Oh…' she said slowly in a tone of great surprise and then suddenly she smiled, her whole face lighting up. 'Like…*right now*?'

Mystified but genuinely excited to hear the voice of her newly discovered half-brother greeting her, Leah moved back towards her bedroom door, amused as Ari apologised profusely for his eagerness to meet her for the first time. He even told her how his wife had tried to restrain him by telling him not to crowd her on the same day that she had already had bad news delivered. A tiny giggle bubbled from Leah's lips.

'I wasn't expecting to hear from you so soon and *this* is good news,' she murmured softly, thinking that he was family and family was something she had craved for a long time. 'Problem is I don't really have anywhere to entertain you here…oh, yes, I can do that… If you feed me as well, I'm yours for ever! Ten minutes? I'll be waiting!'

Switching off her phone, she dug it back into her pocket and turned to look at Gio with colour brightening her formerly pale cheeks. 'I'm afraid I've got an unexpected invitation out that I would like to accept—'

'I was only dropping in,' Gio conceded with a rather jerky shrug of dismissal when all he wanted to know was who had put the blush into her cheeks and lit up her big dark eyes like stars. By her enthusiasm, he assumed the caller was male and he didn't like the direction his thoughts were travelling in one little bit.

He followed her back up the stairs, a knot of trapped rage starting to burn in his gut. He had been right to demand the DNA test and wise to call on her without warning. If he hadn't done so, he wouldn't have realised that she had another man in her life.

'I'll keep in touch,' he breathed tautly at the front door.

'If you like but it's not necessary right now,' Leah told him abstractedly.

Gio strode back to his car in a very bad mood, turbulent emotions washing through him in waves. As the front door shut he stayed static before stretching back in his seat to wait. Barely ten minutes later, a limousine double-parked, and a tall dark male leapt out and strode to the door. A light came on illuminating his features and incredulous recognition gripped Gio. Ari Stefanos! What the hell was Leah doing with a very married Greek billionaire? Could he be the man Leah had fallen for who had lied to her from the day they had met?

Gio watched the front door open, Leah's face unexpectedly serious as taut first words were exchanged and then she started crying and literally hurled herself into Stefanos' waiting arms. Gio wanted to get out and kill both of them stone dead where they stood. The sick sense of betrayal almost ate him alive. He hadn't felt like that since his marriage and bitterness almost consumed him. Why hadn't Leah been honest with him? Was the child she carried the Greek's? And if so, when had she first got together with him? The facts didn't match his suspicions, he grasped dimly.

CHAPTER FIVE

ARI PUT UP with Leah sobbing into his chest remarkably well and once she had recovered from her emotional reaction to his telling her that she reminded him very much of his little sister, who had died when he was a child, she told her employer that she would be back by midnight, before fetching her coat and bag and climbing into her brother's limo with him to be taken back to his London home, where she would meet his wife, Cleo…and some other surprise he had yet to specify for her benefit.

'So, satisfy my curiosity if you can,' Ari urged. 'How on earth did my father and your mother meet? I can't discover any evidence that she ever worked for him—'

'Oh, no, she didn't work for him. They both joined a bereavement group and that's how they met. He had lost your sister and Mum had lost her only sibling to cancer,' Leah explained. 'She told me the whole story shortly before she died. Mum believed that your father was separated from your mother when their affair began but I don't think he was entirely honest with her. Mum conceived my brother and I very early on and their relationship continued. I don't think it was the romance of the century. I think it was more lonely, unhappy people getting together when life was tough. I have vague memories of your father but he's not on my birth certificate and he stopped visiting when I was still very young. To be honest I couldn't even recall his name until the solicitor said it because it had been so long since I had heard it—'

'I don't know what possessed my father. He let you all down badly as a parent and yet—'

'I think your parents' marriage was in a bad way when he first met my mother but then the situation changed—'

'My mother had a nervous breakdown—'

'Did she? Well, anyway, Mum said he pretty much vanished for months and when he reappeared she broke things off with him for good and moved away to make a fresh start. By then she knew there was no future in the relationship, and she didn't want ties with him,' Leah told him wryly. 'Unfortunately, she only then discovered that she was expecting my little sister, Eloise, and Eloise was a newborn when Mum died.'

'Eloise was adopted. I've lodged a letter asking for contact with the agency involved, but she has to ask for contact first. She's over eighteen now, so we'll have to wait and see what happens.' Ari sighed. 'I don't have a lot of patience, unfortunately.'

'Neither do I,' Leah quipped. 'Maybe it's a family trait.'

She was chattering freely by the time they arrived at her brother's imposing town house, and meeting her sister-in-law, Cleo, a warm, welcoming and noticeably pregnant young woman with guinea gold curls, only increased Leah's level of comfort. She was stunned when Ari explained that her late brother and his girlfriend, who had died with him, had had a child together and that he and Cleo had adopted little Lucy. A stinging rush of tears glossed Leah's eyes when Cleo brought a tiny girl into the room to join them for dinner. She was so cute and the knowledge that this child was her niece and her brother's living legacy almost overwhelmed her. She was deeply touched that Ari had had a big enough heart to bring Lucy into his family, fully accepting the bond of blood that some men would have disdained as beneath their notice.

The warmth she sensed in her brother and his wife quickly won her trust, and, when Ari confessed that he had had to have her investigated thoroughly to find her and that he already knew that she was pregnant, she respected his honesty and was willing to give a frank account of what had happened with Gio. Ari invited her out to stay in his home in Greece while Cleo urged her to make an appointment to see the same obstetrician she used.

'I'm giving notice that I'm leaving but I can't leave Mrs Evans in the lurch,' Leah declared apologetically.

Luckily for her, Ari had a solution for every problem. He told her that he would bring in a qualified carer to take her place and free her up from her job sooner. He was very set on taking her and his family out to his Greek island, Spinos, where they could relax and take the time to get to know each other. Leah, in turn, was curious to see the island that her father had once called home and learn more about her paternal background.

When she arrived home at midnight, her thoughts were in a spin and she climbed into bed and slept like a log. Her phone rang while she was bringing Mrs Evans her breakfast tea and toast.

'Excuse me,' she said, stepping out into the hallway to answer it.

'Join me for lunch,' Gio suggested. 'I'll send a car to pick you up—'

'Lunch? I only take an hour,' Leah said reluctantly, wanting to see him and yet not wanting to see him at one and the same time. Where Gio was concerned, she was in total conflict.

'My daughter's coming this afternoon,' Mrs Evans declared from the doorway. 'Take as long as you like. You've already done all sorts of things for me that weren't in your job description.'

Leah agreed to lunch, wondering what Gio wanted even while she wondered if she should have turned him down flat after his insinuation that the child she was carrying might not be his. Ari had counselled her to either take the DNA test or keep her distance from Gio until after she had had her child. It was sensible advice but taking that test would entail sacrificing what little remained of her pride. On her terms, it would mean a climbdown, an admission that possibly there *could* be some doubt about the paternity of her child, and she wasn't prepared to allow Gio Zanetti to believe that.

Why did that matter to her? Why did she care about his opinion? Particularly when she had had a one-night stand with him and flouted her own beliefs in not saving that first experience for a more meaningful relationship? Oliver had utterly destroyed her faith in meaningful relationships, she conceded ruefully, and even as Oliver's indifference had wrecked her pride, Gio's desire for her had finally made her feel like an attractive woman again. But how on earth could she have been such an idiot? So short-sighted? So careless of consequences?

Why had she stopped taking the pill? But beating herself up for what could not be changed was pointless and what Gio thought of her was unimportant when she needed neither him nor his money in her life to survive.

But she did *need* him to be a father for her child, she acknowledged unhappily. She had grown up without a father and throughout her childhood she had longed to have a father the same as her friends. Little glimpses of other men with their daughters had made her envious and sad about what she had missed out on. Even so, would Gio even be willing to take on a paternal role? She supposed she wouldn't know until after her child was born and she supposed that then she would have no choice but to take a DNA test to put his doubts to rest.

She had conceived a child with a distrustful guy, she conceded with regret. He was unwilling to take anything on trust, much like herself, she conceded in surprise at that acknowledgement. Just as she found it hard to trust men, Gio was challenged to trust women. That reality made her a tiny bit more forgiving of his suspicions. Someone or a variety of someones had made Gio reluctant to trust as well. Gio would need proof that her child was his child too and, if she wanted him to bond with their baby and take on a father's role, she would have to provide him with that proof on paper.

And in the meantime, if she truly wanted Gio to be a father for their child's benefit, she needed to make him feel involved in her pregnancy, didn't she? She thought of the appointment with Cleo's obstetrician, which Cleo had made for her for the next day. She would have an ultrasound, Cleo had assured her. Hopefully, she would see the very first picture of her child and find out the sex. Feeling guilty that she had waited so long to have a proper medical examination, she decided simultaneously that she would offer Gio the chance to accompany her and share in the experience. If he said no, well, at least she would have done her best to include him.

Leah changed for her lunch date. Clothes were already refusing to fit her changing shape and she bit her lip in dismay as her best jeans refused to fasten at the waist. Her leggings and her older jeans were shabby and she refused to wear them. Even worse, her once slender waist had disappeared without her really noticing. She hadn't expected those changes to take place quite so quickly and she swallowed hard, knowing she had a shopping trip ahead of her and rustling back into her small wardrobe in search of something a little dressier. A floral maxi skirt with a stretchy waist was literally the only thing she owned that still fitted her. She teamed it with a rather loose white top that concealed the curve of her stomach and winced at her reflection. No make-up. She didn't want him to think she was getting tarted up for his benefit.

A limousine arrived to collect her and her brows vanished into her hairline as it drew up, reeking of money and privilege. She had been taken aback by her brother's limo and it hadn't occurred to her that Gio might use one as well. Of course, they were both very wealthy men. Ari, however, had made a point of reminding her that she didn't need Gio Zanetti for *anything* now, not for money or support, but she had privately thought that she didn't want to take such a combative stance with her child's father. Ari was offended on her behalf by Gio's refusal to accept her word. Leah was offended as well, only rather more willing, having conceded her own flaws, to give Gio a second chance…

This time she entered his apartment block with a firmer, more confident step, straightening her slight shoulders as she stepped into his extravagant penthouse. She was shown straight into a spectacular dining room with fabulous views of the city skyline. As she crossed the threshold, Gio appeared through another door and stilled to stare at her.

'I was keen to have a private meeting with you,' Gio drawled softly. 'Somewhere where we could talk without being overheard.'

His beautiful eyes shimmered and glittered like diamonds in his lean, hard-boned face and she stiffened, immediately recognising the unexpected leaping tension in the atmosphere.

'I suppose that's sensible,' Leah agreed as he pulled out a chair politely for her to sit down.

'Would you like a drink?' he enquired, watching her hitch her long skirt to cross her slender legs, noticing that the top she wore was slightly transparent and merely enhanced the full thrust of breasts cupped in pale lace. As his attention strayed to her luscious pink lips, the thrum of arousal kicked off and he averted his gaze, furious with himself for being so ridiculously susceptible. Didn't he ever learn the lesson that marriage had taught him? It was dangerous to allow himself to be vulnerable with *any* woman. Hadn't his mother taught him that from childhood as well?

'Juice or a soft drink,' Leah responded, striving to relax even in the face of the tension he emanated. Was he angry with her? Had something happened? She was travelling from her earlier calm towards edgy discomfiture, and she resented him for having that effect on her.

He nodded at the hovering manservant and a glass

of chilled orange juice was brought and set in front of her. She felt ridiculously like a condemned prisoner, having a last wish granted as she sat there at the table while Gio remained upright beside the tall windows. It hurt too that she still recognised that his impossible good looks were matched by spectacular magnetism.

'What's wrong?' she asked, driven into speech by the pulsing silence.

'I have only one question to ask you and I expect an honest answer,' Gio decreed arrogantly, the planes of his lean bronzed profile forbidding in the strong light flooding the room. 'What is your relationship with Ari Stefanos? I have the right to know the truth on that score.'

Astonishment gripped Leah and her caramel eyes widened at the demand. How the heck did Gio know about her brother's recent arrival in her life? Her newly discovered ties with her brother and the inheritance that had come with it were a secret and she had no idea whether or not her half-brother had any intention of *ever* going public with their relationship. The night before, Ari had seemed pretty much mortified by his father's secret affair and second family, not to mention being rather ashamed of Christophe Stefanos' undeniable negligence as a parent. Those were not solely Leah's secrets to tell and she did not owe Gio Zanetti a truth that could cause embarrassment for her big brother.

'My relationship with Ari is none of your business,' she told Gio with composed cool.

'Of course, it's my business!' Gio fired back at her. 'Naturally I'm concerned if you are claiming that you are expecting my child when there is *obviously* another man in your life!'

'Oh, so your nasty suspicions have tipped over into

actual fact now that you have apparently established that I really know *one* other man?' Leah rounded her caramel-brown eyes to accentuate her stab at how ridiculous that statement was. 'Do I have to move into a convent to convince you that you have been the *only* man in my life since I conceived?'

Angry colour flushed Gio's hard cheekbones. In the smouldering silence, the manservant reappeared carrying plates. As he uncorked a bottle of wine, Gio informed him gruffly that they would serve themselves and he withdrew again.

'I want an answer,' Gio repeated stubbornly as the door closed.

Leah shook out her napkin with a positive flourish as she lifted her chin, her dark eyes steady. 'You're not entitled to an answer. You're lucky that I was even willing to have lunch with you,' she pointed out, lifting her knife and fork and quite determined to eat the delicious salad on her plate. 'According to you, my claim that I'm carrying your child entitles you to some sort of medieval ownership of my entire person and my freedom. Don't you see how unreasonable an expectation that is?'

'All I asked was for clarification of your relationship with Stefanos, who enjoyed quite a raunchy reputation with women before his recent marriage.'

Leah wrinkled her nose with distaste at that unsought information about her big brother. 'I suggest you look at your own playboy reputation with women before you start throwing insults in Ari's direction—'

'You're not listening to me, are you?' Gio growled, well-nigh incredulous as he watched her continue to eat with apparent composure.

Leah ate quietly for a few moments while she pondered his words. 'You haven't yet said anything which I want to hear. When I met you, you seemed such a straightforward guy,' she confided wryly. 'But I was so *wrong* in that estimation because you're not at all like that. Under the surface, you have more turns and twists than a Gordian knot. You appear to be a womaniser who assumes all women are unprincipled, dishonest and unworthy of trust—'

'That is untrue!' Gio incised in a driven undertone, incensed at that reading of his behaviour.

'From my experience it is totally true,' Leah asserted, crunching through her lettuce with gusto and pausing again to think. 'You invited me here for lunch simply to interrogate me. Even worse, you're demanding answers to questions that you have no right to ask. I'm not married to you. I'm not dating you. I owe you nothing more than the information I've already given you.'

'I am trying to establish a relationship with you—'

'No, you're not. You're accusing me of carrying on with a married man. I assure you that there is no affair, but if you want an explanation of my relationship with Ari, ask him to elucidate. Ironically, he advised me to stay *away* from you—'

'Did he indeed?' Gio slammed back at her rawly, his biting fury at that news illuminating his pale gaze.

'Just until the birth, when I will allow you to have your precious DNA test as proof.' Leah sighed. 'And it was good advice, but I sort of thought I could include you sooner, which just goes to show how naïve I was. I mean, I actually believed I had been invited to a genuine lunch today aimed at improving our tricky relationship.'

'How can it improve when you are determined not to answer my questions?' Gio framed grimly. 'And why are you suddenly trying to include me when you said you didn't need contact with me prior to the birth?'

Leah pushed away her plate and tossed down her napkin. She stood up with thoroughly exasperated dark eyes locked to his lean, darkly handsome face. 'I want my baby to have a father because I barely have a memory of my own. I was afraid that if I excluded you completely at this stage it could damage any potential bond you might develop with our child in the future. I *was* planning to tell you that I'm having an ultrasound screening tomorrow afternoon at Mr Grove's clinic on Harley Street, so that you could attend if you want to be involved. But I can see now that *that* was a very foolish idea,' she completed curtly as she paused only to grab her coat and bag and stalked back into the foyer.

'Leah!'

Leah spun round, her pink pouty mouth compressed into an impatient line, and all Gio wanted to do was chase that expression from her face and erase the lowering thought that he had contrived, once again, to disappoint her. *Per Dio*, since when had he tried to measure up to a woman's expectations when *she* was the one being unreasonable? After all, a simple test was all it would take to remove his doubts that her child was also *his* child. Where was the harm in a basic test?

'I'm sorry, but when I saw you in Stefanos' arms it looked distinctly dodgy,' Gio ground out defensively.

'Ah…that's right, he arrived just after you left and so you saw him.' Leah's delicate brows pleated in confusion. 'But you didn't see any kissing or anything like that,' she pointed out, frowning then before making the obvious deduction. 'You're a jealous toad, Gio.'

A flare of disconcerted colour ignited over his

sculpted cheekbones. 'I am *not* jealous,' he derided incredulously.

'Well, keep telling yourself that if that works for you, but the anger, the suspicion and the interrogation suggest another story. You don't have the right to question me about who I have in my life,' Leah informed him with spirit. 'We are not a couple—'

'We could have been—'

'No...*this*...would have happened.' Leah moved her hand across her abdomen, indicating her pregnancy. 'And it's obvious to me that we would have ended up at each other's throats regardless—'

'I don't think so,' Gio argued, stalking towards her, tall, dark and resolute, his spectacular eyes fierce, making her back up against the wall behind her. 'The passion would have cancelled out our differences—'

'What p-passion?' she dared shakily, her throat tightening, her mouth running dry as he studied her with the incredible intensity that she associated only with him. He looked as though every brain cell in his handsome head were fully concentrated on her and for some reason that sheer intensity of his lit her up inside like a torch. No male had ever looked at her that way until him and it had a power over her that she couldn't comprehend.

She was running out of breath. An intoxicating tension held her still, her breasts stirring inside her bra as she sucked in oxygen, her nipples tightening into straining peaks while a hot liquidity welled at her feminine core.

'Tell me not to touch you,' Gio urged her in a driven undertone.

Why did he have to say that? Nobody had touched her since him. Those words only reminded her of how he had made her body sing and how much she longed to feel that way again. 'I can't do that,' she whispered.

'Why not?' he framed in a sexy purr, leaning over her, resting his hands against the wall on either side of her head, caging her in with his big muscular body. Dimly she could feel his body heat warming her.

'Because…because…' And Leah leant forward and let her hands slide between the parted edges of his jacket and smooth up over his hard muscled chest, the heat pulsing through her metamorphosing into an outright unbearable ache that made her lower limbs tremble. He was so warm and the familiar scent of him that close made her head swim as though she were intoxicated.

Long fingers tilted up her chin; metallic silver eyes inspected hers. 'Your pupils are huge—'

'Are they?' she muttered helplessly as she finally yanked her hands back from him, guilt infusing her at that weakness she couldn't suppress, that wicked and terrible need to *touch* him.

'You want me too,' he husked with a raw edge of confidence.

She stretched up on her tiptoes, small hands reaching up to cup his face. 'We can't do this,' she told him firmly.

With a rough sound low in his throat, he turned his mouth into her palm and slid it down to press against the pulse point on her narrow wrist. As she shivered in reaction, she felt the hard, urgent thrust of his erection against her midriff.

'I've had a lot of cold showers since you went out of my life,' he told her roughly.

'I was barely *in* your life—'

'But you left your mark on me all the same,' he

breathed rawly, reaching down to clasp her hips and lift her up against him. 'And nobody else will do.'

Leah stopped breathing altogether. That physical contact was everything she craved and yet everything she shouldn't allow herself to have. Frustration currenting through her, she let her knees clamp to his waist, and she kissed him, teasing along the edge of his full lower lip, nipping across the upper just as he had taught her that one unforgettable night. He had the most beautiful, perfect mouth she had ever tasted, and she wanted to feel it on hers with every breath in her body.

'Put me down before this gets out of hand,' she muttered tightly.

'I'm already out of hand…feeling reckless.' Gio growled that admission soft and low, bending his head to kiss a teasing, enervating line down over the sensitive slope between her neck and shoulder, awakening a tidal wave of response in her sensation-starved body. 'I want to take you into my bedroom and ravish you. *Madre di Dio*, is that even allowed in your condition?'

'Why wouldn't it be?' she heard herself say.

With a suppressed groan, Gio slowly, carefully lifted her more fully into his arms and carried her out of the hall and down the corridor to his bedroom. She weighed so little and yet he was insanely conscious of the swell of her stomach and of a quite inappropriate desire to shape it with his hands. She was pregnant, definitely pregnant, not lying on that score anyway. And it was *possible* that the baby was his, he reasoned, entirely possible. But it truly didn't matter whether the child was his or not at that moment because it was her whom he was burning up to possess.

'I wasn't jealous,' he breathed against her reddened

lips as he laid her down on a big wide bed and flipped off her shoes.

'If you say so,' Leah mumbled, wondering how they had travelled at such insane speed from discord to passion and why that passion had overpowered her every misgiving and why now she felt crazily relaxed as if she was finally safe. Safe from what? From being alone? She wasn't alone any more. She had Ari and Cleo and her niece now, the family she had always craved. Only for some reason, that wasn't enough for her any more, she grasped dimly.

'It was just anger. You were racing off to be with him when I was there right in *front* of you,' Gio specified without hesitation.

'He offered me dinner—'

'I would've offered you dinner.'

His mercurial silver eyes held hers and heat washed through her as he shed his jacket, wrenched at his tie, all that very formal expensive tailoring of his discarded with disrespectful haste as he stripped. 'I felt challenged, not jealous. I don't share. I don't cheat.'

Leah veiled her gaze and tried not to smile. He was territorial, possessive even, though she had not given him that right. His bronzed chest bare, the rippling muscles of his abdomen taut and evident as he came down to her, he bent his dark head and kissed her with a hunger that raced through her in an incendiary wave of heat. Her fingers speared into his luxuriant black hair as he lifted her up to him and peeled off her top. Her bra fell away. He caught her breasts in his hands, savouring their swollen fullness with an appreciation in his intent gaze that she felt to her very toes, as though her body was his alone to worship and admire.

He rubbed his thumbs over the distended peaks and her breath caught in her throat, making her gasp, and then he lowered his mouth to the achingly sensitive tips and she was lost entirely to the wild surge of desire that ignited the blaze at her melting centre. He found her there, skating across the aroused bud beneath her knickers, making her spine arch and her body jerk as he slid aside the taut strip of fabric between her thighs and found the slick dampness of her arousal.

'*Madre di Dio*, I want you,' Gio growled as he rose over her to remove that last item of clothing.

And then he found the hot, damp, quivering heart of her with his mouth and his fingers and his tongue and she was lost, utterly lost for long moments of blissful sensation that surged through her in gathering waves until she reached a peak that threw her up and into timeless space where she fell apart with sheer pleasure and the lingering deep relief of satisfaction.

Her body still on a high from that overload of delightful feeling, she watched him don protection. She couldn't credit that she had chosen to be with him again but, in that instant, it didn't matter that there were differences between them, it only mattered that he was the father of her child and she craved him like an addictive drug.

He drove into her tender sheath with measured strength, stretching her with a slow burn of wildly electrifying sensation. Her excitement soared to an impossible high because she was ultra-sensitive to every lithe twist of his hips. Heart hammering, body clenching in agonising need, Leah hit another climax and it wiped her out for long timeless moments while she slumped limp and Gio struggled to catch his breath again, finally rolling over to release her from his weight and thrusting his tumbled hair off his brow with a sated groan.

'That was unbelievable,' he muttered unevenly. 'Unbelievably good.'

Leah experienced a painful moment of self-discovery. She wanted to turn time back and find herself leaving the building as she should have done. Should've, could've, would've, she mocked herself bitterly. Everybody had a weakness and evidently Gio Zanetti was hers, only, sadly, he was not a weakness she could afford and, just then, she loathed herself for not turning him down, for not pushing him away. Instead, she had surrendered to her own lust for him.

'You see we have the passion. That's really all we need,' Gio intoned.

Both Leah's hands clenched into tiny fists. He had never come closer to an assault than he was at that moment with her because he was making her taste the consequences of her own poor judgement. He still thought it was acceptable to question her morals and, by succumbing to his appeal, she had betrayed herself, playing into his desired image of her as a woman who treated sex casually. As Gio stalked into the bathroom, Leah was up off that bed within seconds and frantically getting back into her clothes. All that was on her mind was escape at the fastest rate possible. Bare minutes later she was leaving the building, flushed and tousled but too upset to be embarrassed and reminding herself that she could actually afford now to take a taxi.

When he returned to the bedroom, Gio was utterly taken aback to find Leah gone. What was it with her? She had sex and then she ran like a deer being hunted. The first time, well, he had kind of written that up to his having become her first lover. Foolishly he had ignored her insistence then that they could only have one night together. No woman had ever told him that before, so he could forgive his own disbelief. But when it happened a second time and she disappeared, it gave him real pause for thought. What had he done? What had he said? It was hard to escape the idea that in her estimation he did and said everything wrong, and that suspicion hit him like a punch squarely in his pride.

He did not treat women badly. He didn't lie to them, and he didn't cheat on them either. Yet Leah behaved as though he were the worst guy alive. He wondered dimly if it could have something to do with pregnancy hormones, but he knew absolutely nothing about pregnancy, only that he had a friend who had confided that his wife had become very highly strung after she conceived. So, he wasn't about to take offence, he assured himself, immediately ditching his angry annoyance. He would accept her departure like an adult…even if *she* wasn't behaving like an adult? Gio gritted his even white teeth, striving to make allowances when he had never before in his life made allowances for a woman. He liked Leah's chippy feistiness, he reminded himself, he just didn't like the fact that he never knew what she would do or say next. To his way of thinking, Leah, in comparison to all the women he had ever known, might as well have been an alien from another planet.

Leah attended her medical appointment alone the following day. Cleo had offered to accompany her, but Leah had politely demurred. She was a single parent-to-be, she reflected ruefully, and she needed to get used to doing stuff alone. She didn't want Ari and Cleo to start feeling that they were responsible for her in the way that Sally had. She would get through her pregnancy alone fine.

Buoyed up by that belief, Leah was shattered when Gio strolled into the plush waiting room at Mr Grove's clinic while she was waiting to be called for her ultrasound. She wanted to hiss, *What the heck are you doing here?* but it was impossible to do so when they were surrounded by people. It made her feel even worse that she was immediately relieved that she had gone shopping for maternity clothing that same morning and was at least respectably dressed.

Unhappily, Gio Zanetti was the ultimate cynosure of attention in the waiting room. He was sheathed in a tailored navy suit that had probably cost a fortune and that accentuated every line of his lean, strong, muscular physique. It shook her to recognise that his lean, dark features left her bereft of breath and that she was not the only woman present who reacted. Every eye turned and lingered on him as he sank fluidly into the empty seat beside her as though he had every right to be there. And it was all her own fault, she acknowledged, because she had told him where the appointment was and he must have phoned to ask for the time…

CHAPTER SIX

'WHAT THE HECK are you doing here?' Leah contrived to whisper-hiss at Gio in the corridor after the nurse came to fetch them through to the surgery.

Gio sent her a slanting smile that made her treacherous heart skip a beat. 'I realised that you were right. I don't want to miss this opportunity,' he asserted, grateful that she didn't know the story of his marriage.

Of course, absolutely no one *did* know that story apart from Gio and his ex-wife and there was a very good reason for that, Gio allowed grimly. Naturally he had no desire to admit what an idiot he had been at the age of twenty-one. He preferred to forget his marriage had ever happened and, since it had been a dire experience, he believed that few would blame him for that attitude. Only since Leah's arrival in his life and her pregnancy had he begun to appreciate that that disastrous marriage had marked him in ways he had not appreciated.

Leah had already been through a preliminary meeting with the doctor during which various tests had been run and she had been gently admonished for not seeking medical attention sooner. Now, rattled by Gio's unexpected appearance and wondering whether to be grateful or resentful for his presence, she lay down for the ultrasound, striving not to feel awkward as she tugged up her loose top and pushed down her maternity jeans to enable the technician to work, rubbing on the gel and then wielding the transducer wand. Gio infuriated her to the brink of screaming by getting into a technical chat about the equipment with the medics. Talk about a disinterested bystander!

And then the heartbeat sounded very loudly and Gio fell instantly silent.

'Is that the…?' Leah began uncertainly.

'And there is what Mr Grove suspected.' The technician pointed at the screen. 'There are two babies. Would you like to know the gender?'

'Two?' Leah gasped. 'Twins? They run in my family.'

'Twins,' the obstetrician confirmed cheerfully. 'Gender reveal or not?'

'Yes… I would like to know,' Leah whispered shakily.

'Fraternal twins. A little girl and a little boy.'

Just like her and her lost twin, Leah reflected painfully. Sadness tugged at her before she pushed it away to concentrate on the joy of the twins she was carrying. Their lives would be far different from the chaotic childhood she and her brother had experienced, she reminded herself more happily.

Gio was transfixed by the extraordinary 3D screen that showed the babies lying side by side, depicting two little faces. He had never seen anything like it before in his life. But then, he reminded himself doggedly, he had never seen an ultrasound screen before. But it had also not occurred to him that babies could look quite that cute. But then, he didn't think he had looked at many babies before either. Maybe they all looked like that. He blinked while the doctor informed Leah that she would have to take extra precautions as a twin pregnancy would be tougher on her than a singleton one. He experienced an extraordinary urge to scoop Leah up into his arms and take her straight back to his home and it utterly horrified him, putting to immediate flight the temptation to instantly accept that those images were *his* children. *Per amor di Dio…*what the hell was happening to him?

Still very much spooked by that impulse, Gio left the room with Leah in silence and then turned his head to glance down at her, belatedly registering that she had an expectant look in her big brown caramel eyes. 'Are you even thinking about getting that test to sort stuff out?' he enquired quietly, careful not to sound too demanding on that score.

Baulked of her every naïve hope of sharing her pregnancy with Gio, Leah was cut to the quick by that horribly dispassionate question. If that was all he had to say after seeing those wonderful images on screen, there was no hope left for him. She stamped down hard on her disillusionment and told herself that she had got exactly what she deserved for expecting *more* from Gio Zanetti. What she needed and their children would conceivably need in the future, he apparently didn't have to give, and that was, at its most basic, an *emotional* connection.

'No, I'm not thinking about taking that test,' Leah parried brightly with a determined smile. 'You're going to have to wait—'

'I'll take you home,' Gio announced on the street.

'Thanks, but I have someone to meet in half an hour,' Leah told him truthfully and, turning on her heel, she walked away, looking forward to meeting

Cleo for coffee and sharing her news with someone who actually *cared*.

For a split second, sheer frustrated rage over that unhesitating rejection rolled through Gio. The reaction was like a violent rip tide and that unnerved him. The son of a vicious, brutal man, he had learned from adolescence to control his emotions. He had grown up in an abusive home with a father who often lost his temper and responded with his fists. That cautious attitude had bled over into a defensive control that kept any too strong feeling firmly at bay.

He did, however, register that he had got it wrong yet again with Leah and his sculpted jaw line clenched hard. He wished she came with an operating manual he could read and comprehend. He was a male of a technical bent and he liked instructions. Right now with Leah, he felt as if he were stumbling around trying to cope in daylight while he was blindfolded. He was starting to realise that throughout his life he had only ever enjoyed the most superficial of relationships and that belated awareness daunted him. But he could *learn*, he told himself grimly; he could be different if he worked hard enough at it. It wasn't as though he were stupid—indeed Gio enjoyed a genius level IQ, which was what had rescued him from the mean streets of a poor, remote Italian town.

Leah was a little teary-eyed with Cleo. Seeing her babies for the first time had been an intensely emotional moment and she had badly needed to share it with someone, only her children's father had, sadly, been the wrong someone. That closing question about the DNA test Gio had fixated on was the proverbial last straw for Leah. She told her delighted sister-in-law that as soon as it could be arranged, she would be delighted to join her newly discovered family in Greece. After all, Gio had made it painfully obvious that there was nothing to keep her in London…

It took Gio Zanetti almost four months to throw in the towel and admit defeat in his efforts to find Leah. He was a very stubborn man, but she had simply disappeared into thin air. Her former foster mother had confided that she would need Leah's permission to tell him where she was and, since that had not been forthcoming, it had told Gio all he needed to know about Leah's opinion of him. The detective agency he had hired had got nowhere trying to locate her and Gio had slowly come to believe that only someone as wealthy as he was himself could have made it possible for Leah to stage so complete a vanishing act. It was for that reason that Gio had finally bitten the bullet and arranged to meet Ari Stefanos.

Only if he *was* to learn that Stefanos was behind her disappearance, Gio reflected grimly, he was highly likely to slaughter the Greek where he stood. Gio had ploughed through weeks of serious concern over Leah's well-being. He had even gone to the police when Sally had first refused to tell him where Leah was. He had ultimately decided that Leah was almost certainly carrying *his* children because, clearly, Leah wanted nothing to do with him, socially, sexually or financially, so why would she have lied about who she had conceived her babies with? No other interpretation of her behaviour made sense. He thought of her composed response to his suspicion that she had had a past relationship with

Stefanos and gritted his teeth. Whatever the relationship had been, it had obviously not amounted to much when Leah hadn't slept with the other man.

'Mr Stefanos will see you now…' The announcement broke into Gio's intense thoughts and knocked him back to reality.

'To what do I owe the honour?' Ari Stefanos enquired smoothly as he crossed his office and extended a lean hand in greeting.

And that fast, in the other man's decidedly constrained welcome, Gio recognised that he had been entirely correct in his misgivings about the Greek. He shook hands and said without any expression at all, 'Clearly, you know about Leah and I—'

'I do,' Ari confirmed.

'And you know where she is?'

'She's staying on the island of Spinos. But not so fast, Zanetti,' Ari countered with an edge of disrespect that made Gio's wide shoulders straighten into a rigid line, anger firing in his broad muscular chest. 'I have a proposition to put to you and I would like to outline that with you first and hear your answer before we go any further. I've ordered coffee—'

'Not for me, thanks,' Gio demurred curtly. 'What is the proposition? And what is your role in my personal relationship with Leah that you feel you have the right to—?'

'I'm her brother,' Ari declared boldly. 'Her closest male relative and I wish to protect her from further harm and distress.'

Her…*brother*? Gio was astonished. That idea hadn't even occurred to him. Yet he had considered every other possible connection between them from the workplace to a friend of a friend. 'But you're an only child—'

'My father had a hidden second family. In Leah's current situation, I want you to marry her to protect her name and reputation. That may strike you as very old-fashioned but, in some fields, I *am* a very old-fashioned man. Your children should carry your surname and if you do not marry her, they will have mine. I am not asking you to make it a true marriage, but merely to go through the ceremony and part at some mutually agreeable point in the future—'

'*This* is what Leah wants?' Gio interrupted in disbelief.

'Leah doesn't even know we're meeting. Of course she doesn't know, and she would not welcome my interference, but I fully understand what will make her happy and a father for her twins will make her happy,' Ari informed him drily. 'Are you even willing to make that kind of commitment? I do have a small inducement to offer…the Castello Zanetti became my property at the end of last month—'

The urge to knock Ari's teeth down his throat was growing mightily in Gio and both of his hands were slowly clenching into fists. 'How did you persuade the old man to sell to you?' he bit out rawly.

'I'm now a family man. Your lifestyle wasn't to his taste…any more than mine would have been prior to my marriage,' Ari pointed out drily. 'I don't want the property. I merely bought it as an—'

'Inducement,' Gio slotted in with cutting emphasis. 'I don't respond well to blackmail—'

'And I don't respond well to anyone disrespecting my sister,' Ari countered.

'I *didn't* disrespect her!' Gio ground out furiously, outraged at the manner in which he was being condemned when he *had* tried to reach an accommodation with Leah. Admittedly, he had failed in that goal, but he believed that he had been civil and restrained.

Who did Ari Stefanos think he was to try and move Gio and Leah around like pieces on his chess board? He wasn't for sale and Leah and her pregnancy were not a situation under Stefanos' control. Leah was very much Gio's business and he would decide what happened next, *not* her brother!

Leah stretched her toes in her shaded arbour overlooking the sea on her brother's estate and sighed as she slowly wakened. As her pregnancy advanced, she had discovered that she catnapped on a regular basis and now that she was only a few weeks from delivery, that tendency had increased. In her own opinion she was as large as a beached whale and her exhaustion was understandable, only she also knew she was living a life where she was spoiled rotten and waited on hand and foot, so she felt guilty. *Guilty* for lazing about and reading and chatting and eating, *guilty* for not having a job any more, *guilty* for spending the money she had never had before, *guilty* for missing Gio…

And there it was, the fly in her ointment, the shadow on her day, the secret tripwire in her brain…this shameless missing of a guy who had started out as a harmless one-night stand before transforming into the most stubborn, tactless, persistent and hatefully annoying man alive! When had she caught feelings again? After Oliver, she had promised herself that she wouldn't do that again, not at least until a long, long time had gone by and her judgement had improved. But meeting Gio Zanetti had simply upended her life and then Ari had found her and everything had become so complicated that her head ached just trying to think about it. Stress was bad for her and the medics had warned her of the risks, so she breathed in slow and deep to calm herself lest her blood pressure start causing problems again.

While doing that she patted her stomach with a possessive soothing hand, thinking warmly of her babies, active little creatures according to the number of nights they had kept her awake with their squirming and fluttering movements. She was a little envious of Cleo, whose twin boys had already been safely born, two beautiful healthy children called Andreas and Nikolas. Their christening was to be held the following day and Ari and Cleo were flying in to join her that very evening. The island of Spinos was gloriously peaceful, or at least the Stefanos beach house was, she adjusted, thinking of the busy resort at the far end of the island and the equally bustling village nearby. Gradually she raised herself into a seated position and opened her eyes. Midway through reaching for a chilled drink from the cooler at her feet, she froze.

A yacht the size of the *Titanic* was now anchored out in the bay dominating all it surveyed. It was huge, one of those mega yachts she had read about in a magazine but never actually seen in reality, and that was saying something because when Ari was in residence they received some very wealthy visitors, who arrived in their own boats. *Virgo*, it was called, she thought with a frown, wondering why that name seemed vaguely familiar to her. While watching Ari's security men setting off in a motorboat to greet the new arrivals, she watched two other speedboats race from the yacht towards the shore. One veered off to greet Ari's security but the other continued towards the pier.

Leah rested back in the shade and lifted her book, only to blink in surprise a few minutes later when her brother's security chief approached in a beach buggy. She froze when he explained that Gio Zanetti was asking to see her.

'Er…yes, of course,' she heard herself choke out in sheer shock. Gio had arrived on the yacht? Refusing to see him struck her as being childish when she had been hiding away at her brother's home for so long.

Gio, *here* on the island. She could barely get her head around that fact, straining her eyes to stare across at the pier on which a tall, well-built male stood gazing back. Well, the giant silhouette of her even in the distance would identify her, she thought unhappily. She had got even more pregnant and large since their last meeting. Legs feeling weak, she stayed sitting down, watching as the other man used his radio and Gio climbed into another buggy to be driven over to her.

'Would you like me to stay with you, Miss Stefanos?' the security chief enquired protectively.

'Thanks, Dmitri…but that won't be necessary,' Leah declared with a weak smile intended to reassure that Gio might be many things but he was not a threat to her safety…only her peace of mind, she acknowledged as the buggy drew closer and she glimpsed Gio's lean, hard-boned features.

He was still so beautiful that he took her breath away and it stunned her every time she saw him afresh. Yet he lacked that arrogant strut, that unmistakeable conceit that could characterise very good-looking individuals. She had watched every female head swivel, every gaze linger in that doctor's waiting room but she had also witnessed his lack of awareness. Now she saw Gio spring out of the buggy, all six foot plus of him, casually clad in khaki chinos and a black tee, and he looked absolutely breathtaking as she rose to greet him.

'No, sit down…don't let me disturb you,' Gio urged in his dark deep masculine drawl that sent tremors down her taut spine.

Leah's cheeks flamed because she was thinking that he probably thought that she resembled a barrel on spindly legs and looked likely to topple over. The filmy, shapeless white kaftan she wore had not been chosen to be flattering. It had been picked because it was light and comfy in the heat.

Gio, however, was thinking something else entirely. He was transfixed by his first sight of Leah in months. Black hair tumbled round her expressive little face and down her back in a river of glossy curls. With her creamy skin tinted a deeper shade and her huge honey eyes locked to him, she had the rich luminescent glow of a gold ingot in sunshine. The proud swell of her pregnant outline took him aback and he acknowledged that she was carrying part of him, *his* children, and that could only fill him with awe.

'You look incredible,' Gio intoned.

Leah rolled her eyes at him. 'Yeah,' she agreed mockingly.

Gio tensed. 'I wasn't joking—'

'Then say something I can accept. I'm as big as a house!' Leah pointed out tartly and sat down again just as one of the beach-house staff approached to offer refreshments. 'Please sit down and relax,' she added brittly, belatedly recalling her manners.

'I appreciate that stuff is tense between us right now,' Gio remarked.

Leah sighed. 'Understatement.'

'I want to change that,' Gio stated tautly. 'Those babies are mine as well.'

Leah's expressive eyes opened wide in wonderment and she stared back at him.

'I'm not stupid. I worked it out...*finally*. You don't want anything from me. You don't *need* anything from me, so why would you lie?' Gio framed grittily. 'But on another note, when did you change your surname to Stefanos?'

A huge grin lifted the tension from Leah's face. 'As soon as my brother asked me to consider it. I had no special attachment to my mother's name and being a Stefanos, being fully accepted by my brother in public and in private as a member of his family, means a huge amount to me,' she confided. 'I pretty much lost the family I started out with, so it's very important to value the relatives that I have left.'

Gio's brows pleated and he looked unexpectedly grave. 'I feel that way too but the only relatives I have left alive refuse to recognise me because of my father—'

'But why?' Leah cut in, genuinely curious about such an attitude.

Gio breathed in deep. 'He was the worst of the worst. A murderer, an abuser of women, a drug dealer. I can say nothing good about him even now that he's long dead—'

Leah was so hurt on his behalf that she leant across the space that separated them and grasped his hand in her tiny one. 'I'm so sorry. That is very sad and even harder for you to deal with,' she told him sympathetically.

Gio surveyed her anxious, compassionate expression with veiled amazement before he blinked and studied their linked hands. 'Well, if telling you the sordid story of my background wins me a hearing from you, I'll talk about it—'

'Don't you normally talk about it?'

'Why would I?' Gio had been knocked violently off his prepared script because the conversation had not gone in a direction he had foreseen.

'Because talking about that sort of stuff is good and it can help,' Leah remarked ruefully. 'My twin brother became a heroin addict. After my mother's death and our father's abandonment, he suffered from depression and anxiety. I can tell *you* that, but I can't tell Ari that. He feels guilty enough about his father's behaviour without knowing how severely our brother was affected by those losses. Unfortunately, Lucas wouldn't discuss those things when we were teenagers and I barely saw him after that age.'

'I didn't talk to anyone about my feelings or experiences either,' Gio admitted uneasily. 'Perhaps it's harder for men… I don't know. I just wanted to forget about it and move on. That struck me as the healthiest approach. Can we talk about us now?'

'But everything that happened to you when you were young is still influencing you,' Leah pointed out apologetically, already feeling that she understood so much more about him since he had told her about his father and confessed that he believed suppressing bad memories was wiser than acknowledging them and dealing with them in the present.

'I don't do the chest-baring stuff,' Gio told her stiffly.

Leah squeezed his hand and withdrew her own. 'That's absolutely fine as well…whatever you're comfortable with,' she muttered nervously, but feeling rejected that he couldn't talk openly in the way she needed him to, for no difference could ever be resolved without communication and, clearly, he wasn't willing to do it. That did not bode well for the future. 'So…er…*us*? But we aren't an *us*—'

And that fast they were back on track and Gio breathed easier again. 'I want there to be—'

'But how? I don't think you're much interested in the babies inside me,' Leah fielded with regret.

'I am.' Gio breathed in deep and slow. 'I got it wrong before. I kept on giving forth about the DNA test when you were probably hoping I'd say something about what I saw on the screen in that surgery—'

'How did you work that out?'

'By your reaction, your disappearance,' Gio parried stiffly, faint colour larding his spectacular cheekbones, his uneasiness pronounced. 'Obviously, I'd screwed up. I'm not good at the emotional things—'

'Let's not exaggerate. You don't do emotion at all,' Leah countered flatly.

'No, I felt it and I suppressed it because the whole experience with you reminded me of the last time I let emotion carry me away.' Gio gritted his teeth because discussing private matters was for him like stripping his skin off. 'And that sent my life off its rails for a couple of years…and it was *hell*—'

Leah was gripped by that confession. 'Oh?' she said encouragingly.

Gio didn't want to open up but some facts he knew he couldn't hide and had to share. There was no reason to share any more detail, he consoled himself. He sucked in another sustaining breath before forcing himself to continue. 'I fell in love with a woman and married her. Step by painful step I learned that everything she told me was a lie. I divorced her.'

And give Leah her due, meeting those lethal icy eyes of his and reading the shadows and pain still lingering there, she knew that he was sharing to the very best of his ability, every bitten-out word falling from his lips like a bullet. 'I can understand the harm that would do,' she admitted quietly just as the refreshments arrived.

Leah grasped her chilled fruit juice while Gio tackled coffee, as indifferent as her brother was to the intense heat of mid-afternoon in Greece. 'Sally was a therapist before she retired and started the animal sanctuary. She helped me adjust to my past. That's one of the reasons why I said that I was very lucky to have her as a foster mum.'

Gio groaned out loud. 'Maybe you should send her my way… That was a joke!'

'I think for you it would be like tearing teeth out,' Leah said perceptively.

Gio sent her an amused and appreciative smile. 'You get me.'

'Probably for the first time,' she acknowledged truthfully, conceding that she had never considered that he too might have a troubled background, which continued to influence him far into adulthood.

Months after the event, she condemned him less for

the lie he had utilised to conceal his true identity when they first met. He had come clean without being forced to do so. He had apologised. He had explained his behaviour. But Leah had refused to forgive because of her sensitive past history with Oliver, who had hurt her so badly. Regrettably, she had let that experience adversely influence her relationship with Gio. Who could tell what might have happened between them had she simply agreed to see him again and to allow their attraction to progress?

'I'm here on a mission,' Gio explained. 'I want you in my life and I want my children in my life as well. What do I have to do to achieve that?'

Leah stared back at him wide-eyed. 'My goodness, you get straight to the point—'

'*Sì*...that's who I am. Right now…' Gio swept a hand in the direction of the sprawling luxury beach house '… you're the fairy-tale princess in the Stefanos tower and I had to sail a yacht here to reach you because I wasn't sure a helicopter would get permission to land—'

'Fairy-tale princess?' Leah gasped.

'You know, the one with all the hair she had to let down for the prince to get her,' Gio extended in impatient explanation. 'I want you to be *my* princess…'

Leah was aghast at the wash of reactions within her that responded to those words. Excitement, hope, desire. Indeed, a great wave of emotions engulfed her. 'And what would that entail?'

Gio set down his coffee in haste, the cup rattling noisily on the saucer. To her astonishment he dropped down on one knee right there in front of her with a ring he set almost clumsily into her loose-fingered grasp. 'Marrying me. Becoming my wife and the mother of our son and daughter and *sharing* that with me, so that I can be the father my own father and your father refused to be.'

In shocked incomprehension at a development she had not once envisaged, Leah stared down at the magnificent ruby and diamond ring clutched between her fingers. 'But you don't love me,' she mumbled in weak rebuttal.

Gio studied her with intense pale blue eyes that glittered. He had never looked more handsome, with the clean-cut lines of his darkly handsome face enhanced by the sunshine. 'I don't think we *need* love to do this...'

And with that one revealing statement, Gio sent Leah from the height of anticipation and delight down into the dark drowning shallows again, where she felt more for a man than she felt she should.

CHAPTER SEVEN

'Let me think this over,' Leah murmured tautly. 'I wasn't expecting this… I'm in shock, I think.'

'This can work. I can *make* it work,' Gio swore vehemently as she curled her fingers tightly round the beautiful ring, her clear gaze intent on him. 'We can create a loving home for our children together.'

'It's hard enough for couples in love to have a good marriage,' Leah reasoned tightly. 'And we wouldn't have that love even to start with—'

'But we've got the passion and the good intentions. We both want what's best for our children and we want to give them the chances and the stability that we missed out on—'

Leah was tense. He was keen to make the effort, she acknowledged, and unexpectedly serious about what was truly important in life. He had finally come clean with her about his background. He had been honest with her as well about the broken marriage that had soured him on trust, women and love. Was it masochistic of her to now want to know every gruesome detail about his first wife? The *only* woman he had ever loved? Simply human nature, she reckoned ruefully, and irrelevant to their current predicament. She very much wanted what Gio was offering: a father for her twins and a loving stable home. She could provide the home without his help, but she suspected that a caring father figure would be worth a great deal more to her children than she could calculate.

He was giving her a choice, a clear choice. Either she assumed the worst of him and embraced single parenthood or she took a risk on getting hurt and gave marriage a chance. Common sense suggested she go with the flow, but Leah was also uneasily conscious that she was already much more attached to Gio than she should be. And how would that play out in the very sensible but bloodless marital relationship he was suggesting? Her feelings created an inequality she could not deny but surely it was better to have tried than not to try at all, she reasoned ruefully. Trying to protect her own heart when it would deny her children a full-time father would be selfish.

'I… I suppose we should give it a try…at least,' Leah reasoned out loud, only to gasp as Gio dropped down on the seat beside her, plucked the ring from her and lifted her hand to thread the magnificent ring onto the correct finger. 'Gio! For goodness' sake!' she censured then.

'At least I've got enthusiasm to offer, which is more than I can say for you,' Gio riposted in a tone of reproach.

Studying her beautiful ruby ring, Leah flushed to the roots of her hair. 'You took me by surprise and I'm terrified of making a mistake—'

'And how do you think I feel the second time around?' Gio quipped, tugging her closer and losing patience when he failed in that ambition due to the siting of the parasol support. With a ground-out imprecation, he sprang upright and bent to scoop her bodily up into his arms, pausing with a belated frown to ask stiffly, 'Is this OK?'

Wildly disconcerted at finding herself in his arms and striving not to agonise over how much she must weigh in her current condition, for there was nothing slender about a woman due to soon deliver twins, Leah looked up at him with shaken eyes. Their sudden proximity had knocked her even more off balance. 'Depends on what you're planning to do next—'

Gio quirked an ebony brow, an expression of unholy amusement glittering in his eyes and tugging at the corners of his handsome mouth. 'A kiss to celebrate our engagement?'

A faint little quiver rippled through Leah, darting down into her pelvis and tightening every muscle low in her belly. 'I suppose that would be acceptable.'

Gio sat down again with a wicked grin. *'Acceptable?'* he groaned with a shudder. 'Kill me now.'

Her gaze colliding with those wolfish pale blue eyes, her heartbeat stuttered, and her mouth ran dry. 'When have you ever been *only* acceptable?' she whispered shakily, struggling to prevent her body from relaxing too obviously into the coiled virile heat of his lean, powerful body.

'You tell me,' Gio urged.

'I like the ring,' she told him, her hands flying up to frame his sculpted cheekbones, slender fingers stroking down over the rough black stubble beginning to darken his jawline. 'But I don't feel engaged yet—'

Gio shifted her closer and the ache at her liquid core intensified as she felt the unmistakeable thrust of his erection. 'That's not a challenge I can meet in a public place…your brother's security team is watching us with binoculars. The lenses are glinting in the sun. Your brother's not my biggest fan and they know it—'

'Ari will feel different when he knows we're getting married,' Leah forecast, leaning closer, her breasts pushing against his broad chest as she twisted on his lap to fully align their mouths.

Gio rejoiced in the awareness that he would have taken Leah's brother by surprise, which of course had been exactly his intention. He took the initiative then, brushing, tasting, the tip of his tongue delving deep, sending an arrow of stabbing heat to the very heart of Leah and making her tremble. With a gruff sound breaking free of his throat, Gio stood up again and deposited her very carefully back on her seat. 'Definitely not the place,' he told her in a raw undertone of hunger. 'Join me on the yacht for dinner tonight—'

'I *can't*!' Leah confessed in dismay. 'Ari and Cleo are coming back with friends tonight for the christening tomorrow. I have to be here. You'd be welcome as well—'

Gio doubted that possibility when he had told her brother impolitely what he could do with the Castello Zanetti he had bought as an inducement. There was no denying that that unselfish act had cost Gio a pang when he had spent more than half of his life desperate to attain ownership of the only piece of history, family and heritage he was entitled to claim by blood and birth. But Gio *knew* he could not give way to blackmail or hope to hold onto his bride's respect if he grasped at the grubby offer of his mother's former family home. He had tossed that proposal back at the Greek, while knowing that he had every intention of proposing to Ari's sister and refusing to admit to the fact.

'I have a surprise for you on the yacht,' Gio admitted.

'Is this the equivalent of an invitation to see your etchings?' Leah teased with a glint of genuine amusement in her vivid dark eyes. 'The ring was enough of a surprise for one day.'

'I can't get this surprise out from beneath my bed,' Gio confided. 'Although he gets up on the bed in the middle of the night to sleep in comfort. He is the *weirdest* little animal.'

Her startled eyes rounded in disbelief. 'Spike? You've got Spike?' she exclaimed incredulously. 'But he was adopted! A family gave him a home before I moved out here. I was really disappointed, but I was just too late to make a claim on him.'

'Apparently, Spike fell foul of the family cat,' Gio confided. 'They returned him and I have been allowed, not, I stress, to adopt him…but to *foster* him to bring him out here to you. He's had all his jabs but I would hesitate to bring him ashore with your brother's guard dogs patrolling. I think they would traumatise him.'

'Oh, my goodness… Spike,' Leah sighed in a blissful whirl, happy tears stinging her eyes. 'Can we go right now?'

Gio guided her over to the buggy still sitting parked and helped her in. He was smiling. He had never had to seduce a woman onto his yacht before and it had also never occurred to him that he would sink to the level of using a dog as a means of persuasion. But he really didn't care, not when for once he had got it right with Leah.

Evidently alerted by his staff, Ari had phoned Leah before she'd even got into Gio's motorboat at the pier.

She hovered next to it while she answered his questions. 'Yes, he's here and we're going to get married… I think sooner rather than later makes sense,' she told her disconcerted brother, who seemed understandably, she thought, stunned by her announcement. 'Maybe you think this is a little sudden—'

'No…no, I think it's…timely,' Ari selected warmly. 'You can get married on the island this week—'

'*This week…*are you crazy?' Leah gasped as Gio lifted her gently and lowered her down while the crewman held the bobbing boat steady.

'I'll get it organised,' Ari told her cheerfully and rang off.

'Ari wants us to get married on the island,' Leah told Gio with a frown, unsure how well that interference would be received.

'I would've preferred to make our own arrangements but that's acceptable,' Gio assured her. 'I can understand that your brother wants to host his sister's wedding.'

The noise of the outboard motor checked any further conversation. Leah's head was in a whirl. As the breeze blew her hair into a whipping spiral of curls, she put her hand up to restrain it and Gio shot her an amused smile as if to say that she was wasting her time. He was drop-dead gorgeous when he smiled and her heart speeded up. Excitement shimmied through her as he handed her up onto the yacht and ushered her into a lift. 'This is a very big and fancy boat,' Leah remarked and then, with a look of sudden comprehension, she exclaimed, '*Virgo* was the name of the app you designed that made you famous!'

'And very rich,' Gio conceded. 'I had money to burn, hence the yacht. I often live onboard and work though so it hasn't proven to be the youthful extravagance I once feared.'

They emerged into a corridor and moments later Gio swept her through double doors into a massive contemporary bedroom. He bent down to peer beneath the wide divan bed. 'He's still under there,' he groaned in disbelief.

'Spike?' Leah murmured uncertainly.

The little dog shot out of hiding like a rocket and crashed into her legs. Laughing, Leah sank down on the side of the bed to receive his enthusiastic welcome. When she lifted him he gambolled round the bed in mad excitement, finally throwing himself down by her side to loll with his tongue hanging out.

'You're a daft animal,' she told him fondly, stroking his back and smothering a yawn that had crept up on her out of nowhere. 'Sorry, I'm so sleepy these days.'

'I was planning to offer you a tour of the yacht but that can wait. Would you like anything to eat?'

Her brows pleated as she realised that she was really hungry. 'Just a snack… I slept through lunch earlier. I don't sleep well at night and it catches up with me during the day.'

'I'll order something.'

'Thank you for reuniting me with Spike,' Leah murmured appreciatively. 'I can't believe, though, that Sally didn't tell me that his new home had fallen through—'

Gio laughed. 'He was chased out by the cat. He'll never live that down. I asked your foster mum not to mention that I had him until after I had arrived.'

'Neat,' Leah mumbled drowsily, studying him with heavy wondering eyes, committing his bronzed and beautiful lean features to memory. 'You played a blinder with Spike.'

'I play to win,' Gio murmured softly. 'But I'm not playing right now.'

Of course, he wasn't playing, Leah reflected ruefully. Gio was driven by a stubborn ruthless temperament that was very much goal-orientated. Right now, she and the twins she carried were his goal. But once they were actually married, would he retain the same enthusiasm?

A stewardess brought her a light meal and she ate it where she sat. Spike was removed to his 'exercise area' and then returned to her. Leah intended to go off and look for Gio, but a full tummy and growing exhaustion were overwhelming her. She lay back on the gloriously comfortable bed and stretched her toes, kicking off her sandals. She would close her eyes for just five minutes, she promised herself, and then knew no more.

Gio returned to keep Leah company and found her fast asleep, Spike dozing at her hip. Shadows lay like bruises below her eyes in the sunlight and he frowned, quietly slid her sandals off the bed and flung a throw over her. Beside her, her phone emanated an angry buzz and he scooped it up before it could disturb her, striding out to the corridor to answer it, grimacing when Ari Stefanos spoke.

'Leah's asleep. I'm not waking her up. Yes, I do understand that you're entertaining this evening,' he confirmed. 'Thank you for the invitation. Send her outfit out to the yacht and she can get ready here. I'll make sure we're in time for dinner.'

Gio rolled his eyes as Leah's brother grudgingly agreed to his suggestion. He would have to make more of an effort to overcome the hostility between him and

Leah's sibling, he conceded ruefully. Whether he liked it or not, Ari was family, Leah's family. Unfortunately accepting and trusting such a connection was a challenge for Gio, who had never had a proper family and who, after his own childhood experience, was especially wary of relatives. Furthermore, Ari had already offended him, pulling the Castello Zanetti like a white rabbit out of a hat in an effort to persuade him into marrying Leah. For Leah's sake, however, he would have to get over his ire and forgive and forget…not something Gio was good at doing.

When Gio wakened Leah it was dark and she was disorientated, unable to credit that she could have slept so long in an unfamiliar place. 'Gosh, I was great company, wasn't I?' she groaned and then, seeing the time on her watch, she slid off the bed in dismay. 'For goodness' sake, I'm going to be late for dinner!'

'Your maid is here with your clothes to help you get ready,' Gio told her soothingly. 'You have plenty of time and I'm joining you for dinner.'

Belatedly, Leah noticed that he was wearing a dinner jacket and narrow black trousers, tall, dark and impossibly sophisticated, the tanned planes of his stunning face smooth and freshly shaven. By the time she was showered, had done her make-up and had donned the full-length aqua-coloured gown, which did a masterly job of concealing her pregnancy, she felt much better. Gio swiped the pale fringed pashmina lying on the bed and draped it round her narrow shoulders to keep her warm and she stared down at the ruby ring on her finger. Her future had form and focus now. She was going to make a success of their marriage, she promised herself fiercely. He had made a major effort to turn their relationship around and so would she.

A formal dinner was served in the big dining room. Fulsome congratulations were offered and although Leah could see the hints of dissonance between her brother and her future husband, she could also see that both of them were striving to overcome what appeared to be a mutual wariness. Two alpha males, she thought wryly as they stayed up for an after-dinner drink in Ari's study when his other guests had retired to bed for the night, alpha males knocking heads over nothing in particular.

'My legal reps are drawing up a prenuptial agreement,' Ari announced, startling her.

Leah frowned and winced. 'That's not necessary—'

'It is. You are a considerable heiress now that I have...shall we say made the disposition of my father's estate a little more fair to you and your sister?' Ari declared. 'Legal safeguards should be in place.'

'That's only sensible,' Gio chipped in, disconcerting her with his easy acceptance of such an agreement. 'I will alert my team to prepare for a meeting.'

As Gio took his leave, Leah accompanied him out onto the veranda that extended the length of the beach house. 'We don't need a prenup,' she told him awkwardly, afraid that Ari might have offended him with that request. 'I don't know what Ari was talking about when he mentioned our father's estate, but I'll find out.'

'I imagine he feels that you and your siblings were unfairly treated in his father's will and he wishes to redress that. That is between you and your brother. As for the prenup, it is my wish too that we have one in place,' Gio intoned gravely. 'I didn't think of that precaution before I married the first time and I lived to regret the oversight.'

Leah paled and her tummy twisted, consternation filling her. By the sound of it, his first wife had taken him to the cleaners, and he was keen to ensure that if they broke up she could not do the same.

Gio swung back to her, his broad shoulders rigid, his darkly handsome face tense as if the bad memories roused by the conversation had risen to the fore. 'I'm not trying to suggest that *you*—'

'Of course not,' she incised tonelessly, keen now to drop the subject.

'Such agreements deal with more than the disposition of money,' Gio murmured in explanation. 'Were we to separate, the agreement will also specify custody of our children and access to them.'

'What a comforting idea that is,' Leah countered tightly, and she walked back indoors, leaving him to depart without another word.

Gio was an inveterate pessimist, she reflected heavily. Did he think it so likely that they would fail to make a success of their marriage and break up? In her opinion that was absolutely the wrong frame of mind to get married in and she had fled before she told him so. After all, with a divorce under his belt, Gio had to have a more cynical outlook than she had and she couldn't hold his past against him. She didn't want to lose him, not after she had already lost so much of her family and, also, after the pain of Oliver's rejection. She didn't want to demand more and challenge Gio. In fact, she was scared to do so. It wasn't a good idea to rock the boat at this stage either, she reasoned, particularly when he might receive the impression that she was reluctant to sign a prenuptial agreement.

Cleo urged her over to the laptop she already had sitting open. 'Now we get to look at wedding dresses!' she carolled with enthusiasm.

In a daze at the speed of events, Leah allowed herself to be drawn into that challenge. The next five days flew past. Gio attended the christening of her baby nephews, Andreas and Nikolas, before flying back to London for a board meeting. Leah was frustrated by the fact that they spent absolutely no time alone and she was plunged straight into choosing bridal options with Cleo, dealing with the wedding planner and selecting a dress. She also had to persuade Sally to make the trip to the island alone because her sister, Pam, had been swept off on holiday by the new man in her life.

The day before the wedding, Leah flew with Ari to Athens where the legal meeting to settle the prenuptial agreement was being held. She was anxious about what demands Gio's team might make with regard to their unborn children and she wished she had had the chance to discuss those terms with Gio beforehand. The idea of discussing such serious and personal matters on the phone had made her cringe but the concept of discussing those same topics in front of a bunch of legal eagles made her shrink even more, so she had already briefed Ari's lawyers on what she felt she could accept and what she would question.

It was a most unpleasant shock to walk into the spacious office and register that one of the lawyers present was Oliver Bartley, her former boyfriend.

She froze in her tracks. *'Oliver?'* she said doubtingly, the blood draining from her cheeks leaving her pale as he rose from his chair with apparent alacrity, his good-looking face wreathed in smiles below his perfectly styled blond hair.

'Leah?' he questioned with unconvincing surprise. 'I didn't believe it could be you. You've changed your name.'

'Yes,' she conceded stiffly. 'If you're involved in this meeting, you'll want to withdraw.'

Oliver stiffened in dismay, clearly not having foreseen the possibility that she might make that request and annoyed by the threat of exclusion.

'You know this man?' Ari queried with a frown.

'He's my ex-boyfriend,' Leah admitted with a shrug. 'It wouldn't be appropriate for him to take part in this.'

Ari nodded slowly in agreement. Gio strolled in at that point and one of the lawyers on his team inclined his head to bring his client up to speed. Gio settled icy blue eyes on Oliver.

'May I have a word with you in private, Leah?' Oliver enquired smoothly.

'Let's not hold the meeting up,' Leah countered quietly, taking account of their audience, sooner than say that she could not think of a single thing they could have to discuss, considering that they had parted on such thoroughly nasty terms the year before. Not once had he attempted to contact her after the break-up, so he had not a leg to stand on when he suggested they might now want to talk.

Aware of Gio's burning scrutiny, Leah took her seat, nodding as Oliver's boss recognised her with a neat inclination of his head and a broad smile. She might have seemed composed, but she was shrinking with mortification inside herself because she could not look at

Oliver without a sense of burning humiliation, not to mention an unwelcome recollection of the pain he had inflicted on her. He had used and abused her without apology or regret because it had suited him to do so.

As the meeting concluded, Gio closed his hand over hers to help her rise from her seat and murmured, 'We'll have to talk about Bartley.'

'I don't think so,' Leah responded, lifting her chin. 'My past is a closed book, much like your own.'

'But—'

A serene smile lifted Leah's lips. 'It's not on the table for discussion,' she said softly, and it felt good to hold back on Gio for a change, to say only what *she* felt comfortable saying at that moment.

Tension ignited in the air between them. She watched his beautiful stubborn mouth flatten at the corners. Somewhere down deep inside her as she clashed with those silvery icy eyes of his, her body clenched wickedly with piercing sexual awareness. Didn't matter where she was, who she was with or what was on her brain, Gio's raw sexuality engulfed her every time she got close. A flush on her cheeks, embarrassment claiming her at a time when she felt as though she should be more restrained in her responses, she turned away, relieved when her brother intervened and commented on how civilised negotiations relating to the agreement had been.

Leah stepped out of the office to be hailed by Oliver, who was hovering in the foyer. Her soft mouth downcurved. She really didn't want anything more to do with her ex but her pride refused to allow her to avoid him by hiding behind either Ari or Gio. Although she hated being confronted with him again and remained angry with him, in every other way she had moved on.

The young and naïve girl she had been with Oliver had grown up fast.

'You didn't do my career any favours in there. Your brother is my firm's biggest account,' Oliver told her grimly. 'Couldn't you have pretended not to know me?'

'I don't owe you any favours,' Leah replied drily. 'And your boss immediately recognised me, so pretending not to know you wouldn't have worked—'

'You should have told me that you were a Stefanos when we were together—'

'We were never together,' Leah parried, wrinkling her nose with distaste.

Oliver shifted a hand in the air and lowered his voice. 'That business with Celeste…that's all over and behind me. A temporary madness is all I can put *that* down to now. I'm grateful for your discretion.'

Leah discovered that she no longer cared who was in his bed and she made no comment. 'Goodbye, Oliver. All the best for the future.'

And with that, Leah moved back to join Ari, rather than Gio, who had settled glittering diamond-cutting eyes on her for the seeming sin of straying in another man's direction. He was so ridiculously possessive, she thought, although he would never admit it. But he *was*. Oliver was her past and Gio was her future. Why didn't he see that?

Gio wondered why Leah's familiarity with the self-satisfied blond lawyer annoyed him. And the answer came to him fast. Bartley was a man whom Leah had loved. She had gone white at the sight of him and had tried and signally failed to cover up how rattled she was by his appearance. Gio, on the other hand, might be about to marry Leah the next day but he was also the male Leah had cheerfully walked away from after a one-night stand and that was a poor beginning that Gio was unlikely to forget. Nor could he overlook the unlovely truth that had a pregnancy not resulted from their intimacy, she would never have agreed to become his wife. Leah had kept on walking away from him until he'd got that message loud and clear. For the first time with a woman, Gio felt as if he was the one fighting for a more secure relationship.

Gio had invited Ari, Cleo and Leah out to his yacht for dinner that evening.

'Are you cooking for us?' Leah teased before they flew out of Athens.

'No, I don't think your brother would wish to sit in the galley and keep me company while I sliced and diced,' Gio said with amusement. 'My chef will do the honours.'

And Leah cloaked her eyes and thought how right he was. Ari rarely stood on ceremony, but he wasn't given to informality. He had been raised in a very wealthy family and he acted accordingly. Cleo, however, was much more easy-going because like Gio and Leah, she had grown up with very little money.

'I won't be staying late.' Leah sighed. 'I need a good night's sleep before the wedding.'

'Of course,' Gio agreed.

A superb meal was served on exquisite porcelain out on the deck. Ari and Gio talked business until Cleo complained. Over drinks, Ari extended a large official envelope to Gio. 'Our wedding present to you and Leah,' he explained.

Gio tensed and began to open the envelope.

'It's the deeds for the Castello Zanetti,' Ari clarified.

Leah was shocked but Gio froze as if he had been blasted with ice.

'The Castello Zanetti?' Leah questioned Gio. 'Your mother's family home? The one that the current owner wouldn't sell to you?'

'Yes.' That single acknowledgement slipped quietly from Gio's lips as he looked at her brother with cool, narrowed eyes. 'This is by far *too* generous a gift.'

'You're marrying my sister and I'm happy about that,' her brother murmured smoothly. 'I had the good fortune to acquire the property at the perfect time. Let's say no more about it. It *is* your family home.'

There was a tension in the atmosphere that Leah couldn't quite understand. Evidently, Gio wasn't happy about accepting so extravagant a gift. Since he had once confessed to Leah that owning his mother's childhood home was a major ambition of his, she would have expected him to be stunned by Ari's purchase and much more excited, pleased and curious than he appeared to be. Yet Gio's eyes remained cool, his smile distinctly forced as he thanked Ari for his generosity and thoughtfulness and said all that was polite.

'I can't wait to see it!' Leah confessed.

'Perhaps you'll spend your honeymoon there,' Ari suggested.

'Perhaps…' Gio conceded calmly.

Leah almost succumbed to her curiosity and said something when they were alone for a couple of minutes before she stepped into the motorboat to return to the island. At the same time, it was their wedding in the morning and she was cautious, reluctant to tackle what, she sensed was a sensitive subject. She didn't want to make a mountain out of a molehill or give Gio the impression that she thought he had been ungrateful. Possibly he was genuinely embarrassed by so splendid a present or simply annoyed that her brother should have pried so deeply into his background and personal aspirations. Or, possibly he had wanted the thrill of purchasing that family house for himself. Was that the problem? The sticking point?

CHAPTER EIGHT

THE CONSTANT DRONE of helicopters in the sky kicked off Leah's wedding day. Guests were arriving at a steady rate, many of them flying into the resort at the other end of the island until it was time to head for the church.

Her dress was gently gathered under the bust with a lace bodice, a sweetheart neckline and a floaty chiffon skirt. The tight bodice and sleek empire line were tailored to take the focus off her prominent bump and for the first time in months she felt feminine and attractive rather than ferociously, strikingly pregnant with twins.

'You look a treat.' Sally sighed fondly. 'It's a very feminine dress…but you'll never stand those high heels for an entire day.'

'They're gorgeous though.' Leah extended the toe of a pale sequinned shoe with satisfaction. 'I'll take them off during the reception.'

Her niece, Lucy, removed her thumb from her mouth for long enough to touch a reverent finger to the flowing gown and sigh, 'Pretty.'

'Don't touch!' Cleo tugged her adopted daughter back in dismay.

'Don't worry,' Leah urged, smoothing Lucy's tumbled hair in a soothing gesture. 'She's fine.'

Sally anchored the ornate diamond tiara that Gio had sent over for Leah that very morning into her springy black curls. It could only outshine the delicate diamond drop earrings her brother had given her as an equally surprise gift. The trio of women descended the stairs where Ari awaited them.

'You look amazing,' Ari murmured with pride. 'Gio's a very lucky man.'

They left the house at a relaxed speed because it wasn't far to the big church above the village built a generation back by the Stefanos family.

Her heart in her mouth, Leah walked into the packed building on Ari's arm, her bouquet of flowers clutched tightly in her hand. She focused on Gio's tall, elegant silhouette at the altar and wondered who his best man was. She hurt for Gio, though, because he had not a single family member present to celebrate his marriage, and she marvelled at the hard-hearted grandparents who had rejected him for his father's sins. She decided that when she got the right moment she would ask him more about his mother's parents because life was too short for such cold, judgemental separations, she reflected. Perhaps they were terrible snobs who could not overlook his unfortunate beginnings, but Gio was *still* their blood.

She was ruefully amused by her passionate need to protect Gio from anyone who might hurt him. She was beginning to really care about him, to see both his strengths and his flaws, and she supposed that was the proof that she was starting to love him. And wasn't there a possibility that her love would enrich their marriage and make their connection a deeper one? Even though Gio could infuriate her at times, she only had to think of him persuading Sally to give him Spike and his tolerating Spike with all his eccentricities on his beautiful yacht and her heart simply squeezed tight inside her chest.

Hadn't he been hurt enough in life by his dysfunctional background and unhappy first marriage? She had seen those shadows in his eyes, had recognised that he had suffered and that he had learned to guard his heart to protect himself. But he would soon discover that their newborn children's very vulnerability would break through that shell: she was convinced of it.

'You look ravishing, *bella mia*,' Gio murmured as the priest began the ceremony.

Leah looked up at him and meshed with diamond-bright eyes fringed by lush black spiky lashes and her heart speeded up and her thoughts fell into oblivion. She watched the wedding ring threaded onto her finger and then slid on his, laughing when he had to help as the ring caught on his knuckle. And then it was done and they were married and she walked down the aisle again with his hand at her back and she was in a daze as they posed briefly for the photographer. They were wafted back to the house and the smooth service of the wedding caterers waiting to look after them and their guests. A flurry of introductions to Gio's friends followed.

After the wedding breakfast, a nagging ache in her lower back kept her seated when everyone else was on the floor and she blamed herself for standing around too long before the meal. Cleo joined her when she was freshening up and said approvingly, 'I don't think Gio had a single ex on his guest list.'

'Well, why would he have?' Leah asked in surprise.

A glass of wine in her hand and possibly a little merry, Cleo told her the tale of her own wedding when

Ari had happily invited those ex-girlfriends of his who had remained friends. The women had seemingly only attended to make shrewish criticisms of the bride.

'I'm surprised that you didn't strangle him,' Leah remarked with a grimace as the two women found a secluded corner to sit in and watch the festivities. 'Look, I wanted to say something about the wedding gift, which Gio didn't look overjoyed to receive. I think Gio was so *shocked* that—'

Cleo giggled. 'Oh, I don't blame him. Ari *was* overstepping giving the *castello* as a wedding pressie. It was contentious after what had happened beforehand and he did put Gio in an awkward position—'

'What do you mean?' Leah prompted with a frown of comprehension. 'What happened beforehand?'

'Well, you know.' Cleo was slurring a little, clearly struggling to find the right words. 'Ari trying to use the *castello* as a bribe to persuade Gio to marry you… I mean, that wasn't a good idea, was it? It put Gio's back up and, obviously, he was coming here anyway the minute he found out where you were. That's the only reason he went to see Ari in the first place—he was desperate to find you.'

Those explanations fell like stones thrown into a tranquil pond. Listening in shock and disbelief, Leah mentally raced from zero stress to a heightened unbearable level of stress. Her brother had tried to bribe Gio into offering her marriage? That fast, the bottom fell out of Leah's world. Every illusion was shattered and her enjoyment of her beautiful wedding destroyed. How could her brother have dared to do such a thing? To lower her to that level? And how could Gio not have warned her?

'Oh, my goodness,' Cleo framed, her hand flying to her mouth in dismay as she realised what she had let drop. 'Ari's going to kill me!'

'I'll talk to them both when I get them alone…er, later,' Leah mumbled, espying Gio across the room where he was chatting to several men. The truth had knocked her right off her perch, she acknowledged wretchedly. She had been feeling happy, looking forward to the future, maybe she had even been feeling a tiny bit smug as she looked at Gio's beautiful dark angel face and started thinking of him as being *hers*.

Only, by the sound of it, Gio had never been hers, nor had he had any intention of marrying her until her brother had interfered. My word, she had to be stupid to have accepted Gio's sudden volte face. She had miraculously moved from being the pregnant woman whose word he didn't trust to the pregnant woman he believed was carrying his children and badly wanted to marry. How come she hadn't smelt a rat in that sudden transformation?

Once again, it seemed, she had fallen victim to her own poor judgement. She had seen what she wanted to see, discarded anything that hinted at a less positive angle and she had accepted Gio's every word as though each were solid golden proof of truth and honourable intentions. But, evidently, Gio had simply packaged up what he believed she wanted from him and handed it to her complete with a fabulous engagement ring. And who had put the idea of marriage into his head? Her own brother!

A flush on her cheeks, a rage locked in her heart and a tightness in her throat that made it difficult to swallow, Leah fixed a smile to her face as Gio extended his hand to her and drew her under his arm while he chatted. The evocative scent of him, the citrusy tang of some designer cologne overlaying clean, warm male made her stiffen because she was not in the mood to be that close to him or to once again be made viscerally aware of his sexual attraction.

'I need some fresh air,' Gio admitted, walking her out through one of the sets of doors open onto the veranda.

Leah sank down into a comfortable seat while Gio lounged back against the rail opposite her, his long, lean powerful legs splayed. 'You're flushed…are you too warm?'

'A little but it's cooler out here.' She sighed, connecting uneasily with diamond-bright eyes.

'Please don't be offended when I say that I can't wait to get back to the yacht,' Gio murmured wryly. 'I'm not naturally sociable by nature and I would like just to have you all to myself. I've barely seen you since the wedding craziness kicked off.'

She supposed that for him, second time around, all the palaver of a big wedding did strike him as excessive. 'What was your first wedding like?'

'A casual quick thing. We were students. It was a civil ceremony followed by a few friends celebrating together in a bar,' Gio proffered smoothly.

And by the sound of it, much more Gio's relaxed style, although that thought made Leah think that she wasn't really being fair to him. Some men didn't enjoy the fuss of a traditional wedding with all the bell and whistles. Unfortunately, she wasn't in the mood to be fair, she acknowledged. In fact up until the moment that Cleo had wrenched the scales from her eyes, Leah had been thoroughly enjoying her wedding. Her dress, her flowers, even the sparkly shoes that Sally had correctly forecast would be hurting her within hours. She flexed her bare toes, the shoes long since abandoned in favour of comfort. So what if her dress trailed a little? It wasn't as though she was likely to ever wear it again.

'Were you thinking of moving the yacht?' Leah asked tautly.

Gio laughed. 'Of course, I plan to take you sailing.'

Leah tensed. 'I don't want to leave Greece. I've been seeing a very good obstetrician in Athens and I want to stay within reach of him for the next few weeks. Twins often arrive early and I need a C-section.'

A faint flush lit his perfect cheekbones, his lashes, momentarily dipping like black velvet sweeps over his light eyes. 'I'm sorry, I didn't think of that. We'll stay in Greek waters,' he promised. 'We haven't even had the chance to discuss names for the babies.'

'I thought of naming our son after you.'

Gio winced. 'No, it was also my father's name and we shouldn't pass that heritage on to our son.'

'I would like Aurora for our daughter. It's pretty,' she said stiltedly. 'But we'll know better what suits them once they're here with us.'

Some guests were leaving and Cleo came out to warn them. Leah got up, wondering how she was still functioning when she felt stone dead inside herself. It was shock, she reckoned, she was still in shock from the major fault line that had appeared in her fairy-tale marriage. Gio had only proposed because her brother had urged him to do so, and he had accepted a bribe to do it. His family home, the Castello Zanetti, what else was that but a bribe neatly packaged as a wedding present?

And how was she supposed to feel about being bartered off with a property dowry like some medieval bride?

'I'd like a word with you in private,' she told her brother on the way back to the party. 'And it would be helpful if you could bring my bridegroom with you and leave Cleo out of it.'

His brow indented but Leah didn't want to answer questions and didn't linger.

Ari caught her elbow to hold her back. 'My office in ten minutes…'

Leah rubbed her back where the tightening ache was intensifying and paused to speak to her former foster mum, Sally.

'Are you in pain?' the older woman asked with a frown.

'A little. It's my back. It's been a taxing day,' Leah pointed out. 'All of me is complaining—'

'Including those poor tortured feet,' Sally teased, casting a speaking glance down at the bare toes visible below the hem of her gown. 'Are you sure you're not going into labour?' she added worriedly.

'Do you think I wouldn't know?' Leah laughed. 'Of course, I'd know!'

Bracing herself, a cold glass of water clasped in one hand, Leah entered Ari's opulent office. She wouldn't have admitted it to anyone but she was not feeling well and she assumed the nausea and the occasional blurring of her vision meant that she had overdone it a bit. Gio was lounging back against Ari's desk with a drink in his hand, the very picture of relaxation. Clearly having spoken to his wife, Ari, however, was better prepared. He raised both his hands in a surrender movement and grimaced. 'I *know*. Don't say it… I messed up!' he groaned.

'What on earth possessed you?' Leah demanded shakily. 'To try and barter me off like some Dark Ages bride with a dowry?'

Her brother winced. 'It wasn't quite that bad—'

'No, it was worse!' Leah proclaimed. 'You went behind my back to interfere in my life—'

'I was trying to protect you and achieve what I believed would make you happy—'

'No, perhaps you were embarrassed at having an unwed pregnant sister in the family and you wanted me respectably married off,' Leah retorted crisply.

'That's not true,' Ari argued.

'Well, from where I'm standing, it looks like it's true,' Leah reasoned tautly. 'My parents weren't married and it didn't harm me—'

'That's a matter of opinion,' Ari flashed back. 'But it's also a debatable point because your father was already married to my mother—'

'These days women don't need to be married to have children—'

'I'm aware of that but I acted… I interfered if you *must* call it that…because I knew that you wanted a father for your babies. You told me that yourself—'

Leah lost colour and turned away, stiff with embarrassment at that lowering reminder. Even so, she recalled that late-night chat when she had told her brother how guilty she felt about not being able to provide her children with a father and how it had made her feel as though she were failing them as her own mother had failed her and her siblings. 'Yes, in an ideal world, I wanted a father for my kids, but that's not always possible or even desirable. Please tell me how a husband you tried to bribe into marrying me was going to help the situation.'

'But Ari *didn't* bribe me,' Gio incised calmly, entering the conversation for the first time, his cool silvery eyes intent on her furious face. 'He offered me the Castello Zanetti and I refused the proposition and walked away—'

'Only to get it anyway as a wedding present!' Leah fired back, unimpressed by that claim of innocence.

'That was *my* idea,' Ari interposed with a shake of his head. '*Thee mou*, Leah. I don't want the property. When Gio refused the deal what else was I supposed to do with his mother's family home other than give it to him?'

Leah dealt her brother an outraged glance. 'You're not getting the point, are you? And my point is that it was *wrong* to try and trade me off into marriage as though that were the only acceptable thing to do in my situation! The last thing I need now is an unwilling husband—'

'I didn't try to trade you off—' Ari protested.

'I'm *not* an unwilling husband,' Gio slotted in quietly, only to receive a burning look of condemnation from his bride that would have caused spontaneous combustion in a less tough male.

'But the idea of marrying me *didn't* occur to you until Ari tried to persuade and *guilt* you into it!' Leah condemned brittly, a nagging headache tightening round her brow. She lifted a hand to rub at the pain in her shoulder, blaming the joint pain on her awkward gait. Since her third trimester aches and pains had become the norm for her.

'I saw it as the practical solution to our plight. Only marriage met our mutual needs,' Gio commented tautly.

Ari winced. 'You need to up your game in the persuasion stakes.'

Leah felt as though she had been stabbed to the heart. Was that all their marriage meant to him? A business-like bargain to raise their children together? That was so cold, so callous and unfeeling, utterly bereft of any promise of the warmth she felt that she needed to make their relationship a successful one. And yet she had already foolishly begun to believe that they were now sharing things that made their relationship much stronger.

'It doesn't matter. This marriage is over before it even begins!' Leah exclaimed, reacting to the physical discomfort she was in as much as the hurt that Gio had once again inflicted. If it didn't work, throw it away, her pride dictated in an effort to save face in an irreconcilable situation.

He didn't love her and he didn't want her as a wife. She had too much pride to settle for that kind of bloodless marriage and thanks to her inheritance she was a financially independent woman, who had no need to be kept by either her brother or husband.

'You're angry right now. Don't make drastic decisions in this mood,' Gio urged grittily, pale below his bronzed complexion at that sudden threat.

'I don't need either of you to survive!' Leah lashed back at them and headed for the door, perspiration breaking out on her skin.

As she reached the door, her vision blurred and she tripped over her long skirts, tipping forward and landing up hard against the wood, clutching at the handle for support.

Gio scooped her up as she sagged. 'You need to rest

and take a deep breath,' he told her worriedly, settling her down on a sofa.

'I'm not feeling well,' she admitted shakily as a clenching pain gripped her abdomen. 'Oh, no, I think I'm in labour!'

Later she had only a blurred recollection of being bundled out into a helicopter with Gio and Sally accompanying her. She was frightened, frightened that losing her temper so comprehensively had put her unborn children at risk. When they arrived at the hospital she was rushed in the doors as though she were an emergency and when she realised that the twins had to be delivered immediately for both her sake and theirs, she only then realised that she was playing a leading role in a genuine emergency.

Gio's ability to remain wonderfully calm grounded her as she was prepared for the surgery. When he finally reappeared by her side, gowned and masked, she was relieved by the steady pressure of his hand gripping hers. The lights above, the clicking monitors, the number of medical personnel surrounding them unnerved her a little. Gio chatted to her and the anaesthetist and she was grateful for the distraction that allowed her to get her breathing under control.

She felt pressure and then a jostling sensation before her little boy was delivered. He was brought to her all cleaned up for barely a minute before being carried off to an incubator.

'They're not quite happy with his breathing,' Gio explained. 'Seemingly, that's common with a premature baby.'

And then their daughter arrived, squalling, with a

cap of black curly hair like her brother before she too was borne off. It was all over very quickly but Leah felt inadequate and bereft that neither of her babies could stay with her for even a little while. When she arrived in her private room, Gio was waiting for her, Sally having stepped out to give them some privacy. He was not quite as elegant as usual. Black stubble framed his strong jawline, accentuating his mobile mouth and carved cheekbones. Even though he was tousled with his tie loose and his shirt unbuttoned at his throat, Gio still contrived to look drop-dead gorgeous.

'Our children are beautiful. I've just been to see them again…' His dark deep drawl was raw-edged with emotion, his pale blue eyes glossy. 'Aurora is doing a little better than her brother, but the staff think there is no immediate cause for concern for him. Would you consider Luca as a name for our son? It's the name of the priest, Father Luca, the man who encouraged me most during my childhood and adolescence,' he confided tautly.

'Yes… Aurora and Luca. I would be happy with those names,' Leah conceded, studying him closely, shaken by the display of open emotion that he could neither hide nor control, while still struggling to accept that she was now a mother, simply sadly a mother who could not yet hold either of her children in her arms. 'Are you surprised by how you feel about them?'

'Stunned,' Gio confessed with a sudden flashing grin. 'But not in a bad way. I just didn't expect to feel this immediate sense of attachment to them.'

'They're going to be staying in hospital for a while,' Leah muttered, regret, disappointment and reluctant acceptance filling her as she realised that her babies would not be leaving medical care with her.

Gio stood by the door. 'I'm afraid so, but the doctors have every confidence that given time they will gain weight and thrive. Ari's already offered us the use of his city apartment for as long as we need it—'

Her brain felt a little fuzzy but then suddenly she recalled her final threatening words to Gio and she paled, her eyes flying wide. 'Us? I'm not sure we still have an "us",' she framed shakily.

Gio bent to rest his lean hands on the foot rail of the bed so that their eyes were level. His icy gaze was diamond bright with determination. 'You have to give me a chance to prove that this can work. So far, I haven't had that opportunity. You can't hold your brother's crazy attempt at bribery against me when I turned him down,' he told her squarely.

And on the most basic level, he *had* refused that proposition, yet somehow he had still ended up marrying her and magically acquiring the Castello Zanetti all the same, she acknowledged unhappily. Yet right now, with two vulnerable babies to worry about, weren't there more important matters to concentrate on? For the present they were better together, not distracted by arguments and separation, she reasoned.

'We'll talk about all that some other time when we're not so stressed,' Leah murmured, resting her head back on the pillow, exhausted simply from the weight of making that one decision. 'But you should get that DNA test sorted out, so that that's out of the way.'

'I wasn't still planning—'

'You wanted it. Let's not be precious about it now. I agree to the test being done,' Leah framed flatly.

CHAPTER NINE

THOSE FIRST WEEKS after the twins' birth were ever after a blur for Leah. Sally had to return home to the UK within days. Soon after that, Leah succumbed to an infection and was laid low for a week while at the hospital their son and daughter lurched forward one step then back another. Luca only gained weight slowly and, initially, he had feeding problems.

Leah saw very little of Gio. They talked on the phone, they met at the hospital when he was visiting the intensive care nursery to see the twins at the same time, but just as quickly he would be gone on business again. He maintained a punishing work schedule and slept in one of the guest rooms. Occasionally he joined her for breakfast or dinner and, while he was perfectly cordial, they talked about nothing other than their babies. She had no doubt whatsoever that he cared deeply for their children but had no idea how he truly felt about her or a painfully new marriage, which had never even got off the starting blocks. He had told her that he believed their marriage could work and said he wanted the opportunity to prove that to her, but so far he didn't seem to be bothering to try and prove anything to her.

Her reminder about the DNA test he had once demanded had annoyed rather than reassured him and she didn't understand why. She had needed to know that *he* knew beyond a shadow of doubt that he was Aurora and Luca's father but, afterwards, she had worried that mentioning the test again had been provocative and given in the wrong spirit at the ultimate wrong moment.

The first week that Aurora came home, Leah was run off her feet. If she wasn't feeding her daughter, she was trying to soothe her and, after several sleepless nights, Gio strode into the apartment to find her in tears, fatigue and a sense of being a failure as a mother weighing down on her.

'Let me take her now.' Gio sighed, scooping the baby from her with careful hands. 'Go to bed and sleep. I'm hiring a couple of nannies in the morning—'

'I don't need nannies,' Leah protested.

'You need rest and you need help. You have to get your own strength back. Your body's been through a lot these last few months and you're not looking after yourself,' Gio intoned grimly, scanning her bruised eyes and drawn cheeks. 'It's my job to look after all of you and, since Luca will be home with us soon as well, we need extra hands on board, at least until the twins are a little less demanding.'

'I—'

'Don't fight me on this, please,' Gio urged ruefully.

Exhaustion down to her very bones haltered Leah's ready tongue. She slept almost eighteen hours that night and by the following evening the first nanny had arrived, a pleasant girl who in no way made her feel less for not being able to cope alone.

Over breakfast, while covertly feeding Spike forbidden titbits below the table, a habit that had converted

Spike into his devoted mealtime companion, Gio announced further changes. 'We're leaving for Italy as soon as Luca is released from hospital—'

'But we can't leave Athens,' Leah protested, nervous at the prospect of leaving behind the support network she had established there.

'Of course, we can. There is an excellent hospital nearby with a suitably qualified specialist available for any health problems the children might develop. We'll have the nannies with us. We will also have a full staff at the *castello*. They were hired to get the household ready for our arrival. *This* is why I've been working so hard since the wedding, Leah,' Gio stressed, studying her with glittering resolve. 'So that I could finally take some time off to be with my family.'

His use of that word, 'family', cut through Leah's consternation and took the sharp edge off her anxieties. That he was making that effort, had indeed already made such elaborate plans to facilitate their move, touched her heart. The various health crises the twins had endured had made her reluctant to leave Athens, but she recognised that, with Luca's release, the emergency was now over and that it was selfish to expect Gio to stay in Greece.

'And there's no pressure on you, no pressure whatsoever,' Gio emphasised smoothly. 'Your brother did tell me that, basically, you didn't care how long our marriage lasted, only that it took place to legitimise our children—'

Gio breathed in deep and slow, having finally spilt the words that had been burning a hole in his gut ever since Ari Stefanos had voiced them. The last thing he could afford to do was make Leah feel cornered when he needed to show her that he could give her the time and space to find out for herself that their marriage could flourish.

'Ari talked a lot of rubbish, because it's not as though it was something we ever actually discussed!' Leah protested heatedly, pale in receipt of the explanation he was giving her for his casual, distant attitude. He was holding back with her.

Her brother had made it sound as though she would be content with an empty shell of a marriage and now Gio was wondering if that was true, if, indeed, she had only wanted a ring and his name and nothing more. No longer did she need to wonder why he didn't touch her, why he had made no move even to share a bedroom with her. He was following the wretched blueprint that Ari had given him, leaving it up to her to decide what she wanted.

'If you want more,' Gio murmured sibilantly, 'you'll have to tell me. Just as I wasn't an unwilling husband, I have no desire to make you an unwilling wife.'

If you want more... Leah had wanted more from the first moment she'd laid eyes on Gio Zanetti. A lot of women suffered from the same affliction when they saw him, from the nurses in the NICU, who had christened him 'Mr Gorgeous', to the heads that swivelled to get a closer look at his breathtaking features whenever he was in public. Deprived of him, she scrutinised online photos; she had an addiction now, an incurable addiction to Gio. Now, flushed to the roots of her hair, she glanced at him, scanning the cut-glass cheekbones, the carved jawline and the stunning pale eyes accentuated by lush black lashes, and her heart skipped a beat as though she were still an impressionable schoolgirl.

She wanted him, she wanted *more* as much as she wanted air to breathe, but she could no more imagine making an announcement of that fact to him than she could imagine flapping imaginary wings and flying away. She couldn't put herself out there to that extent, risking humiliation and rejection, because he had made no such announcement to encourage her, had he? She had put herself out on a limb with Oliver, had been the first to declare love, the first to seek greater intimacy, and in the end that naïve loving trust of hers had simply become another weapon to be wielded against her and increase her humiliation. And did she really want to take that huge risk anyway when she had already loved and lost so many people, from her parents to her beloved twin?

Maybe Gio already knew that he would be quite content with a shell of marriage, full access to their children and an easy pre-agreed exit when he tired of the arrangement as inevitably any highly sexed male would. But Leah didn't believe that she could detach herself from her emotions to that extent and the prospect of unrequited love only made her tummy sink like a stone… because she had already done that once and she was determined not to do it again.

Surrounded on all sides by a pine forest, the SUV travelled up a twisty steep road into the Italian hills.

'There it is…' Gio indicated the great stone frontage of the *castello* and its massive circular towers where it stood in a dominant position overlooking the wooded valley.

In awe, Leah stared. 'It's a *real* castle.'

'Fifteenth century. The first Zanetti was a soldier

and he built the fortress. His son became a very successful merchant and by the next generation the Zanettis were loaning money to royalty and acquired a title in payment. As the family grew richer their influence and ambition grew and the house became the symbol of their success,' Gio explained.

'How do you know so much?'

'The old man who owned it was a cousin and he wrote an excellent book about the family history. It was fortunate that the property fell into his safe hands after my grandparents sold it. He restored it. I've spent the last decade buying back the original family paintings and the furniture that were auctioned off to finance that restoration.'

'I didn't realise that the last owner was related to you—'

Gio rolled his eyes. 'He refused to acknowledge the blood tie. Like my mother's parents, he was appalled by my father and kept me at a distance. When he told your brother and me that he would only sell the *castello* to a family man, he was denying the ugly truth of his prejudice,' Gio told her tautly.

And Leah wondered what it must have been like for Gio not only to be forced to grow up with a violent, criminal father but also to be punished as though he were of the same ilk even when he reached adulthood. 'That was wickedly unfair,' she whispered.

Gio shrugged a broad shoulder as their car turned up a leafy drive. 'That's life.'

'But even when your life has proved that you're a different man, why don't they recognise it?' she asked in a pained tone.

'Because some people believe that in the end bad

blood will out,' Gio proffered bitterly. 'If I took an axe and murdered someone, many people would nod their heads in satisfaction and say, "Well, he's Giovanni Romano's son. What did you expect?"'

Her heart clenched at the idea of him having endured that bias since he was a child and at the confirmation that his mother's relatives had decided not to give him a chance either.

The SUV drove through a huge archway into a paved courtyard and the whole illusion of the castle that was a medieval fortress melted away as she registered that the towers and the massive walls were only a façade, loosely joined to the far more elaborate and elegant building hidden behind. A great double loggia with a roof spanned the courtyard, linking two wings with lines of windows.

'My word,' Leah remarked, clambering out of the car, feeling the summer heat warm her bare arms, her attention skipping over the beautiful displays of flowers in stone urns. 'It's more of a palace than a castle.'

'It *was* the Palazzo Zanetti for centuries but my cousin reclaimed the original name and opened a museum of medieval weaponry in one of the towers.' A lean hand rested at the base of her spine. 'Let's go inside,' he urged.

'So, this very grand house is where your mother grew up,' Leah murmured, smiling at the older man waiting to greet them at the imposing front entrance.

'Yes, but my grandparents also own a country property outside Florence, which is where they moved when they sold up here. Allow me to introduce you to Jacobo, who is in charge of making everything under this roof run smoothly,' he interposed.

Nothing could have prepared Leah for the sheer magnificence of the *castello* and her eyes steadily widened in growing awe. A spectacular entrance hall with marble flooring was surrounded by room after room of indescribable splendour. Ornate ceilings, glorious colourful frescoes and gilded furniture abounded along with rich soft furnishings. 'Good heavens,' she exclaimed. 'I can understand why you believed the *castello* was far too generous a wedding gift.'

'I've put some very lucrative business deals your brother's way in recent weeks. I can now consider the debt settled,' Gio countered, surprising her. 'In any case, I don't like to admit it but, but for Ari, I *still* wouldn't own this place. My cousin was never going to agree to sell to me.'

'That's sad. Is this the first time you've seen this house?' she asked abruptly.

'No. My cousin held open days in the summer and I sneaked in once when he was in the middle of his grand restoration. I was fortunate not to be recognised.'

Leah found that even sadder and she reached out to clasp his arm and squeeze it in consolation. 'This is your home now. Enjoy it,' she urged soothingly.

'You're the only woman who has ever tried to comfort me,' Gio proclaimed, shaking his handsome head in wonderment as he directed her upstairs while grudgingly conceding that he had never actually shared so much of himself with any woman before Leah.

'That can't be true. What about your mother?'

'She didn't have a nurturing nature. She worshipped the ground my father walked on though, no matter what he did to either of us, no matter how many other women he had. I loved her but she didn't protect me or herself and she wouldn't leave him and save us both,' he divulged grimly. 'He came first with her...*always*. Now enough about me. You've dragged my entire family history out of me, yet you still won't tell me about your ex-boyfriend.'

Leah winced. 'That's different. That story doesn't reflect well on me, while your background is not something you could have changed. So why did you want this castle?'

Gio was disconcerted by her admission about Oliver and he wondered what could possibly lie behind her discomfiture before he answered her question.

'All the miserable years I was growing up I could see this place up on the hill built by my ancestors. It made me feel proud at a time when I had nothing to be proud of. It wasn't its ties with my mother that attracted me, but that sense of history and of previous generations. I felt as though this place would give me a refreshing new focus in my life, while at the same time suppressing some of the shame about my father's criminal activities.'

Leah nodded understanding as Gio pushed open a door to show her the large, well-equipped room that had been prepared in advance for the twins. Loudly complaining, Luca was being slotted into his crib while the other nanny fed Aurora.

'Is there anything you didn't think of?' Leah whispered, impressed to death by the meticulous arrangements that had been made as she scanned the nursery. She soothed her son by gently stroking his head and he gradually settled.

'I depend on you to tell me,' Gio said lightly, guiding her onward to continue the tour of the upper floor. 'Let me show you your room...'

Your room, Leah noted with a sinking heart. 'Where will you be?' she asked lightly.

'Haven't decided yet. There's a dozen bedrooms to choose from.' Gio pressed open a door at the head of the main landing. 'You're in here within easy reach of the nursery, which I know you prefer.'

Leah wandered uncertainly into another large room, adorned with gorgeous drapes and exquisite furniture. Her brain was in a whirl. Any hope of the marital relationship she had dreamt of and hoped to establish was retreating fast. They had been married over two months and he was still treating her like a maiden aunt, keen only to ensure her health and comfort. She glanced at Gio, marvelling at his detachment from her and his blistering confidence in the stance he had taken. Diamond-bright eyes connected with hers and she had an instant reaction, a clenching sensation spearing in her pelvis, her nipples tightening with the instantaneous shock of raw sexual attraction that she could not suppress.

Yet she felt as though she and Gio had grown so much closer in recent days, only it did not seem to be changing his approach to her.

'I turned the connecting bedroom into an en suite bathroom and dressing room,' he explained, throwing open another door for her inspection, and she wanted to scream at him and tell him that she didn't care even if an enchanted wood complete with unicorn awaited her over the threshold.

'I want more,' she heard herself say without any recollection of having decided to utter that sentence.

But there Gio stood, six feet five inches of vibrant masculine energy and an innate authority that made her feel ridiculously safe, as though nothing bad could happen in a world with him beside her.

'More...?' Gio queried, visibly taken aback by that abrupt announcement.

'You said I had to tell you, so I'm telling you!' Leah snapped, her voice taking on a shrill edge of mingled annoyance and embarrassment. '*I want more.* I don't want the separate bedrooms, the cool polite approach or the conversations that only relate to the twins.'

A blinding smile slowly slashed Gio's lean, dark features and it lit Leah up inside like a torch. He strode forward, reaching for her with both hands, drawing her close. 'I had to wait for you to make a decision,' he breathed in a raw undertone. 'That's been a challenge. I'm not patient. I'm not used to letting anyone else have control.'

'But why did *I* have to make that decision?' she asked shakily, the tension of the moment almost overwhelming her.

'Because you chose to walk away after our first night together and when we got together again during your pregnancy you walked away that time too,' Gio reminded her with dark-toned precision. 'I couldn't afford to take anything for granted in this marriage and I need more than your passive participation for the sake of the children.'

'I'm not a passive person,' Leah whispered unevenly.

Her breath caught in her throat as he backed her up against the wall with the stealth and grace of a panther stalking prey, only no prey, she thought ruefully, had ever been more willing to be caught than she was at that moment when she finally understood why he had put her on the spot. For the first time she saw their relationship from his side of the fence and, inside herself, she cringed. She had continually closed him out, shut him down, never giving an inch, never giving him the benefit of the doubt. Unfortunately, the loss of her brother and the father who had simply disappeared had contributed to her insecurity. And then, Oliver had destroyed her ability to trust and she had allowed the impact of that ultimately meaningless relationship to almost wreck her future.

'Prove it,' Gio urged, pulling her close, unashamed to let her feel the bold thrust of his erection.

Leah was done with prevaricating, making excuses for herself and hiding behind her pride. She let her fingers trail from his broad shoulders up into his black hair, tousling the silken strands that she had grasped in rapture many, many months earlier. A pulse of fierce anticipation beat between her clenched thighs, a wanting so powerful it consumed every thought and feeling.

'It's been too long,' she whispered.

'Way too long,' Gio husked feelingly against her soft lips before he parted them and crushed her mouth hungrily with his.

Her senses spun as he bent down, scooped her up and carried her over to the bed. In mid-air she kicked off her sandals, a glorious sense of freedom engulfing her because, for once, she was doing what she *wanted*, not what her zealous inner critic told her she should do. There was not an ounce of self-denial left in her entire thrumming body. 'And don't you ever call me passive again,' she told him in a warning hiss. 'You can blame my inhibitions on Oliver—'

'Oliver…?'

Leah rested silencing fingers against his beautiful

mouth. 'Let's not talk about him today—maybe tomorrow,' she suggested.

'Sore subject?'

'Very much,' she confirmed with a shiver of remembrance, but for the first time grateful that it was all behind her and that she had met someone infinitely superior.

He extracted her from her sundress, his gaze raking over the scarlet silk bra and knickers he exposed and lingering with all-male appreciation. 'You look amazing,' Gio said gruffly.

'Well, I'm not quite pristine any more,' Leah pointed out, wanting to mention her defects to warn him ahead. 'I've got stretch marks now—'

'Makes you even sexier, the mother of my son and daughter and still shaped like a glorious hourglass I can't keep my hands off,' Gio intoned raggedly as he scored an appreciative fingertip over a brown swollen nipple showing through the lace bra and groaned out loud, abandoning restraint to tug down the cup and suck the straining bud into his mouth.

Sensation shot through her quivering length as he pushed her back on the pillows and employed his mouth and fingers on the pointed peaks. The hunger followed in a surge and pooled at the apex of her thighs, a hot, melting liquidity that made her dig her hips into the mattress. The bra got in the way and was swiftly removed while Leah divested Gio of the silk shirt that showed off his well-delineated abs. He scored a teasing fingertip across the damp triangle of silk stretched taut between her legs and her spine arched and she moaned because she was achingly sensitive there. The remainder of their clothing was scrapped in a mutual scramble of seething impatience.

Fully naked, they rediscovered each other with exploring hands and willing mouths.

'I've wanted you for so long,' Gio framed roughly, his touch contrastingly gentle as he dipped a finger between her wet folds, testing her readiness as she arched up to him with a sound of need that she could not suppress.

A savage groan escaped him as her change of position put them into even more intimate connection and he pressed her legs back and forged into her with bold, shuddering force. 'Don't let me hurt you,' he urged.

'I like forceful,' she whispered suggestively in his ear, her entire body clenching in delight round his fullness. 'I'm no delicate flower.'

Gio took her at her word, abandoning the careful approach, locking into the excitement that had ignited in both of them. He twisted his hips, grinning down at her wickedly when she uttered a little cry of appreciation and wrapped herself round him tightly, drawing him in deeper to enjoy the moment more. He was like a well-oiled machine, possessing her with potent energy and strength, setting off fireworks of sensation within her until at last she reached the pinnacle and jerked and cried out as a tide of sweet sensation swept over her.

'I'm not finished yet, *bella mia*,' he told her rawly, flipping her limp body over and urging her up onto her hands and knees. 'Is this OK?'

'Just be warned. It's *so* OK, you're not getting out of this bed for a month!' she teased breathlessly, her heart still hammering wildly with excitement. She was shaken by the sheer heady surge of passion and intoxicating pleasure engulfing her. And there was a glorious enervating flood of joy that she was finally with Gio again and one step closer to achieving the normal marriage she craved with him.

'Is that a promise?' Gio growled.

'If you're up to the challenge,' Leah gasped on the cusp of a moan as his pace quickened, her body tender and incredibly receptive. Sensation jolted her with exquisite reaction, propelling her to an even more intense second climax and an aftermath of drowning delight.

Lying flat on the bed, she whispered, 'I swear that I'm never moving again.'

'Well, I need you to conserve your energies for the month in bed you suggested to me,' Gio teased, flashing her a glittering look of heated possessiveness.

'Jacobo mentioned dinner,' she mumbled.

'We'll eat late. Everything's on our timing here. Go to sleep,' Gio advised, stretching out beside her in complete relaxation.

They ate a snack supper late in the evening and fed the twins together before returning to bed. Leah felt at peace for the first time in months. They were no longer at odds, no longer being polite and careful with every word. Gio had even been generous enough to admit that he would never have been able to buy the Zanetti family home without her brother acting as a middleman. Taking into account Gio's own disastrous childhood, she marvelled at his gentle, loving care of the twins and it continued to trouble her deeply that even his grandparents had rejected him out of hand. She still had questions she wanted to ask him but did not want to tread too heavily on sensitive ground. Gio was still very uncomfortable talking about his mother and she suspected that she could be the only person he had ever discussed his wretched background with.

Breakfast was served in the shade of the rear terrace that overlooked the sunlit gardens behind the *castello*. Gio was smiling, relaxed. 'You never told me when you lost your mother,' Leah dared to say.

'My first year at university. My father had assaulted her and, of course, she wouldn't ever go for medical treatment when that happened lest he be arrested for assault. A broken rib pierced her lung and she died. I never saw him again after the funeral. The one bright moment was when he was finally tried and convicted for his crimes. He had so many enemies that he died within weeks of starting his prison sentence,' Gio imparted grimly.

'Did your grandparents attend your mother's funeral?'

'No. When they cut her out of their lives it was final. I finally met them when I was eighteen, soon after the funeral. I was a student studying nearby. I read in the newspaper about how they raised funds for a local museum and gallery and when they held a meeting I attended it…'

As his lean, strong features tensed, the cool distance of unease and annoyance entered his reflective gaze but that still couldn't conceal the shadows of pain. 'As soon as I identified myself, they turned away. There was no discussion, no explanation, *nothing*. That was that. They didn't want to know me.'

As they walked through the garden beyond the terrace, Leah thought angrily of a teenaged, vulnerable Gio approaching possibly the only civilised adults related to him and being rejected as so many had already rejected him and her heart clenched with hurt on his behalf. By all accounts, his lady mother had been as indifferent to the misery of his life as everyone else around him, yet his grandparents could have turned that around for him had they had the courage, the foresight and the strength to ignore his parentage. Had they ever regretted that negative response? Thought better of it? Wished they had, at least, given him a chance to show them who he was *before* they judged him unacceptable? Gio had taken his grandparents by surprise in a public place. Perhaps had they known beforehand and had there been privacy they might have reacted differently, Leah reflected sadly.

'My grandmother must miss her garden,' Gio remarked with a curl of his lip. 'She went to a great deal of trouble and expense to make a garden here because the only flat land was wooded and the woods were supposed to be conserved at all costs.'

'She broke the rules?'

'I would assume so, but then the woods here stretch for miles. The garden is a little overgrown. The gardeners haven't tamed it yet,' Gio commented.

'It's still very pretty,' Leah countered, fingering the velvety petal of a scarlet climbing rose as she strolled past, enjoying the drenching warmth of the sunlight. 'Have you ever considered going to see your grandparents and giving them another chance?'

'No!' Gio's derisive dismissal of that possibility was immediate, and she spun to look at him in dismay, noting the shuttered hardening of his darkly handsome features. 'That will never be on the cards.'

Her face hot from the sense that she had stumbled badly on a sensitive subject, Leah turned back to study the garden. She had moved too far too fast with him, she told herself soothingly, but she couldn't help feeling hurt that he had been so quick to shut her down just when she had believed that all his barriers were coming down.

'So… Oliver?' Gio prompted, making her tense even more. 'You promised.'

'I met him in a wine bar when I was out with friends. He was good-looking, successful. I was bowled over,' she admitted frankly, thinking that perhaps if she shared freely it would have the same effect on him. 'But from the start he professed keenness without carrying through and I should've smelt a rat when he sometimes didn't phone me for weeks. We had occasional dates in public places and the relationship didn't really take off until he took me to a legal dinner with his colleagues. He made quite a fuss of me in front of them, more than he made of me when we were alone—'

'He gave you mixed signals,' Gio gathered.

'Oh, very mixed. All over me one minute, ignoring me the next, but I was infatuated with him and I just worked harder to impress him. I thought initially that possibly I was competing with another girlfriend…if only I had retained that suspicion. It was a while before I noticed how critical Oliver was. He didn't like the way I dressed, or my accent or my interests and my cooking skills were definitely below his standards—'

An unexpected laugh was wrenched from Gio.

'You see, he wanted me to provide fancy dinners for his colleagues and I couldn't do it. I had to buy ready-made stuff and fake it. I started to change myself to try and please him…' Leah looked sad. 'I was a total push-over for a man like Oliver. He was very manipulative and of course I irritated him because he didn't ever like or want me for myself—'

Gio frowned. 'Then why was he seeing you? Was he gay? Was that what he was trying to hide?'

'No, he was having an affair with his boss's young trophy wife, the gorgeous Celeste, but I didn't find that out until *after* he dumped me,' Leah explained heavily. 'He ditched me by text when the scandal of my employer, Patrick Lundsworth, being arrested broke. I was inconsolable and after a couple of days I realised I had left my raincoat at his apartment and I had to return his key anyway, so I went over there, expecting him to be out at work—'

'And you found them together,' Gio guessed with a grimace. 'You must've been devastated.'

'Celeste laughed in my face. It was her idea that he get himself a girlfriend to act as a cover-up for their affair. But by then she wanted me out of the picture because she and her husband had separated and she was so proud of her power over Oliver,' Leah told him in an undertone. 'She even told me that she had made him promise not to have sex with me.'

'Well, at least she spared you that and he didn't get to use your body as well,' Gio breathed in a raw undertone. 'If I'd known what he'd done to you the day we signed the prenup, I'd have knocked his teeth down his throat!'

His partisanship lightened her humiliation at having to recount the story of Oliver's deception. 'He told me then that he's no longer with Celeste and I was surprised—'

'I imagine the excitement and the challenge went out of it once she was freely available. Nor would being associated with the estranged wife of his superior have done him any favours,' Gio pointed out with innate practicality.

'You think strategically like Oliver,' Leah registered.

'But I would never have done what he did to you. It was callous to deceive you like that.'

It was strange how talking out loud about Oliver had made the entire episode seem infinitely less important and had lessened the sting of humiliation that had been inflicted. The insecurity of her childhood had made her crave love and stability. She had been all too willing to believe in Oliver. 'I was too young and inexperienced to realise that something was seriously lacking in his supposed attraction to me… I mean, he jumped back from me when I tried to touch him—'

'You're a beautiful woman. I imagine he was scared he wouldn't be able to withstand the temptation,' Gio countered with amusement. '*Dio mio*, I'm grateful that he didn't get to touch you…you've only ever been mine and I value that.'

Strong on equality, Leah lifted her chin. 'I would've valued you more if you'd been a virgin too,' she told him.

'Little chance of that after the home I grew up in. I was never innocent in that way because I witnessed sex from an early age,' he admitted in disgust, closing his hand over hers as she mounted the shallow steps of a stone-pillared folly. 'I'll tell you about my marriage some other time. I still don't understand why you're so ashamed of Oliver's deception because it doesn't reflect badly on you at all. You're very straightforward. You wouldn't recognise double-dealing and insincerity until you'd first experienced it. Don't blame yourself for his lack of decency. Sooner or later, he'll get his just reward in life—'

Leah laughed. 'Do you really believe that?'

Gio grinned. 'I like to believe in natural justice.'

She shifted closer and stretched up to taste his mouth with her own. He tasted so good she leant into him, her breath catching in her throat, her heart hammering again on that surge of sexual hunger that only he awakened in her. 'So do I,' she murmured.

'But I imagine Oliver will be most grieved of all that he allowed the Stefanos heiress to slip through his clumsy hands,' Gio derided with satisfaction as he lowered his head and toyed with her lower lip, his words slurring a little. 'His face was a study as you walked away.'

'Do you want to go indoors?'

'Not particularly,' Gio confided, sinking down on a stone bench and tugging her down onto his lap, a lean hand travelling up a slender thigh to tug at her knickers. 'I'm very, very adaptable to new experiences with my wife.'

'I'll draw up a bucket list,' Leah parried with a breathy little giggle and a shiver of appreciation that lit her body up as though she were on fire. 'How long have we got in Italy before you start travelling again?'

'Three weeks and then there's a board meeting I need to put in an appearance at.'

A heady mixture of love and lust shimmied through Leah at the prospect of having Gio all to herself for that long. 'I hope you don't get bored with us.'

'The one thing you never do is bore me, *bella mia*,' he swore as he unzipped his chinos and rearranged her, bringing her down on his engorged shaft and making her moan with startled pleasure.

Afterwards, she lay in his arms, relieved that they were able to confide in each other and feeling a sense of peace spreading through her. In time, she was convinced, she would know everything there was to know about Gio Zanetti.

Almost three weeks later, Gio flopped back on the picnic rug under the tree. 'I was a student and I fell like a ton of bricks for Gabriella. I'd had a lot of sex, but I hadn't been in love before. I'd just created my first app, Virgo, and it had gone viral. Money was pouring in and, to be honest, at first, I didn't know what to do with it—'

Leah was thrilled that he was finally willing to talk about his first marriage to her. 'It must have been an exciting time.'

His lean dark features tensed. 'When Gabriella told me that she was pregnant, it never occurred to me to ask her to prove it. It never crossed my mind that a woman would lie about such a thing.'

'I can't imagine you being that trusting.' Leah sighed, running a hand slowly down over a muscled forearm.

Gio grimaced. 'I was twenty-one. I thought I knew it all and I married her the same week she told me she had conceived because all I could think about was that my father had never cared enough for my mother to marry her. I wanted to be there in every way for her and my child,' he confessed ruefully. 'Gabriella assumed she'd be able to fall pregnant *after* the wedding, but it didn't happen and eventually she got tired of the pretence and started drinking and going out again when I was working. There were rows. Some time after that she brought another man home and banged him and I walked in on it…'

'That was some wake-up call. I'm sorry,' Leah murmured, belatedly realising why he had wanted her to prove that her child was his to allay the fears and doubts that Gabriella's lies had bred in him. Belatedly, now that she understood the man she had married a little better, she appreciated that he hadn't told her about his marriage in any detail before because he was ashamed of how trusting he had been at twenty-one, and that saddened her.

'She came clean then. I'll give her that,' Gio told her grudgingly. 'She admitted that she'd thought I was a great financial bet for the future and that she had never been pregnant. The divorce took for ever and cost me a fortune because there had been no prenuptial contract. It left me bitter and distrustful and determined not to get seriously involved with a woman for a long time. Do you realise you're the first person I have ever told that story to?'

Leah rubbed her brow tenderly against his shoulder. 'I'm touched. But no wonder when I told you *I* was pregnant it pushed all your panic buttons.'

'I *didn't* panic,' Gio asserted, sitting up and pouring a fresh glass of wine.

Leah grinned. 'As far as you are capable you *panicked*,' she contradicted, sipping at her wine while Gio's wolfhounds tried to sniff out and chase Spike, who was hiding under a shrub.

As Spike emerged, he made a run for a stone bench and jumped on it to start madly barking. The wolfhounds careened back at speed and, accustomed to the terrier's excitable nature, flopped down on the ground beside the bench. Spike joined them, scrambling up onto Lupo to lie down on his big shaggy back. Gio's dogs treated Spike like a puppy and let him take all sorts of liberties.

The past three weeks had been full of new experiences for Leah and her dog. She had explored picturesque San Gimignano, lunched in Pisa and toured the gothic cathedral in Siena. Gio had very kindly encouraged her to play the tourist. She had enjoyed a picnic in the Chianti hills and toured the highly successful organic vineyard there, which Gio owned, and she had got sunburned on a charming boat trip along the beautiful coastline of the Cinque Terre. She had seen museums, old buildings, fabulous craft galleries and had revelled in incredible meals in wonderful restaurants. He had taken her around Florence on a motorbike, showing her the places he had favoured as a student, and she had been silently, ridiculously jealous that Gabriella had shared his life back then.

Thinking about how much she loved Gio sometimes made her head spin because she knew how vulnerable her emotions made her. She hadn't told him that she loved him because she believed that if she didn't lay that guilt trip on him there was more chance that he would learn to love her in the future. He had been in love with his first wife when he'd married her and he was clever enough to eventually recover from that bad experience. Why shouldn't she be optimistic? Particularly when Gio was steadily becoming more open with her and sharing all his secrets?

After all, right now, Leah was incredibly happy and the twins were thriving and slowly falling into a routine as they began to sleep longer at night. To her surprise,

Gio revelled in the ordinary family stuff and he gladly joined in with bathing their children, feeding them and taking them for walks in their pram. Of course, he enjoyed all that, she conceded. Never having had the benefit of a normal childhood for himself, he loved seeing the twins enjoying that security and the love and appreciation that went along with them.

Leah still longed, however, to give Gio the blood connection that his Zanetti grandparents had denied him and, pondering that thorny problem, she had decided to approach them for him because he was too proud to risk rejection a second time. She had searched online to discover their names and, since their palatial country home was occasionally open to the public, discovering their address had not been much of a challenge. And after a great deal of thought, she had printed a photo of the garden his grandmother had created and had written a letter, identifying herself, mentioning their great-grandchildren and asking to meet them at their home to tell them about Gio, the grandson they had refused to acknowledge. If they ignored the letter, she would have lost nothing by making the effort on her husband's behalf, she reasoned ruefully.

She was convinced that his grandparents' acceptance would mean a great deal to Gio. Whenever she mentioned the older couple, she saw the pain in Gio's eyes and, even though she knew he would probably be angry about her interference, she thought that if she could help in any way it was worth that risk.

A response to her letter awaited her back at the *castello* and she hid it in her sleeve before Gio could enquire about it because she didn't want to tell him any lies. She was shaken that she could have received a reply so soon and nervous in the sense that she had now started something that was no longer wholly in her control. Opening the letter in private, she found a formal reply inviting her to visit and giving her a phone number. She immediately decided to visit the elderly Zanettis while Gio was in the UK on business.

Gio's grandparents, Eufrasio and Matalia Zanetti, the Conte and Contessa Santastino, lived in a country house only marginally less imposing than the *castello* they had sold.

The week after that letter arrived, Leah stepped out of the car that had brought her to the house outside Florence and lifted her chin. Now she would discover whether or not Gio was correct in his conviction that the older couple were inveterate snobs obsessed with their pedigreed lineage and, even decades on, still painfully sensitive to their daughter's fall from grace.

What worried Leah most of all was the horrid suspicion that Gio would kill her if he knew where she was and what she was trying to do for him. They had grown so close and now she was doing something he probably would disapprove of and he might well be furious with her, she reasoned nervously. Gio, after all, had a great deal of pride. He didn't look back with regret to the past because he was too busy moving forward at speed. He didn't give those who wronged him a second chance, didn't believe in it but, even so, he had given Leah more than one chance, hadn't he? Had that only been because she was pregnant? His dreadful childhood and his resolve that he would make every possible effort to be a good and active father to his own offspring? Was the wedding ring on her finger only there for those most basic reasons?

She was probably kidding herself if she allowed herself to believe that she was anything more important to Gio than the mother of his children, the wife he required to create a secure traditional home for the twins. He made her happy and he seemed happy with her, but he had told her from the start that he wasn't offering her love, so she couldn't say she was being shortchanged, could she?

Sadly, when she had told Gio that she wanted *more* she had truly meant that she wanted a great deal more than his wildly entertaining expertise between the sheets.

Admittedly, he was incredible in bed, she thought, her cheeks warming at the reflection that Gio had needed to go away for a night or two to allow her to catch up on her sleep. And it was not as though intimacy were confined only to the night hours. Once Gio had registered that Leah was fascinated by encounters in unexpected places, he had ensured that he delivered on that score as well. Their only disappointment had been making love in the Maserati when they had ended up getting out of the car and using the bonnet instead, but by that stage of the proceedings Leah had been so consumed by giggles that Gio had marvelled at his ability to save the day.

Her body still heated by her recollection of that episode, Leah entered the classy drawing room of the Conte and Contessa's home with a straight back and a composed expression. Dealing with guests by Ari and Cleo's side had given her a great deal more social confidence than she had once had but facing up to Gio's blood relatives still demanded considerable courage. Although they were now in their late seventies, his grandparents were elegantly dressed and still upright and strong.

'Please sit down, Leah. We do appreciate your visit,' Gio's grandmother said in accented English.

'Hopefully you are not as hot-headed as the man you married,' her husband remarked, provoking his wife into a staccato burst of Italian.

'You see how hen-pecked I am,' he lamented with a glint of amusement in his creased eyes.

'You're not hen-pecked, you're grumpy because you haven't had your afternoon tea yet,' his wife told him roundly, pressing a bell by the fireplace.

Moments later a maid came in carrying a tray and a very formal afternoon tea session commenced, complete with bone-thin porcelain, cloth napkins, minuscule sandwiches, even tinier fancy cakes and solid silver cutlery. Leah was grateful that Gio wasn't with her. His tolerance threshold for extreme formality and exaggerated old-style courtesies was low. While her brother was very much at home with such customs, Gio, denied such experiences when he was younger, was aggressively contemporary in his habits.

'At that first meeting with him at the museum we weren't prepared and we didn't know what to say. One moment he was there and then he stomped off and that was that,' the older woman explained heavily.

'I was concerned to see that he had the hot temper his father was famed for,' her husband added.

'Gio doesn't lose his temper,' Leah responded carefully. 'He's very controlled, very cautious. I think his background made him that way.'

'It doesn't help that he's the very picture of his father,' Gio's grandfather admitted, compressing his lips. 'But it was unreasonable to judge him for that.'

'His father *was* a vile character,' Matalia Zanetti murmured tightly. 'We did everything within our power to try and persuade our daughter to leave him, but she was as addicted to him as some were to the drugs he sold. Nothing would move her and in the end we had to accept that she was where she wanted to be.'

'The town priest, Father Luca, came to us when Gio was a boy and told us that he was being neglected and he asked us to consider fighting for custody.'

The old man looked very sad. 'We felt we could not face another scandal in the newspapers and the dragging out of all that dirt concerning our daughter again. We also thought the priest was exaggerating but stories came out after Gio's father's imprisonment and subsequent death which horrified us. We let Gio down badly and from what we read about him, he deserved so much more from us.'

'But by then it was too late and Gio had come to Florence as a student and we had simply stared dumbly at him as though he were an exotic beast when he approached us.' Gio's grandmother's eyes were bright with unshed tears, her deep sigh one of regret.

'Well, all that's behind you now,' Leah pointed out, keen to inject a more positive note into the conversation but suddenly very pleased that she had taken the risk of visiting on Gio's behalf. 'I'm suggesting a fresh start and staying away from the past because everybody is sure to have a different opinion on that. Gio loathed his father, but he wasn't close to his mother either because she didn't ever try to protect him from his father. It's better for you to know that in advance.'

'You're a very sensible young woman,' the Contessa told her. 'How do you suggest we go about meeting our grandson?'

'We're holding the twins' christening in the *castello* chapel in ten days. That gives me plenty of time to explain to Gio that I visited you. I brought an invitation for you,' Leah admitted, digging into her capacious leather bag to extend it.

'Do you have any pictures of the twins…? Oh, yes, I have kept up with the news,' Gio's grandmother admitted with a smile.

Smiling back, Leah extended her phone and brought up the most recent photos. There was one of Gio holding Aurora and she noticed his grandparents lingered over that one the longest. 'He's a wonderful man,' she said quietly. 'Very clever, generous and caring. I think the only lessons he learned from his father were how not to be like him.'

'Your love for him shines in your eyes,' the Contessa said softly.

Leah was in the best of good moods and feeling sentimental when the limousine delivered her home to the *castello*. She walked in the front door held wide by a curiously tense Jacobo and glanced up with a smile as Gio stalked into the hall.

'My goodness, I wasn't expecting you back until tomorrow,' she told him chirpily.

'Was that why you felt confident enough to believe that I wouldn't realise that you'd betrayed my trust?'

CHAPTER TEN

AND, THAT FAST, Leah knew that somehow Gio also knew where she had been and her tummy sank like a stone to her very toes. 'How did you find out where I was?' she almost whispered, horror gripping her when she collided with the biting, stinging chill of his glittering wolfish gaze.

In all their relationship, Gio had never looked at her like that: with raging hostility, fierce condemnation and an even more terrifying coldness. It suggested that in his eyes she had put herself beyond the pale and done something absolutely unforgivable. Her tummy twisted, sudden pallor now stamping her taut features.

'It wasn't difficult. You hadn't bothered to cover your tracks because you didn't know I'd be arriving back early. I wanted to surprise you.' Gio visibly gritted his even white teeth at that recollection. '*Dio mio*, didn't that turn out well? Almost as well as when I decided to surprise Gabriella. I don't learn, do I?'

'Gio,' she began breathlessly.

'I called your driver to ask where you were. In the future if you're trying to hide something, you need to bribe your driver,' Gio warned her flatly.

And it was only at that moment that she truly understood how very shaken up and upset he was underneath that cold front of control. He was, after all, standing in the hall loudly saying private things where anyone might have overheard them, but she rather suspected Jacobo had guessed that trouble was in the air and he had quietly removed himself and every other staff member from the vicinity.

'Come into the drawing room.' Leah's voice was almost a whisper because tension had stolen the breath from her lungs.

'Oh, you've definitely been visiting the *grand*parents,' Gio derided. 'This is a living room.'

In a daze, caught unprepared as she had been, that statement of reverse snobbery made her spread her gaze round the confines of the vast opulent room, with its huge wooden carved hearth bearing the Zanetti coat of arms, ornate tall ceiling and decorative drapes. 'No, it won't ever be a living room unless you deconstruct it. It's a drawing room because it was made like this to impress and intimidate visitors. Ordinary people don't have spaces like this in their homes,' she told him as though they were having a perfectly normal dialogue instead of a heart-wrenching fight that was tearing her apart inside herself.

That Gio could be hurt and angry enough to compare her to his ex-wife, who had lied about her pregnancy and slept with another man, appalled her. 'I would have told you that I was planning to visit your grandparents, but I didn't want to do it until I'd met them and sussed them out… I didn't want them upsetting you in some way,' she admitted doggedly, determined to explain her reasoning. 'I was sort of vetting them for you in advance.'

'Naturally, it wouldn't have occurred to you that,

ironically just like them, I had a certain prejudiced reason to keep my distance?' Gio raised an ebony brow enquiringly. 'They brought up my mother and she was a sociopath who didn't have a single drop of love or compassion in her heart, even for her child. Why would I seek them out now that I am no longer vulnerable enough to actually need them?'

Leah bit her tongue, unwilling to get into such a discussion when it was for him and his grandparents to bridge all the unmentionable things that had happened to him. She didn't think his mother's parents would be that surprised to find out how she had treated him. She had noticed that they had not uttered a word in their daughter's defence and had not referred to her as a victim either. 'Perfectly normal, decent people end up raising sociopaths. It's not their fault any more than it's yours that your parents were...unpleasant—'

'*Grazie mille* for that vote of confidence,' Gio mocked that understatement. 'But it doesn't excuse your betrayal in any way.'

Leah thrust the door shut behind her and protested, 'I didn't betray you... I would *never* betray you, Gio!'

'But you did,' Gio threw back at her with icy bitter precision. 'You betrayed me the instant you went behind my back to see my grandparents without my knowledge. I trusted you, Leah. Do you know how long it's been since I trusted a woman?' he demanded. 'I trusted you with all my secrets and you deceived me today.'

Leah lifted her head high. 'No, that's not how it was. There was no betrayal of trust involved—'

'How can there not have been when you went to see *them*?' Gio accused with wrathful emphasis. 'You didn't even mention what you were thinking about doing and you didn't discuss it with me—'

'How the heck could I discuss it with you when you're not rational about it?' Leah slammed back at him, her own temper finally sparking in self-defence. 'You lit up like a firework whenever I tried to talk about them!'

'And you're surprised? After the rejection I had from them?' he parried rawly.

'No, I thought about that. You were young, Gio…you didn't think it through…approaching them when other people were around and without warning. They got it wrong and they *know* they got it wrong that day—'

'It's best that they remain in the past alongside my late parents,' Gio opined curtly.

'I assure you that I didn't share anything you've ever told me about either of your parents with them. I didn't spill any secrets and neither did they. That wasn't my business and I knew that. I only said that you were a wonderful guy—'

'You expect me to believe that?' Gio raked back at her. 'You positively bounced back into this house looking very pleased with yourself. So, I assume your visit to them went well on your terms. It won't get you anywhere because I want nothing to do with them. So, why did you do it?'

'I—'

'I noticed that your brother was somewhat impressed by the fact that my grandparents were titled,' Gio continued harshly. 'And they do have an elite standing in social circles. Is that kind of social status and acceptance so important to you that you would rate that higher than my wishes and needs?'

Leah was utterly savaged by such a suspicion. Did

he know so little about her? How could he even suspect her of such superficiality?

'I went to see them for your benefit. I told them nothing private—'

'How was it for *my* benefit when I've done without them all my life?' Gio flung at her in scornful condemnation of that statement.

'They're your family and I think it would do you good to have family other than me and the twins,' Leah declared clumsily, her eyes stinging with tears because that was not something he would easily hear or something that she had wished to be forced into saying. 'I know how much Ari finding me meant to me…discovering my brother was a *huge* thing for me and wonderful! I know you're probably not Ari's greatest fan, but the knowledge that he searched for me because I was his half-sister meant the world to me.'

'Ari *searched* for you. My grandparents always knew where I was,' Gio responded deflatingly. 'You can't compare the situations. But you do know me well enough to know that taking it upon yourself to seek them out and visit them without my agreement or approval was a deception and a piece of disloyalty I cannot *accept* from someone as close to me as my wife.'

Nausea bubbled in Leah's tummy. She felt sick. She felt threatened. The man she loved was lacerating her for sins she would never ever have considered committing against him. Love, not disloyalty, had driven her. Her optimism, sparked by her brother's generosity, had persuaded her to go that extra mile in the hope that a solution could be found to grant Gio a connection with his grandparents.

'Sometimes you're so stupid, Gio. You're clever

about so many things but with emotions…or, apparently, possible motivations, you're hopeless. Why do you think I sneaked off to see your grandparents? What was in it for me?' Leah asked flatly. 'In reality, there was nothing in it for me except the chance of a nasty reception from your grandparents or a humiliating rejection because I was married to you. I took a risk for your benefit, not for my own. I couldn't care less about their social status. I gain nothing by you having a relationship with your grandparents—'

'So, why the hell did you do it, then?' Gio launched at her in a furious attack.

'Because I love you, and when you love someone you want them to have everything that can make them happy. You want a sunny perfect world for them and you want no bad things to happen,' Leah muttered while Gio stood staring at her, suddenly frozen to the floor by that astonishing declaration. 'That's why I did it, and I didn't tell you about what I was doing because I knew that if it went badly, it would only increase your bitterness.'

Tears sprinkling her cheeks, Leah spun and left the room to head upstairs to take refuge in the nursery. She hadn't intended to tell him how she felt about him, but it would have been worse to allow him to assume that she had decided to court his grandparents because they were titled, influential people. When misunderstandings occurred, honesty was the only solution, she reasoned wretchedly.

Unfortunately, she felt as though she had abandoned her dignity and humiliated herself because the last time she had told a man she loved him, Oliver had been the target. And Oliver had reacted as non-committally as if she had told him it was raining. How she had cringed from that memory after finding out about his affair with Celeste! She stared down into the cots where her children slumbered, peaceful and unaware of the world beyond their cosy cocoon. Slowly she backed out of the nursery again, reminding herself that the twins were the main reason she had married Gio. She had wanted them to have a father, and in that line Gio was amazing, she reminded herself doggedly.

Oh, stop kidding yourself, she urged herself impatiently. She had married him because she wanted him, because she loved him. She almost collided with the man himself on the landing but when he tried to catch her arm, she shook him off and headed straight into her bedroom, her bedroom which had steadily become *their* bedroom. Of course, what highly sexed male was likely to say no to the sex?

Gio stood in the doorway. 'I overreacted—'

'You think?' Leah parried without looking at him, stripping off the more formal outfit she had worn to visit his grandparents and ignoring him.

'I'm sorry,' he breathed stiltedly.

'Right,' Leah said tightly.

'I lost my head, my temper… I never do that. I watched my father do it too often, saw him lash out with abuse and his fists,' he admitted in a tortured undertone.

Leah breathed in deep and slow, fiercely resisting the urge to move closer and wrap her arms round him. 'You didn't use fists and you weren't abusive. You said how you felt and that was betrayed. I underestimated the level of your sensitivity…and, no, please don't tell me that you're not sensitive, because you've got triggers as we all have. You trusted me and I shocked you by doing something you see as unforgivable—'

'I don't see it that way any more,' Gio sliced in, his dark deep voice raw and rushed. 'I reacted badly because you mean more to me than anything in this world and I'm hopelessly in love with you and the thought that you could be disloyal simply devastated me.'

Leah stilled halfway into the sundress she was putting on. That garbled surge of confession in which he barely seemed to draw breath took her so much by surprise that her tongue was glued to the roof of her mouth. Clad in floral lingerie, she turned to focus on him with wide, disconcerted dark eyes. 'Hopelessly in love with me?' she echoed in a slightly strangled voice. 'Since when?'

'For ages. But I wasn't going to tell you, wasn't going to put myself in a weak position like that again.' Gio grimaced. 'You're braver than I am. I sort of thought you'd guess and I wouldn't have to say it.'

'Idiot,' Leah pronounced, finally donning the dress she had been holding in frozen hands at her waist.

'Possibly,' Gio conceded with a slow-burning smile that tugged at the corners of his tense mouth. 'But very much *your* idiot.'

'I wasn't ready to tell you either,' Leah conceded grudgingly, and the whole time there was this surging inner joy interfering with every other thought process. He loved her back. This time she had gone out on a limb and it had paid off because Gio loved her. Every insecurity fell away, every fear was vanquished. 'But you are pretty special…in some ways,' she added, not wanting to flatter him too much.

Gio gave her a wide slanting grin. 'I suppose I could

say the same thing about you. You're not quite so special when I'm tripping over the shoes you leave lying around or when you leave make-up cluttering the bathroom—'

'Don't be so *literal*!' Leah shot at him. 'You're not supposed to tell me that you love me in one breath and then in the next tell me what I do that irritates you.'

Gio's grin grew even wider as he crossed the distance separating them and tugged her into his arms. 'Clearly, I need training—'

'You do,' Leah agreed, rather covertly leaning into the heat and strength of him, still not quite accustomed to the idea of actually being loved back, accepting that she needed a little time to luxuriate in that security before she could overcome her defensiveness. Her hands slid up from his shoulders into his black hair, flirting with the tips of the silky strands. 'But you're very sexy. That comes naturally.'

Engaged in unbuttoning the straps on her shoulders, Gio glanced up with his stunning eyes semi-screened by lush ebony lashes. It was a look that made her heart skip a beat and butterflies go crazy in her tummy. 'Well, you did once give me the feeling that all you wanted from me was sex…'

Leah flushed to the roots of her hair. 'But…er—'

'You slept with me and kept on walking away again. What else was I going to think?' Gio chided. 'It was a new experience for me not to be chased. Being challenged didn't do me any harm at first, but then I saw you with Ari and assumed he was a rival and that was hell. I've never been jealous before. By the time I found Gabriella in bed with another man, the marriage and any feelings I'd had for her were dead. I'd realised I'd married someone I didn't have a thought or feeling in common with and it was a sobering experience—'

'And yet you married me—'

'By that stage I knew I didn't want a life without you or our children—'

'It was the same with me for you when I agreed to marry you. You weren't offering me love,' Leah admitted, feeling a swell of happiness rise inside her like an unstoppable tide because everything she had ever wanted with Gio was suddenly right there in front of her, 'but there was this enormous need to be with you and I couldn't resist it—'

'Why should you have been able to resist it when I couldn't?' Gio asked, efficiently removing her last item of clothing with the single-minded resolve that was so much a part of him. When he set his heart on something he would do anything to win it and she felt so lucky that he had fallen for her. 'That's what love is…'

'Where do you think we'll be twenty years from now?' she asked him sunnily, positively buoyant with joy and optimism now that she had his heart and appreciation.

Gio laughed. 'We'll be the same. People don't change but I bet we have more kids. And in the near future I imagine I'm going to meet my grandparents…am I right?'

Leah went pink. 'I invited them to the christening.'

'Clever, enough people around to avoid each other if we don't click but the chance to connect if we do and take it further. You really are amazing,' Gio told her, pressing her down on the bed to cover her with kisses and show her all the ways in which he was also amazing.

Seven years later, in honour of their wedding anniversary, Gio and Leah and the family were in Norfolk staying at Shore House. Sally was coming to dinner with Tom, the widower who had recently become her regular companion, and Gio was cooking. It would be one of those relaxed, informal evenings that they both so much enjoyed but rarely experienced.

As she finished dressing, she glanced out of the window to check her family, who were all on the beach. They were all so active and athletic that they put her to shame. Aurora and Luca were squabbling over a ball game.

She could tell by their stances with each other, and then Aurora went to thump Luca, who always wound her up into a rage, and Gio was suddenly there, pulling the twins to him and, no doubt, once again explaining why it wasn't all right to get physical when someone annoyed you. Luca was laughing because he loved to see his sister get mad and have to deal with her frustration. Luca was far too clever for his own good. Their five-year-old, Talia, named for her great-grandmother, tugged at her father's jacket to get his attention because her siblings' argument had interrupted her seashell gathering. Their three-year-old, Rocco, was hanging onto Talia. The little boy followed Talia around like a puppy dog.

For a moment sadness shadowed Leah's eyes as she remembered Spike, who had had a very good innings, who indeed had lived to a very old age and passed away peacefully. Leah had shed many tears over his departure and Gio's surviving wolfhound had been so devastated at the loss of his only companion that they had had to replace Spike with another rescue dog, which Sally had been delighted to provide them with.

Their family was complete, both animal and child,

Leah mused. But there had been losses from the family circle as well. Gio's grandfather, Eufrasio, had died two years earlier and, several months ago, Matalia, Gio's grandmother, had agreed to move into their home in Italy. She had her own annexe at the *castello* but loved being within reach of a busy household again with plenty of visitors, many of the child variety, and assistance if she needed it. Leah had never regretted going that extra mile to reunite her husband with his grandparents and over the years since he had thanked her many times for taking the risk of losing face that he himself could not bear. Gio hadn't had that long with his grandfather, but they had become close during the time they had been blessed with and Matalia, well acquainted now with Gio's kind heart and attachment to his family, adored her grandson.

And the family circle had grown and not only with children, Leah mused fondly. She had rediscovered her lost kid sister, Eloise, as well. Eloise, however, was no longer called her original birth name and the trials and tribulations that had brought her to her current status were another story entirely. Leah saw her sister as regularly as she saw her brother, Ari, and his family. Every Christmas they took turns and staged a family festive celebration and the next Christmas, it would be Leah and Gio's home that housed everyone.

Gio strolled into the bedroom and found Leah on the window seat, a favourite spot of hers where she tended to daydream. She wore a beautifully tailored casual blue top with her favourite jeans, the top outlining the swell of her breasts, the jeans showing off her shapely thighs, and that fast he wanted her again with the seething hunger that only Leah had ever inspired in him. The more time he had with her, the greedier he got, he conceded with a slanting grin.

'What are you doing?' he asked, and she turned her head, black curls bouncing on her shoulders inciting his hand to rise.

'Being lazy, watching the rest of you on the beach.' Inured to Gio's every move, Leah jerked her head out of reach of his fingers. 'No, I finally got the frizz out—'

'Only you see the frizz in your hair. I only see glossy ringlets,' Gio confided truthfully.

'I love you, but I want my hair nice for this evening.' Leah rested big caramel eyes on him, her pink mouth pouting, and it was too much for him.

'Gio!' she shrieked as he grabbed her up into his arms and kissed her breathless.

'You see, you should've let me stroke your hair. I would've been satisfied with that,' he teased her as she came back at him for another kiss.

'Liar,' she muttered against his lips.

Gio smiled down at her, his black hair tousled from the beach, his stunning eyes glittering with energy. He smelled of the sea and the outdoors and she drank in the scent of him like the addict she was, slender fingers tracing that very kissable mouth of his as she rejoiced in the reality that he was hers, all hers, as much hers as he could be. He was never off the phone when he was away from her. He took interest in every little thing that she and the kids did. She couldn't have found herself a better man and was still grateful that he hadn't given up on her, because she didn't want to think how empty her life would have been without him and the children.

'You are wearing your new pearls,' Gio finally noted with satisfaction, fingertips brushing the perfectly matched string at her throat, his gift for their anniversary to match the heavy pearl drop earrings he had given her for her last birthday. 'I want to see you in them naked in the pool at midnight to commemorate the way we met—'

Leah adored him but she rolled her eyes as if she had never heard anything so ridiculous. 'We do that every year—'

Glittering eyes intent, Gio ran the tip of his tongue across her collarbone, making her quiver with anticipation. 'I've got game to bring—'

'You've always got game to bring,' Leah murmured cheerfully, her body melting, but they both knew that their guests would be arriving soon and then there would be the fuss of the children going to bed and there just wasn't time unless they left it all to their nanny, and they only liked to do that when they had no option. They were both aware from watching some of the kids in the family circle that children grew up terrifyingly fast and they didn't want to miss out on the cuddles and the bedtime-story phase.

'Is that a fact, Signora Zanetti?' Gio teased, hungrily assessing her with his eyes. '*Dio mio*, I love you…'

'And I love you too,' Leah told him softly, scrambling off the bed before she gave way to temptation, which was so easy with Gio. 'Until midnight…'

* * * * *

THE BILLIONAIRE'S ONE-NIGHT BABY

JOSS WOOD

MILLS & BOON

PROLOGUE

Five years ago...

Jago found her in her grandmother's bedroom upstairs, seated on the end of her bed, slim arms wrapped around a framed photograph of Lily, her red head bowed. She'd refused to wear funeral black and Jago thought that she looked even smaller in her simple ecru dress and low heels—if that were at all possible. Smaller, defenceless, broken.

He watched a tear drop from her nose onto the old wooden floorboards and swallowed, fighting the urge to turn around and rejoin the wake downstairs. What was he doing here? Sure, he'd known her for years and, through Thadie, interacted with her at Le Roux family functions, but they weren't *friends*. The best he could call them was friendly acquaintances. But he'd had his eyes on her all afternoon and when she ran up the stairs, obviously needing a break from her grandmother's mourners, he found himself following her.

Jago pushed his hand through his hair and rubbed his jaw, unable to take his eyes off her bright, bowed head, her pale profile. Love—that messy, uncontrollable, bewildering emotion—and its sidekick, grief, annihilated people. Like a lightning strike, it was powerful and destructive, diving towards its destination, fast and unforgiving, incinerating anything and everyone in its path. It was merciless, thoughtless, devastating.

Was it any wonder he avoided it?

Jago laid a broad hand on Dodi's head, and she looked up at him, her nose red from weeping and those marvellous grey-blue eyes drenched with tears. Despite the gravity of the occasion, her eyes held all the impact of a pole slamming into his stomach. He wished he could describe the colour accurately, but he wasn't a writer or a poet and the best he could come up with was that the smoky blue reminded him of sun-and-rain-splattered mist.

The first time he'd noticed her, six or so years ago, he'd been walking into a restaurant, his new bride, Anju, on his arm. He immediately noticed the redhead laughing with his sister, dressed in a short, boldly patterned sundress. Pretty, he'd decided. Young, and if she was a friend of his sister's, probably a little rebellious. Then someone had congratulated him, and Dodi was forgotten.

Too many deaths had occurred between that low-key celebration of his marriage to Anju and today: too many tears had been shed, too many floors paced and too many nights spent awake and grieving.

Jago gently pulled the photograph from her grip and placed it on the dressing table behind him. Having buried his wife and father months apart, Jago knew what Dodi was going through and what her immediate future held. After their funerals, he'd spent so much time dissecting his intellectual marriage, based on friendship and mutual interests, and examining his relationship with his volatile father. He knew that Dodi, in the weeks and months to come, would also do some intense soul searching.

But, unlike him, Dodi would grieve solo, without the support of family or siblings. Thadie, lovely and loyal, was trying to fill in the gaps but she couldn't be there twenty-four-seven for Dodi.

His heart, withered as it was, ached for her.

Jago sat down on the bed next to her, sliding his hand up and down her back, his hand connecting with every bump in her spine. She was so slight, so petite. Still, at only twenty-four, so damn young. 'How are you doing, Elodie Kate?'

He felt, rather than heard, her emotional hiccup to his using her full name. He had decided, years ago, that her old-fashioned name suited her ethereal face and slim build. And, as far as he knew, he was the only person who called her by her birth name. Jago knew it frustrated her but that wasn't a good enough reason for him not to use it. He liked her full name, so he'd use it.

Obviously exhausted, Dodi simply rested her head on his shoulder. Death, he realised, tended to put inconsequential arguments into perspective.

'I feel like a part of my soul has been amputated. It's just such a damned waste, Jago. Lily wasn't that old.'

Jago silently agreed. He didn't know Dodi's grandmother well but, from what he'd heard from his sister Thadie, he understood Lily to have been a vibrant and charismatic woman, energetic and charming. She'd taken Dodi in when she was a teenager and Dodi adored her, as did his sister. Lily's death would leave a huge hole in Thadie's life and a crater in Dodi's.

Dodi curled into his arm and lifted her hand to his

chest. Despite the sombre moment, he couldn't help his immediate reaction to her touch, the electric current to his groin. What on earth…?

This was his sister's best friend, someone he'd come up here to comfort, not seduce. She was grieving, sadness rolled off her in waves, but all he could think about was whether her mouth was spicy or sweet and whether her skin was as silky soft as it looked.

Jago shook his head, annoyed with himself. What was he thinking? Not only was Dodi grieving but she was also nine years younger than him and his sister's best friend, and his wife had only been dead a year. His reaction to Dodi annoyed and upset him—he loathed feeling out of control. He was not his father, easily able to move on from grief and loss.

But holding Dodi like this was torture.

Jago ran a tired hand over his eyes and shifted away from Dodi, who promptly followed and cuddled closer as if seeking his warmth.

Dodi wiped her eyes with the heels of her hands. Jago managed a tiny smile. It was the same gesture his nephews used when they were upset or tired.

'She left me her business, but I don't think I can take it on, Jago,' she murmured.

Jago sighed, wrapped his arm around her shoulder and tipped his head sideways so that his head touched hers. 'Why not?'

'Because it makes me feel trapped,' Dodi whispered. Before he could ask her to explain her strange comment, she spoke again. 'We did everything together. She was my anchor.'

What was he supposed to say to that? He was self-sufficient and unemotional, deliberately so, and he had no words of comfort.

Dodi hiccupped a sob. 'God, Jago, what am I going to do?' she wailed as tears rolled down her face and storms rumbled in her eyes.

He felt out of his depth, uncomfortable, but what did that matter when he'd do anything to alleviate the emotional storm sweeping through her? 'What can I do, Dodi? Tell me, sweetheart, how can I help you?'

Dodi lifted her incredible eyes, and they collided with his, sparked and held. Half turning to face him, she rested her forehead against his. 'Help me forget, Jago, if only for a little while. Please, just give me that.'

He was shocked when her lips brushed his, transferring lightning from her mouth to his. He tried to pull away, but she just followed, her hands stroking his chest, her tongue in his mouth. Suddenly it was too much, she was irresistible, and his arm banded around her and he tumbled into a world he didn't know existed.

She tasted of mint and madness, grief and sadness. He knew this was the wrong time and place, that she was feeling overwhelmed and out of control, but he needed to learn her taste, have her scent lodged in his nose, feel her slim body pressed up against his. Her bottom was fuller than he'd expected, her hips curvier, and her breast filled his hand perfectly.

Jago pulled her dress up her slim thigh, sighing when she shivered, feeling more like a man than he ever had before. And yes, her skin did feel like warm silk, her hair smelled like sunshine and underneath his hand her heart, like his, triple-thumped.

He, suddenly and powerfully, longed to see her naked. He needed to know her, to count every freckle, to stroke every curve. He craved the feel of her long legs around his waist. It was vital to experience her feminine heat, to lodge himself inside her.

Forgetting where they were, who he was, Jago pulled her down to the bed, his hand encircling her thigh, his mouth fused to hers. Time stopped and the world stopped turning and there was only Dodi…

But Thadie, calling Dodi's name, shattered the moment. Dodi reacted quicker than he did, bolting off the bed and running for the bedroom door. He was still trying to process why his arms were empty when Dodi stepped out of the bedroom to meet Thadie in the hallway, pulling the bedroom door shut behind her and keeping his presence a secret.

Jago sat on the end of the bed for a long, long time, his head in his hands, mentally whipping himself for his lack of self-control. Then he left the bedroom and walked out of her house and out of her life.

Dodi had made him lose control. That was unacceptable and so she must be avoided.

CHAPTER ONE

DODI DAVIS STOOD just inside the front door of Love & Enchantment, the bridal shop she had inherited from her grandmother, Lily, and tried to ignore the familiar burn somewhere around her heart.

Wasn't it the law somewhere that the owner of a shop providing wedding dresses and accessories to excited brides be…well, excited?

Or, at the very least, believe in marriage and love and happy-ever-afters?

Dodi didn't.

'Dan didn't work out, but when you find the right man you'll feel differently, darling,' Lily had said, sounding completely convinced days before she died five years ago. Dodi hadn't wanted to argue with the woman who'd been her port in every storm, the one adult in her life who'd given her love and attention, who'd made her feel safe. A few weeks after her devastating diagnosis, they'd discussed her dying—her doctors had suggested she had just three months, if that—and what came next. It had been a horrible, awful, wretched conversation. Tears streaming, she couldn't tell Lily that she'd seen the worst of love, that she didn't believe in it and certainly didn't want to spend her life promoting the scam.

Lily, ravaged by cancer, hadn't needed the reminder that her son and daughter-in-law's lives had been a roller coaster of never-ending drama.

Dodi's parents had separated when she was three, divorced when she was four. Remarried when she was twelve and divorced when she was fourteen. In between their marriages and affairs, her dad had married once and her mother twice. Dodi vaguely remembered her one stepmother and two stepfathers but had lost count of the number of partners and lovers she'd met along the way.

Her parents liked variety and lots of it. To her parents love was possession and passion, and she was collateral damage—a human pass-the-parcel—lost and forgotten in their quest to chase down their next sexual or emotional high.

About a month before Lily's death, Dodi had got a call that rocked her world, shattered her soul. The caller told her that she'd been having an affair with Dan—her first real friend, her first lover and the man she'd thought she'd be with for ever—and that she wasn't the first lover he'd had...*that year.*

Dodi had immediately launched into a 'stand by your man' and 'he wouldn't do that' series of protestations, but the caller had proof, photos and text messages, and credit card receipts for hotels and dinners for two at places she'd never visited.

Dan's lover, sick of playing second fiddle, had also gleefully informed her that he'd played a series of mind games with her since the day they met and that his proclamations of love and forever were a lie. She'd had to face the hard truth that her best friend, the person she trusted and loved, second only to Lily, had cheated on her, more than once and with more than one woman.

Emotionally numb, she'd delayed confronting Dan until after Lily's death, partly because she couldn't deal with another emotional fallout as she watched Lily die, and partly because she hadn't wanted to upset Lily, who'd adored Dan.

Lily had had a near-perfect marriage, cut short by her grandpa's heart attack, and she'd loved love, loved her store and loved her only grandchild. So, to Lily, it made sense for Dodi to inherit Love & Enchantment, her renowned bridal boutique situated in Melville, an arty and bohemian suburb of Johannesburg, South Africa's economic powerhouse.

She loved this city, built on gold and one of the biggest on the continent. She loved its vibrancy and its crazy drivers, its fast-paced hustle and its blend of communities and nationalities. She loved the vitality of Soweto, the messiness of Alex, the gentility of Rosebank. She adored its cold winter days and, when the wild storms pounded it during its hot summers, its unapologetic in-your-face energy.

Love & Enchantment contained the largest selection of sample wedding dresses and bridesmaid gowns in the country and showed off the skills, artistry and creativity of the most elite wedding dress designers in the world.

Dodi appreciated the product but wasn't a fan of what the dresses, and all the other accessories—bridesmaid and flower girl dresses, veils, shoes and bling—represented. Standing in the empty salon, Dodi felt like a fraud, trapped and frustrated.

Just once, she wanted to *choose* the situation she found herself in…

She'd been bounced between her parents' homes, and when she was sixteen she'd been, without discussion or warning, dumped with her grandmother, someone she'd never met. Dan's cheating and gaslighting had devastated her and Love & Enchantment had been forced on her…

Okay, enough, stop! You sound like an ungrateful brat!

Her childhood was *over*, Dodi told herself, and Dan was a mistake she'd never repeat as she was done with relationships. Moving in with Lily was the *best* thing that had ever happened to her and how *dared* she complain about inheriting Lily's considerable assets and fantastic business? If she hated the shop so much, then why hadn't she sold it, moved away, done something different?

She'd studied design at university, then pursued an additional business degree, thinking she'd like to travel before joining an upmarket retailer as a trend-spotter or a buyer for retail fashion. She'd travel the world, wear designer threads, liaise with the top designers in the world…

She was months off graduating when Lily had died, and she'd inherited Love & Enchantment. Her two degrees enabled her to run the business without making too many mistakes that might have been hard to come back from, and provided her with a healthy income. Her house was paid for, as was this building.

But she still felt resentful of having her choices ripped away from her.

Get over yourself!

L&E was her link to the one person who had loved her unconditionally, who'd been her port after a lifetime of storms, her true north… Her loyalty to Lily was absolute. In life and death.

Dodi raised a bottle of water to her lips, sipped and eyed the big clock on the far wall. She had a half-hour before her after-hours, top-secret appointment. All her staff, except for her most experienced fitter, had left the premises and she was going to deal with the next bride, and her entourage, all on her own.

Dodi smiled, thinking of the uptick in appointments at L&E since Thadie Le Roux, body-positive influencer, socialite and heiress, had announced on Instagram that she was acquiring both her wedding gowns—one for the church, one for the reception—through Love & Enchantment.

Everyone wanted to follow in Thadie's footsteps and Dodi didn't blame them—her best friend was not only beautiful but also funny, down-to-earth and genuinely lovely.

And she was getting married at the end of May, tying herself to a famous and revered rugby-player-turned-sports-commentator. Clyde, having taken his young, inexperienced team to a World Cup Rugby win, was a national treasure and universally adored. Dodi rested her water bottle against her forehead, wishing she could warm to Thadie's fiancé.

Clyde had never been anything but charming to her, his future wife's closest friend. He was always thoughtful, considerate, respectful, but something about him bugged her.

Dodi bit her bottom lip and rocked on her heels. Did she automatically distrust every man she met because of her parents' dysfunctional relationships and because of what Dan had done to her? Was she projecting her fears about relationships and marriage onto Thadie?

She didn't know. Maybe. Possibly.

Dodi looked through the floor-to-ceiling windows and noticed the tall figure of Jago Le Roux crossing the road, looking ever so fine in his custom-made Italian suit, as well as crisp and cool despite its being a warm summer evening in Johannesburg. She immediately thought of her favourite broody heroes—Heathcliff from *Wuthering Heights* and Oliver Mellors, Lady Chatterley's gamekeeper. Like them, Jago was a corralled tornado of darkness and intensity.

Every time she saw Jago she was immediately whisked back to Lily's wake, remembering their passion-filled kiss, the strength of his arms as he had held her to his very fit body. For days, and weeks, before and after Lily's death, she'd felt as though she was encased in a cold, wet bubble, the real world distorted and distant. Jago's kiss had pierced her balloon of grief and loneliness and for five minutes—ten?—she'd felt alive, feminine, strong. Free of grief.

If Thadie hadn't interrupted them, God knew how far they would've gone. Pretty far, she reluctantly admitted.

God, he was good-looking. Tall, broad, fit, debonair, suave, her best friend's older brother turned heads, produced swoon-worthy sighs, and caused cars to crash into lamp posts. Dodi desperately wished she was immune to his sex appeal.

But, from the first time she'd seen him, and every time since, tingles raced along her skin, and fireworks exploded deep inside whenever she laid eyes on him. Yeah, she was attracted to Jago Le Roux—any woman with a pulse would be. But, she reminded herself, it was inherited lust, something left over from Neanderthal Dodi, whose survival had rested on mating with the most alpha of alpha men.

It was biology. It didn't mean anything. One of the lessons she had learned from living with her lust-soaked parents and cheating ex was that desire was ephemeral, as tangible as the early-morning mist hovering at the beginning of a hot summer's day. It could alleviate boredom, scratch an itch, be entertainment or, like their hot encounter after Lily's funeral, be a means of distraction and comfort. It didn't mean anything and never lasted.

Dodi flipped open the lock on her door and pulled it open to allow Jago to step through. She caught the delicious scent of his cologne and noticed his broad hand as he pushed his long fingers into his light brown hair, short at the sides, wavy on top, sun-kissed. The late-afternoon sun turned his three-day stubble to a deep gold.

It was early evening, but the dipping African sun sent bright yellow rays, tinged with pink, through her extensive showroom, dropping a flushed hue onto the bridal gowns hanging off copper pipe railings encircling the room. With its exposed wooden beams and skylights, the room looked huge, with clusters of vintage designer furniture in front of many floor-to-ceiling mirrors. Flowers, roses, sweet-peas and peonies gently scented her luxurious boutique.

Jago, so masculine, should have looked out of place in the faded peaches, creams and pinks of the bridal salon but, annoyingly, didn't. If anything, the super-feminine room just highlighted his masculinity.

'Dodi.'

'Jago.'

Their eyes collided and held, his gaze mesmerising. His eye colour ranged from pewter to steel to iron, occasionally shot with lightning, frequently rumbling with thunder. Hypnotic and spellbinding.

Despite being friends with his sister since they were in their late teens, she'd had little to do with the older of Thadie's brothers. Micah, his minutes-younger twin, was the more charming of the two. Jago was the string pulled too tight, about to snap. He was aloof, abrupt, introverted and broody, and those silver eyes, the irises surrounded by a black ring, were too scalpel-sharp for comfort.

He made her feel off centre, squidgy, jittery, and his effect on her irritated Dodi. She was almost thirty and should be able to admit that she was sexually attracted to the man and then move the hell on. But no, just looking at him made her feel like she was riding an out-of-control roller coaster.

Sanguine she was not.

'I'm glad I caught you alone,' Jago said, his deep baritone sending a shiver up and down her spine. He had the ultimate bedroom voice, rich and dark, like the Belgian chocolate she so adored. Great, now she was thinking about him in a bedroom, about pushing that jacket off his shoulders, pulling his shirt from the band of his trousers, laying her hands on his hot skin.

Argh! Seriously, what is wrong with you, woman?

Dodi folded her arms against her chest, conscious of her messy hair—it always was by the end of the day—and that the minimal make-up she wore had probably disappeared hours ago. She pushed the front door closed, locking it, and turned to walk into her salon, her right ankle slightly twisting and causing her to stumble. Jago reached for her and stopped her from falling flat on her face. Dodi found herself up close and personal with him, and God, he smelled so good. Of rich soap and laundry detergent, of a citrusy cologne and male skin. She wanted to bury her nose in his neck and commit his scent to memory. And Lord, every inch she touched was hard muscle and the hand that held her hip, steadying her, was big and broad and seared her skin.

Dodi looked up, and up, saw that his eyes were on her mouth and sparks skittered up and down her spine. She wondered whether he still tasted as deep and dark as she remembered, his kisses as rich as velvet, as smooth as heavy silk. For a moment, just a couple of seconds, she saw temptation in his eyes, desire deepening the silver to slate-grey, and in a flash his expression turned impassive, his eyes shuttered.

Right, the moment had passed but Dodi suspected her fair skin remained fire-red, almost the same colour as her hair. She remembered his earlier comment about being alone. 'Um…right…why did you need to see me alone?'

Jago took a moment to answer her. Was he also feeling caught off guard? No, not possible. Jago Le Roux, Johannesburg's toughest deal-maker, was always in control.

He hadn't been in control in Lily's bedroom… Stop it, Dodi!

'I wanted to catch you before the others arrived because I need to pay for Thadie's wedding dresses,' Jago told her, reaching into the inner pocket of his jacket to pull out a slim wallet.

Right. Of course!

Dodi nodded, remembering Thadie's offhand comment that her mega-successful brothers would be paying for her dresses, the bridesmaids dresses and all the wedding expenses. Her brothers had accompanied Thadie months ago to help her choose her dress, both feeling out of their depth and trying to hide it. It was a testament to the siblings' close relationship that they were back for this final fitting.

They were there as a stand-in for their dad, who had passed away five years ago. That had been a terrible year for both her and the Le Rouxs with Anju, Jago's wife, dying in January, Theo, the Le Roux patriarch, in March, and Lily six months later. They'd all attended far too many funerals that year.

But even before Anju died, and possibly due to the nine-year age difference between them, Dodi hadn't had much to do with Jago and had seen little of him. Thadie had had nothing in common with Jago's highly intellectual, aloof wife and tended to avoid her. Because Thadie and Anju weren't close, Dodi had only seen Anju a few times a year when she was invited to a function at Hadleigh House and, beyond saying hello, they didn't engage.

'Can I pay by credit card?' Jago asked her, pulling her attention back to their conversation.

'Absolutely,' Dodi replied, relieved. She'd paid the designer for Thadie's dresses earlier this week and had winced at her low bank balance after the transaction. She'd emailed both Micah and Jago, gently requesting payment, and here Jago was, thank God. Wedding dresses for high-society influencers were not cheap and she'd prayed one of the brothers would offer up his credit card this evening.

Someone upstairs had been listening.

'My office manager isn't here but I have a card machine in my office,' Dodi said. She thought about asking him to follow her and quickly discarded that idea. Her office looked like a bomb had hit it. Books of sample fabrics were stacked high, client folders needing to be filed were stacked even higher and her desk was covered with papers and coffee cups. It looked nothing like her exquisitely decorated showroom. 'Let me get it and the invoice.'

Luckily Thadie's file was on the top of the stack, and she'd printed the invoice out earlier. She grabbed the credit card machine, returned to the main salon and sat down at one of the many sofas in the room, all grouped around daises and oversized mirrors. She gestured for Jago to take the seat beside her and waited as he shed his jacket and slowly rolled up the sleeves of his cotton shirt, revealing tanned, muscular forearms lightly dusted with bronze hair. He had great hands, broad and strong. His fingers were long, with neatly clipped, clean nails. She had a thing about hands…

Dodi sighed. *Face it, Davis, you have a thing about Jago.*

Jago sat, pulled the knot of his tie down and flicked open the button holding his collar closed. Tearing her gaze away from his tanned throat, Dodi flipped open the file and picked up the invoice. She mentally grimaced at the total and handed it over.

There had been no discussion about what the wedding gowns would cost—Thadie had ordered two, one for the church and one for the reception—and, despite their wealth, she had no doubt the total would be a shock.

Jago looked down at the invoice in his hand and his eyes widened. 'I think you've made a mistake, Dodi.'

She shook her head, keeping her face impassive. 'I really haven't. And that's the discounted price as I gave you my friends and family rate.' Because Thadie was her best friend and she'd garnered an enormous amount of publicity having her as her client, she'd only added a small mark-up onto the cost, just enough to cover the expenses of shipping the dresses from Milan to Johannesburg.

'Forty-two thousand *US* dollars? Twenty for one and twenty-two for another?'

Was his deep voice suddenly an octave higher or was she just imagining it? Dodi nodded. 'They are Paulo Du Pont creations, Jago. He's one of the best wedding dress designers in the world. If not *the* best.'

'Holy crap. I could buy a very decent car with that sort of money,' Jago said, sounding a little strangled.

Dodi leaned back and crossed her legs, not worried. Jago, along with Micah, having inherited the extensive multinational company his father built from a small corner grocery store he established when he was twenty, was an exceptionally wealthy man. The Le Roux twins owned mines and manufacturing plants, shopping malls and farms, hotels and chain stores, both in Africa and overseas.

Dodi found running one business strenuous enough. She had no idea how the brothers kept track of multiple businesses, thousands of employees, managers and billions in assets. But their long hours working were paying off because Le Roux International was still expanding and was, thanks to Jago's and Micah's hard work as co-CEOs, stunningly successful.

As shareholders, Jago, Micah, Thadie and Liyana—Theo's second wife and Thadie's mum—topped the richest people in the country list. Dodi was pretty well off—she'd inherited all of Elodie's wealth, a house in a gated community in the wealthy area of Blair Atholl, northeast of the city centre, and this building—but the Le Rouxs operated in another stratosphere.

Dodi knew Jago's credit card could handle a forty-two-thousand-dollar charge. Hell, she was pretty sure it could handle any amount thrown at it. With certain cards, unlimited meant exactly that and she was pretty sure Jago owned one or two, or ten, of those types of credit cards. And a mega-healthy bank balance to support his purchases.

Dodi heard Jago's sigh and watched as he pulled a card from his wallet and handed it over. It was sleek, black and heavier than any other bank card she'd ever handled. She recognised the familiar logo but not its weight. 'Why is it heavy?' she asked as she swiped the card through the machine.

Jago shrugged. 'It's made from titanium.'

Even her machine was impressed by the card because it pushed through Jago's transaction at double its normal speed. Dodi pulled off the receipt and handed the card and paper back to Jago, her fingers brushing his. Sparks danced along her skin as desire flared in his eyes and she fought the urge to kiss his sexy mouth.

Nobody, before, or since, had kissed her the way he had. With casual confidence, incredible skill and soul-deep passion.

Jago's eyes dropped to her lips and all the moisture disappeared from her mouth. 'Do you ever think about the kiss we shared back then?' he asked, his thumb caressing her index finger, which was still holding his card. How could such a small amount of skin on skin cause such havoc?

Of course she thought about it! Every day. Sometimes more than once. But she couldn't tell him that. 'Do you?' she countered on a whisper, still unable to pull her hand away.

'Yes.'

How often? When? What do you remember? It took all her willpower to keep her questions behind her teeth. And even more not to dive in for a repeat performance. It had been so long since she'd been kissed by anyone, let alone someone with superior skill.

Jago tugged his card from her grip and Dodi blinked, then blushed. She sat back and pushed her hand through her hair, telling herself to stop acting like a complete dolt! It was a quick kiss, nothing special…

If she'd been kissed more, had more people kiss her, she wouldn't think about him so often. It was simply a question of numbers…

Right.

Dodi needed to put some distance between them, some time to gather her thoughts. Dodi folded the invoice in two, handed it to Jago and tapped the credit card machine with her finger. 'I'm just going to put the machine and Thadie's folder away, so that she doesn't see either when she arrives.'

Jago nodded. 'Good idea. If she sees what the dresses cost, she'll insist on paying for them herself, and that's not going to happen. Her wedding is our gift to her and Clyde.'

Dodi saw doubt flicker in Jago's eyes at the mention of his soon-to-be brother-in-law and tipped her head to the side. Did Jago not like Clyde or was her imagination running wild? She dismissed her suspicions, thinking she was doing Clyde a disservice. As she well knew, breaking into the Le Roux inner circle was incredibly hard and Thadie's brothers were intimidating. They were both tough, take-no-prisoners direct. They were successful, supremely wealthy, incredibly powerful men and Thadie wasn't a shrinking violet either.

She'd known the family for a decade and when she attended the odd function at Hadleigh House, the Le Roux family home, she still felt like an outsider looking in. Clyde needed time to fit in.

'Paying for her wedding is an incredibly generous gift,' Dodi commented.

Jago shrugged. 'It's what my father would've done. He wouldn't have spared any expense, and neither will we.'

Dodi kept her eyes on his tanned face, taking in the finer details of his masculine features. He was in his late thirties—thirty-eight to be precise—and long hours working had put tiny lines next to his eyes, grooves next to his mouth. He was a stunningly good-looking man, but even hot guys couldn't stop life from leaving its marks on their faces.

And why did she feel the urge to smooth his frown, to kiss his tension away? To wrap her arms around his very broad back and hug away his stress? And then take him to bed to make him forget?

Wow! Where had all that come from?

They'd been talking about Thadie's wedding and her out-of-control imagination—or her libido—had steered her in a completely different direction.

Enough of that, Davis!

They'd had a moment years ago, for God's sake! Jago Le Roux was her best friend's brother and completely out of bounds. And way, *way* out of her league.

Walk away, dump your stuff and find your brain, Dodi.

CHAPTER TWO

DODI WALKED AWAY and Jago tipped his wrist to look at his watch and wished he were back in his penthouse office suite, working. He felt out of place in this peach and pink feminine room, and a huge sneeze, brought on by the subtle scent of what had to be dozens of cut flowers, threatened. Pushing it back, he rested his forearms on his knees, and swiped his thumb across the screen of his smartphone. Within the emails he saw one with the subject name 'Lagos' and his thumb hovered over it, poised to open it. He knew the email pertained to a shopping mall they were building in the city and scrolled down. The real estate, retail and hospitality arms of the business were Micah's baby and he had enough on his plate dealing with the mining, manufacturing and agricultural businesses in their portfolio. Jago watched as new messages and emails landed, feeling incredibly weary. Needing a break, he pushed the side button and his screen turned black. He placed his phone on the cushion next to him and rubbed the back of his neck. Work never stopped and he took calls and received emails and texts twenty-four-seven.

He and Micah could both do with a clone, or three. And that was why he didn't have the time or energy to waste looking at wedding dresses in ultra-pretty salons. He wouldn't be here for anyone else but Thadie. He—and Micah—would move mountains stone by stone for their baby sister.

Jago watched as Dodi crossed the room to a wedding-dress-lined hallway. This was only the second time he'd been in her shop—or any bridal salon. Anju, the least interested bride in history, had worn a cream trouser suit to their civil wedding and hadn't bothered with a bouquet. Afterwards, they had both gone back to work and met up with his family later for dinner at a local restaurant.

They'd spent nothing on their wedding, but Thadie's wedding was edging close to a million. If not a lot more. Dodi's wedding dresses cost the price of a small car. *Each.* The champagne was imported, as was the caviar. The caterers were the best in the country and the entertainment was a hot Los Angeles singer-songwriter he'd never heard of.

It was pure insanity. Jago rubbed his jaw and reminded himself that his dad would've paid anything to give Thadie what she wanted. And more. There was no doubt that Thadie had been his favourite child, the apple of his eye, the one who could do no wrong. And, in this instance, he agreed with his father. Thadie, along with her twin boys, was—and always would be—the best part of their lives.

Jago looked at Dodi's slim back, his eyes trailing over the loose curls of her long hair as she stopped in the hallway and straightened a picture frame. Over the years her bold red hair had deepened to a deep Titian red and yeah, with her willowy build, pale skin and flowing locks, she looked like a muse of those pre-

Raphaelite artists. She was missing the melancholic expression though, as her feelings raced across her face and jumped into her smoky blue eyes.

And yes, she had freckles—how could she not with her complexion? Lots and lots of them, darker on her straight, haughty nose, paler across her cheeks and forehead.

After losing his self-control after Lily's funeral, Jago had deliberately avoided Dodi. When he had to be in her company, he ignored her as much as possible, acting as if their kiss hadn't redefined the word for him. Before that sad day, the connection of lips had been another GPS point on the route to the destination—a great orgasm. It was enjoyable, sure, but not, to his mind, necessary. Everything had changed when he kissed Dodi. He'd never admit this, not even under extreme torture, but as his mouth had met hers he felt the DNA that formed the stars and the starfish, the mammoths and man, luminesce deep inside him. When he had kissed her, touched her fabulous skin, he felt for the first time in months and years alive and connected.

And utterly out of control.

He still thanked God Thadie had chosen that moment to call Dodi, to break their passionate connection. She'd saved him when he hadn't been able to save himself…

But, damn it, his attraction to her hadn't faded, not even a little. When he'd caught Dodi after her stumble earlier, his body immediately sat up and started taking notes. Sexy mouth, great breasts, long legs he wanted to feel wrapped around his hips. She smelled of soap and lemongrass, of blue skies and fresh air, and the combination of her slim body, her scent and those witchy eyes stopped him in his tracks. And sent his blood rushing south.

Jago rubbed his hand over his face. What was it about her that turned him inside out? Could it be because he hadn't had sex for a while? Damn, he hoped so! Maybe he should schedule a visit to one of a handful of old friends who knew the score, a woman happy enough to share his bed and who wouldn't sulk when he left it a few hours later. Sex had always been—yeah, even with Anju—a physical release, a way to blow off steam. As necessary as exercise and sleep.

The fact that he'd reacted to Dodi—his sister's best friend!—was a solid clue that he needed to get some. And soon.

Jago looked around the expensive salon and curled his lip at the wedding dresses on rails encircling the three walls of the room. There were hundreds more in the back, simple and stylish, splendid and luxurious. Shapes and cuts and decorations to suit every taste, ranging from mildly expensive to eye-wateringly and budget-blowingly insane. He could not understand why women put so much stock in looking like a hyped-up, photoshopped version of themselves, why they put so much time and effort and money into one night, the adult equivalent of their first school dance.

Why they even wanted to get married in the first place.

Having been there, done the whole thing, he knew of what he spoke. Would he marry again? No. Not because he'd been unhappy in his marriage—he hadn't been particularly happy either, truth be told—but because marriage was an outdated institution that had little relevance in today's world. He'd been twenty-seven when they married. They made their relationship legal because Anju, despite being a brilliant neuroscientist with a glittering future ahead of her, craved financial security, a legal document, and a solid prenup agreement.

Because she was what he'd wanted, an unemotional woman who didn't demand love, loved sex, good food and travelling, he agreed to her terms. Fiercely intelligent, she wasn't interested in having kids, and apart from having enough money for a roof over her head and food in the fridge, didn't care that he was the son of a multibillionaire. She also had an equally low tolerance for drama. They'd loved each other, he supposed, and he'd grieved for her when she died. But life went on and here he was, five years after her death, still single, and still allergic to drama.

He'd had so much of it as a kid, before and after his mum died when he was nine. They said that his father was larger than life, charismatic and compelling, brilliant, but, to Jago, he'd been intensely volatile, a bully and a bastard. For his entire early childhood Jago stood on the lip of a volcano, constantly scanning the horizon for trouble, for a hard wind or quick tap that would push him—or his mum and brother—into the lava that was Theo's temper. They never knew where they stood with him, and their home swung from laughter to tears in the space of a heartbeat. His father could slow dance his mum around the kitchen one second and throw a crystal glass against the wall the next.

Jago did everything he could to keep the peace and, before his tenth birthday, became adept at scanning his environment, looking for problems and trying to head off trouble. But, as hard as he tried, he couldn't anticipate that his mum would die in a head-on collision or that Theo would start dating six weeks after her funeral. His marriage to Liyana, four months after his mom's death, rocked him. And once Liyana moved into their home, it was as if his mum had never existed. Theo, his dad, refused to talk about her and redecorated their home top to bottom, expunging everything she'd done to make their house a home. Theo donated everything of hers—from jewellery to art to clothes to trinkets—to charity. He tossed out all the family photographs, effectively erasing her presence in their life as a surgeon would cut out a cancerous tumour.

Before Jago had hit puberty, he decided that love equalled drama and he wanted nothing to do with either concept.

Jago heard a brisk knock on the front door and looked around to see his twin, Micah, and Thadie standing under the rounded peach portico above Dodi's front door. Seeing no sign of Dodi, he stood up and walked across the salon, twisting the key and pulling open her door. Thadie stepped into the salon, followed by one of her bridesmaids—Alta, Clyde's stepsister, agent and publicist. Having only met her once before, he stuck out his hand and internally sighed when Alta kissed his right cheek and then his left. He caught Micah's eye and frowned at his twin's knowing smirk.

Micah knew better than to think he had the hots for the very spiky Alta: she was too in-your-face and too abrasive for him to make a move in her direction. He had no idea why his laid-back sister had included her in the wedding party. It had to be a request from Clyde. Nothing else made sense. And Alta, he was sure, had only agreed to be a bridesmaid to stay in the wedding loop and to make sure nothing tainted or tarnished Clyde's glittering reputation.

Thadie pulled him into a hard hug. She had her famous mother's cut-glass cheekbones, warm brown skin, face and height but Jago still saw her as a wide-eyed kid with knobbly knees. In his head, she definitively wasn't old enough to be a mum or to get married.

He adored her.

Thadie stepped back from him and looked around the salon, before releasing a long sigh. 'I love this place, and I still expect Granny Lily to walk in from the back with a huge smile on her face.'

His sister had the biggest heart in the world. 'You really liked her, didn't you?'

Thadie sent him a soft smile. 'I did. She was truly lovely. Dodi is a lot like her.' Thadie looked past him, and her smile rushed into her eyes. 'Hey, you!'

Jago knew, without turning, that she was talking to Dodi, as they were always excited to see each other.

Jago moved and saw Dodi standing there and his heart rate, stupid thing, accelerated. She'd tidied her hair and reapplied her lipstick and her right arm was fully extended over her head. Two clothing bags brushed the floor. Jago quickly moved towards her and took the bags from her, his height making it easy to hold them off the floor.

Dodi thanked him, greeted Micah and Alta and smiled at Thadie, who was hopping from foot to foot in excitement. 'Are those my dresses?' Thadie demanded.

Dodi mock frowned at her. 'Your dresses? What dresses? Did you order a dress from me?'

Thadie rolled her eyes at Dodi's teasing and reached for the zip of one of the bags. 'Lemme see.'

Dodi gently smacked her hand away. 'Be patient, Thads.' Dodi gestured to a whitewashed credenza standing against the far wall. On it stood a silver ice bucket containing a bottle of champagne and champagne flutes. 'Have a glass, then join me in the first dressing room on the right and let's see what they look like.'

'I hope they are perfect,' Alta commented. She tapped the face of her watch with a red-tipped fingernail. 'You're running out of time, and you'll be in a world of hurt if they don't fit.'

Jago watched, fascinated, as Dodi's eyes cooled, and her expression flattened. 'We're not in the habit of making mistakes, Alta.'

Alta lifted her too-thin eyebrows. 'I hope not because, as you know, this is the wedding of the year.'

Jago watched the storm brewing in Dodi's eyes and waited for her sharp comeback. But instead of issuing a harsh retort, she pulled up a smile and took Thadie's hand. 'Lily would haunt me if we messed up your dresses, Thads, you know that.'

Her gaze moved from Thadie to the front door and Jago saw the rest of the bridal party, his stepmother Liyana and Thadie's two other bridesmaids, approaching the salon.

'Micah, if you could open the front door for me, that would be wonderful and then give the ladies a glass of champagne, please. I'm going to help Thadie change into her gowns, and then we'll choose the mother of the bride and the bridesmaid dresses. Sound good?'

No, Jago silently replied. It sounded like hell, actually.

Dodi didn't wait for their agreement, she just led

Thadie out of the room, their hands linked. Dodi's melodious voice drifted back to him as he followed them to a changing room with the wedding dresses. 'We might have to make some very minor adjustments, Thads, just to make sure the gowns fit beautifully. But, because they are Paulo Du Pont gowns, I'm not expecting any problems.'

At twenty thousand US dollars a dress, Jago bloody well hoped not.

Dodi closed the door behind Thadie, Micah, Liyana and Thadie's other bridesmaids, flipping the lock and her sign to *CLOSED* to keep out any late evening shoppers or spur-of-the-moment drop-ins.

Kicking off her heels, Dodi moved over to the seating area and jerked when she noticed Jago standing by the window that looked out onto the small garden to the side of the property. She'd had her hands full with Thadie's mum—the very discerning ex-supermodel Liyana—and the ultra-picky Alta, who had something negative to say about every bridesmaid dress she suggested. Micah excused himself after seeing Thadie's dresses and she'd thought that Jago left too, so she was very surprised to see him in her now empty salon…

Surprised and excited. Seriously? Excited by Jago Le Roux? Was she losing it? Yes, he was stunningly sexy, but she'd sworn off men, and relationships. Because, really, she never knew what to expect from people in general and men in particular.

'You're still here,' Dodi commented as he picked up a champagne glass.

'I thought I'd help you clean up.'

Since Jago Le Roux had been raised with a full set of

silver cutlery in his mouth, his offer came as a surprise. The Le Roux family employed a butler and a houseful of servants. Had the man ever made a bed, washed dishes? She didn't think so.

'Where do you want them?' he asked.

Dodi looked at the delicate glasses he held and thought that with one small squeeze from those big hands they would shatter. 'Uh… I'll get a tray from the break room.'

He picked up the other glasses. 'No point, I'll just carry them through. Where to?'

Dodi gave him directions—down the hallway, last room on the right—and he was back within a minute, his face bemused. 'I feel like I've been sucked into an alternative world of silk and satin. How many wedding dresses do you have in stock?'

She wrinkled her nose. 'Including the stock that came in today, probably close to three hundred.'

His eyes widened. 'Seriously?'

'Some, depending on the designer, are hugely popular, some aren't. Some, not many, thank God, don't have any takers at all. We auction those online to raise money for women's shelters and organisations dealing in domestic violence.'

He sat down on the ottoman she had used earlier. 'Do you pick the dresses yourself or do the designers just send you a range of their designs?'

Dodi was bemused by his interest. She'd never imagined that Jago Le Roux would be interested in her shop and that he would engage her in a getting-to-know-you conversation. She didn't know what to make of it. 'A mixture of both. I sit down with my head of Sales, and we choose what we like and what we don't, taking into account what's hot and what's not. We then order sample dresses of the designs we like. We also allow the designers to send us a few dresses they think we should stock. The brides try on the sample dresses, and if they want that particular style we measure them and put in an order for the dress. Six to eight months later, the dresses arrive, and we pray the bride hasn't lost or put on too much weight.'

'Thadie's wasn't predesigned, was it?'

She smiled. 'No, Thadie's was specifically designed for her.'

He jammed his hands into the pockets of his trousers and rocked on his heels. 'Can you explain how a dress can cost so much damn money?'

She heard the puzzled note in his voice, the confusion. And yeah, she got it, it was an insane amount of money to spend on a dress, but she'd had brides who'd spent more. Not many, admittedly. 'Real pearls and Swarovski crystals, high-grade silk, handcrafted embroidery, French Chantilly lace and fabric. Shall I go on?'

'No, you are giving me a headache.'

She smiled at his low rumble, knowing that it wasn't the money he was complaining about, because Jago wouldn't deny his sister anything. He, like most men, simply didn't understand that beauty and craftsmanship also applied to clothing and not just to things with engines.

Thadie's dresses were works of art, completely stunning. They were some of Paulo's best work. And, because they were incredible and for a VVIP client, she'd lock the dresses in the walk-in safe in her office before she left for home. Her staff had all signed non-disclosure agreements, but anyone could take a sneak peek of the gown and snap a photo on their phone. She had over thirty consultants and knew that most had offers from tabloid reporters to spill the beans on their high-value clients.

Not on her watch.

Dodi perched on the arm of a wingback chair, swinging her bare foot. She really should slip on her heels, but this was Jago, the shop was closed, and she didn't think he cared. He took a long moment to answer, and she was fascinated by the emotion in his normally unreadable eyes. 'She's going to make the most beautiful bride,' he stated. Thadie was lovely, inside and out, but it was nice to hear Jago state the obvious.

'She really is,' Dodi agreed.

'And you handled Alta well,' he told her, surprising her. 'She was demanding and annoying, but you didn't lose your cool.'

Dodi shrugged, then smiled. 'I've had a lot of practice at not losing my cool. Trust me, she wasn't the most difficult client I've had this month. Or even this week.'

Jago winced. 'I would've lost patience five minutes in,' he admitted. She didn't doubt it. In the business world, Jago wasn't someone to be messed with. He had a reputation for being cold, unfeeling, decisive and determined. It was commonly accepted that, with Jago, you had two choices: either move out of his way or get run over.

'Good job, Elodie Kate.' Elodie Kate? Her grandmother was the only person who had ever called her by her full name—Dodi was a nickname everyone used—and she swallowed, emotion closing her throat. Man, she still missed Lily with every beat of her heart. She should be here, running this shop, bestowing her wide smile and good sense on neurotic brides, scared brides, spoiled brides. She could charm bridezillas into behaving better, shy brides into happy conversations and tame off-the-wall brides.

Unlike Dodi, she hadn't pulled on a mask and gritted her teeth as brides gushed and giggled, cried and cooed.

Really, what the hell had Lily been thinking, leaving her L&E?

And why did Jago's compliments make her feel warm and wonderful? They had a tenuous connection because of her friendship with his sister, and shared a brief kiss years ago, nothing more. They were, essentially, little more than strangers.

Maybe it was because he was so difficult to impress. He set, as she'd heard from Thadie, impossibly high standards for his employees.

And himself.

Jago looked at the expensive watch on his wrist and grimaced. 'I should go. I still have a lot to do tonight.'

She looked up to find his eyes on her face and she sucked in a sharp breath, unable to look away. Those eyes! Intense and piercing and so very, very captivating. He had the eyes of a warlock, she decided. And his face and body weren't too bad either.

Not bad? He was utterly gorgeous! Why did her skin feel too tight for her body? Why did she suddenly want his lips on hers, his hands on her back, her breasts, her bum? What was happening here?

His gaze travelled up and down her body, and flames licked her skin. Her feet were glued to the floor and the room felt smaller. And a hundred degrees hotter. Dodi heard Jago release a small expletive, and within a second, maybe two, he crossed the space to where she sat, slid his hands under her elbows and lifted her to her feet. His big hand slid around to her back, and he held her against him, but Dodi knew that with a small push he'd release her and step away.

Honestly? She rather liked where she was, thank you very much. His chest was broad, hard muscles covered by hot skin and fine Egyptian cotton. He smelled like summer, of thunderstorms and hard rain, lemons and deep forests.

She lifted her hand to touch his jaw, trailing her fingers through his surprisingly soft stubble, enjoying the feel of his hard, square jaw. Her thumb brushed over his bottom lip, and she heard his low growl again, the one that made her feel squidgy and soft, super-feminine.

This was crazy, this was wrong…this was Jago! But she couldn't, wouldn't, step away, not until she'd reacquainted herself with how he tasted, until she'd discovered whether there was still passion behind his inscrutable, abrupt facade.

Despite being tall, Dodi still had to lift onto her toes for her mouth to reach his. Please, please don't rebuff me, she silently begged. Give me this one kiss, this one moment out of time.

She tasted his sigh, sweet and a little desperate, and when his lips didn't move to meet hers she thought, for one awful moment, that she'd miscalculated, that he didn't want to kiss her.

But she caught the smallest twist of his lips, a flash of lightning in his eyes, and his mouth covered hers, a petrol bomb tossed into a dry wooden shack. Flames, hot and insistent, scampered across her body, and her nerve endings caught fire. Dodi slid her hand under the collar of his shirt to find warm male skin and curled his fingers around his strong neck. She sighed, and when Jago's tongue painted the seam of her mouth with need and fire she opened her lips and…

Boom! Electricity shot to her toes, up her legs, into her womb. She wanted to protest, rail at him for making her feel so out of control—no one had ever made her feel so alive!—and at the same time she wanted to climb inside him, be part of him. His arms tightened around her, and his big hand slid down, cupping her butt and pulling her closer so that her stomach pushed into his heavy, hard erection, as he easily held her against his hard, muscular frame.

This was heaven, she decided, and hell. Heaven because his kiss was more powerful than the one they'd shared before. Hell because she knew they had to stop before they went too far. She couldn't make love to her best friend's brother on her shop floor on a Wednesday evening in late summer.

She couldn't make love to her best friend's brother at all!

This was an aberration, a crazy, tiny rip in reality. And this didn't mean anything, it couldn't. She wouldn't let it.

But surely she could keep kissing him, just for a little while longer?

His stubble tickled as he dragged his lips to her cheekbone, teased her jawbone. Keeping one hand on her butt cheek, he moved the other between them and found her breast. The material of her dress and bra was an unwelcome barrier as he massaged her nipple and teased it into a hard peak. She felt her panties dampen and when his hand rucked her dress up her thigh and his fingers encircled the top of her leg she knew they had to stop because if he kissed her one more time, if he touched her there, she would be lost…

And she didn't know if she'd be able to find her way home.

Dodi, reluctantly, it had to be said, pushed her hands against his chest. 'Jago, stop.'

It took a couple more kisses and his fingers skimming the front of her panties before her words registered. He pulled back and glowered at her, disappointment in his eyes and rushing across his face. 'We're stopping?'

'Yes.'

He dropped a harsh curse into the heavy silence that followed her answer. *'Why?'*

Dodi stepped back and shook out her skirt. 'Because I'm not making love in front of floor-to-ceiling windows, because you're Thadie's brother, because, despite that connection, you're just one step up from being a stranger!'

'I've known you since you were eighteen years old! We've even kissed before!'

'That kiss didn't count!' Dodi retorted. 'I was sad and hurting and you were trying to comfort me, to make me feel better. And in the ten years we've known each other,' Dodi added in a rush of words, 'we've never had a conversation that went beyond *Hi, how are you?* I don't know what madness this is but it's stopping right now. I'm not interested in a relationship—'

'It was a kiss, not an invitation for you to move into my life!' Jago responded, his eyes reverting to their normal sub-zero silver.

She ground her back teeth together, quite sure enamel

was flying from her teeth. 'I don't do one-night stands, Le Roux, and I know that's all you do.'

'Have you been following my love life, Elodie Kate?'

Oh, he was now starting to annoy her. But, unlike when she was with her picky brides, she didn't have to keep her sharp tongue behind her teeth. 'In your dreams, Jago. I don't care who you sleep with, as long as it's not me.'

'Your kiss two minutes ago tells me that statement is a lie. This time, you're not sad or in need of a distraction. Are you?'

She winced and felt herself flush. She *so* wasn't going to answer that question! Their conversation was getting out of control, and she needed to shut it down. Pronto.

Dodi lifted her nose, spun on her heel and walked over to the front door, flipping the lock to open. She yanked the door wide and gestured for him to leave. 'Let's pretend this never happened, Jago,' she said, injecting a healthy amount of frost into her words.

He took his time walking towards her, reminding Dodi of a stalking cat, leashed power about to erupt. He reached her, looked down at her and then, surprisingly, his mouth twitched in amusement. He dropped his head to speak in her ear. 'This is far from over, sweetheart.'

CHAPTER THREE

JAGO THREW HIMSELF into his brand-new Range Rover Autobiography and scowled at the passing traffic. He pulled his hand down his face, rubbing the palm of his hand along his jaw. What the hell was that?

Stupid question, Le Roux.

That was lust. Flat out, intense desire. Drop-her-to-the-floor-and-take-her-now attraction.

For the past five years, he'd made a conscious effort not to think about Dodi and their kiss, to ignore her as much as possible. But their collision just now—what else could he call it?—blasted through his carefully constructed shields. Thoughts he'd pushed away came rushing back in with the force of a nuclear-powered rocket…

He adored her thick, dark red hair that made him think of Ireland and mystics and magic. Her voice held a hint of gravel, a rasp that deepened when she was turned on, and her eyes were a lovely, strange shade of smoky blue. Or were they wispy grey? Her young, too-thin frame had slid into curves, and her legs went on for ever, legs he wanted to explore with his hands, then his mouth and his tongue.

Jago leaned back in his seat and gripped the steering wheel, his knuckles white against the black leather. Annoyingly, he could still taste Dodi on his tongue, almost feel those full, soft lips against his, her nipple spiking the palm of his hand. Today's kiss had nothing to do with grief, wasn't a way to ease her sadness. No, what happened earlier was pure, clean desire…

And deeply dangerous.

She was his sister's friend, someone who'd hovered on the outskirts for years, but here she was, front and centre, in his life. Jago tightened his grip on the steering wheel, holding on so that he didn't fling himself out of his car, run across the road and finish what they had started. Oh, he'd never force her—he wasn't, and would never be, that guy—but he knew that a few hot kisses would melt their clothes away.

He wanted that more than he wanted to take his next breath.

He didn't like feeling so out of control, being at the mercy of his emotions and desires. He operated best when he had mental and emotional guardrails in place, and to keep them erect and functioning meant keeping control.

Kissing Dodi—Dodi herself—blew a series of holes through those barriers. And that was utterly unacceptable. Control was everything.

He'd seen how destructive it was living with a mercurial and volatile personality, so when he'd met Anju he'd known she was exactly what he wanted, what he needed. Someone cool, detached, someone who abhorred drama. From their first date, he'd known their life together would be calm, smooth sailing, unaffected by high emotion. He'd liked her very masculine way of looking at life, that she was always rational.

They hadn't needed to have intense, soulful conversations—Anju was very like his father in that regard. Theo hadn't been one to interrogate feelings, to acknowledge hurts, to admit anything in his perfect, perfect world was wrong. His father had the incredible ability to compartmentalise his life, and if a person or a set of circumstances didn't fit into his worldview he was quickly able to move it into his not-important-enough-to-waste-energy-on box. Anju had been the same, adept at moving on. But, because their relationship was based on mutual respect, equal intelligence, shared priorities, he didn't feel the need to be constantly on the lookout, waiting and watching with anxiety, and they made their marriage work. Theirs had been a meeting of minds…

Unlike his encounter with Dodi. He felt unhinged, out of control, as if he'd been plugged into an electrical socket. Jago pushed his thumbs and index fingers into his eye sockets, hoping to push away his sudden headache.

Dodi was unexpected, their kiss unanticipated, his world a little shaken.

Jago had no problem admitting he felt uncomfortable with change, with the unforeseen, was easily rattled when situations didn't play out as expected. He'd spent his childhood and teenage years trying to anticipate trouble, trying to prepare for a change in his mercurial father's mood. Overanalysing everything in an attempt to avoid emotional meltdowns from his father. That was why Anju had been perfect for him. She was constantly calm, effortlessly undramatic. She'd been a respite from a stormy life spent with his father.

The hoot of a car horn, then the shouts of a taxi driver half falling out of his window in an attempt to attract some customers, jerked Jago back to the present. How had he gone from thinking about his volcano-hot encounter with Dodi to thinking of his past, his father and his wife? He must be more stressed than he thought. Tired too.

But if being around Dodi triggered these reminiscences then maybe it was better if he avoided her from now on. They'd had little to do with each other since they met. Surely they could carry on that fine tradition?

Except that he and Micah were part of the wedding party, Dodi was Thadie's maid of honour and they'd have to be in each other's company more than usual in the build-up to the wedding. Thadie's engagement party, delayed because of Clyde's work commitments, was this coming Saturday, then there were the hen and stag parties, both of which he'd have to attend.

He'd rather shove a lump of burning coal in his eye.

But his non-appearance would hurt Thadie, and he refused to do that. He'd do anything and everything for his siblings.

And if that meant feeling like he was dancing on the edge of a razor-sharp blade or connected to a thousand volts of electricity whenever he came within a few feet of Elodie Kate, then he'd just have to deal with it.

He was a big boy. He could handle it. And her.

'I thought redheads weren't supposed to wear red. Or pink.'

Dodi turned at the deep, rich voice in her ear, cursing the goosebumps pebbling her skin. A few words, two short sentences and she wanted to melt into a puddle at his feet. Utterly ridiculous. Could she be any more asinine if she tried? She was almost thirty and a hot guy in a designer suit shouldn't have this mind-melting effect on her.

Dodi touched the pleated skirt of her halter-neck,

sleeveless cocktail dress, a bright, bold red ending with an eight-inch block of bright pink. It was, she admitted, a bold choice but Liyana, Thadie's mum, reassured her that the dress looked fabulous, and the colour suited her complexion. Since Liyana was fashion-obsessed and had exquisite taste, Dodi trusted her assessment.

'I seldom do what people expect,' Dodi told him, thinking how amazing he looked in his custom-made, perfectly fitting dark grey suit, striped shirt and a tie the colour of a rich, fat aubergine. A paisley handkerchief peeked out of the pocket above his heart. He had what Lily called a clotheshorse body: wide shoulders, slim hips, long legs. Honestly, Jago could make a priest's robes look sexy.

Her inner fashionista nodded in approval. 'Bold colour combination, Le Roux. I didn't think you had it in you.'

He touched the knot of his perfectly formed tie. 'Credit to my stylist. She puts these combinations together. I just take the complete outfit off the hanger and pull the clothes on.' He straightened his waistcoat before shrugging his shoulders. 'I don't care much about clothes.'

Sacrilege! 'I do. I love fabric and fashion, clothes, interior design. Anything that's design-led.'

Jago snagged two glasses of champagne from a passing waiter's tray and passed one to Dodi, who shivered when his fingers brushed hers. How old was she? Twenty nine or nineteen?

Sipping, Dodi looked across the entertainment deck of Jago's childhood home and into a garden filled with shadows, smiling at the fairy lights wound around the trunks and branches of the old oak trees. She wasn't a regular visitor to this house and the last time she'd been here was to attend Theo's post-funeral wake.

Hadleigh House was one of the great historic homes of Johannesburg, built in 1904 by one of the city's first mining magnates. She'd always loved this house, constructed in Arts and Crafts style with touches of the Art Nouveau movement. It was an enormous double-storey house with a shingled roof, and some windows still sported leaded light glass within their frames.

She remembered hearing that the first owners of the house were, like Jago's parents, incredible hosts and the Hadleigh House balls, tennis parties and Sunday luncheons were the stuff of legend. Most of the original grounds surrounding the house had been sold off but the extensive garden was still wonderful, with old oak trees standing sentinel over wide, thoughtfully planted wide beds. The entertainment area ran the long length of the house and flowed onto an enormous pool, and at the end of the garden stood a tennis court and pavilion. Tonight their guests, immaculately dressed, stood around the pool or sat on comfortable sofas and chairs, enjoying the warm, scented air, excellent canapes and the steady supply of expensive alcohol. Occasionally they wandered down paths leading to secret gardens and courtyards, complete with deep ponds housing fat, and happy, koi fish.

Dodi saw Thadie standing next to the dessert buffet laid out by the pool, Clyde's proprietary arm around her waist. They were talking to Liyana, a grey-haired man and a woman who had the look of a long-distance runner. Wait, wasn't that…?

'I didn't know Thadie was friends with the British ambassador and the country's favourite Olympian,' Dodi commented, tipping her glass in their direction.

'She isn't. But Liyana, with input from Clyde, drew up the guest list,' Jago replied. 'The opportunity to network must never be missed.'

He definitively sounded cynical. 'And you? Don't you need to network?' Dodi asked him.

'No,' Jago stated. 'People either want to do business with me or don't. I'm not the type to schmooze.'

'You really need to work on your confidence, Jago,' she sarcastically murmured.

He flashed that rare smile, the one that hit his eyes, and Dodi had to look away. That particular smile could be used as a weapon of mass destruction.

Right, moving on…

Dodi's eyes bounced off more guests and then she saw Micah talking to Alta, Clyde's stepsister dressed in a barely-there mini-dress. She grinned. 'Your brother doesn't seem to have the same problem.'

Jago's thick eyebrows pulled together. 'He'd better be careful because she is actively looking for husband number three.'

'What happened to numbers one and two?'

'Both marriages ended in divorce. Hopefully, the third time is the charm but she's wasting her time looking for a commitment from Micah.' Jago took her hand and led her to a quiet corner of the expansive entertainment area, pulling her behind two huge Ficus trees so that they were half hidden from curious eyes. He nodded to her dress. 'You do look amazing, Elodie Kate.'

He had once told her that her old-fashioned name suited her and, as he was the only person who called her by it since Lily, and both times in private, she didn't mind. Pleased by the compliment—such an ego boost coming from the super-sexy, normally reserved Jago—Dodi hoped the darkness hid her heightened colour. 'Thank you.'

They were silent for a few moments before Jago spoke again. 'You said you loved fashion, clothes…'

'I do,' she replied when his words trailed off.

'But not wedding dresses?'

Surprised by his prescience, she felt her champagne glass wobble in her hand. 'I don't know what you are talking about,' she stated, cursing the unsteady note she heard in her voice.

Although he stood in the shadows, she saw his small shrug. 'I think you do.'

Was he just shooting in the dark or was her antipathy towards Love & Enchantment not the closely held secret she thought it was? She'd never spoken to anyone about her feelings towards L&E, not even Thadie. Admitting that she hated weddings, and wedding dresses, made her feel disloyal to her grandmother, as if she was throwing Lily's hard work and sacrifices in her face.

Dodi sighed and stared out into the darkness. Nobody understood how difficult it was to be the object her parents fought over, not because they loved her but because they didn't. Neither had they wanted to be saddled with her. She'd learned some major life lessons before she hit double digits: that nothing was permanent, that relationships were only temporary and that getting attached was a good way to get hurt. She'd loathed her life, being bounced between her parents' houses, and frequently wished she lived anywhere else.

She got that wish when her father—Lily's only child—had left her at Lily's house without forewarning or an explanation. Up until that point, shortly before her sixteenth birthday, she hadn't known of Lily's existence. After a few weeks and being unable to contact either of her parents, Lily enrolled her in school, and she was given chores and rules and regulations.

She wanted to hate Lily and her new life, but she didn't, couldn't. Lily was lovely, kind but firm, and so very normal. Life with Lily was so much better, more stable than what she'd ever experienced before. But what she did hate was her lack of choice, the fact that her path had been chosen for her and that her future had been moulded by another's hand. Being bounced between her parents, coming to live with Lily, inheriting the business…none of those life-changing events was her choice.

After Dan's infidelity and Lily's death—the first a real betrayal, the second that felt like one—she vowed she'd never allow anyone to dictate the terms of her life again, to make decisions for her.

But Jago's sensing of her feelings towards her business was a red flag, an indication that he saw too deeply and too much. *So why did he think that?*

He shrugged at her question. 'When you get excited, your eyes turn a deeper shade of blue…some of the smoke clears.'

What was he talking about? 'My eyes change colour?'

'Mmm.'

'You're talking rubbish, Jago.'

Jago leaned his shoulder into the wall and crossed one ankle over the other. 'No, I don't think I'm off base at all. The other day your eyes were a flat grey. I think you appreciate the dresses for their workmanship and beauty but they don't touch your soul. Do you only feel like that about Thadie's dress or *all* wedding dresses?'

'I don't feel like that at all,' Dodi told him, irritated.

'Liar,' Jago softly responded. One corner of his mouth kicked up. 'And, since those dresses cost me a fortune, I'm bloody offended.'

He was nothing of the sort, he was just teasing her. And that was a surprise because she hadn't thought Jago Le Roux knew the meaning of the word. She knew him to be terse and abrupt, aloof and distant. She didn't know how to handle a teasing Jago and, because she also wanted to move the conversation along, she thought it prudent to change the subject.

An obvious choice was this house and its recently completed renovations.

'Why did you decide to renovate the house? It was pretty wonderful before.'

Jago narrowed his eyes, obviously debating whether to pursue his interrogation. Thankfully, he looked around and nodded. 'It had some structural issues. The roof needed replacing, some of the foundations were sinking. The house, originally, had eight bedrooms but some of the rooms were dark and gloomy so we created five suites, all with en-suite bathrooms. We also created two separate wings at the back of the house with two master bedrooms and two lounges, and separate entrances so that Micah and I can have some privacy when we want it.'

'And Liyana lives in the house behind this one.'

Jago nodded. 'When she's in the country, which isn't that often, to be honest. Our stepmama is a bit of a social butterfly.'

Since it wasn't unusual for Liyana to be photographed at an event in Monaco on Wednesday and in New York on Friday, that was the understatement of the year.

'We wanted Thadie to move in, but she said that living with Liyana, or us, would drive her mad. She compromised by buying her place just down the road.'

Yeah, there was a reason why this street in the ultra-wealthy suburb of Sandhurst was unofficially known as Le Roux Drive.

'What will you do if either you or Micah marry? Who gets the house?' Dodi asked, intrigued.

'Technically, as the older son, I inherited the house,'

Jago replied. 'But this is Micah's childhood home too so we designed the renovations in such a way that we both, should that ever happen, could easily have two still ridiculously big but separate homes. We'd share the hall and the entertainment deck and, obviously, the pool and the grounds. And Jabu.'

They both turned to look at Hadleigh House's butler, a distinguished gentleman who'd been with the family since the twins were toddlers. Jabu, hands behind his back, was watching the hired catering staff with an eagle eye as well as waiting for orders from any members of the Le Roux clan.

He was, she knew, adored by everyone in the family and was, as Thadie informed her, constantly bombarded with offers of employment. Jago followed her gaze. 'He had two job offers this week,' Jago told her. 'One from a Japanese businessman who spends half a year in Joburg, another from the Bahraini ambassador's wife. One of these days he's going to leave us for a more exciting position.'

'What makes you say that?' Dodi asked him, touched and a little amused at his glum tone.

'He's made it very clear that we don't entertain enough, that there's not enough to do, that Micah and I work too hard, and that this house needs a young family. Or families.'

Yep, definitely morose. 'And do you plan on doing something about his demands?'

'I'm smarter than that,' Jago told her, his expression turning sly. 'His biggest complaint is that there are no small children around, so whenever he gets broody I send him around to Thadie's place and she lets him look after the twins for a day. He comes back shattered and doesn't nag us for a week or two.'

Dodi's laugh tumbled over her lips. She'd seen the normally staid and distinguished Jabu running after Thadie's Energizer Bunny three-year-old twin boys but hadn't realised how they exhausted the older man. Or the motivations behind why the brilliant butler was playing nanny.

'He desperately wants more Le Roux grandchildren, but he's equally terrified he might be saddled with more boys. After all, the man barely survived Micah and me.'

Dodi shook her head, still laughing. 'C'mon, you couldn't have been that bad!'

'We were his worst nightmare. Frogs and sugar in beds, sliding down the bannisters in the great hall, throwing darts at old paintings,' Jago told her, his affection for Jabu shining in his eyes. 'What else? Food colouring in the pool, dyeing our white Labrador green. Making chlorine bombs and trying to jump off the turret roof onto mattresses—'

Dodi grimaced. 'No way!'

'We were monsters. Occasionally, I remind him of how bad we were and that also shuts him up for a while,' Jago said, smiling. He really should smile more often, Dodi thought. Smiles belonged on that sexy face.

'Do you want a tour?' Jago asked, standing up straight. 'Would you like to see what we've done to the house?'

CHAPTER FOUR

Dodi nodded and Jago plucked her glass from her hand, placed it on the nearest table and, taking her hand, led her around the corner of the house. It was darker here in the shadows and she tightened her grip on Jago's hand, trusting where he led.

He tested a handle, a door opened and Jago tugged her into another dark space. He told her it was their home gym and sauna. 'I'm not going to turn on the lights—I don't want to attract attention.'

He pulled her past a kick bag hanging from the ceiling, and as her eyes adjusted she noticed the different machines, all top of the line. Right, that explained his beautiful body under the excellent suit.

They emerged into a hallway and to the right, at the end of the passage, she saw a chic, extra-large kitchen—black granite surfaces and matte black ply doors and drawers—filled with the catering staff. Jago turned left and Dodi followed him, idly noting the incredible art on the walls. She passed a Tretchikoff, a massive Blessing Ngobeni, and an exceptional William Kentridge. The passage bent right and ended in a rather prosaic set of stairs, the exact opposite of the magnificent, hand-turned wooden staircase dominating the main hall of the residence.

'This was originally the servants' staircase. There's another one on the other side of the kitchen. We can, obviously, access our suites via the main hallway but this is a more private entrance.'

Dodi licked her lips as she followed him up the stairs onto a landing that overlooked the hallway that doubled as a fantastic space for entertaining. Keeping to the shadows, they looked down at the guests below, some of whom were listening to the four-man jazz band playing in the corner, some quietly talking in small groups. Dodi allowed her fingers to drift over the shoulder of a bronze sculpture of a Khoisan hunter, his eyes squinting against the sun. She'd forgotten that Theo Le Roux had been such an avid collector of art, sculpture and ceramics.

'Your house is amazing,' Dodi told Jago, still conscious that her hand was in his. She tried to tug it away, but he tightened his grip as he led her down the gallery and another hall, passing a series of closed doors.

He stopped at the end of the passage, pushed open an oversized door and stepped back to let her walk inside. The door clicked closed behind him and Jago tapped a screen on the wall next to the door and a soft, warm light filled the room. Dodi looked around, intrigued. Like the rest of the house, his sitting room was exquisitely decorated, with rich cream walls featuring amazing seascapes from artists at the top of their game. Two leather sofas and an oatmeal-coloured wingback chair faced a massive flat screen on the wall.

But, unlike the rest of the exquisitely decorated house, this room looked lived-in, loved. A haphazard pile of books sat on the coffee table, there was a dirty coffee cup on the side table and a sweatshirt lay across the back of the chair. A pair of top-of-the-range trainers sat on the ancient, massive Persian carpet. A sleek laptop lay on the cushion of one of the sofas.

Jago shrugged out of his jacket, pulled down his tie and opened the buttons to his waistcoat. 'Take a seat,' he told her, heading to the corner of the room, where two walls filled with bookshelves met. Pulling a bottle of red wine from the built-in wine rack, he held it up. 'Would you like a glass?'

Dodi narrowed her eyes at the expensive label. 'I'm not a wine connoisseur, so maybe you shouldn't waste your good wine on a plebeian like me.'

Jago gave her another half-smile, efficiently removed the cork and poured wine into two huge glasses. He walked over to her, handing her the glass before sinking into the depths of his enormous sofa. She could imagine him falling asleep there, weary after a long workday.

Dodi, still standing, sipped her wine—fruity and rich and, yes, delicious—and sauntered over to the bookcases to inspect his reading material. Books on politics were mixed in with crime thrillers, autobiographies stood alongside business tomes. 'How on earth do you find a book?'

'I have a photographic memory,' Jago replied, crossing his feet at the ankles. 'I know where everything is, mostly.'

Dodi walked across the carpet to the open doors, which led to a small patio. Peeking outside, she saw a wrought-iron table and a lovely, plump sofa squatting on the balcony—good grief, what was a Fendi Casa sofa doing on a balcony? It was a perfect place to drink an early morning coffee. She could hear the distant sounds of the party but, because they were on the other side of the house, the noise was a gentle wash in the background.

'Aren't your guests going to miss you?'

Jago shrugged. 'Micah did a "welcome to the family" speech on our behalf—he's better at that sort of stuff—and Liyana is playing hostess, backed up by my twin. And they know I hate crowds and won't be surprised by my disappearing act.'

She looked down at her feet. 'I can go if you want to be alone.' She forced herself to smile. 'But you might have to draw me a map so that I can find my way back to my car.'

Jago's eyes slammed into hers. 'I wouldn't have brought you up here, to my *private* living space, if I didn't want you here, Elodie Kate.'

Right. Well, then.

'Why don't you take a seat, kick off your shoes?' Jago suggested. He looked at her spiky heels and pulled a face. 'Those heels are super-sexy and do amazing things for your butt and legs, but they have to be as uncomfortable as all hell.'

She started to protest, saw the amusement in his eyes and shrugged. 'You're right, they are uncomfortable. But also very gorgeous.'

'That they are,' Jago agreed when Dodi sat down on the edge of the sofa and bent down to unbuckle the strap around her ankle. She murmured her relief and slipped off the other shoe, rotating her feet at the ankles.

'Pretty, pretty little instruments of torture,' Dodi murmured.

'Is there any point in asking why you wear them if

they hurt? Or is that one of those inexplicable things women do that we will never understand?'

'As you said, butts and legs.' Dodi grinned, picked up her wine and pulled her feet under her bottom, her dress flowing over her knees and down her legs. Jago slid further down the sofa and rested his head against the back, looking relaxed for the first time that evening. Dodi tamped down the urge to run her fingers down his jaw, to rub her nose in the stubble on his cheeks.

By being here with him, feeling so comfortable in his space, she was playing with fire. If he kissed her, there was a very good chance of their clothes flying off. She wasn't sure if the idea excited or terrified her. Or both.

She nodded to a door on the other side of the room. 'Your bedroom?'

'Walk-in closet, bedroom and then a bathroom,' Jago replied. 'Feel free to take a look.'

Curious about him, and his space, she stood and walked into his bedroom, taking in the textured, deep navy walls and the enormous bed covered in white linen. Yet another wall was covered in shelves, the verdigris copper pipes and wooden shelves adding warmth to the room. A trio of atmospheric charcoal sketches in matt black frames caught her attention. They were, she quickly realised, abstract portraits of Jago and his siblings.

This was another room that was lived-in. A jacket lay across the arm of a navy-and-grey-striped armchair. A book was face down on the side table. A huge window led onto yet another private balcony that looked over the back garden.

'Like it?'

Dodi felt his breath skimming across the top of her

head, the words warming her from the inside out. She turned and found herself just an inch from him. One tiny step and she'd be in his arms, one lift of her toes and her mouth would reach his. Like before, the urge to kiss him was overwhelming, the need to be in his arms, her mouth under his, urgent.

He muttered a low, indistinguishable curse and placed his hands on her hips, gently pulling her towards him. She wanted to be sensible, to step away, but her body had other plans and she all but fell into his arms in her eagerness to get closer to him.

He looked down at her mouth before dragging his eyes up to slam into hers. 'I've told myself, over and over, that this is crazy, I have no idea where this need for you comes from but I'm tired of talking myself out of having you,' Jago murmured. 'I think I should and *must* kiss you…everywhere. Tell me you want me to do that.'

'I shouldn't but I do,' Dodi told him, reluctance tinging her words.

'Thank God.'

Jago nibbled her jaw, and she inhaled his cologne, and her mind went fuzzy. She lifted her chin to give him better access to the spot where her neck met her jaw, and he dropped an open-mouthed kiss on her skin.

Dodi released a turned-on groan. 'I want you, but I don't think this is a good idea, Jago.'

'Best idea I've had for a long time. Stop thinking, Elodie Kate, just feel.'

This wasn't her. She didn't find herself in the bedrooms of sexy billionaires who smelled of midnight and looked like temptation. She knew she should walk away, find her way through his enormous house and back to her car, but being sensible wasn't what she wanted to be tonight. She wanted to be a little wild, throw caution to the wind, step away from the reality of her life—working too hard and playing too little—and *feel.* She wanted to feel like a woman again, sexy, desired, wanted.

But…

Jago placed a hand on her heart, and her nipple under his hand reacted immediately, instinctively. 'Your eyes are blue fire and your heart is pounding. You want me, Dodi, as I want you.'

'I don't want to want you,' Dodi replied, sounding cross.

He smiled, amusement flashing in his eyes. 'Don't deny yourself—don't deny this, us. And, for God's sake, stop thinking. Give me one night, and we'll go back to normal tomorrow…whatever normal is.'

His words reassured Dodi a fraction, and she knew that Jago always kept his word. They could have their moment out of time and then it would be done, a nice memory, something to remember when she was old and grey. He wouldn't hassle her for another round, demand more, allude to it in conversation. Jago might not talk a lot, or hardly at all, but she trusted every word out of his mouth.

In the morning, when she was back at her house, this night would be a secret the two of them shared.

Dodi tapped her fingers to her mouth, knowing that she was on the slippery slope to saying yes, to sharing her body and this experience with a man who'd been on the periphery of her life for the last decade. She wasn't someone who indulged in casual encounters, who had one-night stands—this would be her first—but it had been so long since she'd been held, since she'd had her body stroked, since she'd heard a masculine voice in her ear telling her she was beautiful, how good she felt…

So long since she'd experienced the tangle of limbs, the rough texture of a man's skin, being rocketed up and up and feeling as if she could touch the stars.

She was a strong, independent, modern-day woman but even a strong woman needed to feel, if only for a few hours, sexy and desired, to lie within a strong man's arms.

'Come to bed with me, Elodie Kate,' Jago said, taking her hand and pulling her to the end of his massive bed. She expected him to kiss her, to follow up his suggestion with a sexy swipe of his lips, his tongue twisting around hers, but he pulled her against him, cuddling her to his chest, allowing her the space and time to make up her mind, to get her jumbled thoughts into some sort of order. Dodi slid her hands up and down his ribcage, feeling his hard muscles under the thin cotton of his shirt. She rested her nose in the vee of his open shirt and inhaled his scent—soap and cologne and a deeper note that was pure Jago. She touched her tongue to his skin and felt him shudder, relieved to know that she could make this terse, uncommunicative man tremble.

Emboldened, she pulled his shirt out from the band of his suit trousers and slid her hand under the fabric, allowing her fingers to skate over his ridged abdomen, his ribcage, through a light smattering of hair and over his flat nipples. She felt his tension, knew he was holding his breath, and when he spoke his voice was growly with frustration.

'Are we doing this or not, Dodi?'

Oh, yeah, they were. She couldn't *not*. She looked up at him through her long lashes and started to undo the remainder of his shirt buttons, pushing aside his shirt and vest to lie her hot mouth against his skin.

Jago placed his hand against her cheek, his thumb gently lifting her chin so that she had to look into his eyes. 'I need you to *tell* me that I can take you to bed, Elodie Kate.'

She nodded, but his eyes told her that her gesture wasn't good enough, so she licked her lips and forced the words over her dry tongue. 'Yes, Jago, just for tonight.'

'Thank God,' Jago muttered. He stepped closer to her, his fingers dipping down and lifting the hem of her dress to her thighs, and slid his thigh between her legs, creating a little friction, a lot of heat. Passion clouded his eyes as her hands skated over his wide chest. He brushed his thumb against her lip, over the throbbing pulse point in her throat, across one erect nipple.

So good, so amazingly wonderful.

Dodi didn't know that she'd spoken aloud until he responded. 'You are the sexiest thing I've ever seen. I can feel your heat on my leg, and I bet that if I put my hand between your legs I'll find you wet.'

Dodi released a breathy whimper.

His hand on her lower back pulled her against him and his erection jumped against the fabric of his suit trousers. 'Let me see you. I need to see if my imagination matches up to reality.'

His hands found the side zip to her dress, and he slowly, tantalisingly pulled it down, allowing the warm summer air to touch her skin. He unhooked the catch at the top of the zip and lifted the halter-neck over her head, exposing her pale cream braless chest to his heated gaze. She wanted to cover up but the admiration in his eyes gave her courage. He smiled as he skimmed his finger over her freckle-covered chest. 'You are more beautiful than I thought. And I love every dot,' he murmured, curling his hand around one of her breasts, always smaller than she'd like. He bent his head, sucked her nipple inside his mouth and Dodi whimpered with pleasure, sliding her fingers into his hair to hold him there.

Her dress whispered away, and Dodi found herself lying against the cool fabric of his duvet, with Jago exploring her body with his tongue and lips and those large, gentle hands.

She could lie here for ever, a goddess being worshipped, feeling languid and loved.

Jago pulled away from her to kick off his shoes, to discard his shirt and vest. She half sat, resting on her elbows as he revealed his big, beautiful body, fascinated by his arms bulging with muscle, the raised veins under the skin, his long, powerful legs. Broad hands and feet, and his fallen-angel face.

He was every inch a man and she felt feminine and powerful, a combination of goddess and muse.

Jago joined her on the bed and leaned over her, his mouth an inch from her own.

'One night, Elodie Kate, and let's make it one to remember.'

'One night, Jago. Kiss me…please.'

His eyes slammed into hers and she pushed her head back into the pillow, stunned by the blistering heat in his gaze. He wanted her. She was astonished by how much. Was there anything as wonderful as being the object of a hot, sexy guy's complete attention? She didn't think so.

Dodi ran her hands down his chest, her fingers flirting with the snap on his trousers. Jago looked down at her hands and smiled. 'Feel free to explore.'

'I would, but you haven't kissed me yet,' Dodi murmured.

He didn't need to be told twice, and as his skilled tongue slid into her mouth she—somehow—managed to push his trousers and his underwear down his hips, exposing gorgeous masculine skin she couldn't wait to explore. The dip of his spine, his long muscles flowing over his hips, his firm and masculine butt. After he removed the last of his clothing, Dodi lifted her hand to touch his face. She stroked her thumb over his jaw, along his cheekbone, explored the shell of his ear, dragged the tips of her fingers through the scruff on his face. If she only got to do this once—whose stupid idea was that?—she wanted to be able to pull up this memory. In years to come, she wanted to remember how he smelled, the heat of his skin, the rich taste of his mouth.

Dodi sighed as Jago's hands moved up and down her back, over her butt, up her sides, and onto her breasts. His touch was confident and assured. He was a man who knew how to touch a woman and make her burn.

Jago's fingers speared into her hair and he gripped the back of her head, taking their kiss deeper. With her entire focus on him and what he was doing to her, Dodi felt her control slipping away, superseded by the need for her to know him, in the most intimate way a woman could know a man. She tilted her hips up, needing to connect with his erection, to feel his need. For her.

So much need.

Jago moaned, a deep, guttural grunt of approval, and Dodi felt her panties slide down her hips, and, with no hesitation, he parted her legs and dragged his fingers across her feminine folds. Dodi whimpered and then gasped when his finger pushed inside her, his thumb on her tiny, responsive bundle of nerves.

'Condom,' Jago panted, pulling back to reach over her to open a bedside drawer. He pulled out a packet, ripped it open with an impatient curse and rolled it down his shaft. Resting his hands on either side of her head, he stared down at her, his eyes the colour of molten silver. 'You are exquisite, Elodie Kate.'

Emboldened by his compliment, Dodi streaked her hands over his upper body, trying to touch him wherever she could. She was burning up, a rocket flying through the atmosphere, and she needed him to push her through to the other side. 'Jago, I need you. Inside me. Now!'

He didn't argue, didn't hesitate, just entered her with one long, sure, perfect stroke. Dodi's legs encircled his hips and she pushed her nails into his firm butt, groaning with approval as he kissed her mouth, his tongue winding around hers.

He didn't move, but Dodi could feel his arms shaking, felt the tension in his neck, his back. Dodi jerked her hips up, trying to find her release, and softly cursed when Jago pulled back, keeping her hovering on the edge. Ducking his head, he pushed her breasts up so her nipples could meet his mouth.

Pleasure peaked and peaked again. She was so close. All she could think about, concentrate on, was the sizzle, waiting for the moment she burst into flames.

As if sensing she couldn't take any more, Jago drove into her, deeper and harder, demanding more from her. Her lungs tightened—who needed to breathe anyway?—her skin flushed, and her channel throbbed as she teetered on the edge of an earth-shattering climax.

He did something, she knew not what, and then her orgasm hit, incinerating her. But, strangely, she still needed more and she begged Jago not to stop. Knowing her body better than she did, he pushed his hand between them to find her nub while his hips pistoned into her. Dodi felt herself reignite, and when she felt his release she stepped into another fire, this one filled with pyrotechnics. She became colour, luminescence flowed through her veins, kaleidoscope patterns formed on her skin. Magic, witchery, sorcery…

She'd thought of him as a warlock and, man, maybe that description was closer to the truth than she'd realised.

CHAPTER FIVE

A LITTLE MORE than a month later, Jago looked up at the sharp rap on his door, looked through the glass—all the walls to their offices were glass—and gestured for Micah to come inside. He held up his index finger, asking Micah to wait, and returned his attention to the high-pitched squawking in his ear.

His head of Human Resources had a dozen reasons why her weekly report wasn't in his inbox and none of them held any water. Jago ended the call and shook his head. 'People,' he told Micah, knowing he'd understand his frustration.

'People,' Micah agreed.

Jago looked across the room to where Micah stood by the window, taking in the view of the sprawling city of Johannesburg from his admittedly impressive office. Both he and Micah negotiated with some of the most powerful men and women on the continent—politicians, dignitaries, and deal-makers—so when they'd had their offices redecorated a year ago they had wanted to impress. They'd demanded clean and streamlined decor, offices with the most up-to-date technologies, including touchless computing and big screens for remote conferencing. His space was elegant, luxurious but, because it was where he spent so much time, also comfortable. He liked it.

It was coming up for noon and the midsummer heat rising off the buildings made the dusty, smoggy air shimmer. Micah looked harassed, Jago realised, an unusual state for his normally sanguine twin. His hands were in the pockets of the grey designer chinos he'd teamed with a light blue shirt and a navy jacket. Because he had a meeting with conservative investors later, Jago wore another expensive suit—a navy blue stripe with a white shirt and burgundy tie. Boring as hell, he admitted. Dodi would not approve, but he looked sober and serious, exactly the impression he wanted to convey.

'What's up?' Jago asked Micah, forcing a memory of Dodi, lying naked on his bed, her red hair rippling across his pillow, freckles flowing across her satiny skin, away. It had been four, nearly five weeks since she'd left his house as the rising sun shattered the night, got into her car and driven away. Thirty-three days of silence, seven hundred and ninety-odd hours of trying not to think about her.

Of wanting her again, wishing he could have a replay of that truly spectacular night…

He saw Micah's mouth moving, realised he hadn't taken in anything and held up his hand. 'Sorry, say that again?'

Micah frowned at him. 'It's not like you to ask me to repeat myself…'

'It's been a long morning.'

Micah walked towards his desk and gripped the back of one of his leather and chrome visitors' chairs, a deep frown pulling his eyebrows together. 'Thadie called me, in an absolute state. Someone cancelled their booking at the wedding venue.'

He didn't understand. 'What do you mean?'

'Somebody called up the venue, said she was Thadie's wedding planner—she actually used the wedding planner's name—and explained that the wedding was off and that they should keep the deposit for the inconvenience. The venue, as you know, has a waiting list a mile long and they've already slotted someone else in.'

It took Jago a few seconds to understand what he was hearing. 'Jesus…are you being serious?'

'Deadly.'

'But surely they'd check? The wedding is one of the biggest in the country—why would they dismiss such a huge event on a phone call?'

'Ah, it was followed up by an official-looking letter from the wedding planner and a fake email from Thadie.' Micah looked as if he was grinding his teeth. 'Could they have tried harder to confirm? Sure. But they had the deposit and another function to fill the space, so they weren't too concerned.'

What fresh hell was this? Jago rubbed the back of his neck as his brain kicked into gear. 'What now?'

'Well, apart from tracking down the person who sabotaged her big day—'

'Who would do that? And why?' Jago demanded.

'She's had an uptick of trolling on her social media accounts since their engagement was announced. There's been a raft of nasty comments but nothing that grabbed her attention. Unfortunately, she did name the venue on her social media feeds, so the world knew where they were going to hold the reception. Anybody could've cancelled it.

'We could sue, kick up a fuss, but it doesn't change the fact that we need to find a venue that can accommodate a thousand people in less than six weeks,' Micah pointed out. 'Thadie asked me for help. Thank God we own an events company so I'm roping in one of their top consultants to help me find a venue.'

'Great idea,' Jago replied. He looked away from Micah and through the glass walls of his office saw a flash of red hair topping a pale face. His heart pounding, he watched Dodi cross the large reception room, stopping to talk to his PA.

What the hell was she doing here? They had an agreement...*one* night. Then nothing. No contact.

And why did he feel so damn glad to see her? Why was his heart skidding around his ribcage?

Micah turned to see what had caught his attention. 'Dodi looks like she's in a strop,' he said. 'Thadie must've told her about losing the venue.'

That didn't explain why she was at Le Roux International, and not with their sister.

Dodi turned to look at him through the glass panes and their eyes clashed and held, hers turbulent. She looked paler than normal and had dark stripes under her eyes. He stood up, pushing his chair back so hard that it crashed against the credenza. He skirted his desk and yanked open his office door.

'Let her in,' he told his assistant.

'Your investors will be here in five minutes, Mr Le Roux.'

'I know,' he replied, his eyes not leaving Dodi's face. Yep, she looked as if she'd been handed a bag of Cape cobras or a pipe bomb. 'Come, Elodie Kate.'

The last time he'd said those two words aloud had

been when he'd been painting her skin with his words and his kisses. She'd exploded on his mouth seconds later.

Not helpful, Le Roux.

Dodi nodded briefly and walked into his office, stopping in front of Micah to plant a kiss on one cheek, then another. He didn't get as much as a 'hello, Jago', never mind a kiss.

'I presume you are here to talk about the venue disaster,' Micah said, gesturing for her to take one of the two Wegner swivel chairs.

Dodi frowned, looked from Micah to him and back again. 'I'm sorry…what are you talking about?'

'Someone, a very cruel, malicious someone, cancelled the wedding venue and now Thadie and Clyde have nowhere to hold their wedding reception,' Micah explained.

'What?' Dodi's eyes widened and her freckles stood out against her white skin. She raised her fingers to her mouth, genuinely horrified.

'Didn't Thadie tell you?' Jago asked, puzzled. Didn't they share everything?

Dodi pulled a face. 'Uh…my phone has been off.' She bit her bottom lip. 'What are we going to do? How are we going to find another venue?'

Okay, it was obvious that she had no idea of the cancellation, so that begged the question…why was she here, in his building, demanding to see him? He thought they had an agreement that they'd only see each other when they both had to attend wedding-related events.

It was bad enough having her invade his thoughts and dreams at inopportune moments—or all the damn time—but seeing her in the flesh just made him want to strip her of that black sheath dress and wedge shoes, pull out the pins securing her messy hair to her head and lower her to his office sofa.

Again, not helping yourself, Le Roux.

'I'm on it,' Micah told her. 'I'm going to make some calls and get some help from another event planner.'

'I can ask some of my wedding contacts whether they have any ideas for a venue, if that will help,' Dodi suggested.

Micah nodded. 'Good idea, thanks.'

'But who would do this?' Dodi demanded, turning her clear gaze back to him. '*Why* would they do this? Thadie is the sweetest, nicest person around. She doesn't have enemies!'

It was a good question. Someone disliked his sister enough to cause her a lot of stress and anxiety and to spoil what was supposed to be the wedding of the year. Who? And why? And how the hell did they unmask someone working in the shadows?

They were burning questions, good questions, but another question was also burning a hole in his soul.

'If you didn't come here to discuss Thadie's wedding dramas, why are you here, Elodie Kate?' Jago asked as he resumed his seat behind his streamlined, modern desk, also a Hans Wegner design, linking his fingers across his stomach.

Every drop of colour disappeared from her face and anguish dropped into her smoky blue eyes. Jago, reading her body language, abruptly sat up and frowned. 'What is it, Dodi?'

Dodi looked at Micah and bit down on her bottom lip. 'Micah, would you mind giving us a minute?'

Micah's expression turned stubborn, a look Jago knew

well. 'If this has anything to do with Thadie, then I have a right to know.'

Dodi shook her head, the fingers gripping the arm of her chair turning white. 'I promise you, it doesn't. I just need a private word with Jago and then I'll be on my way.'

Micah shot her a disbelieving look, but he did, thank God, walk to the door and yank it open. He shut it behind him and Dodi closed her eyes. Her lips moved silently, and Jago felt his heart sink to his toes.

Whatever she was about to say was going to change his life for ever. Of that he was sure.

Dodi lurched out of her seat and stomped over to the floor-to-ceiling window of his incredibly luxurious office, resting her throbbing head on the cool glass, oblivious to the amazing view of Johannesburg from the massive tinted windows. After a few days of feeling bone-deep tired, headachey and frustrated by a constant horrible metallic taste in her mouth, she'd decided a visit to her doctor might be in order. Since Dr Kate was one of her grandmother's oldest and best friends, her father's godmother and the woman she was named after, she could kill two birds with one stone: see her old friend and also get a Vitamin B injection to lift her energy levels.

But because Kate was the type of doctor who insisted on thoroughly checking her over she was there for the best part of an hour instead of a quick in-and-out visit. She'd also given her an astounding piece of news and Dodi, not thinking, had immediately turned her car around and headed into the city to Le Roux International's headquarters.

She now regretted that impulsive move. She wasn't

ready to share her life-changing news with Jago. Oh, she'd have to, at some point, but she needed time to wrap her head around it first.

She needed to think, to assess, to make sense of it all.

She was pregnant, with Jago's baby.

She understood the individual words, but the sentence still didn't make sense. How had this happened? Why? Why her? Why with him? Dodi wanted to release the pressure pressing against her ribs, to unravel the constrictor knot that was now her twisted intestines.

She had so much to consider but, as hard as she tried to push them away, the words *I didn't want this* and *This isn't what I want* rolled around her brain. Yet again, she'd found herself in a situation she hadn't chosen.

She was starting to think that her face was printed on Fate's personal dartboard.

Dodi walked back to the chair she'd used and bent down to pick her large tote off the floor. She pulled it over her shoulder and forced herself to look at Jago. He wore his usual implacable expression, and she couldn't read any emotion in his eyes. 'Sorry, barging in here was a mistake. I should go.'

'Sit down, Elodie Kate.'

She glared at him, ignored him and turned to make her way to the door. She couldn't do this, not now. She needed time to think, to plan, to consider her options. Space.

'I swear, if you leave I will follow you, pick you up, toss you over my shoulder and bring you back here,' Jago stated, his voice calm but determined.

Dodi whirled around to face him, her mouth falling open at his ridiculous statement. 'You wouldn't dare!'

'Try me and see,' Jago softly replied. His low tone

and determined expression convinced her there was a better than excellent chance of him doing exactly that.

'Sit down, Dodi, and tell me why you are here.'

Dodi tapped her foot and looked past him to the huge seascape on the wall behind his desk, feeling as if she was tumbling in those waves crashing onto the shore. She couldn't breathe. It was all too much. Why did this always happen to her? Why did her life tend to skid sideways? What was she doing wrong?

Dodi felt the room sway and dots appeared behind her eyes. Her throat started to close. God, was she having a panic attack? If so, she didn't want to have one in front of the imperturbable Jago Le Roux.

A strong hand on her shoulder pushed her down and her bottom hit the seat of a chair. Jago's big hand forced her head to her knees and his rough voice commanded her to take big breaths, slow and deep. After a couple of minutes—years?—her chest and throat loosened. Dodi slowly lifted her head and speared her fingers into her hair, holding her pounding head.

'I swear to God, if you don't tell me what's wrong with you, I'm going to call an ambulance and have you hauled off to the emergency room to be checked over.' She didn't doubt he'd do exactly that.

'I was at my doctor's this morning,' she told him, her voice raspier than usual.

'And? What's the problem? Are you ill?'

Was that a hint of worry she heard in his growly voice or was she imagining it? No, he was just frustrated she was wasting his precious time. Annoyed at him and irritated at herself, she lifted her head to see him leaning his butt against the edge of the desk, his feet crossed at the ankles. His suit trousers brushed her bare knee and she wished she could touch him, just to anchor herself as she delivered her conversational hand grenade.

She could put this off and tell him later…

No, she had to tell him some time and it might as well be now. Dodi pulled in a deep breath, forced her eyes to his face and rubbed the back of her neck.

'I don't know how it happened because we used condoms, except for that one brief moment, but… I'm pregnant. And the baby is yours.'

A heavy, tense, painful silence dropped between them. Jago didn't pull his eyes off her face, neither did his expression change, but she sensed that every muscle in his body contracted, that a nuclear bomb had just been detonated in the depths of his soul.

She started to speak, but before she could she heard a faint buzzing noise.

He grimaced. 'Hold on, my PA needs me.' He issued a voice command to open his intercom system and a few seconds later his PA's voice came through on hidden surround-sound speakers. 'Your investors are downstairs, Mr Le Roux. They'll be here in three minutes.'

Without dropping his eyes from hers, Jago spoke again. 'Put them in the conference room and tell them I'll be a few minutes late.'

He issued another command to mute their conversation, ran his hand through his hair and shook his head, looking only mildly harassed.

Nobody would ever guess that she'd just told him he was about to become a father, that their impulsive one-night stand had resulted in a great big 'oops'. He jammed his hands into the pockets of his trousers and stared at her, his gaze shuttered. Jago was so good at hiding his emotions and she couldn't tell if he was sad or mad, flummoxed or resigned.

She couldn't read him, and a little part of her loathed him for being able to conceal his emotions so well. In contrast, her face was the emotional equivalent of Times Square.

Jago, after many minutes of contemplation, spoke again. 'Are you planning on keeping the baby?'

Dodi threw her hands up in the air. 'I heard I was pregnant a little over an hour ago—I'm still coming to terms with the idea!'

'But you came here, to me, straight away.'

Why had she done that? Why had she run to him? She should've gone home, taken some time to let the news settle, to make sense of this three-sixty turn her life had taken. But her need to see Jago, to share this moment and news with him, had been overwhelming.

'I have no idea what I'm doing, feeling, to be honest. This is all a bit surreal.'

Jago touched his tie, started to pull it down and dropped his hand. Did he need air? She sure did.

Another buzz, followed by the words, 'Sir, you are now more than a few minutes late.'

Jago grimaced at the admonishment coming from the hidden speakers and stood up to walk around the back of his desk. He pulled on his jacket, ran his hand over his head and looked at Dodi from his great height. He gestured to the door. 'I'm sorry but I have to go. This is important.'

And having his baby wasn't? *Seriously?*

Dodi placed her hand on her sternum, trying to physically push back the rolling wave of pain and disappointment. She hadn't expected him to jump for joy, for him to take her in his arms and hold her close—she wasn't that much of a fool!—but she hadn't expected to be dismissed a few minutes after dropping her bombshell news.

And in that instant she was a child again, desperately waiting for her parents to see her, to acknowledge her, to interact with her. To pay her some attention, *any* attention. Then, like now, she'd been treated as an afterthought, a pesky fly that could be ignored, waved away. She wasn't anyone's priority and was of little, or no, importance.

She'd lived with self-involved parents, and after watching her grandmother die had broken up with her long-term boyfriend when she was informed he'd been pathologically unfaithful and emotionally manipulative. She'd experienced grief and loss, heartbreak and betrayal, but she'd never felt as alone as she did right now.

And there was nothing she could do to change it. Dodi pulled in a deep breath, straightened her shoulders, and planted her feet on the floor. Pulling her bag over her shoulder, she stood up, feeling her thick hair falling out of its hastily pinned bun.

Jago placed his hand on her lower back, physically encouraging her to head for the door. She flinched, pulled away from him and quickened her pace. His arm shot past her to open the door and she didn't bother to thank him, choosing instead to walk out of his life with her head held high and her back straight.

'I'll call you later and we can discuss this further,' Jago murmured in her ear.

'You now know, so there's nothing more to discuss.' This was her baby, her body, her life. Had he had anything but a calm, unemotional, almost non-reaction she would've agreed to another discussion, to try and find a way forward together. But because he'd been so damn robotic, practically uninterested, she knew she, and the baby, were problems to be solved, an obstacle to overcome.

Well, at least she knew where she stood. She was on her own.

And that was okay. Being alone, being independent, was what she did. The essence of the person she was.

Hours later, Jago sat on the expansive deck overlooking a waterhole within a private game reserve on the outskirts of Muldersdrift. He tipped his beer bottle to his lips and listened to the shrill song of the cicadas, interspersed with the occasional croak of a bullfrog. The sun was sinking behind the acacia trees, and he heard a group of laughing guests heading towards the open-top game-drive vehicle which stood outside the pub. The place would be quiet for a while—exactly what he needed.

He needed to think, dammit.

After the meeting with his investors finished, he'd driven out to this extensive property, forty minutes northwest of the city, windows down and hoping the hot air would blow the cobwebs from his groggy mind. He owned a half-share in this five-star boutique safari lodge and came here, as often as he could, to this place where the air was clean, the traffic minimal and the birds, animals and insects were frequently his only company. This was his thinking place, a spot with no mobile-phone reception and where he couldn't be disturbed. After taking a beer from the bartender, he had found the most isolated, out-of-the-way corner of the deck and propped his feet up on the railing, desperate to make sense of his suddenly topsy-turvy world.

He leaned back in his chair and tipped his head up to look at the bright stars appearing in the purple-blue, velvety sky. It was past seven and he was exhausted. Physically and mentally drained.

He guessed that was a natural outcome of splitting your thoughts and attention between a complicated business deal and imminent fatherhood. Business was easy…

He'd been working on acquiring a platinum mine for more than eight months, one of the biggest in the world, but he couldn't leverage enough funding for Le Roux International to buy the mine without partners. Few people in the world could. So he'd looked around for investors, found businessmen he knew and trusted, and pitched his idea. He could've easily postponed the meeting this afternoon, citing a personal emergency, and his colleagues would've understood.

But, feeling sideswiped and off-balance, not knowing how to respond to Dodi's declaration and close to panic, he'd turned to work, something he could control.

But he was done with work and meetings and had run out of excuses, so he had to face Dodi's out-of-the-blue announcement.

She was *pregnant*. The baby was *his*.

Jago stood up and walked along the wooden deck, noticing but not paying any attention to the two kudu bulls approaching the waterhole for an evening drink.

He had not seen this coming. At all.

Anticipating trouble—change—was what he did, who he was. He planned his life, every detail, and he didn't allow life to throw him curveballs. Fathering a child wasn't a curveball, it was a goddamn asteroid strike.

A baby had never been part of the plan. With his wife or anyone else.

His marriage to Anju had been a head decision—he'd liked her mind, they'd both had fun in bed, they'd both agreed love was a myth—and her wish to remain childless and pursue her career had been a stance he fully supported. She'd understood the Le Roux empire required an enormous amount of his time, and neither of them had envisaged his changing nappies while negotiating multi-billion-dollar deals.

But his reluctance to be a dad went deeper than that. He knew himself well, and he was too controlling and analytical to be a father. Because of his need to anticipate trouble, change and potential emotional comet strikes, he constantly scanned his environment, overanalysing and overthinking. He put up barriers, rearranged situations, and either ignored or manoeuvred people to make life easier.

For him.

Children deserved, demanded, and required a father who could engage with, relate to and talk to them, not someone who was rigid and dogmatic, someone who'd stifle their creativity and enthusiasm. He was skilled in many facets of business but being a dad, raising a child, wasn't something he knew how to do. He wouldn't even know where to start and he could see himself screwing up. Badly. To Jago, failure, of any type, was unacceptable.

And frightening.

Children also required emotional availability and he wasn't that type of guy. Smothering his feelings, pushing down his expectations of people, keeping a solid emotional distance between himself and the world had been his coping strategy since he was a child, a way to deal with the vagaries, temper and instability of a volatile father. Hardening his heart was also the only way he could cope with his father's quick remarriage, and the way he'd erased his first wife from his heart, his memories and his life.

Being emotionally distant was a habit now, something he was familiar, and comfortable, with. Something he had no intention of changing…

Except that he had a baby on the way. *Madness.*

But also, weirdly, a little exciting, in an 'I'm about to bungee jump and I don't know if the rope will hold me' type of way. There was a little person on the way who would, at some point, call him Dad. Did he, would he, deserve that title?

And while he was on the subject of questions he couldn't answer, how the hell had Dodi fallen pregnant? As she said, they'd used condoms, every time they made love that night. Hadn't they? Yes, he was pretty sure…

Jago stopped pacing and frowned. He recalled their passion, her frantic demands for him to come into her, and he'd done as she asked, sliding inside her, just once, without being covered because he'd needed to know how she felt without the barrier of latex between them. But he'd pulled out before he'd come, of that he was sure. Had that tiny contact resulted in a child? Could something so life-changing be the result of his need for there to be no barriers between them, just for a minute or two?

Could life be so capricious?

And wasn't that a stupid question? He knew, from experience, exactly how unpredictable life, and people, could be.

And talking about unpredictable, he needed to get back to the city and face the woman who'd turned his world inside out. They had plans and decisions to make.

Lives to reorganise.

CHAPTER SIX

DODI PULLED HER T-shirt off, pushed down the band of her leggings and stood in front of her free-standing mirror to stare at her still flat stomach. She turned sideways but, as far as she could tell, her breasts weren't any bigger or her stomach any rounder.

She laughed at herself, remembering she was only a few weeks pregnant. Her baby couldn't be bigger than a full stop, less than one millimetre in length, and weighing less than a gram. She'd only start picking up weight in a couple of months and it would be a long time before she felt her baby move.

Her baby.

Emotions, dark and light, battered her from all sides, a constantly changing flow of happy and sad, fear and excitement. Anxiety and anticipation. She was going to be a mum. She was growing a little human she could love. Was she good enough to be a mum? Could she do this on her own?

As a child she'd imagined having a family, being someone's mother, but she'd pushed aside those dreams to focus her attention on how to navigate life with uninterested parents. She'd thought she might, some time in the future, have kids with Dan. But Lily's death, Dan's infidelity, her single status, and the responsibility of running a business had pushed any thoughts of motherhood away. Over the past few years, becoming a parent wasn't something she'd considered. Now it was all she could think about…

Dodi looked at her fingers resting lightly on her stomach, knowing that she was looking for a physical connection to the tiny, tiny human developing inside her. The one she and Jago had made. How she still wasn't sure, but if this kid could fight his or her way past condoms, punch through their protection, she thought the little speck had earned its right to be here, to make its way onto this crazy planet.

And yeah, its father was an unemotional jerk, easily able to brush her and The Speck away, but she couldn't do the same. Wouldn't.

She was keeping this baby…

Excitement and terror gave way to red-hot anger. And all of it was directed at her baby's DNA donor. How dared Jago blow her off, give her life-changing announcement no more attention than he would a memo that crossed his desk? His priority had been his imminent meeting. Hers had *only* been the rest of her life.

She wanted to strangle him…

For being so cool, so unaffected…for transporting her back to her childhood when nothing she said or did resonated with her parents. She'd brought home brilliant report cards. They didn't care. She was hauled into the principal's office—not her fault!—and they'd never bothered to respond to her request for a meeting. They'd shipped her off to live with a stranger…

If she hadn't gone to live with Lily, she might've grown up thinking that her life with her parents was normal, that all mums and dads were uninterested and that kids were supposed to raise themselves. But Lily's deep interest in every facet of her life—her achievements but also her feelings—only highlighted what dreadful parents they were, how much love she'd missed out on. Was it any wonder that she'd fallen into Dan's arms? She'd been a needy, lonely schoolgirl, so empty of love. And he'd been so attentive.

Was she repeating her past mistakes?

Had she slept with Jago because she was lonely, looking for a connection, needing to feel as if she mattered to someone? Oh, of course she mattered to Thadie, but she was, naturally, low on her list of priorities right now. Thadie had the twins, Clyde, a wedding to plan, a new life to embrace. They'd always be friends but her boys, and Clyde, would always come first.

A small part of her, the piece that wasn't cynical and untrusting, wanted to be someone's beginning and end, have their complete attention, be the focus of their interest. Dodi sighed, reluctantly admitting that she'd had that with Jago. For one night she'd been the object of Jago's intense focus, and she'd loved it. But one night had led to enormous consequences…

But not all consequences were terrible. Okay, she was super-angry that she hadn't *chosen* to fall pregnant, but, on the other hand, this baby would be the one person who'd be fully hers, someone who couldn't leave or be taken away, someone she could safely love with all her heart.

She and The Speck would be a team…

And she didn't need Mr 'Nothing Rocks My Boat' Le Roux.

As a single parent, she could control her world,

her Speck's world and keep them safe, emotionally as well as physically. By calling the shots, she would always know the ground beneath her was stable, that she wouldn't be forced, manoeuvred, or negotiated into a situation she didn't choose or feel comfortable in. She could work with that…

Dodi heard the chime of her gate's intercom and cocked her head, frowning. She looked at her watch. It was past ten—who on earth would be visiting her?

Jago. It had to be. He was the only person arrogant enough to ring her doorbell nearly half a day after being a cool, dismissive arse.

Picking up her white T-shirt, she walked into the passage, pulled it on and stopped by the stairs to look at the security screen attached to the wall. Yep, that was his swanky car parked in front of their communal boom gate. She swiped the screen to give her a view of the camera pointed at the driver's seat and could see his tense, scowling face.

Dodi watched as he ran a hand across his eyes, pushed it through his short hair. He looked as shattered as she felt…

His hand came out of the car to push the button again and Dodi jumped. He looked directly into the camera, somehow sensing she was watching him.

Dodi picked up the receiver. 'That was a long meeting, Le Roux,' she told him, not bothering with a greeting.

'Let me in, Elodie Kate.'

When hell froze over. 'It's late. Go away.'

He didn't drop his gaze from the camera, and even though the feed was black and white she caught the irritation in his eyes. 'I can sit here all night with my finger on this buzzer. We can do it now or at four in the morning, your choice, but I'm not leaving until we talk.'

Dodi didn't doubt his words. She knew how determined the man could be. He never gave up and he never backed down so, yeah, he'd stay there until she either called the police or her neighbours did, or she let him in.

She cursed and spoke again. 'I'm number ten in the complex. Go right, right again, and left. I'm at the top of the hill.' She slammed the phone down, hit the button to raise the barrier and rested her forehead against the cool wall at the top of the stairs.

The man was infuriating. Sexy as hell but simply exasperating. And, dammit, irresistible.

There was something magical about a single woman's house, Jago decided as he stepped into Dodi's small hallway. That element of enchantment had something to do with the feminine scents that hit his nose, a combination of her perfume, laundry softener and handpicked roses in a fat glass jar.

Removing his phone from the pocket of his trousers, he placed it, and his car keys, on the small table in the hall and followed Dodi into a vibrantly colourful room. The walls were a rouge pink, the L-shaped sofas a bold blue, and mismatched prints of flowers and figures covered the main wall. Six, no, seven clay-fired pots held luscious plants and the room led into a small conservatory holding a small wooden desk and sixties-style chair. Nothing matched, everything clashed, but it worked. It shouldn't but it did.

'Let's sit outside,' Dodi said, leading him through her conservatory and onto a small outside deck. She gestured to a small wrought-iron table painted in a bold shade of tangerine and rocked on her feet, obviously uncomfortable. Or annoyed. Or a combination of both.

Frankly, he didn't blame her. He'd reacted badly earlier, and he'd barged in here tonight.

'Got anything to drink?' he asked, keeping his tone mild. 'I think this conversation calls for alcohol.'

Politeness warred with fury, but she eventually wrinkled her nose. 'White wine? A light beer?'

'Wine will work.'

Dodi nodded and spun around on her pretty bare feet to walk back into her house. He watched her slim form until she disappeared into the house, thinking that she had the perfect figure to wear tight leggings. Rounded hips and butt, flat stomach, long, long legs. Then he recalled those legs wrapping around his hips, and her breathy moans and how she had dug her nails into the base of his spine.

But their mutual delight and pleasure—he was in no doubt that she'd enjoyed their time in bed as much as he had—resulted in her falling pregnant, and that was what he had to focus his attention on. Not her lovely breasts under that tight white cropped T-shirt, or his quest to discover where else she had delightful freckles…

Dodi placed a bottle of white wine, glistening with condensation, on the table and handed him a wine glass. Lifting the bottle, she started to dash some into her glass before pulling a face.

'Problem?' he asked.

She nodded. 'Being pregnant, I shouldn't be drinking alcohol…'

He was desperate for the soothing effects of the fermented grape, but if she had to have this conversation sober then so should he. He pushed the wine bottle back into her hand, asked for a glass of water and tried not to think about the case of Domaine de la Romanée-Conti he'd received just yesterday. Rare and fabulous in contrast to the fruity combination of chemicals Dodi had just offered.

She went back inside to get his water and he wondered if he was turning into a snob. No, thanks to a lifetime of privilege, he'd probably always been one. He'd grown up as a child of extreme wealth and was used to the best money could buy. His father had many faults, but Theo had worked hard and insisted they did too, at school, university and then in the business. Theo hadn't made any allowances for his sons—if anything, he was a lot harder on them than on his other employees.

There was one element of his father's life that Jago wouldn't emulate: he'd vowed not to have children. He refused to inflict another generation with a screwed-up father.

But one tiny mistake, one impulsive action had led to the creation of life, and he'd been, without any warning, promoted to being a trainee father. He wasn't ready, didn't want the responsibility. Was scared to his soul.

Jago rubbed his hands over his face and when he dropped them he looked at Dodi, who sat down opposite him.

For the first time in what had to be years, decades, he didn't know what to say, how to act. What to think. He felt as if he was standing in a dense web, unable to think, breathe, speak. What was the next step? Where did they go from here?

Dodi broke their tense silence. 'Why are you here, Jago? You made your feelings very clear this morning when you hustled me out of your office.'

He hadn't known what to think, had still been processing her news, trying to understand, so there had been no feelings to transmit. He'd still been trying to wrap his head around her grenade-exploding news. He frowned. 'I didn't say anything,' he protested.

'Exactly!' Dodi hotly replied. 'I told you I'm pregnant with your child and you told me that you had a meeting. Hell, Jago, that reaction would've made a robot proud!'

He was robotic? Her words were a whip slicing across his soul. He was aloof, distant, standoffish but he hadn't always been that way. As a child, he'd been more communicative, quick to laugh, to have fun. To give and receive affection. But after his mum's death he'd started to retreat from people, made sure to keep his distance, and made it a habit to scan the horizon for potential emotional traps.

Drama—verbal, physical, emotional—had become something to avoid.

Dodi closed her eyes, took a deep breath and linked her hands across her flat stomach. 'Finish your water, walk out of my house and out of my life. Neither of us needs you.'

He lowered his glass. Had he heard her properly? 'I'm sorry?'

Dodi rubbed her forehead with the pads of her index finger and thumb. 'I'm going to keep this baby, Jago, but that's my choice. I can afford to be a single mother, to give this baby everything it needs. We agreed to a one-night stand and I'm not looking for more. Go back to your normal life and pretend this never happened.'

What. The. Hell.

She couldn't possibly think that he'd stroll out and

leave her, well, literally holding the baby. He knew he had a reputation for being ruthless, driven and obsessed when it came to his family and Le Roux International, but he also took full responsibility for his actions. And he certainly wasn't going to allow her to dictate the terms of this strange situation, to kick him out of her and his baby's life.

She was the mother of his child, and he was tied to her, in a fundamental way, for the rest of his life.

He swallowed some hot words and hauled in some air. 'There's no way in hell that's going to happen.'

'You only wanted a one-night stand, so I'm not stupid enough to believe that you suddenly want to play daddy.' Dodi narrowed her eyes, now as cold as a Highveld winter's morning.

He'd never wanted children so he couldn't argue with her reasoning. 'True enough.'

'Well, then, for God's sake, go! I'm giving you permission to walk!' Dodi cried, her voice rising with frustration.

Jago felt his temper bubble. 'Firstly, I don't need your permission to do anything. Secondly, there's another option.' He needed to have her close, for how else would he be able to protect her from anything ugly heading her way? Like Micah and Thadie, she and his child were now under his protection. How could he do that if he wasn't close by?

'What? Are you going to tell me we should get married?' she asked him, her expression mocking.

The thought was initially, just for a few seconds, jarring.

'Yes.'

The axis holding the earth in place shook and he

wondered what entity had taken control of his mouth. He'd never intended to marry again or planned on having a child, but once his shock had receded the thought, surprisingly, didn't scare him.

Or didn't scare him as much as he thought it *should.*

He sent her a steady look. 'We're *going* to get married, you're *going* to move into Hadleigh House, and we're *going* to raise this child together.'

Her mouth dropped open and her eyes clouded over with confusion. He waited for his words to register and when they did, instead of blasting him, she released a belly laugh. 'Oh, that's too funny.'

Really? Strange, but he couldn't find anything amusing about their current situation. Was he missing something here?

As she took in Jago's thundercloud face, Dodi's laughter faded away. God, he was being serious! He actually expected her to marry him, after just a few conversations and a night spent in his bed.

What an insane idea!

Having witnessed her parents' lackadaisical approach to marriage and commitment, and knowing the detrimental effect it had on her, Dodi took the idea of being legally and morally linked to another person extremely seriously. Marriage was a commitment that should be separate from pregnancy, and one shouldn't influence the other. Outside forces or circumstances shouldn't play a part in any decision to commit to spending the rest of their lives together. She'd been a 'mistake', an unwanted pregnancy, and her parents had married because they'd thought it the right thing to do…

It hadn't been, not for them and not for her.

And what was Jago thinking with his 'going' to do this, and 'going' to do that statements? She was not *going* to allow him to push her into a relationship, house or situation she didn't want to be in, one she hadn't chosen. She was a grown adult, perfectly able to make her own decisions, one who didn't need a man to support, protect or dominate her.

Who did he think he was?

Exasperation, impatience and fury sparked her temper to life. Standing up, she stomped over to the French doors and gestured for him to leave. When he didn't move, she forced the words past her gritted teeth. 'Get out.'

Jago folded his arms across his broad chest, stubbornness turning his eyes to the colour and texture of slate. 'No. We're talking about this.'

'We're not talking, you're dictating!' Dodi shouted at him, vibrating with outrage. 'That might work at Le Roux International, but it won't with me! I am not one of your employees and you don't get to tell me what to do!'

She clenched her fists, her nails biting into her palms. Stomping back over to the table, she placed her hands flat on the surface and leaned forward, bending her head to stare into Jago's eyes. 'You are *not* the boss of me.'

Blue and grey eyes clashed and held. Jago eventually broke their stare by rubbing his hand down his face, across his mouth and briefly closing his eyes. He sat back, breathed deeply and Dodi knew that he was trying to harness his temper.

Maybe she should do the same. Standing up straight, she paced the small area of her deck before turning her back on him and looking to the small water fountain in the corner of her enclosed yard. The pretty garden, overlooked by a memorial plaque she'd put up for Lily on the back wall, looked ragged and overgrown. She hadn't tended the garden for weeks and her fingers itched to dig in the soil, to pull out weeds, to tidy it up. To restore a little bit of order to her chaotic world.

Feeling a smidgeon calmer, Dodi turned back to Jago and rocked on her heels.

'This could be so much worse, you know,' she told him.

He looked at her in disbelief. 'It could? How?'

'I could be a teenager, with absolutely no resources, pregnant by a boy who didn't have a job, couldn't be bothered to find one, couldn't be bothered about me or the baby. I could be a mum with four kids to feed, with no money to raise another. But I'm a wealthy, privileged woman, who has the money to raise this child on my own. I'm healthy, I have a house, I have medical. I own my own business and have fabulous staff, so I can pick and choose the times I go to work and take the baby with me when I do.'

'You seem to have it all worked out,' Jago stated with an edge to his voice. 'What do you want from me?'

'Right at this moment, I don't want or need anything from you, Jago,' Dodi quietly told him. 'I don't need you to rush in and rescue me, to marry me or do anything equally stupid. I've been on my own for a long time and I'm perfectly happy to walk this path alone.'

She read the expression on his face as clearly as if he'd spoken: that's not going to happen. Dodi rubbed the back of her neck, exhausted. She didn't want to argue any more. 'Look, if you want to claim this baby as yours, you can put your name on the birth certificate. If you want to see the child, have him, or her be part of your life, we can talk about that…visitation rights, et cetera. But I'm not forcing you to be, or do, anything that makes you feel uncomfortable. I expect you to treat me the same way.'

'That's all very well, Elodie Kate, but you have the right to ask me to step up to the plate, to take responsibility and to play my part. I was there. You didn't get pregnant on your own!'

He was overbearing and bossy and was used to getting his way, but he was, in his screwed-up way, trying to be the good guy, to do the right thing. She had to respect that. Then she caught the flash of determination in his eyes and knew that he wasn't backing down, he was just trying to find another way to get what he wanted. Not going to happen, bud.

'You are thinking that you will work around me, to manoeuvre me into, at the very least, moving in with you.'

He didn't deny her accusation. 'I live in a huge house with servants, a massive garden, a pool and a gym. Your meals will be cooked for you, your laundry and cleaning done. At Hadleigh House, you'd be looked after, by me and my staff.'

'I don't need to be looked after!' Dodi wailed. 'That's not your job!'

God, how was she going to get through to him?

'Jago, you are very used to getting your way,' Dodi told him, her voice taking on a hard edge. 'But I am not your brother, sister or one of your many responsibilities. Yes, I'm pregnant, with your child, but that doesn't mean you get to swoop in and start arranging my life.'

She walked over to the French doors and waited as he followed her to his feet. 'Don't make decisions for me.

I don't want you to, and I don't need you to. If you decide to be part of this baby's life, I will discuss that. But I will not be dictated to, manipulated or manoeuvred.'

Dodi rocked on her heels, feeling like a battery that was drained of power. 'I need you to go, Jago. It's been a long, long, emotional day and I'm wiped.'

'We'll talk soon,' Jago said, nodding. 'Hopefully we'll make more progress next time.'

He wasn't backing down or giving up. God help her. Jago surprised her when he lowered his head to place his lips against her temple. 'Call me if you need me, Elodie Kate.'

Dodi stepped back and looked up. 'I make it a point of never needing anybody for anything,' she informed him.

He brushed his thumb over her cheek and Dodi fought the urge to step into his arms and seek his warmth and strength. 'Start thinking of what you want to be moved into Hadleigh House, sweetheart. And as soon as you give me the word, I'll send the movers to pack up your stuff.'

'I am not—' Dodi bit off the words and pointed in the direction of the front door. 'Out! Now!'

Luckily, this time he listened. Dodi didn't expect him to do it again.

CHAPTER SEVEN

SHORTLY BEFORE LUNCH the next day Jago slipped into Love & Enchantment unnoticed. The place was packed to the gills with prospective brides, bridesmaids, family members and the odd male hanging around looking uncomfortable.

His eyebrows rose as a slim, willowy blonde walked out from the dressing rooms in a strip of feathers covering her breasts and her hips. It was white, so he assumed it was a wedding dress. Look, he wasn't a prude, but surely a wedding dress required a little more fabric?

And God, he hoped the priest, the groom or the best man didn't have any heart issues, because they'd need a defibrillator when they saw that…*thing*…she was *almost* wearing.

Jago stepped to the side, hid behind an enormous bouquet of white lilies, happy to watch the mayhem. A pretty girl across the room stared at her meringue-like dress in the mirror, swishing her skirts as a four-year-old would.

A Goth-looking bride—black-as-coal hair and even blacker lipstick—stepped up onto a dais and cocked her head to look at the Morticia Adams-style wedding dress. Black, of course.

Her voice drifted over to Jago. 'Could I wear a witch's hat?'

Honestly, he thought she should. The dress certainly called for it.

Jago leaned his shoulder into the wall. This was actually fun. The customers seemed to be enjoying the experience and Dodi's staff appeared relaxed and efficient and had perpetual smiles on their faces. And yeah, he was happy to stand here as he worked out how to apologise to Dodi. Apologies weren't something he often did, and he sucked at them.

But he'd properly screwed up last night. He'd been tired and wired, upset and off-balance, and that made him rude. He should've taken some time to decompress and think before confronting Dodi.

And what had he been thinking when he demanded that she marry him or, at the very least, move in with him? He had a lot more finesse than that. He still wanted her living at Hadleigh House, sharing his bed, but her back was up and he'd have to work twice as hard to get her there.

He genuinely thought that moving in with him—he conceded that mentioning marriage had been a step too far—was a reasonable, sensible option. She was pregnant, owned a business and lived alone. And, being as independent as she was, she found it hard to ask for help, he suspected. He had the money, power and resources to make her life easier, to smooth away the obstacles that made life difficult and tiresome.

It was for her own good…hers and the baby's.

But he'd have to tread carefully. Dodi wasn't a pushover and had more pride than most.

Jago's eyes moved around the room and his heart

kicked up when he saw Dodi walking into the salon from the staff area, a fixed smile on her face. In her white silk T-shirt tucked into wide-legged trousers, she looked professional and sophisticated, but under her pleasant expression he could detect her frustration.

Something was wrong. He knew it the way he knew Hadleigh House.

As if sensing him, she jerked her chin up and looked around, immediately zeroing in on him standing in the corner. Those perfect, russet eyebrows lifted, silently asking why he was standing in her salon on a Friday afternoon, one of the busiest afternoons of the week.

Handing the dresses she carried to an assistant, she crossed the room to him. Standing close to him, she tipped her head to the side. 'What are you doing here, Jago?'

He couldn't tell her that their situation was all he could think about. And they weren't just thoughts about the baby, but also thoughts of *her*. What she tasted like, how she smelled, how he felt as if he was home when her arms wrapped around him, connected to her body. How much he wanted to be with her again, making love or just talking. He didn't care which.

'I need to apologise for my behaviour last night,' he quietly stated.

She waited, her eyebrows still raised. He rubbed the back of his neck. 'I'm sorry, I was out of line.'

She nodded. 'You were. Apology accepted.'

That was it? Two words? He frowned, unsure of her brief response. Did she mean it? 'Let me take you to lunch so I can apologise properly.'

'You just did, and I really can't.' Dodi gestured to the packed room and shook her head. 'It's crazy busy,

Jago, as you can see. I'm not going anywhere, not for a while yet.'

Now that he was here, he desperately wanted to spend some time with her. He glanced at his watch. 'How long until the madness dies down?'

'An hour, maybe two?' Dodi replied before shaking her head. 'But I can't leave the premises today. I have so much to do.'

'It's Friday, Elodie Kate, and work will still be there on Monday.'

Dodi reached up to lay the back of her hand against his brow, his cheek. 'Are you feeling okay? Who are you and what have you done with Jago Le Roux, the workaholic?'

'Funny.'

'I thought it was,' Dodi told him, a small smile touching her sexy mouth.

'That dress looks like a bowl of cat sick,' a female voice stated.

Dodi widened her eyes at Jago before turning to look around at the group closest to them. Three women stood in front of a cross-looking blonde woman, sitting back in the chair as if she were a young queen, disdain on her face. It was obvious to Jago that she held the power in the group and had every intention of wielding it.

Jago fought the urge to bolt for the door. He didn't belong here. Weddings, love, frippery and fancies weren't his thing. But he still wanted to take Dodi to lunch, get some food in her. She was looking too thin and a little washed out.

Was she taking vitamins? Getting enough sleep? Looking after herself? He needed to know…

But only because she was having his baby.

Lying to yourself now, Le Roux? That was a new low.

'I hate my job,' Dodi whispered, seemingly to herself.

Jago looked down at her and saw the truth of that statement reflected in her face. She looked as if she'd rather be anywhere but here…

But why? Surely not because some drama queen was being nasty to one of her bridal party? This should be a happy place to work, with people wanting to be pleased, enjoying the experience, content to spend money on their fairy-tale dress. But Dodi wasn't as enamoured with running the shop as everyone thought. Interesting.

Then again, everything was interesting about this woman. And that was…interesting in a terrifying kind of way.

Dodi left his side, bent over the shoulder of the bridezilla and murmured in her ear. The woman shot up, spun around and slowly stood up, her eyes wide. She followed Dodi over to a quiet corner and, with Dodi's back to him, he watched her face pale, flush and pale again. Then her shoulders slumped, and she stared at her feet, her expression now miserable.

Right, there was no doubt that Dodi had just informed her that bitchiness was not permitted in her salon. Good for her.

Dodi and the bride-to-be walked back towards him and the group. 'Ladies, Dana would like to take you all to lunch and then, after you've had something to eat, we'll resume the appointment. Is that okay with you?'

The three women looked at the prospective bride. Her bottom lip wobbled, and a tear slid down her face. 'I'm sorry but I miss my mum and I just want her here!'

The bride opened her arms and the group huddled together, laughing and crying. Dodi rolled her eyes at Jago and, taking his hand, pulled him back to the entrance of her salon. 'Drama, drama, more drama. It never stops!'

'You certainly talked the Bridezilla around.'

'She's young, scared, missing her mum and desperately hoping that a lovely wedding will make her feel happy again. That her boyfriend will provide the happiness she so desperately craves,' Dodi replied, with a bite in her voice.

'Wow, cynical.'

'No, truthful. Other people—friends, lovers, husbands—can't make you happy. A person has to make their own happiness.'

Jago looked around the room before connecting with her smoke-blue gaze again. 'And this doesn't make you happy?'

She stared at him, moved from foot to foot and dropped her gaze, as if she was trying to find a way to avoid his question. Her shoulders lifted to her ears and stayed there. 'No, it doesn't, not particularly.'

Dodi reached around him and opened her front door. 'Thanks for stopping by and the offer of lunch. But as you can see, I have fires to put out.'

He smiled at her. 'Don't make any more brides cry.'

'I'll try not to.' Her smile turned brighter. 'Although someone—a father, fiancé or the bride herself—might weep when I present them with the bill.'

He smiled, enchanted by her. 'I'll pick you up here at six, take you for an early meal.'

'I can't, it's—'

He cut off her words by dropping a kiss on her nose. 'Six o'clock. Be ready.'

He felt her eyes boring into his back but didn't turn

around to look at her. If he did, he might be tempted to take her into his arms and kiss her senseless.

Not what her clients needed to see on a sunny, late summer day.

The only reason she was going out for an early meal with the very high-handed Jago was that she was starving—she'd missed lunch—and because she didn't have any food in the house. And, even if she had, she didn't have the energy to cook it.

Sliding into his car, something stupidly low and ridiculously expensive, Dodi pulled her seatbelt across her stomach and clicked it into place. She was only five, nearly six weeks pregnant, but man, the hormones were rocking around her system. She was tired, more exhausted than she ever recalled being in her life, constantly nauseous, and yeah, her patience levels, never good, were running low.

She remembered Jago's offer to look after her, for her to move into Hadleigh House and to have his butler and staff take care of her. He wanted to wrap her in cotton wool and smooth her path through life. Tonight, she was tempted to let him do that. She was *that* tired and overwhelmed.

'You doing okay?'

Dodi slowly rolled her head in his direction, lifting a hand to smother her yawn. She couldn't let him know that she was feeling vulnerable and emotional, she couldn't give him that much leverage. 'Just tired. It's been a long day, a long week.'

Jago nodded. 'For me too. Let's find a pub, get a drink and, more importantly, some food into you.'

Food, a bath, and an early night. It sounded like bliss.

She should work—her paperwork was piling up—but, right now, she didn't care. Dodi, enjoying the light, cooling air coming from the vents, slid down further in the seat and felt her eyelids dropping. She couldn't fall asleep, shouldn't, but it was so nice being in this car. It was a cool, cosy, comfortable cocoon…

Dodi woke up to the sound of a car door closing, the smell of good quality leather and the seatbelt digging across her chest. She blinked, disorientated. Where was she?

She looked out of the front window at the modernistic, L-shaped house with its flat roof and banks of tinted floor-to-ceiling windows, and it took her a minute to recognise the house Jago lived in when he'd been married to Anju. She'd only ever visited once, with Thadie. Anju, she recalled, hadn't invited them in.

So Jago still owned this house. Why hadn't he sold it? And why were they here?

Releasing herself from the seatbelt, she saw Jago talking to a large man wearing body armour, a huge pistol on his hip. Opening her car door, she climbed out and walked over to them, pulling the band to release her falling-down hair.

'What's going on?' she asked, confused. Why were they here and not at the pub? And this house was at least a forty-five-minute drive from her salon…had she been asleep all this time? And why had Jago let her sleep?

She caught his eye, the warmth in his small smile, and felt her heart quiver. She didn't need him looking at her like that. Neither did she need him to be caring and considerate. It both warmed and confused her and, worse, tempted her to let him take over.

Jago gestured to the security guard. 'This is Bheki,

from the alarm company. An alarm was triggered here so he asked me to meet him here.'

It took Dodi a moment to connect the dots. 'Someone has broken in?' she asked, moving closer to Jago.

Jago lightly touched her back with the tips of his fingers. 'No, no one is here,' Jago replied. 'It must've been a glitch in the system.'

Bheki nodded. 'I'll get going, then, Mr Le Roux.' He nodded to the open front door behind them. 'Don't forget to lock up.'

'I won't. Thanks.'

Bheki hopped into his response vehicle, reversed and drove away. Jago looked down at Dodi before lifting his hand to run his thumb across her cheekbone. 'Did you have a good nap?'

She blushed. 'I did. I can't remember when last I slept for forty-five minutes.'

He grinned. 'It was closer to an hour, actually.'

'You drove me around for an hour?'

He shrugged. 'You needed sleep, so I gave it to you.'

It was a sweet gesture, considerate and very kind. And very unexpected coming from the terse 'time is money' billionaire.

Jago smiled. 'And you snore, by the way.'

Really? No, she didn't! Needing to change the subject, she gestured to his house. 'I thought you sold this place.'

His expression clouded and he shook his head.

She took a step towards the open door, then stopped. 'Can I look around inside? I remember Thadie raving about the design.' Seeing that he was about to say no, she carried on quickly. 'Just a quick peek, Jago.'

He pulled a face before taking her hand and leading

her up the three shallow steps to the oversized front door. 'It hasn't been opened for a while, so it will likely smell musty,' he said, leading her into the two-storey rotunda. The deep grey floors were highly glossy and complemented the light grey walls and a modern floating staircase.

Dodi walked across the rotunda into a massive open-plan living, dining and kitchen area, minimalistic, elegant, and very, very cold with its silver and white accents. She noticed the hand-painted cushions on the sofa and the large and expensive coffee table books stacked neatly on the glass table. It looked like a show house, waiting for its new, wealthy owner to arrive. It didn't look like a house that had stood empty for years.

On the other side of the rotunda was a high-tech media and games room with a huge, wall-mounted TV and a full-sized billiard table. The bi-fold doors opened up onto a long entertainment deck edged by a two-person lap pool. Beyond the pool was a well maintained, manicured garden.

She could see signs of Anju everywhere and it felt as if she'd just left the room. There was a book on neuroplasticity sitting on a side table, a bookmark peeking out from between its covers. There was even a cream cardigan hanging over the back of a chair, something Jago must've missed when he'd packed up the house.

If he'd packed up the house…

'Can I look upstairs?' she asked.

Jago nodded and followed her up the floating stairs to the second floor. To her, it felt as if the house was holding its breath, as if it was full of tension, desperate to exhale. It felt cold and lonely and, despite the slick decor, expensive art and high-end furniture, oozed neglect. Houses needed human energy, and they needed to be lived in.

At the top of the stairs, Dodi turned right and poked her head into three luxurious, huge guest rooms, all with en-suite bathrooms. Hotel rooms, she decided. Moving to the other side of the hall, she opened another door and blinked at the floor-to-ceiling bookshelves containing, well, books, arranged alphabetically. She also noticed a closed laptop, a stack of notebooks, pottery containers holding pens, a stack of folders. A shelf containing files lined the wall above the desk and a corkboard was covered in sticky notes in elegant handwriting, a reminder of appointments and oft used phone numbers.

It looked as if someone, a feminine someone, had just stepped out of the room and had run downstairs for a break.

This was, had to be, Anju's study. But why hadn't Jago cleared it out, packed up her things? Puzzled, Dodi left the study and eyed the room at the end of the hall, deciding whether she should go in or not. It was where Jago and Anju had spent their most intimate moments together and she wasn't sure she wanted to see where they'd loved and, hopefully, laughed.

But she was curious to know whether Jago had cleared this room or whether it was a shrine to his dead wife.

Sucking in a deep breath, she opened the door and slipped inside, her eyes rising at the massive bed that dominated the stark white room. Floor-to-ceiling windows on two sides allowed the light in, but it was so cold and clinical it reminded her of a hospital room. Walking around the back of the bed, she found a bathroom with a huge two-person shower and twin granite basins.

Putting her finger on the cupboard below one basin, she pulled it open and saw that the shelves were bare. Unable to stop snooping, she popped open the door under the other basin and saw that it was filled with high-end toiletries and expensive make-up, two-thousand-dollar bottles of perfume.

Jago had cleared out his stuff but not Anju's.

There was a walk-in closet leading off both the bathroom and the bedroom, but Dodi didn't need to look inside it to know that she would find Anju's clothes, her handbags, shoes and accessories.

Biting her lip, she walked back into the bedroom and over to the corner of the room to look down onto the entertainment deck and the landscaped garden. Was Jago in a holding pattern? Had he still not accepted Anju's death? Not moved on? Was he still living in the past?

Dodi heard Jago's footsteps and turned to watch him enter the room. He wore his normal impassive expression but his eyes seemed darker, a little more turbulent.

He joined her at the window and leaned his shoulder into the glass, folding his arms across his wide chest, the fabric of his shirt tight across his big biceps. And Dodi felt that familiar rush of heat, that weird *I want you now* feeling.

Her body wanted his again, over hers, under hers, hot and hard. But her mind was flashing huge red warning lights, telling her to be very, very careful. He was a complicated man, one fighting demons. She had her problems. She didn't want to help him fight his. Not that he would let her. Jago was the most emotionally distant person she'd ever met and wasn't one to invite confidences.

'Do you like the house?' Jago asked her, a slight frown pulling his eyebrows together.

She wished she could say that she did, but she didn't, not at all. Oh, it was innovative and thoughtfully designed, with super-luxurious finishes, but it was cold and stark and every room made her want to pull on a cardigan or wrap her arms around her torso to contain her shiver.

She looked for a diplomatic way to tell him that she didn't.

The corner of Jago's mouth lifted in that sexy almost smile. 'Don't hurt yourself trying to be kind. I can see that you don't.'

Oops. She shrugged. 'I far prefer your family home,' she admitted. 'It's…warmer.'

Dodi walked over to the bed and sat down, crossing one leg over the other. Should she ask him why he hadn't sold the house and cleared out her things? Did she have a right to question him, to pry into his life? No, probably not. They'd only slept together once, had a few conversations. They weren't friends…

But they were also going to have a baby together.

She'd ask. He'd either answer her or not. 'Why haven't you emptied the house, Jago? Packed up Anju's stuff, sold the property? Why leave it?'

His hard eyes slammed into hers and Dodi saw the turbulence within all that grey. He didn't speak and she bit down on her bottom lip, wondering whether to push forward or retreat.

His body language screamed for her to back away, to give him some space, that he wasn't ready to discuss his dead wife with her or, knowing Jago, anyone at all.

This was a no-go area, a field pitted with conversational land mines, and Jago was on the other side of the fence.

Safe but still so very wounded.

So why did she want to push him? She had no right to, and she hated it when people tried to do a deep dive into her psyche. She prized her emotional privacy, and she should respect Jago's.

It was only fair.

She stood up abruptly and lifted her hands in a conciliatory gesture. 'I'm sorry, I have no right to pry. It's got nothing to do with me.'

Jago didn't reply and after staring at his still form for a minute she grimaced, then sighed. 'I'll wait for you downstairs and, if it's okay, I think I'll skip dinner. I'm pretty tired.'

Dodi turned to walk out of the room, her heels echoing in the empty space. She was at the door when Jago cleared his throat.

'I didn't want her forgotten. That's why I haven't packed up the house.'

Turning, Dodi put her hands behind her back and rested her open palms on the wall behind her. She looked across the room and saw that Jago had pushed his hands into the pockets of his suit trousers. His shoulders were still raised, and his eyes were filled with emotional whirlpools.

'You must've loved her so very much, Jago. And I'm so sorry you lost her.'

Jago's head snapped up, his expression puzzled. He looked as if he wanted to disagree with her, to tell her that she had it wrong. No, that didn't make sense at all. He'd married Anju, and the few times she saw them together they'd seemed happy in a busy, modern, non-affectionate way.

What was she missing here? 'You did love her, right?' Dodi asked, confused.

Jago shrugged. 'Love never really came up.'

What?

Jago removed the gold cufflinks holding the cuffs of his shirt together at his wrists and shoved them into his pocket, quickly rolling his shirtsleeves up his muscled, tanned arms. His veins under the skin were raised, the way they always were on super-fit guys. Sexy.

Don't get distracted, Dodi.

Jago looked around the room and shrugged. When he spoke again, his voice was rough with pain. 'Within two, three weeks of my mum dying, my dad had the staff pack up everything that was hers, every last thing. He didn't consult us or ask us if there was anything of hers we wanted.'

Dodi's head jerked up, and her lips parted in surprise. Partly because he was opening up, partly because his words were so bizarre.

'Sorry?' she asked, not sure she was hearing him correctly.

His small smile was sour. 'He stripped the house of her, basically eradicated her presence from his life, from our lives. He donated all her clothes to charity, sold her jewellery at a specialised auction, burned her diaries and personal documents.'

Odd, Dodi thought. And so, so sad.

'And six weeks later he was dating Liyana,' Jago said, his voice flat and emotionless. Right, she was beginning to realise that the less emotion there was in his voice, the more deeply ran his emotions.

Jago looked around his old bedroom. 'I suppose that's the real reason I haven't packed up this house. I didn't want Anju forgotten.'

Dodi tipped her head to the side. 'I think that's part of it…but that's not the only reason.'

Jago gripped the bridge of his nose. 'Jesus. How did you figure that out?'

Not having an explanation, Dodi shrugged. He could see below her surface as well. Fair was fair, she thought. 'Will you tell me the other reason you've held on to this house?'

He pushed his hand through his hair. 'Ah…that would be Theo's fault. My father didn't approve of me marrying Anju. He said that I didn't know what I was doing and that I was making a mistake. He refused to help me buy a house and wouldn't let me stay in any of the many rental properties Le Roux International owned. I refused to listen to him, and our relationship, never easy, soured. By marrying, I was defying him, and he was determined to make it as hard as possible for me to do that.

'I used the money my mum left me, took out a huge mortgage and bought and designed this house,' Jago explained. 'It's the only asset I have that's not tied into the complex web that is Le Roux International, that isn't connected, in any way, to the business or the family. It's mine. In every way.'

'And why is that important to you?' Dodi asked.

'It's my back-up plan. If anything, and everything, goes wrong with the business, with us, I have this property to fall back on. I can live in it or leverage it to start something new. I always anticipate trouble, Elodie Kate, and I consider the worst-case scenarios. And then I prepare for them.'

Wow. That was a hell of a way to live. And this had to be a deep-seated belief because Le Roux International was one of the biggest and most stable companies in the country, on the continent. It would take an event of epic proportions to collapse it.

She could poke holes in his theory but wouldn't. She had no right to. This was his journey to walk, his road to map out, his emotions to walk through.

She wouldn't offer unsolicited advice. She had her hang-ups and issues and couldn't judge his.

'No comment?' Jago asked her.

Dodi shook her head. 'No. Anju was your wife, this is your house, and they are your mental processes.'

She wouldn't judge him. She had her own defences and walls and was still trying to deal with her past—Lily's death and Dan's deceit.

The combination of her parents' craziness and emotional neglect, Lily dying, and Dan's infidelity and mind games made her accept—once and for all—that love was a fairy tale, concocted to sell Valentine's Day cards and chocolates, engagement rings and wedding dresses.

No wonder she felt like such a fraud, owning, working at and making money from Love & Enchantment.

But this discussion wasn't about her, it was about Jago and this house and his past. Dodi forced a smile onto her face and gestured to the door. She wanted out of here and felt a little claustrophobic, her chest tight. 'Shall we go?'

Jago nodded and followed her path to the still-open front door, noticing that dusk had fallen and that the temperature had dropped, from hot as hell to hot. She pushed a tendril of hair behind her ear, thinking that she was due to give birth at the beginning of December, one of the hottest months of the year. Carrying a bowling ball around in that heat wasn't going to be fun.

Jago punched a code into the alarm panel at the front door and locked the door behind him. Placing his hand on Dodi's lower back, he steered her to his car, reaching around her to open the passenger door for her.

In the car, he started the engine, turned the air-conditioning up and they both sighed when cool air hit their faces. Jago flicked on the headlights before turning to face her. 'I asked you to share a meal with me tonight so that we could talk more about the baby, and the future, but we haven't even come close to broaching that subject.'

But she didn't want to, not tonight. She was tired after a long week, and she was taking tomorrow off, leaving the salon in the capable hands of her second-in-command. Tonight, all she wanted was a cup of tea, a shower and to sleep.

'I'm really tired, Jago, and not up for an intense discussion.'

He nodded before expertly reversing his car and pulling away. 'I figured. But we're going to have to talk about it some time, Elodie Kate.'

But not tonight and that was all she cared about.

Jago navigated his way through the suburb and within minutes they were on the freeway, and he was weaving his way through the evening rush-hour traffic. After a few minutes of silence, he spoke again. 'Have you told Thadie, or anyone else, about the baby?'

No, and she did feel guilty about keeping such a huge secret from her best friend. But Thadie had so much on her plate right now. 'I haven't. I don't want my news taking away from what should be Thadie's time and moment. And I think it's sensible to, at the very least, wait until I've seen the heartbeat before I say anything. Most women are told by their doctors to wait until three months have passed before telling anyone, as most miscarriages happen early,' she added.

He sent her a quick but intense look. 'Is miscarrying something you're worried about?'

Dodi shrugged. 'I'm healthy but a lot of healthy women miscarry. Let's wait for the first scan before we say anything. That will happen around eight weeks. If everything is fine at that point, we can talk about telling your family. And maybe we should delay the how-we're-going-to-go-forward conversation until then, as well.'

His family. She didn't have any of her own. God, she missed her grandmother.

She felt his eyes touch her face. 'I'll agree to keep the baby a secret until then but not the conversation. We are going to talk, Dodi, sooner rather than later.'

Ack. Well, she tried.

Jago took the exit that would take her home and stopped at the traffic lights, tapping his finger on his leather-covered steering wheel. 'What are you doing this weekend?' Jago asked her.

'Pottering, mostly. Hopefully, I'll catch up with Thadie and the twins, too.'

'I'm heading to Cape Town tomorrow for a conference. Next weekend?' Jago asked, pulling off.

'Uh…' God, it was embarrassing to admit that her social life was a wasteland. That she spent most weekends catching up on chores or binging series on Netflix. 'Nothing exciting…why?'

'There's a wine and appetiser reception I've been invited to, to raise funds for a cancer research charity, at Moon next Saturday night. Would you like to come with me?'

To Moon? One of the swankiest venues in the city? *Uh...*

It sounded as if Jago was asking her out on a date, that he wanted her with him on the night. But why? They'd just slept together, weren't planning on doing it again and were now—*eek!*—having a baby together. Why was he complicating an already complicated situation by asking her to upmarket events at a luxurious rooftop venue?

Jago placed his hand on her knee and squeezed. 'Stop overthinking this, Dodi. I need a date, and you, I think, need to get out of your head and your house. Come with me, meet some new people, plug your business. God knows there is always a bride or two wafting around looking for their first, second or third wedding dress. You might as well be the one to provide them with what they want.'

He sounded so cynical, Dodi thought. Is that how she sounded about marriage, about weddings? Sceptical and harsh? If yes, then she needed to tone it down a notch or four hundred.

Jago squeezed her knee again and Dodi realised that he was waiting for her reply. 'Um… I don't know, Jago. We said one night, nothing more.'

'Nothing was written in blood, Dodi, and we can spend an evening together without us ripping each other's clothes off, right?' Well, maybe he could. She wasn't so sure about herself.

'And I'm thinking that, if we are going to be having

a child together, we should at least try to be friends,' he added.

She heard his logic, understood it, but her heart, soul and body didn't want to be friends with Jago. Friends meant that he wouldn't stroke his big hands over her bare skin, drop kisses on her lips, skim his mouth across her stomach, down the inside of her legs.

'Say yes, Dodi. Don't make me go alone.'

'I'm pretty sure that you have at least fifteen women you can call up right now who would be happy to be your date.'

'Sure. But you're so much more interesting,' Jago said, his deep voice raising goosebumps on her skin.

Interesting, Dodi thought as he swung down her road and approached her boom gate. Was interesting a good or bad thing?

She didn't know and she wished she did.

CHAPTER EIGHT

JAGO PULLED UP in front of Dodi's double garage door, cut the engine to his car and raised his hand off the wheel, puzzled to see it trembling. Why?

He couldn't be nervous. He didn't get nervous. Scared? No!

Excitement, he eventually decided after picking up and discarding other emotions. He was excited to pick up a woman, to go on a date.

No, that was wrong. He was excited to see *Dodi*. To spend some time with her.

He hadn't seen her for ten days, but his mind often wandered in her direction, and he frequently had to resist the urge to check in with her, to see what she was up to, to see how she was doing, to make sure she was feeling okay. At the end of the day, it took everything he had not to head over to the salon or her house so that he could look into her smoky eyes, count the freckles on her nose, feel her luscious mouth under his.

And his nights were pure torture. He took a long time to fall asleep, and when he did he had X-rated dreams with Dodi in a starring role. This wasn't like him. He didn't get excited over a woman, didn't let anyone upset his equilibrium. He *never* allowed them to distract him from his work.

But Dodi frequently strolled into his mind during business meetings, plopped down and made him lose his train of thought. And when he wasn't trying to work out how she got him to talk about his dad and the past—subjects he never discussed—he still scanned the horizon for Dodi-related trouble. What could go wrong with her pregnancy, her business, *them*? And after the child was born, what then? How were they going to raise a kid together, how might they disagree, what were the potential obstacles and how could he solve them now…?

He'd never spent this much time thinking about a woman, ever. He should nip his little Dodi obsession in the bud before it got out of control.

He refused to fall under her spell and be at the mercy of any sex-, lust-or attraction-induced craziness. He'd seen how his parents had acted—hot, cold, on, off, up, down—and he liked stability, things to be even keel, no drama.

That was why he'd married Anju, remember?

And really, he had so many other things in his life demanding his attention. Micah and an employee from the events planning company they owned—a business his father had acquired for Liyana to run years ago, and which hadn't held her interest for long—had yet to find another venue for Thadie's wedding and they were rapidly running out of time.

Thadie had more online threats than usual and the attention from the media and general public had ramped up exponentially, so much so that Thadie had employed a bodyguard from the local arm of an international company specialising in personal protection.

Her stalker/harasser had managed to cancel the wedding venue and tried the same scam on the caterer and Thadie's florist. Luckily, they both called for confirmation, so those disasters were averted.

Thadie, and by extension he and Micah—and Dodi, he supposed—were all living on tenterhooks, waiting for the next axe to fall. And, honestly, his sister was looking like anything but the radiant bride. She was thinner than she'd been since she was a teenager, her face looked gaunt and her eyes haunted.

Thadie, her wedding, and his inconvenient attraction towards Dodi all took up a lot of mental energy, so much so that he hadn't spent a lot of time thinking about the fact that he was going to be a father, that Dodi was carrying his child. Or maybe he'd deliberately avoided thinking about his being a father because the idea scared him stupid.

He liked Thadie's twins, he really did, but he had no experience with kids and had never planned to have any—that was a very deliberate choice he had made early on. He was far too much like his dad. Theo had been more of a business coach and hard taskmaster-motivator than a hands-on father. He didn't know what a good dad looked like. He was abrupt and terse, impatient and competitive. What if he was as bad a father as his own had been?

Worse?

What if he failed at this most important of tasks? What then? Could he live with himself? He didn't think so. But neither could he walk away from his child, from Dodi—that wasn't an option! So here he sat, in no man's land.

Jago scrubbed his face with his hands and pushed his hand through his hair, before rubbing the back of his neck to ease the tension in his neck. He could either, he decided, sit in his car overthinking and overanalysing or he could get out, ring Dodi's doorbell and take an exceptionally attractive woman out to a charity event at a lovely venue in the heart of the city.

Leaving his suit jacket in the car, Jago walked up the path to Dodi's front door and rang the doorbell. He heard her shout telling him she was coming and a few minutes later she yanked the door open, dressed only in a short, silky nightrobe clinging to her damp body.

Jago's eyes skimmed her body. She was not wearing anything under the thin fabric and immediately felt aroused. He swallowed and shoved down the urge to yank her into his arms, kiss her senseless and drop that gown to the hallway floor.

'God, I'm so late! I'm so sorry!' Dodi told him, pulling him inside the hall and slamming the door closed behind him. Her messy hair was piled up on her head, water ran down her skin into the vee at the bottom of her throat and her dark copper eyelashes were beaded with droplets. She'd literally just stepped out of the shower.

'Can you give me fifteen minutes…twenty?' Dodi gabbled.

Discombobulated, Jago stared at her profile, fighting the urge to kiss her. Then Dodi yawned and Jago noticed her pale complexion, the puffiness of her red eyes, her trembling lower lip. All thoughts of taking her to bed fled—well, okay, receded—and he placed a hand on her shoulder to halt her progress up the stairs. He turned her to face him and lifted her chin when she wouldn't meet his eyes.

'Hey, what's wrong? You look like you've been crying.'

Dodi nibbled on her bottom lip before shrugging. 'It's been a stunningly difficult day.'

Yeah, he could see that. It was in her dark, sad eyes, in the way the skin pulled across her high cheekbones, in her wobbly lip and chin. 'Workwise or pregnancy-wise?'

'Both. I've started with morning sickness, but my body seems to think it's something I should do a few times a day. And God, I'm tired. I've never known tiredness like this, ever.'

If she lived with him, he would've known about this. He could've called a doctor, made sure she got to bed early, helped her, dammit! Not wanting to start a fight, he swallowed down his irritation. 'Is that normal?'

Dodi shrugged. 'Apparently so. It hits some women harder than others.' She pulled a face. 'Lucky me.'

Dodi moved away from him to continue her dash up the stairs, but Jago stepped in front of her. 'Wait, what happened at work?'

Dodi closed her eyes and shrugged. 'Bad brides, horrible brides, demanding mothers, whiny bridesmaids.' She patted his chest. 'If I don't go on up, we are going to be late. Very late.'

He didn't care. 'They'll survive.' He was lucky enough to have carte blanche entry into all the best parties and events in the city, in most cities, and nobody would complain if he was late. The fundraisers knew that the presence of any Le Roux attending a charity event was a stamp of approval and he could walk in at any time he liked and they would welcome him with open arms.

It was the power his surname commanded.

Dodi swayed on her feet and Jago grabbed her by the hips to steady her. If anything, she looked paler than she had a few minutes before. 'When last did you eat, Elodie Kate?'

She scrunched up her nose, trying to think. 'Breakfast? An apple midmorning?'

He ground his teeth together. Not good enough. And he couldn't take her out until she felt a bit steadier on her feet, with a bit more colour in her cheeks. She needed food, stat.

And maybe an early night.

'Go on up, pull on something comfortable and I'll call Jabu and get him to bring us some food.'

She looked at him as if he'd grown an extra eye. 'You will not! Your butler doesn't need to cook me a meal and then drive forty minutes across town to deliver it.'

'There are at least a dozen meals he can whip up in a heartbeat. He loves to drive, and more than that, he loves to be useful. If I call him now, we can eat in about ninety minutes.'

Dodi shook her head, looking bemused. 'You could just order a takeout.'

'With no nutritional value? I don't think so.'

She looked at him, bemused but wide-eyed and lovely. 'What about your charity event?'

'I'll write them a bigger than expected cheque to compensate for my non-attendance.'

Dodi's eyes slammed into his and a small smile touched her lovely mouth. 'You keep surprising me, Jago.'

He was so tempted to pull her into his arms, to lower his mouth to hers. Not only because he wanted her—and he always wanted her—but because he wanted to give her a little comfort, some tenderness. And that was strange, weird, because tenderness wasn't something he was familiar with. Soft emotions made him feel vulnerable and uncomfortable and he tended to avoid them as much as possible.

Yet, around Dodi, they kept welling to the surface. And, for the first time ever, he didn't mind too much. The feelings he'd avoided for so long—vulnerability, tenderness, a hatred of being out of control—weren't quite as frightening with her as they'd been before.

Jago watched Dodi walk up the stairs, slower than normal, holding onto the bannister. He couldn't ask her to go out with him tonight. He could see that she was at the end of her tether, emotionally and physically. He couldn't expect her to do her hair, put on some make-up and be charming.

And he was more than okay with spending the evening in her colourful, slightly bohemian house, inhaling the calming scents of roses, perfume and beeswax, and the warm Highveld wind blowing in from the open doors leading to her courtyard. He was used to the best money could buy, beautifully designed furniture and eye-catching art, *space*, but he had no problem with sitting down on her bright red sofa and putting his bare feet on her coffee table, sipping on a beer as he watched a rugby match on TV. Or listening to music.

Or just talking to the woman carrying his baby.

Jago made his call to Jabu and pulled off his tie, dropping it onto the hall table, along with his phone, keys and wallet. After rolling up his sleeves, he walked into Dodi's kitchen and found a nearly full bottle of white wine in her fridge. He found a wine glass and poured himself a healthy measure.

He felt at home here in her quiet, fragrant house, he realised as he sipped his wine. He could hear Dodi moving around upstairs, the murmur of the turned-down stereo, the distant sound of a dog barking.

It felt normal and natural. He liked it.

He liked it a *lot.*

Dodi made the mistake of lying back on her bed, where she promptly fell asleep. She woke up to the sound of voices downstairs and low male laughter. Then her front door closed, and she heard a car starting up and accelerating away. Jago's butler had come and gone…

How long had she been upstairs?

Dodi, dressed in black three-quarter leggings and an oversize off-the-shoulder slouchy top the colour of oatmeal, pulled her hair up into a high, messy ponytail and headed downstairs. She placed her hand on the door frame to her kitchen and looked at Jago, who was standing at the island in the centre of the room, on which sat two ornate silver cloches.

'I fell asleep.' Dodi grimaced, walking over to the island. 'Again.'

Jago smiled at her. 'I know. I was worried about you, so I went up and saw you passed out on your bed.'

She looked at the clock on the wall and saw that nearly two hours had passed. 'What have you been doing with yourself?'

'I grabbed my laptop from my car and did some work,' Jago explained.

Dodi winced at her lack of hospitality. 'I'm so sorry.'

'You needed sleep—and I'm a big boy. I can look after myself.'

When it came to Jago Le Roux people thought him abrupt and cold, terse and tense, but under the designer suits he was nothing like that, Dodi decided. Six weeks ago, she'd thought him to be unemotional and a little robotic. Hot but austere. She now believed that his impassive facade hid a deeply feeling and sensitive man.

Jago had hidden Mariana-Trench-deep depths and she, damn her, wanted to dive. Dodi folded her arms across her chest and pinched the inside of her left arm, reminding herself that that way madness lay.

It would be so easy to fall for Jago, she thought, to allow herself to be swept away in the fantasy of falling in love with her baby's father. He was outrageously sexy, a fantastic lover, wealthy as Croesus and more thoughtful than she gave him credit for. But Dodi knew, better than most, that good things didn't last. She'd never felt secure with her parents, and she'd spent the bulk of her childhood and teens constantly worried whether one or the other parent would permanently abandon her, and which adult she'd be left with.

Lily's taking her in had been an offer from heaven and she'd only had eight years with her grandmother before she died, eight short years of being loved and adored before she was ripped away from her.

Dan, before they became lovers, had been her best friend since she was sixteen, her lover since she was eighteen, but he'd lied to her, constantly and consistently about so much over a long period. Along with cheating on her, he'd also sabotaged her friendships to ensure that she remained emotionally reliant on him. Had his lover not brought matters to the head, she might, by now, be married to him, not knowing he was manipulative and untrustworthy.

She adored and trusted Thadie but the only person she could fully count on was herself.

Dodi felt the headache building up behind her eyes

and pushed her fingers into her temple, feeling a little lightheaded. A heartbeat later, Jago's arm encircled her waist and with no effort at all, and using only one arm, he lifted her off her feet and walked her over to the small, two-seater dining table tucked up against the wall and deposited her into a chair.

Stepping back, and efficient as always, he poured her a glass of ginger beer and pushed it into her hand. 'Drink that,' he ordered in a brusque voice.

Dodi sipped, felt the bubbles in her nose and sighed when the tart liquid slid down her dry throat. In a few minutes, the sugar would hit her system and she'd perk up. Maybe even enough to go to Jago's charity event.

Jago slid a small plate of crackers adorned with finely sliced tomatoes, grated cheese and chives in front of her. 'I made these earlier because I was starving. Get some food into you, Dodi,' he gruffly told her. 'You look like a puff of wind could blow you away.'

Fair assessment. Dodi picked up a cracker, popped it into her mouth and chewed. She'd eat one, two if Jago gave her the beady eye, but probably no more. Food, generally, held no appeal.

Then the tart, slightly spicy mayonnaise hit her tongue and she moaned in pleasure, closing her eyes at the flavour bomb on her tongue. Swallowing, she picked up another cracker and demolished that. Soon, most of the crackers on the plate were gone and she felt, almost, like herself.

Jago flashed his devastating half-smile. 'Enjoyed that?'

She nodded and picked a crumb off her plate with the tip of her finger. 'They were delicious.'

He shrugged. He pointed to the cloches which still sat on the island. 'Are you ready for dinner or can you wait?'

Dodi lifted her feet to place her heels on the edge of her chair. She wouldn't be able to sit like this in a few weeks or months. 'I can wait.'

Jago refreshed her glass with ginger beer, added some mint picked from the small bush growing on her windowsill and finally some ice. After refilling his wine glass, he joined her at the table, resting his back against the wall and stretching out his long legs. 'Tell me about your horrible day.'

Dodi grimaced and shook her head. 'It's over. I'd rather move on.'

'Tell me, I want to know.'

Dodi ran her finger up and down her glass, breaking up the droplets of condensation. What to say? How to start? It had been a disaster of epic proportions. 'Saturdays are busy days at the salon but today was insane. We were slammed from the moment we opened, with both walk-ins and brides with appointments.

'Two of my consultants didn't arrive—they both sent me messages telling me that they had stomach flu.' She felt the same familiar spurt of annoyance she had earlier. 'But, since they are best friends and both previously asked me for the weekend off, I think them having stomach flu was a lie.'

Jago didn't suggest that she fire her staff members or discipline them, which she appreciated.

'Anyway, we were slammed, and I think the heat and the crowded salon started to work on everyone's nerves, from the staff to the brides to the brides' entourages. As the day went on, everybody started getting rattier and things started going wrong.'

'Like?' Jago asked when she stopped talking.

'Ah…well, a bride picked up five kilograms and couldn't fit into her very fitted dress. She blamed my most experienced dressmaker for taking the wrong measurements. A bride and her bridesmaid got into a heated argument when the bride chose a hideous colour and style for their dresses, and they ended up screaming at each other.'

Jago turned to face her, placing his bent forearms on the table, looking sexy and interested and…hot.

Concentrate, Dodi.

'Another bride insisted on a dress that was three times her father's budget and he tried to pay for it using three different credit cards and all of them were declined. She flounced off in tears and he wasn't far off.'

Jago moved his hand so that he could run his finger on the inside of her wrist. It was, she was sure, a gesture of comfort, but it sent sparkles of desire rushing up her arm.

'It was a mess, all around. At one point I went into my office, put a pillow over my face and screamed at the top of my lungs.' And cried.

'Tough, tough day.'

It had been, Dodi agreed. But she'd made it through without killing or maiming anyone, so that had to be a win. So she just needed to keep doing that for the next, oh, thirty years or so.

'Can you hire someone to help you?' He closed one eye and grimaced. 'Can *I* hire someone to help you?'

She rolled her eyes at his suggestion. 'You cannot. And I don't need physical help, not really. Sometimes I'd just like to step away from the responsibility of it all.'

She could see the understanding in his eyes. Jago's responsibility wasn't to thirty people but to many thousands. God, how did he sleep? Jago sipped from his wine glass, and when he lowered it he looked thoughtful. 'Tell me the real reason you don't like the wedding dress business.'

Because it was a question she hadn't expected, it felt like he'd rammed a probe up her spine, sending two thousand volts of electricity through her body. Nobody but Jago suspected her of having a dislike-hate relationship with Love & Enchantment, knew that she dragged her butt to work every day. She'd adored her grandmother and knew how much she loved the salon, and the thought of anyone knowing how much she hated pouring brides into white-after-white-after-cream dresses made her feel sick to her stomach.

Lily had saved her from a dead-end life, given her a profitable business, a house, security, and telling anyone how she felt, really felt about the salon, made her feel intensely disloyal.

She sucked in a deep breath, prepared her lie. 'I just had a bad day, Jago, nothing more.'

He cocked his head to the side and touched the tip of his finger to the side of his nose. 'You always scrunch your nose up, just on the one side, when you lie.'

She did not! Did she?

'But I'm not lying,' she stated, forcing herself to look him in the eye. 'Bad day, annoying people. Let's move on.'

Jago dared to smile. 'Let's not. What's your problem with the business, Elodie Kate? And what would you be doing if you weren't a bridal salon owner?'

Oh, God, that was easy to answer. She might hate wedding dresses, but she loved fashion and she'd open a vintage clothing shop and decor shop. She could just see it, full of mid-century Swedish furniture and Italian lighting, Art Deco glass and great clothes from fantastic designers.

She sighed, reminding herself that she had a shop, one that she'd been given by a woman who loved her, who'd rescued her. Who'd expected her to carry on her legacy.

Dodi dropped her feet and faced him, placing one elbow on the table and resting her temple in the palm of her hand. She wanted to tell him, she realised. She wanted to unburden herself, to share the messy feelings of gratitude and resentment and discontent, hoping that he would understand.

'You're right, I have issues with the salon,' she quietly told Jago and immediately wished she could pull the words back. Because she felt colder now, swamped with an icy blanket of guilt and ingratitude.

Jago didn't look surprised. He slowly nodded. 'I've known that for a while. At Thadie's dress fitting, you were all business, totally in your head and on a mission to make sure the dresses were perfect. You seemed almost unmoved.'

Dodi grimaced. 'Dammit, I hope Thadie didn't realise that.'

'Nah, it was because I was watching you so closely that I noticed.'

'Why were you watching me so closely?' Dodi asked, confused.

Jago sent her a soft, heat-filled smile. 'Because I had brushed up against you earlier and I was transported back to that kiss. I was not only fighting my impulse to drag you into my arms but also trying to work out how my sister's best friend morphed into an even more stunning woman than the one I kissed five years ago. And why you did strange things to my blood pressure.'

His voice was like hot chocolate after playing in the snow, tart lemonade after swimming in the sea. Soothing and rather wonderful. And he'd felt all of that? Really? 'Ah… I don't know what to say to that.'

But damn, I could kiss you. I could kiss you for the longest, longest time.

Jago cleared his throat, stood up and picked up his glass. He yanked the wine bottle out of the fridge and filled his glass before briefly resting the cold bottle against his forehead. He released a deep, loud sigh before replacing the bottle in the fridge. But instead of returning to his chair opposite her, he leaned against the island, crossing his ankles.

How she'd love to see him in jeans and a T-shirt, wearing board shorts…barefoot and bare-chested. He had a clotheshorse body and looked good in anything, even a pair of smart black trousers and a white shirt, but man, she'd love to see him in something different.

Naked. Naked would be good.

'Why do you hate working at Love & Enchantment, Dodi?'

Damn, they were back to this. Dodi wanted to deflect the question, tried to think of a subject change but couldn't raise the energy. And really, did it matter if Jago knew? He was the one person in the world who never blabbed—hell, he was so far from being a Chatty Kathy it wasn't even funny, and she knew he'd never share her secret and her shame.

'I feel like a fraud.' There, she'd said it.

Jago frowned, instantly puzzled. 'A fraud? Why?'

Dodi dragged her finger across the table, drawing

imaginary pictures in her head. She couldn't look at him. If she did, she'd never get the words out.

'My grandparents had a fairy-tale relationship. By all accounts they were soul mates. My grandfather died when my father was young. Lily already had the bridal shop and she adored helping brides, loved hearing their 'meet-cute' stories and hearing about their fiancés and their weddings. She was so into love and weddings and happily-ever-afters. I used to tease her, tell her that she lived in a romance novel, that the real world didn't work like that,' Dodi said, smiling at the memories of her gran's outrage. 'She told me that one day I would fall in love, and I'd see what she was talking about.'

'I take it that didn't happen? Or maybe it did, and your relationship went sour?'

She wished she had such an easy explanation. 'Not exactly.' Dodi tapped her finger against the table, the sound of her nail hitting the wood filling the silence. 'To explain, I need to tell you about my parents. My father was Lily's only child, and he was...different. Difficult. Fantastically intelligent but impulsive and free-spirited and stubborn. He met my mum at university. Met? No, that's too tame a word. I sensed that they collided, smashed into each other. Two wilful, spoiled, sexual creatures who wanted what they wanted when they wanted it.'

She stopped, feeling like a cork about to shoot out of its bottle. She'd never spoken to anyone about her parents and how she felt about them.

'Get it out, Elodie Kate.'

'I was an afterthought, something or someone they were burdened with. A drag.' Dodi felt a cold hand clutch her heart, and she was a child again, feeling helplessness and bone-deep fear. 'They hated being lumbered with me and didn't bother to hide their frustration from me.

'They wanted to be free, to circle each other, to move away, to come back, but I was the unwanted heirloom they didn't want and couldn't get rid of. Neither of them wanted me permanently. They took turns leaving, both married and divorced other people, remarried each other, divorced, and their biggest arguments were over me and who had custody of me. I was never sure where I would live, on whose doorstep I'd land, whether I'd like my new stepmother or stepfather.'

'Jesus, Dodi.'

'My father cut off all communication with my grandmother around the time my parents married, and Lily lost track of them. She wasn't even aware she had a granddaughter until I landed on her doorstep.'

He frowned. 'I don't understand.'

Why would he? 'Shortly before my sixteenth birthday, my parents concocted a plan. They were done with me, that much they agreed on. My dad told me to pack a bag, that we were taking a trip. We landed at Lily's, he told her I was his granddaughter and that he was going out for a while, to give us time to become acquainted. He didn't return, didn't answer our calls, and two days later the rest of my stuff arrived by courier.'

As she'd expected, Jago looked horrified. 'That's… diabolical,' he stated, anger in his voice.

'I later learned that Lily was as caught off guard as I was but, God bless her, she rallied and she let me stay,' Dodi explained. 'Living with her was like entering an alternative reality. I had chores and curfews and had to go to school every day and bring home decent reports. I had to do an extramural activity and some sort of exercise, eat healthily.'

'And you rebelled?'

She grinned. 'On the contrary, I loved every rule, every regulation. I'd had none, so I loved the rules, knowing what I could and could not do. And Lily's rules made me feel secure, loved, cared for. Can you understand that?'

Jago rubbed his jaw. 'I guess. So, you were happy with your gran?'

'Happier than I'd ever been in my life. I met Dan, at uni I met Thadie, and my life was truly excellent, you know?'

'Who is Dan?'

No, she couldn't talk about him, not yet. Maybe not ever. She waved his question away. 'I was so happy with Lily and we were close. We often spoke about my parents and the shop. She told me I was too young to be so cynical about love and marriage, I told her she was living in La-La Land. She told me I would change my mind at some point.'

'But you haven't.'

She shook her head. No, thanks to Dan, she was even further away than she was before. 'Sometimes I look at those starry-eyed brides and I want to shake them and tell them that a gorgeous dress and a stunning wedding means nothing, and that it won't always lead to sunshine and roses.'

Jago's intense eyes were laser-like on her face. 'Do you not think they realise that? That they just want the experience of their union being celebrated before they settle down to the hard work of marriage?'

Dodi jerked her shoulders up to her ears. 'I don't know.

Did Anju feel like that? Was your marriage hard work?' she asked, curious.

The skin tightened across his face and his lips thinned. 'I wasn't in love with Anju, and she didn't love me. We didn't have a white, church wedding. Our marriage was a marriage, I suppose, of convenience. Both of us were very clear about what we wanted from each other.'

Wow.

'And that was?' Would he answer? She wasn't sure.

'A meeting of minds. We were very good friends who shared a lot of the same interests. Good sex…we were very compatible in bed. Neither of us wanted children and we were both focused on our careers. She was unemotional, as am I. Our lives were a drama-free zone and that was important to me.'

'And it worked for you?'

'Yeah, it did. Maybe we weren't happy, but we were content.'

He dropped his head to look into his half-empty wine glass, idly swishing the liquid around inside. He opened his mouth to speak, then shook his head. 'I think that's enough for now, Dodi. Maybe we should eat.'

She wasn't hungry…well, not for food anyway. And yes, maybe they should stop talking because he was fascinating mentally *and* emotionally. She couldn't afford to start having feelings for him, to fall in love with him, to be anything but his friend and the woman who was carrying his child. Too many people had smacked her heart around, and she would not allow Jago Le Roux the same opportunity.

No, she wouldn't allow herself to think like that, to let thoughts of fascination and fondness settle in her mind. She was attracted to Jago, that was all that was happening here. She was conflating sex with emotions, and that was a very dangerous thing to do.

She had to separate the two, now…*immediately*.

To remind herself that she was in control, that she knew what she was doing—that she knew the difference between sex and love—Dodi approached him and placed her flat hand above his heart, her other hand sliding up his chest to curl around his neck. She wanted the crackle and the fizz, to be hit by lust and passion. And if feeling like that pulled her out of her bleak mood and from reliving her tiresome day, then she considered that a bonus.

'Will you kiss me, Jago?' she murmured, looking at him from under her lashes.

He put his hands behind him and gripped the edge of the island's granite top, holding on tight, as if he was forcing himself to stop himself from reaching for her. 'I don't know if I'll be able to stop myself from doing more,' Jago admitted.

Dodi rested her forehead on his sternum, inhaling his fresh, clean scent. 'I'd like you to take me away from today. Take me out of my head and take me to bed, Jago. Please?'

She'd beg if she had to, she needed him that much. Needed his confident and clever hands, his deep voice painting words on her skin, his mouth trailing fire over her body. The perfection of him sliding inside her, the intense explosion he pulled up inside her.

She needed the distraction, but more than that, she needed him.

The thought scared her, but when he bent his legs and carried her over to her sofa, it didn't scare her enough to resist.

CHAPTER NINE

MAN, HE WAS LUCKY.

Lucky to be here, having Dodi look at him with fire in her eyes, want chasing need across her face. He couldn't wait to get his hands on her, to cover her body with his, to slide into her. But between now and then, there was a wonderland to explore. And Lord, what a place it was.

He loved every single freckle, perfectly imperfect dots on her pale skin, he thought as he gently pulled her top up and over her head, revealing her pretty mint-green lacy bra. Through the lace, he could see the outline of her nipples and he had to restrain himself from pulling her bra cup aside and taking her in his mouth.

This evening he wanted slow and sexy. To discover and to delight.

Her eyes met his and he lost himself in all that blue, smoky and intense. His breath caught in his throat, his heart-rate increased and he forced himself to look away, uncomfortable with the emotion bubbling away in his chest. This was sex, he reminded himself. A physical connection between two people who were attracted to each other…

Then why did it feel like something so much more? Something deeper, darker, intense?

Dodi curled her hand around his neck and pulled his head down to hers, a silent entreaty to kiss her. Soft lips, a spicy mouth, heat. Kissing wasn't something he usually enjoyed—it was usually a means to an end—but he could kiss Dodi for hours without needing a beginning or an end.

But soon his hands itched with impatience, and he moved his fingers to her lower back, down her fabric-covered butt. Her leggings had to go, so he gently pulled them down her hips and over her pretty feet, tipped in pale pink polish, dropping them to land on the floor next to the sofa. He felt Dodi's hands working his shirt buttons and, impatient with the delay, Jago reached behind his head to grab the back of his collar, pulling off the shirt in one movement, sighing when her hands stroked his chest, the ball of his shoulder.

They spent long, drugged-out moments kissing and touching, exploring, using their hands and mouths, teeth and tongues. It was sexy and seductive, a world of sensation. Jago placed his hand on her bare knee and slowly worked his way up her thigh, his fingers brushing the fabric between her legs. He knew she was damp and hot and, judging by the way she softly panted, in need of what he could give her. She lifted her hips and he pulled his hand away, wanting to delay her satisfaction, knowing he could take her higher and faster. He palmed her butt with his hand, kneading her, smiling when she released a little growl of frustration.

Using his other hand, Jago pulled her hairband loose and shoved his fingers into her heavy mass of hair, clasping her head and angling her face to receive his no-holds-barred kiss. Tongues danced as he devoured her mouth, learning her, tasting her, pushing her for more.

The last of her inhibitions left her and, encouraged by his passion and groans of appreciation, Dodi let her hands streak over his body, tracing the rows of his stomach and the long muscles covering his hips, brushing over his hard erection.

Such a brief touch but it sent reverberations up his spine, shooting pleasure into his brain. He must've said something, he knew not what, but she touched him more firmly, dragging her thumb along the length of his fabric-covered shaft.

'I love the way you touch me,' Jago muttered against her now bare breast, before sucking her nipple against the roof of his mouth. She arched her back, and fumbled for the clasp of his trousers, equally frustrated with the barriers between them.

Needing a minute to slow down, to lower his racing pulse, he looked down at her, his eyes skimming over her breasts, over her still flat stomach to her long legs. Those pretty feet.

'Perfect. You are so very lovely.'

'You're pretty hot yourself, Le Roux,' Dodi told him, sliding down the zip of his fly. 'But I think this would work better if we got rid of these.'

That made sense. Pulling away from her, Jago yanked off his shoes and socks and pushed his underwear and trousers down his hips in a quick, efficient slide. Stepping out of the fabric, he lay on his side next to Dodi, resting his hand on her stomach and sliding his mouth across her lips. He briefly thought about getting a condom—protection was a habit—remembered they didn't need one and smiled. He couldn't wait to make love to her with no barriers between them.

Jago slid his hand between her legs and cupped her,

his thumb immediately finding and brushing her hot core through her thong, causing her to gasp, then sigh.

'That's so hot and I want more.' Dodi moaned the words. 'I need more… I need *you*.'

He tested her again, knew she was ready for him, dispensed with her panties and, with one hand under her hips, moved her under him so that she lay in the centre of the sofa. He wished he were in her bed—he needed space to move and briefly considered carrying her up the stairs but knew he couldn't wait, not a second more, to slide inside her and to make her his.

But he had to be careful, to take it slow. He was long and thick, and her taking him inside her meant she would have to accommodate and stretch and…man, she felt so amazingly good.

He'd never felt like this before, when being inside a woman felt like coming home, the best place to be.

On that thought, Jago hooked his big hands under her thighs and lifted her, spreading her legs so that he could fill her completely, as well as making contact with her ultra-sensitive clitoris.

Jago pinned her down with his body, pulling back and sliding into her again with one long, sure stroke. He felt himself dissolving from the inside out as his world narrowed to what was happening between them. Everything faded away and there were only her hands on his butt, nails digging into his flesh, her tongue in his mouth as he kissed her endlessly, the upward thrust of her hips as she met him stroke for stroke.

She needed to come because he was fast losing control. 'I'm not going to be able to hang on,' Jago told her, his forehead against hers. He moved his head to talk in her ear. 'Take all of me, darling. Yeah…use me… Fly, dammit!'

'Harder…' Dodi told him, her body arching as she reached for her release.

Jago rocked into her, as hard as he dared, and she shouted as she clenched around him. Stars exploded behind his eyeballs, at the base of his spine, as his body splintered into a million pieces. He vaguely heard Dodi panting beneath him, knew that she'd lifted her arm to place it over her eyes, but he was in another dimension, someplace indescribably lovely.

Yet, for some reason, he knew this wasn't the end, not quite, so he moved his hips again and, still hard, touched something deep inside her. Dodi slammed her head back into the cushion, scrunched her eyes shut and screamed his name before she fractured again. He orgasmed again too, not so big and bold this time but still crazy good. Two orgasms, one massive…had that ever happened to him before?

He didn't think so.

Minutes, hours or years might have passed before they returned to reality, came back down to earth and Jago rolled off her and pulled so that she lay on top of him, her cheek resting above his heart, his arms cradling her close.

Dodi yawned and then he heard the unmistakable sound of her stomach rumbling. He laughed and patted her bottom. 'I need to get some food into you. You need your strength.'

She yawned and nodded. 'Mmm, I have to start eating better. This baby saps me of all my energy.'

'That's one reason. The other is that I intend on taking you upstairs and doing this, and more, again. Are you up for that?'

She lifted her head to look at him, her eyes soft and sweet. Then her smile turned wicked. 'Oh, I'm up for anything, Le Roux.'

The next morning, Dodi agreed to accompany Jago to an upscale farmers' market north of the city, where he was meeting his twin, and Thadie and her kids, for breakfast. It was family time, he explained, something they did every month or so.

Dodi knew of their monthly breakfast date and was honoured to be invited to join them. She just didn't know how she was going to explain why she was with Jago, how she was going to answer Thadie's curious questions.

She wasn't ready to tell Thadie that she was sleeping with her brother and was definitely not ready to tell her that she was carrying his baby. Partly because Thadie was stressed out of her mind and partly because she didn't know how her relationship with Jago—could it even be called a relationship?—would affect the most important relationship in her life.

She couldn't lose Thadie. It would kill her.

Walking alongside Thadie, who was dressed in a short, pretty, lime-green sundress, enormous sunglasses and flat sandals, Dodi waited for the interrogation to start. Any minute now Thadie would ask her why she and Jago were together so early on a Sunday morning.

I was in the shower with him just a couple of hours ago and he had his hands…

No, she couldn't tell her that. There were some things her best friend didn't need to know, especially when it came to her older brother.

Thadie stopped to look at leather handbags and Dodi looked around, her eyes immediately going to Jago's broad back. They'd briefly stopped at his house so that he could change into a loose, linen shirt and tan cargo pants. He wore expensive leather flips-flops on his feet and a pair of dark sunglasses covered his eyes. Micah wore board shorts and a green T-shirt, and he was pushing the double pram holding the chattering twins, who were dressed in cute matching outfits of denim shorts and patterned T-shirts.

Thadie's bodyguard hovered a few steps behind her, dressed casually but on high alert.

'I need coffee,' Thadie declared, gesturing to a stall selling upmarket coffee. 'Do you want a cup?'

Dodi just managed to stop herself from shuddering. The smell of coffee made her want to hurl. 'I think I'll have fruit juice instead.'

Knowing that Thadie would ask her what was wrong with her—up until she'd fallen pregnant, coffee was her favourite food group—Dodi attempted to distract her. 'Where's Clyde?'

Thadie pulled her towards the cart selling coffee. 'He plays golf every Sunday.'

Dodi didn't think the world would stop turning if Clyde skipped golf once in a while.

'Besides, I told him I needed to spend some time with my brothers before the wedding, as a family. I haven't seen much of them, or you, lately. It's *so* nice to see you.'

Dodi pushed her hand into the crook of Thadie's elbow. 'I know, I'm so sorry. It's been mad. Are you okay?'

Thadie joined the line for coffee and stared down at the dusty floor, her shoulders lifting. 'I don't know. I'm getting married in a month and it's starting to get real, you know?'

A bit too real? Real enough and scary enough for her

to call it off? She was debating whether she should verbalise her concerns about Thadie's marriage when she saw a very familiar person, walking hand in hand with a dark-haired woman. She sucked in her breath, feeling a little lightheaded.

She'd hadn't seen him since the day she broke up with him, a couple of days after Lily's death and before her funeral, and Dan looked just the way she remembered him, with his thick hair and his glasses falling halfway down his nose. He was dressed in his usual summer uniform of shorts and a boldly patterned printed shirt, this one in bright yellows and greens.

As if feeling her eyes on him, Dan looked around and he jerked, just a little, when he recognised her.

He lifted his hand, sort of waved and sent a swift smile. God, Johannesburg had a population of six million people and she had to run into Dan at a farmers' market outside of the city. What were the chances and why was life punishing her like this?

Dan mouthed some words and she wished she could pretend that she couldn't understand him. *Are you okay?*

No, I'm not okay, she wanted to scream. *You cheated on and lied to me, played mind games with me!*

Dodi closed her eyes and shook her head, instinctively wrapping her hands around her middle, feeling as if she was about to fall apart. Losing his friendship, that closeness, still made her heart ache, dammit.

When she opened her eyes, she saw a woman tugging him away. He looked back, just once, his face filled with sadness and regret. But Dodi knew he wasn't sorry. He'd loved making her life hell. Dan was an excellent actor.

'Dan doesn't look a day older,' Thadie commented.

She nodded, unable to speak.

Thadie rubbed her upper arm, giving her comfort. 'Still hurts, huh?'

'I think it always will,' Dodi reluctantly admitted. She wished she could forget about him, forgive him for what he'd done, but she couldn't. He'd played with her mind, her life and her emotions, and betrayed their friendship.

She'd never allow anyone to do that to her again. She'd never give anyone that amount of emotional power over her again.

Dodi glanced over to Jago and saw that he was standing a little way from them, talking to the bodyguard and Micah. The three men, tall, fit and devastatingly good-looking, were garnering a lot of attention, mostly female. There was a lot of hair-twirling, flirty smiles, looks over shoulders. None of them noticed.

Dan was in the past, and she had a baby to focus on, so Dodi pushed back her shoulders and decided to forget about her waste-of-oxygen ex and enjoy the time with her best friend.

Thadie pulled her glasses off her face, folded the arms and tapped them against her palm. 'So, did you hear that Jago has rented out his house?'

It was a blatant change of subject but one that made Dodi's mouth drop open in shock. Hadleigh House? His family home? 'But that house has been in your family for decades! Where are he and Micah going to live? What about the staff?'

Thadie rolled her eyes. 'Not Hadleigh, goose! His own house, the one he lived in with Anju.'

Oh! *That* house. Dodi raised her eyebrows. 'Really?'

'Mmm. He sent in the movers, and they packed everything up. He asked me where he could donate her clothes, sent her books to a second-hand shop, sent other stuff to her family. He took a couple of days off work last week to sort through the house.'

Really? *Wow.*

'My oldest brother is different,' Thadie commented after a short silence. 'More relaxed, warmer. Would you know why?'

Oh, God, the interrogation was about to start. Dodi placed her hand on her heart, forcing her eyes wide. 'Why would I know?'

Thadie narrowed her eyes at her. 'You suck at lying, Do. What is going on with you two?'

Dodi was about to reply when Jago's familiar scent hit her nose and his hand landed on her lower back. 'The boys want to visit the mini petting zoo, so Micah and I thought we'd head over there. It'll give you two a little time alone,' he said.

She scowled at him. Honestly, this wasn't the time for him to be considerate! Dodi widened her eyes in panic, desperately hoping Jago would read her mind and suggest something they could all do together. Anything to prevent the cross-examination she was bound to face if she and Thadie were left alone.

Thadie sent her a wicked grin. 'What a wonderful idea! Dodi and I have so much to catch up on and we'd love a little girl time!'

Dodi grimaced. Thadie was her best friend and she loved her, but knew how relentless she could be when she knew something was afoot. Dodi looked at the broad backs of the departing Le Roux brothers and wished she were going with them. Dragging her feet, she followed Thadie to a table under a white tent and knew that within ten minutes Thadie would know that a) Dodi was sleeping with her brother, and b) she was going to be their baby's aunt.

She and Jago wanted to keep the news to themselves for a bit longer, but that wasn't going to happen because there was no way she was going to lie to her best friend. Oh, well, Dodi thought, shrugging.

It was all Jago's fault for being kind and thoughtful. As they said, no good deed went unpunished.

'I cannot believe you didn't tell me earlier! How could you keep this from me?' Thadie demanded via a video call, later that evening.

They'd covered this ground earlier when Dodi finally admitted that she was pregnant and that Jago was the father of her baby.

'You have a lot on your plate, Thads, and I didn't want to take attention away from you and your wedding,' Dodi explained, *again*.

Thadie waved her words away. 'My best friend is having my brother's baby! That's something I needed to know.'

'Sorry,' Dodi apologised. Again. For what felt like the hundredth time. But she knew Thadie was more excited than mad, and that there wasn't any heat behind her accusations.

'I hope you have a boy—I really do. But I also hope you have a girl…oh, a girl would be magical!' Thadie rattled on, her dark eyes dancing with joy. 'Maybe you'll have twins!'

Her heart lurched in fear. Two babies? No, thank you! 'Shut your mouth,' she told Thadie.

Thadie's laugh sounded a little wicked. 'Twins are exactly what you deserve for keeping this news from us.'

When Jago, Micah and the twins had rejoined them

this morning at the market, Thadie immediately asked Jago whether he had something to tell Micah and Jago instantly knew the game was up. Their eyes had connected, she'd shrugged and, after scowling at Thadie, he told Micah that she was pregnant and that the baby was his.

Micah, to his credit, had simply raised his eyebrows, kissed her cheek and given Jago one of those half-hugs men excelled at.

Dodi had no doubt Jago had received a *What the hell?* phone call from his twin.

'So, I'm still not clear on something…'

Oh, God, she knew what was coming.

'Are you and Jago together or not?' Thadie demanded.

How could she answer that question when she had no idea what they were, nor how they were going to be?

The best way to answer Thadie was, Dodi quickly decided, to distract her. 'Your bridesmaids' dresses arrived. We need to arrange a final fitting.'

'Stop trying to change the subject! Are you and Jago—?'

Dodi slapped her hand to her mouth, faked a heave and waved her hands in the air. 'Got to go! Morning sickness!'

Thadie still managed to get a few words in as she fumbled to disconnect the call. 'You are such a liar, Elodie Kate Davis!'

She was. Absolutely.

Exhausted by the long day and Thadie's interrogations, she walked from Jago's private sitting room onto his balcony and saw that he was talking on his phone. Seeing her, he wrapped up his conversation.

'That was Micah, checking in.'

Dodi dropped into the sofa next to him, sighing at

how comfortable it was. The space was protected from the elements but still, a sofa this expensive, this lovely, shouldn't be outside. Ever.

'Let me guess…he wants to know whether we are together or not.'

'Yep.'

Dodi narrowed her eyes. 'And I bet your nosy sister nagged him to call.'

'Yep.'

Dodi pulled a face. 'God, she's relentless.'

Jago stretched out his long legs, linking his hands on his stomach, his expression thoughtful. 'We're all determined people—having a father like Theo, it's inevitable. But Thadie got a double dose. It's the only trait she inherited from our father, thank God.'

'You didn't like him much, did you?' Dodi asked.

'Did you like him?' he countered.

'I hardly knew him,' she replied. 'But he was always charming to me.'

'Of course he was—that was how he was with most people,' Jago bitterly replied. 'That wasn't the person he was at his core.'

'So who was he, Jago?'

Jago ran his finger up and down the side of his cold beer bottle. 'Theo established Le Roux International himself. He didn't have any family money behind him. He hustled and lied, ducked and dived, made promises he couldn't keep, over-promised and under-delivered. But somehow, because he was so damn charismatic, he made it work. Even when the business took off, even after he made his first million, billion, he still couldn't stick to the truth. Sometimes I think he lied to keep people unbalanced, because it was fun, to see if he could get away with it, and he always did. He was

Theo Le Roux, wealthy, successful, with this huge personality and he was feted and adored.'

Dodi heard the bitter tone in his voice. 'Did he lie to you? To your siblings?'

Jago's expression tightened. 'All the time. He made promises to us, and my mum, that he never kept. He said we could get a dog one day, changed his mind the next. Said that if I got a B plus for maths I could get a motorbike, the next report card I needed to get an A, then when I did the goalposts moved again. He promised to join us on holiday, never did. Promised us he'd be there for Christmas, missed many of those.'

So much bitterness, so much pain.

'He treated my mum badly, kept her constantly off-balance, neurotic. Praising her one moment, belittling her the next. He did that to Micah and me as well. One day we were his favourite child, the next day we were scum on his shoe. He pitted us against each other, created competitions, fostered enmity. He hated that we were so close and tried whatever he could to come between us, between us and our mum. Everything was always about him, all the time.

'My father fed off drama and he loved arguments, fights, confrontation. His volatility was the reason I learned to read people and situations. I learned to anticipate trouble and how to take control of a situation, how to make it work for me, and, more importantly, my siblings. Because of him, I have back-up plans for my back-up plan.'

Dodi winced. She hadn't had the most functional of childhoods, it had been ridiculously unstable, but she hadn't lived in a war zone. Theo had been an emotional abuser, she realised. She wondered if Jago knew and accepted that.

Jago picked up his beer bottle and pointed it at her

stomach. 'He's the reason I'm terrified of being a father. I'm scared I will do to my kid what my dad did to me.'

Dodi's mouth gaped open in shock. 'That's the most ridiculous thing I've ever heard!'

'Why? I am very like my father,' Jago replied, sounding super-reasonable. 'I'm demanding, competitive, married to my job. I'm impatient and abrupt.'

'You also love your brother and sister and treat them with kindness and respect. Sure, you're very straightforward, but you aren't cruel and you don't play mind games!' Dodi protested.

'How do you know, Dodi? You haven't spent that much time with me.'

How did she know? She wasn't sure, but she did. She'd somehow managed to pull away some of that hard shell and peek below the surface, and the man underneath the tough exterior was softer and more sensitive than the world realised. Someone who wanted a family, to love and be loved in return.

But he, like her, was too scared of taking that chance, of being hurt again.

'Who was the guy at the farmers' market today?'

Dodi blinked at his change of subject and flushed when his words sank in. 'Uh…who?'

Jago glared at her. 'Don't treat me like an idiot, Dodi. You and Thadie were both staring at him like he was a threat.'

Dammit! She'd hoped Jago hadn't noticed. A stupid wish because there was nobody more observant than the older Le Roux twin and she now knew why. It was because his father had made him that way.

'Dan? Well…uh…that's a long story.'

'I'm not going anywhere,' Jago told her.

Dammit.

CHAPTER TEN

ONLY THADIE KNEW the whole story, knew how Dan had blindsided and betrayed her. How much it hurt and that she felt like the world's biggest idiot for not having seen through him years ago. That thinking of him, what he'd done, was like taking a knife to her belly and slowly cutting herself open.

'Please tell me, Do.'

It was that soft 'please' that did it, the look in his eyes telling her she could trust him. But could she, though? She didn't know…

But Jago had been brave enough to tell her about his father and his childhood. Surely she could tell him about Dan's betrayal?

Where to start? When they'd met was as good a place as any. 'Lily sent me to a high school down the road from her house, a huge school with thousands of students. I'd only ever attended small, rural schools, so I was lost and scared and completely overwhelmed. Dan found me, scooped me up and took me under his wing. He wasn't the most popular guy around, but neither was he bullied…he was normal, I guess. He had a group of friends, guys and girls, and he pulled me into his group. I felt blessed and grateful to have a group.'

Jago's gaze was steady on her face. 'That sounds pretty normal.'

One would think. 'Yes, it does. Except that I'd make a new friend or be invited out on a date, and it would be fine for a week or two and then I'd be dropped like a hot potato. It happened a few times and I couldn't understand it because I didn't do anything wrong. Dan would hold me while I cried and tell me not to worry about them, that he and I were friends and nothing else mattered. It happened five, maybe six times, and I stopped going on dates, trying to make friends, because it hurt so much. Dan became my only friend, and he was my lifeline, my support structure, everything that mattered to me. We became lovers in my final year of school and remained together until just before my grandmother died.'

'So what happened that caused you to break up?'

Right, straight to the heart of the matter. 'A couple of weeks before Lily died, I was trying to nurse her, run her salon, and also trying to come to terms with her imminent passing. One day I got a call from a woman telling me that she and Dan had been having an affair for a few months.'

Jago winced. 'Ouch.'

'Yeah. Naturally, I didn't believe her, but she sent me pictures of them together, text messages, emails. Dan had told her that he didn't love me, couldn't stand me but he was worried I'd do something if he broke up with me. Some of the things he said about me were truly horrible.'

Jago said something indistinct but distinctly uncomplimentary about her ex and Dodi almost smiled.

She might as well tell him the rest, although it wasn't

a pretty story. 'His lover, mistress, whatever, then told me something else that rocked my world.'

Jago's eyebrows rose, waiting for her to continue.

'So, back at school, those friends I made? Well, Dan bragged to her that he poisoned the well. As soon as he saw there was a connection, he went to them and quietly told them I was talking about them behind their backs, that I was playing with them, that I thought they were trash. He said that I was a little unbalanced and that they shouldn't confront me, that it might push me over the edge. Naturally, they dumped me, and I had no idea why.

'It kept happening, even at university—Dan and I went to the same one—and into my twenties, and I eventually stopped trying to make friends altogether. I didn't want to get hurt any more. I thought I was destined to have one friend, one lover.'

'But you and Thadie remained friends. He didn't manage to come between you.'

She shrugged. 'We shared a flat. He couldn't be there all the time. He and Thadie hated each other. She tried to tell me he was separating me from people, that he was trying to isolate me, but I didn't—couldn't, wouldn't—believe her.'

Jago grimaced.

'He saw me as *his*, his project, his property. He didn't particularly want me, hence the many flings and affairs, but he didn't want anyone else to have me either. If his lover hadn't called me, I would've married him,' Dodi admitted. 'It scares me to think that he would've manoeuvred me into marrying him.'

Dodi looked at Jago and tried, and failed, to smile.

'I have this thing about being pushed where I don't want to go, Jago.'

Would he hear her message, understand what she was trying to say?

Jago took a sip of his beer, looking thoughtful. 'Doesn't everyone want to make their own decisions, be in charge of their destiny?' he quietly asked.

'I'm sure they do.' Dodi leaned forward and captured her hands between her thighs. 'But it's a big thing for me because I've found myself in situations that I didn't choose, and they changed my life.'

'Being sent to live with your grandmother without warning, being cheated on, inheriting a business you didn't want,' he mused.

Exactly! 'I promised myself I wouldn't allow myself to ever be put in a situation that wasn't of my choice again.' She looked down at her hands and sighed. 'That's why this…this…thing with you is so hard. I didn't choose to have this baby—'

'I thought you said you wanted it,' Jago interjected, frowning.

Dodi waved her hands around, frustrated. 'I do! I'm just getting used to the idea and the fact that it's, once again, something that's been thrust on me.'

'And on me,' Jago pointed out.

Fair enough.

'I hear you, Elodie Kate. The thing is, we don't have to figure everything out right now. We have time.'

Seven months could, and would, fly past. They didn't have as much time as they thought.

The sound of Jago setting his beer bottle on the wrought-iron table disturbed the quiet, lazy summer evening. Here at Hadleigh House, she could pretend they weren't in the middle of a metropolis, living in a sprawling city. She felt as though she were on a country estate, far away from the hustle of city life. It was fast becoming her favourite place to be.

But this place wouldn't mean anything if Jago wasn't in it. It would be just another house filled with expensive stuff, but Jago made it home.

Home. Dear Lord…*home?* Or was home wherever Jago was, where she wanted to be? She thought it might just be because… Oh, *God.*

'Dodi?'

She blinked, trying to focus and his intense expression came back into focus. 'I am your baby's father and yes, while the thought of raising a child scares me, I do want to be part of the process. Don't doubt that, sweetheart. I'm not going anywhere.'

She saw the sincerity in his expression and the tenderness in his eyes. She was starting to trust him, she admitted silently. Panic coated her throat and lodged on her tongue. She loved being with him, sleeping with him, enjoyed their chats, but it would be stupid to trust him, or anyone else, with her very fragile heart.

She should tell him they couldn't go anywhere, that they'd run out of road. She wanted to suggest that they be lovers until they tired of each other…

She scoffed at her thoughts. She doubted she'd ever tire of having Jago in her arms, in her body or her bed. Because…

Could she say it, even to herself? Could she even think it?

Was she, maybe, possibly, falling for Jago? Could she be falling in love with him?

Dodi stared at him, knowing she needed to try and

talk herself out of the notion but knowing it was impossible. Some part of her—whether it was little or big was yet to be decided—was in love with Jago. God help her.

He couldn't know, not yet…possibly not ever. Would he hear it in her voice, see it in her eyes? She couldn't let that happen, not before she regained control, pushed it away.

She finally, finally, found the courage to meet his eyes and was surprised to see an understanding smile. 'It's overwhelming, right?' he softly asked. He was talking about the baby, thank God. He had to be.

'Very,' she admitted. She sighed, thinking that she could do with some time alone, to think.

Jago stood up and picked up his empty beer bottle. 'It's been a long day and we're both tired, played out.'

How did he do that? How did he know what she was feeling, what she needed without her having to say a word?

'Okay,' Dodi agreed, following him to his feet.

Jago walked around the table to where she stood and gently gripped her chin in his big hand and looked down into her face, his expression intense. 'You're going to have to trust someone at some time, Elodie Kate. I hope that person is me.'

She managed a small smile, a quick nod and tried not to sigh when Jago dropped a hard kiss on her open mouth. 'Come to bed now,' he softly suggested.

She stared at his broad hand for a moment before sliding her own hand into it and following him back into his sitting room, and then into his bedroom, wishing she could tell him that trust was an essential part of love, and if she couldn't trust him, she couldn't love him.

Wouldn't let herself love him.

Because loving, and losing, Jago would destroy her. There would be no climbing out if she toppled into that deep abyss.

Unable to sleep, Jago left Dodi in his bed, walked outside, and dived into the pool. After swimming for nearly an hour, and still feeling edgy, he sat on the side of the massive pool, his feet dangling. Water ran down his body, from his hair, and his limbs felt hot and heavy.

Normally exercise cleared his head, sharpened his thinking, but that hadn't happened tonight. If anything he was more confused than ever.

And it was all Dodi's fault.

The woman disoriented him, made him feel a hundred emotions at once, spun him in a thousand directions simultaneously.

Leaning back on his hands, Jago looked up at the bright moon, immediately seeing the rabbit shape on its surface, something one could only see from the southern hemisphere. He inhaled the fragrant air, heat mingling with the smell of roses from the extensive garden to his right. He smiled at the deep bellow of a bullfrog. Even in the city, he still felt connected to primal Africa. It was in her heat, her smells, her sounds and her essence. But saying that, he needed to get into the bush, somewhere wild, and he wanted to take Dodi with him.

Would Dodi agree to step away with him, to go to an unknown place with few roads, no mobile phone reception and no people? He wasn't sure. After hearing how her piece-of-crap ex had treated her, he finally understood Dodi's reluctance to trust, didn't blame her for being wary about people and men.

But he still wanted her to trust him, to know, deep

down, that he would never, ever hurt her or their child. She needed to accept that she was under his protection and that he'd rather die than see her in any sort of distress.

Yes, he was protective of her, would be protective of his kid, but there was so much more to his feelings for his sister's best friend than his need to shield her.

He adored her body and loved being naked with her. He'd enjoyed a healthy sex life with Anju, had had many sexual encounters since she'd died, but with Dodi, the act seemed deeper, more mysterious, intense. The physical release wasn't the end goal. She wasn't a way to blow off steam. With Dodi, it was the journey, not the destination that was important.

And that was very, very new.

He couldn't help but compare her to Anju—his wife was the only long-term partner he'd had and, as such, his only reference.

He'd enjoyed Anju's astounding intellect and their highbrow conversations about politics, neuroscience, chemistry and astronomy. But they'd never laughed or joked around, discussed the mundane and the ridiculous, the normal and the nonsensical. There was a good chance that he and Dodi would never talk about the latest brain-imaging techniques or scientific discoveries, but they could discuss books and music and movies, politics and religion.

She'd make him laugh, and curse, and she would challenge him to feel more, be more, *engage* more.

And that wasn't a bad thing.

He'd thought he'd been so clever, constructing his life and his marriage to be safe, to be stable. In trying to avoid drama, he'd created a life that was, in all honesty, stiflingly boring. It was hard to admit that he'd been living on the edge of life, scared to swim to the centre. In the middle of the pool of life were the currents, the whirlpools and rapids, where things got interesting. It was safe at the edges, but it was also deeply uninteresting, and mind-numbingly predictable.

The centre held energy, it demanded you engage, be present. Dodi was turning out to be his centre, his favourite whirlpool, the current taking him on a new journey.

Her dropping into his life, with her vibrant looks and personality, had flipped his world upside down and yeah, she was everything he needed. Up until now, he hadn't *lived* life, he'd operated to the side of it, scared to wade out of the shallows.

Sure, his childhood had been tough. He hated the way his father had acted, and the way he had raised them…

But he wasn't his dad, didn't have to make the same choices his father had and wasn't obliged to *be* his father. His childhood was over, and he couldn't keep living in the past or letting his father and his actions affect what he did today, how he lived his life.

And, since he was going to be a father, he needed to teach his kid to be brave, to live authentically, to take chances, to engage with the world. If he kept himself separate, remained on the sidelines of life, then that was what his child would do too…

No, he wanted his child to grab life by the horns and go on a wild ride, skidding in at the end on a whoop and a grin, yelling that he'd had a hell of a ride.

Actually, that was how he wanted to be. He'd wasted so much time looking for trouble, trying to keep himself safe…and he was done. He wanted to live, dammit. Feel. Be present. If he was going to have another relationship, create a family, then he had to do it properly, go all in and skip the emotional guardrails and airbags. If he wanted to live the rest of his life with Dodi, with his kid, creating a life and a family with her, he needed to be brave, open, fully present, and God…emotionally available.

The thought made his hands tremble.

If he wanted the happy-ever-after with Dodi, he first had to get her to trust him. But she was as emotionally wary, as scarred as he was. Could they build something new, start afresh, or was he tilting at windmills, setting himself up for a sky-high fall?

He didn't know, couldn't predict the outcome. But when faced with the alternative—living a half-life, with Dodi on the periphery of it—he knew that he had to take this huge, crazy, scary leap.

And hope like hell that Dodi would catch him.

'I do want to be part of the process. Don't doubt that, sweetheart. I'm not going anywhere.'

Dodi stood in her shower stall, her hands flat against the wall, her lips pursed, deep in thought as she remembered Jago's words from their intense conversation two weeks ago. Did she believe him? Would he stick around?

She trusted Jago, as much as she trusted anyone, and she knew he was a straight-shooting guy, someone who didn't mince words and who did what he said…

He was also considerate and thoughtful, and since telling him she was pregnant he'd shown her that he cared for her. He'd looked her car over, decided it needed new tyres, and loaned her another car while her tyres were being changed. While her car was in the workshop, he'd also arranged for it to have a top-to-bottom service. Frankly, she was surprised he hadn't replaced the thing!

Jabu, his butler, was now a frequent visitor to her house, always accompanied by a Hadleigh housemaid. She hadn't cleaned her house or done her laundry in over a month. Her freezer was stocked with nutritional meals, easy-to-heat food full of all the nutrients she and the baby needed.

Jago was taking care of her and, God help her, she liked it! She shouldn't, but she did. But she still harboured a deep-seated fear of being abandoned and couldn't shake the voice of doom that kept insisting that this couldn't last, that Jago would hurt and disappoint her. It was, after all, the pattern of her life.

She wasn't being fair to him. He hadn't done anything to deserve her mistrust and she wanted to enjoy their growing closeness, the intimacy that had sprung up between them. But something kept holding her back…

Her heart and her head were at war, that much was clear. Her heart was head-over-heels in love with the man, while her brain was asking if she was off her rocker. Her heart wanted to tell him how she felt about him, and her brain wanted to slap a gag over her mouth.

Her heart insisted she could trust him. Her brain was deeply concerned that she was losing her capacity for rational thought. She felt as if she was playing host to two squabbling teenagers, both determined to be in control, to have the upper hand.

She did love Jago but she also wanted to stay safe. She wanted him in her life, to share her life—for her to share his—but she didn't want to open herself up to being disappointed, to be let down by him. She wanted his beautiful body, to feel his touch every day and in every way, but she needed to keep her heart encased in Teflon. She wanted everything to change but she also wanted things to stay the same.

But she wasn't the only one with skin in the game, so what did Jago want? Did she even have the first clue? Dodi snapped her thumbnail against her front tooth, deep in thought.

He wasn't interested in love. He'd said as much. He didn't want the messiness and the drama of being in a relationship. He'd married Anju to have a drama-free, cleverly constructed life with someone whose company he enjoyed, whose body he loved. They'd entered into a well-thought-out arrangement, and it seemed to have worked.

Why couldn't she and Jago have something similar?

She wasn't talking about marriage—that was too complicated—but maybe they could live together, sleep together, raise their child together. They could sleep in the same bed, have hot sex, which they both enjoyed.

And, if they felt like it, they could talk about their lives, thoughts, and feelings.

Could it work? Was she brave enough to suggest such a thing?

A hard rap on the bathroom door made her jump. She spun around as Jago opened the bathroom door and stepped inside, dressed in dark suit trousers that hugged his muscular thighs and a white button-down shirt that skated across his broad chest. A mint-green tie, still to be knotted, hung down his chest. He'd shaved and his hair was carefully tousled. Lord, he was hot.

Jago flashed her a smile. 'No, I'm not getting into the shower with you, temptress. I've got to get moving.'

His ability to read her mind still disconcerted her. Jago waited for her to turn off the water and then opened the shower door and handed her a towel. 'I'm running late but I need to talk to you before I go.'

She caught the worry in his eyes and frowned as she wrapped the towel around her torso. She was about to ask him what was wrong, but he walked back into her bedroom. Concerned, Dodi quickly dried off, ran a comb through her hair and pulled on her dressing gown. In her bedroom, Jago stood by her window, frowning as he gulped from his steaming coffee cup. 'I made you some ginger tea.'

'Thank you,' she said, sitting down on the edge of the bed before picking up her cup. 'What's up? You're looking quite grim.'

'Have you seen the weather report this morning?'

He knew she hadn't. They'd woken up, rolled towards each other and made love. Then she'd dozed as he showered and changed. Then she'd showered…

Besides, she wasn't someone who routinely checked the weather. It was summer in Africa and that meant heat and the occasional thunderstorm. What was the point of routinely checking something she couldn't control?

'They are predicting a torrential downpour this afternoon, with the possibility of huge hail.' Right, Jago did check weather reports. That made sense, as he had a habit of scanning his world for potential disruptions and changes.

'It's going to cause havoc on the roads. I don't want you driving in it.'

She'd navigated the crazy roads of this city for a long time and she wasn't worried.

'Can you leave work early today?' Jago demanded, and Dodi bristled at the command she heard in his voice. 'They are expecting the worst of it to hit around six, but I'd prefer it if you were off the roads way before then.'

Dodi pushed her hand through her wet hair. 'I'll be fine, Jago. They always exaggerate!'

She could see the irritation in his eyes, the tension in his jaw. 'I don't want you driving in torrential rain,' he stated through gritted teeth. 'Close your business early and get home. Please.'

The *please* he uttered didn't detract from the force of his order. How she hated being told what to do, being made to do something she didn't want to do!

Deciding to play him at his own game, she tipped her head to the side and narrowed her eyes. 'Okay, then you get home before the storm strikes too. I don't want you driving in torrential rain either. Blow off your appointments and get home early.'

'I have a board meeting at five that's going to take about five or six hours—'

'Five or six hours? What are you discussing, how to rule the world?' she asked, trying to lighten the mood.

He didn't smile. 'Micah and I are presenting some new projects to the board, some of which will take the company in a whole new direction. It's a meeting that will have massive consequences for the company and will present some significant risks. It's probably the most important board meeting since my father died. But I wish we could delay it.'

'Why don't you?' Dodi asked.

'It's difficult to find a date that suits all the board members, and some of the projects are time-sensitive. If we don't get their approval tonight, we'll miss our window of opportunity,' he explained. 'I have to be there. It's vitally important.'

And her business was vitally important to her. 'I have brides coming in at four. I can't leave L&E either.'

Jago slammed his coffee cup down and rubbed his hands over his face. 'I just want you to be safe, dammit.'

'I'm a grown woman, Jago—I can make my own decisions about my business, my safety and my actions.'

'You're pregnant!' he yelled.

She was, but so what? 'I didn't lose my ability to act independently, or to think, when you impregnated me, Jago.'

He released a low growl and stomped over to the walk-in wardrobe, where he'd hung his suit jacket. He returned, pulling it on with jerky movements. 'I'm just trying to look after you, Elodie Kate! I'm concerned, that's all.'

She was pretty sure he was, but it felt as if he was trying to bend her to his will. Maybe she was overreacting, maybe not, but she couldn't allow him to bark orders at her and expect her to obey. She was perfectly capable of looking after herself, and she didn't need a big, bossy billionaire telling her what to do and how to do it! Jago stopped in front of her and glared down at her.

'Will you, at the very least, let me know your plans? I need to know when you leave and that you are safely home. I'll be in the board meeting, so I won't be able to respond, but I'll see your message.'

He still looked frustrated, but his suggestion was reasonable, so she nodded. 'Okay.'

Jago bent down and dropped a hard kiss on her mouth. 'It would be so much easier if you just did as I asked, Elodie Kate.'

'I'd bore you within a week if I did that,' Dodi informed him. *And I'd lose all respect for myself.* 'You should go, Jago—you said you're already late.'

Jago nodded and walked to the door. He placed his hand on the doorframe and looked back at her, his expression hesitant. 'I'll probably only make it home by midnight tonight, if I'm lucky. I'll see you later, okay?'

He thought of her home as his and she thought of his as hers. Was he, maybe, feeling something more for her? Could he, possibly, be having feelings for her? The thoughts made her stomach fizz, her brain a little fuzzy from happiness. She knew hope was dangerous, that she was setting herself up for disappointment, but Jago was a deliberate guy who was careful not to raise expectations. What he said, he meant…

'Do not drive in that storm!' he told her again, the command in his voice unmistakable, and her excitement fizzled and died. She heard the sound of his size thirteens running down her steps, the slam of her front door. Dodi shook her head, bewildered by their argument, the confusion it raised, and the highs and the lows of their interactions. Ten minutes ago, she'd been considering a life with this man, living together, trying to build something. She'd thought that he might be feeling the same, just a little. But then his commands and demands, his banked frustration at not getting his way, made her wonder if she could be with him, whether they had a future together.

It made her question whether he'd ever consider her an equal partner and not someone under his protection, someone whose life he wanted to manipulate and direct, someone who'd manoeuvre her into situations she didn't want or choose. And if she didn't do as he wanted, if she baulked too often, would he decide that she wasn't worth his effort and time? Would he think that his life was better off without her in it? Would he abandon her, leaving her holding her shattered heart?

Maybe it was better not to take that chance, maybe it was better to keep her emotional distance, to erect her emotional guardrails again.

Dodi flopped back on her bed and turned her head to look out of her window. She scowled at the blue sky. There was a storm on the way, and not just in the meteorological sense.

CHAPTER ELEVEN

DODI, HER HEART in her mouth, hands wet with perspiration, peered through the driving rain, and crawled down Jago's street, looking for the gates to Hadleigh House. It was shortly after six and yes, the storm had rolled in, more vicious than she'd expected. Jago had called it and she wished she'd left work early because the visibility was dreadful, the roads were river-like and there was still, so she'd been told, an excellent chance of hail.

Dodi heard the sharp crack of lightning, felt the fizz of electricity and jumped at the boom of thunder. She needed to get off the road as soon as possible… where the hell was Hadleigh House?

She'd been annoyed earlier when a Le Roux intern dropped off an envelope from Jago containing the remote control to an electric gate and a set of keys.

His terse note was not a heartfelt love letter.

If you're going to be stubborn and stay at work, at least drive to Hadleigh House instead of trying to make your way across town to your place. It's closer. Let me know when you leave and when you arrive. Also, Jabu is on holiday, so the house is empty. Alarm code below.

She'd been leaving work when the heavens opened and she quickly decided that driving to Jago's house was the sensible option. She was stubborn but not, she hoped, stupid.

Dodi gripped her steering wheel tighter and narrowed her eyes, trying to get her bearings. Forty-eight, fifty…she was getting close. Her windscreen wipers were operating at full speed and her windshield was steaming up, and she lifted her hand to clear a small circle in front of her. As she caught sight of the gates to Jago's house, she heard the sharp ping of something hard hitting her roof and she cursed. Hail! Dammit!

She swung into Jago's driveway and fumbled for the remote control to open the gates, cursing the pebble-sized hailstones bouncing off the bonnet. Her car was going to look like a golf ball after this.

The gates opened and Dodi crawled up the drive. She usually parked to the side of the house but tonight she was going to get as close as she could to the entrance, and when the hailstones stopped she'd run up the stone stairs and into Jago's house.

Dodi waited for five minutes before the worst of the hail stopped. The rain was still bucketing down, and lightning and thunder still chased each other around the sky. She'd get wet—why wasn't she one of those organised people who kept an umbrella in her car?—but that was okay. It was just water. She'd survive. Deciding to leave her bag in her car, Dodi wrapped her phone into the hem of her shirt to protect it from getting soaked, grabbed Jago's bunch of keys and pushed open her car door, fighting the wind wanting to slam it closed.

Bending her head, she ran through the hard rain, wincing as the needle-hard droplets slammed into her face and plastered her hair and clothes to her body. By the time she reached the stone steps, she was soaked through. She slowed down as she hurried up the steps, wiping her eyes and pushing back her wet hair. The huge front door was just there, and, behind it, warmth and safety. She'd send a message to Jago telling him she was safe and then she'd dry off, make herself some tea. And when the storm died down she'd take a long, hot shower. Bliss…she couldn't wait.

Dodi stepped onto the slate floor of the portico, took two steps, maybe three, and then her feet slid out from under her and her butt slammed down, bouncing off the tiles. Her back hit the floor and then her head. Burning pain ratcheted up her spine and she released a high-pitched scream, which was immediately sucked into the storm.

Her last thoughts as she passed out were a quick prayer that her baby was okay. She needed Jago…and she needed him *now.*

Jago opened the door to Dodi's private hospital room and leaned his shoulder on the doorframe, happy to watch her sleep. The past twelve hours had been some of the worst of his life and he'd felt as though his heart had started and restarted a hundred times.

He never, ever wanted to relive last night. And he'd do everything in his power to make sure that Dodi would always be safe and protected, dammit.

He could've lost her last night and the thought made his heart drop like a stone to his shoes and his throat close. It was time they stopped mucking around and she moved in with him, where he could look after her and love her.

Because love her he did. More than he'd ever believed possible. He'd been fighting his feelings, ignoring the sensations he didn't recognise—and therefore weren't, in his rational mind, valid—determined to keep things between them under control.

Her falling, cracking her head—the possibility of losing her—was a wake-up-and-face-the-music call. For the first time in his life, he felt as if his life was incomplete, that up until now he'd been unaware of the Dodi-sized hole in his life. He needed her: she made him a better man. A life without her in it was a wasteland, grey, wet and utterly miserable. She was light, colour, fun, laughter…love.

She was his everything. Dodi sighed, her eyes opened and she turned her head to the door, a soft smile on her face. 'Hi,' she murmured.

Jago walked over to the bed, sat down next to her and stroked his thumb over her still pale cheek. 'Hi back. How are you feeling?'

'A bit of a headache…' Dodi's eyes widened, and she shot up, panic on her face. 'The baby…is our baby okay?'

He gripped her shoulders, gently squeezed and bent his head so that he could look directly into her eyes. 'The baby is fine, Dodi. Relax.'

It took her a few deep breaths for his news to make sense. 'Are you sure?' she demanded, her voice shrill.

'Very. They did an ultrasound, and all is well.'

The panic in her eyes receded and was quickly replaced by tears. Of gratitude, he presumed. She flopped back on the pillow and closed her eyes. 'Thank God, thank God.'

He wholeheartedly agreed. Thank God. Jago found

the remote control and lifted the bed so that Dodi sat upright. He resumed his place next to her and placed his hand on her thigh. 'Don't you remember having the ultrasound?'

The doctor said that some of her memories might be fuzzy as she'd cracked her head quite hard. She hadn't needed stitches but she did have a large goose egg on the back of her head.

Dodi shrugged. 'I remember bits and pieces of last night, not much. I remember running up the steps, slipping, my butt hitting the floor and how sore it was.'

'You bruised your coccyx and smacked the back of your head,' Jago told her. 'You have a minor concussion.'

'That explains the headache,' Dodi commented. 'Who found me?'

'I did. You didn't let me know that you were home and I felt uneasy.' Jago brushed her hair off her forehead and tucked it behind her ear. 'I couldn't concentrate, at all, so I excused myself from the board meeting and left the room.'

Dodi winced. 'Were they mad?'

He shrugged. 'It was at a crucial point in the presentation, so they weren't impressed, but I couldn't continue, I couldn't focus on anything but my rising dread. I tried to call you but your phone just rang and rang.'

'I'm sorry, I didn't mean to scare you.'

'You took ten years off my life,' Jago ruefully told her. 'I used an app to find your phone, saw that you were at my house, but you weren't inside because the alarm was still on. I checked the camera feeds and saw you lying outside the front door. My heart stopped.'

She winced and gestured for him to continue. 'I

called for an ambulance, told Micah I was leaving and raced home.'

Despite the torrential rain, he'd made the trip home in ten minutes instead of his usual fifteen. It had been a hair-raising trip, not knowing how seriously she was injured.

'You left your important board meeting for me?' Dodi asked, linking her fingers in his.

He'd move mountains for her if he could.

'I thought it crucially important that you were there.'

Not as important as her. He shrugged. 'Micah handled it.'

'And did they vote for your changes?' Dodi asked, tipping her head to the side.

He didn't know and didn't much care. Not at this moment, anyway. She was all that was important, his entire focus. 'I have no idea.'

Dodi sighed, sat up and draped her arms around his neck, snuggling in. 'I remember you looking over me last night, your hand stroking my hair back. I was so very glad to see you, to have you there.'

His hand drifted up and down her slim back. 'I'll always be there, Elodie Kate. And last night made me realise that it was ridiculous for us to live apart. I can't do that any more—I need to have you close by, need to be able to protect you.' He shuddered. 'I can't go through that again.'

She rubbed her hand over his back. 'It was an accident, Jago and I'm fine. The baby is fine.'

This time. He couldn't lose her, wouldn't take that risk. 'The doctor said that you can be discharged but he wants you taking it easy for the rest of the week.'

She nodded, wincing. 'I can do that.'

Progress, Jago thought on a smile. 'Then let's get you dressed, and I'll take you home.'

Dodi nodded and pushed back the bedcovers, trying to hide her wince. 'I can't wait to be in my bed, sleeping on my pillow.'

He shook his head. 'You're not going home. You're coming back to my place. Jabu and one of the maids are packing up your clothes and toiletries as we speak, and when you are up to it you can tell me what furniture you want to be moved to Hadleigh House. I know it's Lily's house and you might not want to sell it but maybe you can rent it out, partially furnished. Or we can store the stuff you don't want to get rid of.'

She stared at him, a frown pulling her eyebrows together. 'I'm sorry, I don't understand.'

Jago dumped the small overnight bag he'd brought with him, containing a change of her clothes. He pulled out a pair of loose summer trousers, a comfortable T-shirt, clean underwear. 'What's to understand? You're moving into my place, with me.'

Her fists bunched and the colour drained from her face. Her eyes turned a deep, hard blue and it was at that moment that Jago realised that in his haste to have her with him, to look after her and to love her, he'd badly miscalculated. He'd made a major decision without her input....

He rubbed his jaw, his mind going at a mile a minute, trying to work out how he could extract himself from the quicksand he'd blindly walked into.

'Please, please tell me that you didn't just say what I thought you did. You couldn't possibly have done all that without consulting me,' Dodi said, her voice ultra-polite. 'I told you how I feel about being pushed into situations not of my choosing, how I hate being manoeuvred, so you couldn't have done something so idiotic.'

He had. Jesus. Why hadn't he remembered that?

Because all he wanted this morning—after a night of sitting by her bedside staring at her, imagining a life without her in it—was to bind her to him, to hold her and keep her and protect her. She'd scared him senseless, and he'd just wanted her with him.

He hadn't thought further than meeting that objective. Stupid. So stupid.

Dodi bit down on her bottom lip and stared at her tightly linked hands. 'For a minute there, I was so happy, despite feeling like I've been run over by a truck. Our baby is fine and you prioritised me over your very important board meeting. You came to find me, and you were there for me. I felt at peace, knowing and trusting that you would be there for me, that you'd never let me down.'

But...because, hell, there was a great big but to follow.

Dodi rubbed her hands over her face and when she dropped them she looked stricken. 'But despite that, you still don't *get* it, you don't *get* me. I promised myself I'd never allow myself to be pushed around again, would never permit someone to force me in a direction I didn't want to go.'

God, he was a moron. Why hadn't he considered that? What the hell was wrong with him?

Dodi met his eyes, and hers were filled with pain. And not because she was physically hurting. 'Give me a reason why you'd do this, Jago. Please.'

Jago cursed the fact that he had no defence, that he could find no words to make it right. He wanted to tell her that he loved her, that he'd acted out of panic and passion, that he couldn't imagine not having her in his life so he'd taken steps to get her there. But the words stuck on his tongue, and he was unable to push them past his teeth. He'd never told a woman that he loved her, didn't know how. He could negotiate multi-billion deals, had, reputedly, balls of steel, but not when it came to love.

He didn't know how to explain, what to say. What words to use. How to *do* this.

Dodi shook her head, closed her eyes. 'This isn't going to work, Jago, it can't work. We've been kidding ourselves, confused by the attraction between us. You need to have control, and to plan and protect and I can't or won't be controlled, shoved into situations you think are best for me.' Dodi's voice was soft but strong and very, very resolute. She slid out of bed, gathered her clothes and nodded to the small bathroom. 'I'm going to change and you're going to leave.'

He opened his mouth to tell her that she didn't have a ride home, but she held up her hand and shook her head. 'I'm going to call Thadie, ask her to come and get me. And no, I won't badmouth you to your sister. But you'd better call Jabu and tell him to replace my stuff, and inform him, and anyone else you told, that I will *not* be moving in with you. Not today, tomorrow or any time in the future.'

Well, that sounded bloody final. Jago rubbed the area above his heart and watched her walk into the bathroom and close the door behind her. When he heard the lock engage, he knew that it was over and that he'd lost the only woman he'd ever loved.

And he'd done it within two months. He knew how to work fast, but that had to be a record…

Dodi walked into her busy salon and handed the sample dress to a consultant, watching the bride's eyes light up when she presented the frothy princess-style ballgown. She danced on the spot and her smile was as big as the sun.

She ran a reverent hand over the puffy tulle, her expression wondrous. 'I've been dreaming of this moment since I was eight. Trying on a dress, looking like a fairy-tale bride.'

God, another one who was so caught up in the nuptials and wasn't looking beyond the big day. Dodi handed her a tight smile and did an internal eye roll. 'I think it will look wonderful on you.'

She watched the bride walk towards the dressing room and rubbed the region above her heart. Since leaving Jago's house nearly a week ago, her heart felt heavy and full. She had acid in her stomach, and tears gathered in her throat. She missed him, so much. She felt like she was walking around with a red-hot heart, one that was, at all times, one bump away from disintegrating.

'She might be young but she's not rushing into this with her eyes closed.'

Dodi turned to look at the bride's mother, sitting on the two-seater sofa next to where she was standing. She hadn't even noticed the well-dressed woman sitting there, hair and make-up perfect. What else hadn't she noticed while she was wallowing around in her Jago-induced funk?

Dodi pulled up a polite smile. 'I'm sorry, I don't know what you mean.'

The older woman cocked her head to the side. 'Now, that's not true. You think she's only thinking of the wedding, hasn't paid any attention to being married, to being in a committed relationship for the rest of her life…'

Dodi rubbed her fingers across her forehead and gestured to the seat next to her. 'Do you mind?'

'Not at all. I'm Dee.'

'My name is Dodi. I own this salon.'

Dee peered at her. 'Are you Lily's granddaughter? You look like her!'

Dodi smiled. 'I am. I inherited the store when she died.'

Dee scrunched up her nose. 'I'm so sorry to hear that. Lily fitted me with my wedding dress and she's the reason why I'm celebrating my thirtieth wedding anniversary this year.'

Dodi turned to face her, her attention snagged. She loved hearing stories about her grandmother. 'Really? What did she do?'

'She talked me out of my grand five-hundred- person wedding,' Dee said, her eyes alight with amusement.

Dodi's mouth fell open. 'What?'

'Mmm. I was one of those brides, so caught up with the wedding and the pomp and ceremony, that I didn't think of anything else. Your grandmother sat me down, asked me about my fiancé, what he did, what he liked, his hobbies and his politics. I couldn't answer any of her probing questions about him and it irritated me.

'Then one day my then fiancé's brother gave me a lift to this salon and walked in with me. Your gran asked about him and I could tell her his favourite colour, that he hates olives, that he's allergic to bees and that Faulkner is his favourite author. She let me rattle on about Grant and, without her saying a word, I realised I was marrying the wrong brother.' She winced. 'It took about three years before the family forgave me for ditching one brother for the other. Four years later I returned here to buy dress number two.'

'That's such a lovely story,' Dodi said, conscious of how much she missed Lily. What she wouldn't do right now for one of her hugs.

Dee crossed her legs. 'I spent quite a bit of time here, back in the day. I used to make excuses to come here, to be around Lily. I felt a real connection to her, and I loved listening to her stories, hearing about her life.'

Dodi felt tears gathering in her throat. 'What sort of things did she tell you?' she asked.

'Ah, she'd tell me about her childhood, her friends and how much she loved the store. But the stories I loved best were about Tim, her husband.'

The grandfather she had never met. 'They had a fairy-tale romance. I've seen pictures of him, and he was good-looking, as well. I've always imagined him to be the perfect groom, an absolute Prince Charming,' Dodi said.

Dee widened her eyes. 'Are we talking about the same guy? Because that wasn't how your grandmother saw him.'

Dodi frowned, puzzled. 'Lily adored Tim, she told me that often. They were deeply in love.' She couldn't bear it if the *one* love affair she believed in wasn't true. She wouldn't be able to cope with knowing that!

'Oh, I agree with that, they were in love. But your grandfather wasn't anything like Prince Charming,' Dee explained.

'Really?'

'He was, as Lily often said, the strong but silent type. He found it very difficult to express his emotions and she said that he wasn't good at verbalising his feelings. Tim didn't drop *I love yous*, but Lily had no doubt she was loved, deeply and completely.'

Dodi was fascinated by this insight into her grandmother's life. 'Did she tell you how she knew he loved her?'

Dee smiled. 'I asked her the same question and I'll never forget her answer…she told me that love sometimes speaks in different languages. Someone might not say "I love you" but they might check whether you've eaten, or whether you had a good sleep, offer to help when they see you are struggling. She said that some people's love was spoken through actions, not words.'

Dodi stared at her, a bankload of pennies dropping into her brain. Jago didn't speak of love, had never suggested or hinted that he was in love with her, but his actions spoke a million words. He often checked in to see how she was feeling, allowed her to sleep when she was tired, brought her ginger tea when she was feeling nauseous. He sent his staff to clean her house and do her laundry, trying to lighten her load. He made sure her car was in peak condition, that her tyres were new and that everything was reliable and safe. He'd been insanely worried about her driving in that horrible storm, and he'd rushed out of a crucial, company-defining board meeting to check on her.

His actions spoke of his love…

But he'd tried to rearrange her life and wanted to shove her into a situation without consulting her. She'd been incredibly angry because she'd *told* him she loathed being placed in situations not of her choosing, where she had no control. He'd forged ahead anyway…

But maybe, just maybe, Jago had been terrified by the events of the previous night and he'd been scared, of losing her, losing what they had. It was in his nature to scan his world for things to go wrong and he'd seen the possible consequences of the storm and he'd asked her to take precautions. She'd ignored him, and when his fears came true he reacted by trying to control the situation, by gathering her closer, fuelled by his need to protect her…

Because he'd been petrified of losing her.

Could that be true? Or was she conning herself, desperate to find an excuse to be with him again?

Dee cleared her throat. 'One more thing, Dodi. My daughter isn't a silly bride—'

Dodi winced, excruciatingly embarrassed. 'God, I'm so sorry—'

Dee placed her hand on hers and squeezed. 'I'm not trying to make you feel bad, I just want to explain why your assumption was so very wrong. Courtney has been with Drake for eight years and he stood by and supported her while she underwent a mastectomy and a year of chemotherapy. He made her laugh and held her while she cried. He made her feel beautiful when her hair fell out, before she had reconstructive surgery. And Courts, well, she came face to face with her mortality and she wants to grab life by its neck and live it. But she wants to do it with Drake.'

Dodi felt tears burn her eyes and placed her hand on her chest, as if to stop her heart from climbing out through her ribs. Okay, maybe she did judge her brides far too quickly. And, obviously, erroneously. 'I'm so sorry. I shouldn't have rushed to judgement.'

Dee's smile was soft and full of sweetness. 'Your grandmother loved weddings, but she didn't wear rose-coloured glasses. She knew who would make it and who wouldn't…what it took to be happy,' Dee told her, giving her hand a quick squeeze. 'She was a wise woman, your Lily.'

Dodi nodded, smiled and stood up. 'Thank you for sharing your memories of her with me. It means a lot. And I do hope you visit again, with or without your lovely daughter.'

Her eyes burning, Dodi walked away from Dee, blinking furiously. She turned down the passageway, marked Staff Only, and leaned back against the wall, able to see her busy shop, her consultants, and her excited brides.

Did she hate the shop and her job because she didn't believe in love or was it because she *did* believe in love and she hated the fact that it never stuck around for her? Was she jealous of her brides' happiness and security? Did she actually, somewhere deep down, want to be married, be part of a couple, be wrapped up in another person, in every way possible?

Would she want to be married to Jago?

Hell yes. A thousand times.

So maybe it was time to stop fudging, to tell herself the truth without embellishments, without trying to protect herself. She loved Jago, with every atom of her being, every cell, every breath she took. And she did trust him because he'd shown her, time and time again, that he was there for her, that she was a priority.

She finally understood his love language…

More than anything, she wanted their lives, hearts, bodies and feelings to be tangled up in each other. She wanted to be in love, a bride excited to get married, to be part of a couple, to start a life with someone she adored.

One of her consultants hurried past her and Dodi reached out to stop her. She braked, turned and smiled. 'How can I help, Dodi?'

'There's a bride in changing room number three by the name of Courtney. Her mum's name is Dee.'

Her assistant nodded. 'Dark hair, huge smile?'

Dodi nodded. 'Yeah. She's trying on a Pablo dress, but I don't think she can afford it. She'll probably settle for a cheaper dress in the same style. Sell her Pablo's sample dress, at cost.'

She saw her assistance's confusion, understandable because they never sold the sample dresses, as the brides needed to use them to make their initial choices. She'd just spent a little under forty thousand with Pablo. He could send her another dress in the same style.

Her assistant nodded. 'You're the boss.'

Yes, she was. And this was her business, one that helped make a bride feel beautiful, contributed to a magical start to what was supposed to be a magical life. Oh, it wouldn't be, not every day, but one started as one meant to go on. She wasn't ever going to sell or dispense of Lily's business, so maybe it was time to change her attitude towards it and try to love it instead.

And if she was going to fix her relationship with Love & Enchantment, then she was also going to fix her relationship with Jago. Or, at the very least, she was going to try.

CHAPTER TWELVE

A FEW DAYS LATER, Jago stepped onto the entertainment area at Hadleigh House and saw his twin sitting on the edge of the pool, his feet in the water. They'd returned from a ten-kilometre run a half-hour ago and, like him, Micah had showered and changed into a pair of shorts and a T-shirt.

'Want a beer?' Jago asked.

'Sure.'

Jago took two bottles out of the fridge and walked over to where Micah sat, dropping down to sit next to him, feet in the water. He handed over his beer, placed his bottle on the paving next to him and leaned back on his hands. Night had fallen and he could hear the sound of the cicadas and the frogs. It was a stunning night and he wished he were spending it with Dodi and not his twin. He liked Micah but…

'Thank you for running the board meeting the other night and convincing the board to go along with our plans. That was all you, and I am grateful.' Micah had done a hell of a job and the future direction of Le Roux International, cleaner and greener, was all down to his brother.

Micah tapped the neck of his beer bottle against Jago's. 'I'm not just a pretty face,' he quipped.

He most certainly was not.

'I know you have a lot going on, but have you found a venue yet for Thadie's wedding?' Jago asked, rolling his tense shoulders.

It was still light enough for him to see Micah's wince. 'No. Maybe.'

Jago lifted his eyebrows at Micah's non-answer. His brother was normally more decisive. 'What does that mean?'

'It means that Ella, the event planner I'm working with, might have a lead on a property that could be very suitable, but it isn't currently being used as a wedding venue,' Micah told him.

Jago had a million questions and started to ask the first one that came to mind when Micah held up his hand. 'Not in the mood for the third degree, Jay. You'll know, as soon as I do, as soon as Thadie does, whether it's an option or not.'

His brother looked shattered, Jago realised. Almost as tired as he did. 'Everything okay?'

Micah shrugged and Jago knew, without his saying anything, that things weren't okay, but Micah wasn't ready to talk. Not yet.

But he was. He felt like a volcano ready to erupt and he needed to talk to someone. No, he needed to talk to his brother, his twin, the person who knew him best. But Micah beat him to the punch. 'Can you believe that by this time next year you're going to be a dad?'

He couldn't. But he could. Both at the same time. He took a long sip of his beer, trying to get his erratic pulse under control. 'I can't wrap my head around it, to be honest.'

'You've always said that you didn't want kids, so are you okay with it?'

Very okay. 'I am. Dodi made me realise that I'm not Theo, that I don't have to be the father he was.'

Micah nodded. 'Just do the exact opposite to what he did, and you'll be awesome.'

That was the plan. Jago felt Micah's eyes on his face, could almost hear the wheels turning in his brain. He braced himself for his next question. 'I haven't seen Dodi around lately. Everything okay between you two?'

'No.'

Micah grimaced. 'What happened?'

Jago released a long sigh. 'I messed up. The morning after the storm, I arranged, without talking to her, for her to move in here, with me.'

Micah scratched his chin. 'Sorry, but I'm not seeing the problem here.'

'What you don't know is that Dodi has a deep-seated, understandable hatred of having her life arranged without her input. She was furious that I didn't consult her before sending Jabu over to pack up her stuff. She told me that it would never work between us and basically, dumped me.'

Micah's eyebrows shot up. 'Really?'

No, he was making things up as he went along… 'Yeah, *really*.'

Micah held up a placating hand. 'So your controlling behaviour finally came back to bite you?' he asked, amusement coating his words.

'I'm not controlling…' Jago's words trailed off and he dropped his head. 'Of course I am, but I don't do it to be a jerk. I just wanted what I thought was best for her. I'm crazy in love with her and I genuinely believe that living here, with me, would be the best thing for her and the baby.'

'Did you tell her that?'

'No.'

'So what did you say to her?' Micah asked.

Jago looked away. 'Nothing. I couldn't find the words. I just let her walk away.'

Micah released a low, pained groan and buried his head in his hands. 'Jago, seriously? What is wrong with you?'

'I tried to do the right thing with the best intentions, but it backfired. Maybe it's the wrong time, she's the wrong person. Maybe I'm just really, really bad at this.'

'I only agree with your last statement,' Micah informed him.

Jago shrugged. 'The more it means, the harder it is to say. Dad was a master of words, but he treated people terribly, especially those he was supposed to love. I never wanted to be like him, so I hold my words in, and it's become a habit.'

'What do you want to do, Jago? What do *you* want from *her*?'

Time to get real, he thought. Jago lifted his beer bottle and took a long sip. 'I want the emotional connection, to be able to love her, for her to be my wife in every way, good, bad and ugly. I want to spend my life talking to her, loving her, protecting her and our child, and the other kids I want to have with her!'

His voice was climbing higher and higher, and by the end of his sentence he was practically shouting.

'Don't you think Dodi needs to hear this, not me?'

Micah nudged him with his shoulder. 'Let me put it another way… She can't read your mind, Jago, and even I find it difficult to read your feelings and we rented a womb together! Trust me, she has no idea that you love her. And by not consulting her about moving in, it looks like you don't give a damn about her past and that her feelings aren't valid or important. You are such a useless communicator, twin,' Micah added.

He was. And by not being brave enough to tell her the truth, the whole truth, to be vulnerable, he'd not only hurt her but also disrespected her. And that was utterly unacceptable.

'I need to talk to her,' Jago told Micah, sounding a little stunned.

'I think that's a damn good idea,' Micah replied. Then he lifted his empty beer bottle. 'But before you rush off, can you get me another beer?'

Where are you right now?

Dodi, about to get in her car after dinner at Thadie's house, looked at the message from Jago. She'd been trying to find her courage to contact him for days but kept finding excuses not to. She was tired, she was busy, she wasn't ready.

But what she was, was a complete coward. She was still terrified of love, still scared of making a mistake, of being hurt.

But he'd reached out first. Why?

Dodi's heart lurched when her phone rang and his number popped up on her screen. She'd just been thinking about him…okay, in fairness, she was never *not* thinking about him. Waving at Thadie through the window, she pulled away, her phone tucked between her ear and shoulder.

'Jago?'

'Don't give me a hard time, just tell me where you are,' Jago said. God, he sounded…luscious.

She could argue but she didn't have the energy. 'I'm leaving Thadie's. Why?'

'I was going to ask you if I could come over to your place, but, since you are down the road, it would be quicker if you came here.'

Her heart jumped at the thought. She missed him, wanted to see him, wanted to inhale his amazing scent, lose herself in his eyes and his arms. 'Um…why?'

Jago didn't answer straight away, and when he did his voice sounded rough. 'Because I need to talk to you, and I'd prefer to do it now rather than make a long drive across town to talk to you in forty-five minutes.'

Dodi approached the end of Thadie's drive and hesitated. Left to go home or right to go to Hadleigh House?

'Are you coming or not?' Jago asked, his tone gentle but utterly determined. 'If not, I'll see you at your place.'

Dodi frowned. 'It's that important?'

'Anything to do with you, or us, is important,' Jago quietly told her. 'Please come, Elodie Kate. I can't do another week like this last one, another minute.'

It was the please that did it, the sadness she heard in his voice. 'Okay. I'll be there in a minute or two.'

She heard his relieved sigh. 'The code for the gate is the same. Come in via the side door and I'll be in my apartment waiting for you.'

'Okay.'

A couple of minutes later, Dodi parked her car in its usual spot under the willow tree and, leaving her bag and phone in the car, walked up to the side entrance and tested the handle to the door. It was unlocked, so she stepped into his house and immediately turned to walk up the old servants' passage. Could it only be ten weeks since she'd first walked up these stairs, her hand in his? So much had happened in those few short weeks: she'd fallen pregnant and fallen in love with Jago.

And, strangely, fallen back in…well, not love but like with her little store.

Since her chat with Dee, she'd stopped judging her brides and was actively trying to learn their stories. She was asking them about their lives and the men they were going to marry.

Oh, she still encountered the occasional shallow-as-a-puddle entitled bride-to-be, but most of her clients were normal women, excited, nervous, insecure. Some of them were downright petrified of the massive decision they were making. It was weird but their nervousness and insecurities made her feel calmer, better, more accepting of herself.

Everyone had their issues…they were all human with human fears. As was she.

Reaching the landing, Dodi wiped her sweaty hands on her white shorts and headed for his door. She lifted her hand to knock, but before her fist made contact the door swung open and Jago gripped her wrist and pulled her into the room.

She bumped up against his chest, releasing a tiny squeal of surprise, but before she could say anything he took her mouth in a dazzling, desperate, so-good-to-see-you kiss. Dodi melted against him, wound her arms around his neck and fell into his kiss, her tongue dancing with his.

His arms were where she needed, *wanted* them to be.

It was Jago who broke their kiss, who pulled back and rested his forehead against hers, breathing heavily.

Dodi lifted her hand to her mouth. 'What was that?' she asked, panting.

'That was my way of telling you I miss you, that the last week has been hell, that I can't last a day without having you in my arms.'

Dodi blinked and blinked again, not recognising the need in Jago's voice, the blatant emotion. 'You missed me?' she asked.

'Every minute, every day,' Jago assured her, holding both her hands in his. 'I've been comprehensively useless at work, grumpy as hell and haven't been able to concentrate on anything.'

Dodi tried to process his words as he led her to the sofa and gestured for her to sit. Right, it was obvious that he'd missed her but as what? Did he miss his lover, the sex? Or did he miss *her*? There was a massive gulf between the two.

Dodi perched on the edge of the leather seat and draped one leg over her trembling knee. She forced herself to look at him and ask the question that was burning on her lips. 'Are we talking about you missing the sex we shared, Jago?'

He frowned at her before scratching the underside of his chin. 'Of course I miss the sex. We are brilliant together.'

Dodi's heart sank and she stared down at the carpet, her eyes burning with tears. What an idiot. What had she expected him to say? That he missed her laugh, and smile, missed talking to her?

'That came out wrong,' Jago said on a heavy sigh. He

sat on the seat next to her and shook his head. 'You know, I'm pretty good at words. I can hold conversations, generally get my point across without misunderstandings, but when it comes to you and feelings I'm useless. My words get jumbled and I either say something I don't mean or don't say anything at all…'

'Are we still talking about you missing sex?' Dodi asked, puzzled.

He sighed and shook his head. 'I'll get back to that in a minute, but first…' He shoved his hands into his hair, his eyes filled with emotion. 'I messed up at the hospital. I was tired, scared and emotional. I wanted you with me and I made that happen without taking your feelings or opinion into account. That was wrong of me, and I will never do that again.'

She wanted to believe him, she did. 'Never is a long time, Jago.'

'I promise, Elodie Kate. And I don't make promises easily and often.'

The knots around her heart started to loosen and she took in the first deep breaths for hours, days.

Jago rubbed his hands over his face before dropping them to dangle them between his knees, his face turned to look at her. 'As I was saying earlier about the sex… yes, I miss sleeping with you, but I miss waking up with you more. I miss hearing about your day and your crazy brides, seeing your smile and have been irrationally worried about whether you were eating enough, sleeping, taking your vitamins. I love the sex, Dodi, but I love you more.'

His words were sweet, a balm to her scoured soul. He'd mentioned her smile, was worried about her…wait!

What? Had she heard him correctly?

'Did you just tell me you love me?' Dodi demanded, her voice nearly drowned out by the roaring in her ears. She must've heard wrong. Jago didn't believe in love.

'Of course I love you,' he stated calmly. 'I think I have since the first moment I kissed you in your salon. Maybe even when I kissed you all those years ago.'

Right, she'd fallen down a rabbit hole. 'You don't believe in love, remember?' Dodi told him, scooting away from him and holding out her hands.

'I do when it comes to you.'

Dodi stood up and started to pace the area next to the sofa. She waved her hands in the air. 'I'm feeling a bit overwhelmed here, Jago!'

Jago leaned back into the sofa and placed his bare ankle on his knee. 'Tough,' he gently said, smiling. 'And, at the risk of overwhelming you some more, I don't want a loveless, tidy union with you, I want a messy one.'

'A messy one?' And yes, she really should stop repeating his words.

'I want the fights and the hugs, the laughter and the disagreements. I want the drama love brings, the excitement you bring to my life. I most definitely do not want a quiet life. Not with you.'

'I… What…? You're not making any sense!' Dodi wailed.

'I am and that's what's scaring you,' Jago calmly told her. 'You're scared, just as I am, of being with me, of loving me, of being in a relationship that makes us feel like we're riding a roller coaster. You're scared of being hurt, of trusting another man, another person. Scared that I will disappoint you and hurt you.'

All true, every word.

'I won't, you know. Hurt you or disappear on you or

disappoint you, not in any of the big ways. Oh, I'm going to mess up, of that I am sure, but I will always be in your corner, Elodie Kate. I will always be there, standing by your side, carrying you when you need me to, standing behind you if you don't. I'll be the rock you need.'

Dodi lifted her fist to her mouth, startled to find tears running down her cheeks. 'Don't… Jago, please.'

Jago stood up and walked towards her, his thumb brushing the tears off her cheek. 'Don't what? Love you? Too late for that. Stand behind you? I'm going to do that whether you marry me or not. Even if you can't love me, you're the mother of my child and I'll do anything and everything to give you what you need, including my friendship and protection.'

Dodi looked up at him, his lovely face blurry from her tears. She sniffed. 'You want to marry me?'

'More than anything in the world, sweetheart.'

'But *why*?'

'Because with you I feel like I'm Jago, not the corporate shark or Theo Le Roux's son or Micah's twin. I feel like me. You make me better, lighter, so damn happy.'

She bit down on her bottom lip. 'So, this has nothing to do with the baby?'

He shook his head. 'I'm excited, still a little scared about becoming a father, but right now I'm talking about you and me. And our feelings for each other.' He pulled a face. 'Though so far I've been rambling on, and you've mostly just repeated my words.'

Dodi winced. 'I have, haven't I?'

'Well, here are some words I wish you'd repeat… I love you too, Jago.'

Dodi tipped her head to the side, not fooled by his small smile, the cockiness on his face. His eyes reflected his worry that she didn't love him back. The muscle in his jaw told her how tense he was. He was uncertain, feeling vulnerable, scared of her answer. Seeing this big, bold, tough-as-leather man vulnerable brought home the reality of his words. He did love her, he did want to be with her. He would stand beside her, next to her, he wanted to do life with her.

All he needed was her trust and her assurance that she loved him too.

'I trust you, Jago.'

She saw hope jump into his eyes. 'You do?'

'I do. With my heart and my feelings, with my opinions and my life. Lily was my rock, the one person I trusted implicitly, no questions asked, with every fibre of my being. But I've realised that you show your love through actions. You've shown me that you love me, in so many different ways. I do trust you, Jago, just as I did her.' She saw his Adam's apple bob, saw the hint of moisture in his eyes and, feeling brave, and powerful, and oh-so-feminine, she placed a hand on his heart.

There were more words she needed to say. Good words, strong words. Important words. 'I love your body. I love making love with you. I'm already crazy about our child. But you, Jago, *you* make my heart sing. I look at you and I feel both excited and content, jittery and calm. And I feel love, so much of it. You own my heart, Jago, and I love you.'

Jago's big hand covered her cheek. 'Sweetheart...those words... I didn't think I needed them, and I didn't, not from anyone else but you.'

Dodi's bottom lip wobbled. 'Did you...did you mean it?'

Jago lifted his eyebrows. 'Mean what?' he asked, his eyes dancing with happiness and amusement.

'What you said about wanting to marry me?' Dodi asked in a small voice. Was she pushing too hard again? Asking for too much too quickly?

'Did you want me to mean it?' Jago asked her, his voice suddenly serious.

She looked up at him, doubts swirling. Then she realised that she couldn't keep hiding her feelings, she needed to tell Jago exactly how she felt—he couldn't read her mind. Honesty was always cleaner and led to fewer misunderstandings.

'Yes, I want you to mean it,' she replied. 'Did you?'

He sent her a tender smile. 'Very much so.'

Relief washed over her. 'Good,' she told him, with a huge smile. 'Because I still want a decent proposal—nothing too over-the-top—and a kick-ass ring. And we are getting married in a church, by a priest, Le Roux, and I sure as hell want a honeymoon.'

Jago cupped his hand behind her head and bridged the gap between them. 'Proposal, ring, church wedding, honeymoon… I'm taking mental notes. Anything else, my darling?'

Dodi's hand snuck up and under his shirt, revelling in the feel of his hot skin, his hard muscles. 'Just for you to love me, Jago, every day and in every way.'

'I do, I will, Elodie Kate. That's a promise.'

Jago dropped his head to kiss her, but before he could, Dodi took his hand and placed it on her small bump. 'We're a family, Jago. *Finally.*'

He kissed the corner of her mouth. 'That we are. And you are, and always will be, the centre of our world.'

* * * * *

CINDERELLA IN THE BILLIONAIRE'S CASTLE
Clare Connelly

"You cannot leave."

"Why not?"

"The storm will be here within minutes." As if nature wanted to underscore his point, another bolt of lightning split the sky in two; a crack of thunder followed. "You won't make it down the mountain."

Lucinda's eyes slashed to the gates that led to the castle, and beyond them, the narrow road that had brought her here. Even in the sunshine of the morning, the drive had been somewhat hair raising. She didn't relish the prospect of skiing her way back down to civilization.

She turned to look at him, but that was a mistake, because his chest was at eye height, and she wanted to stare and lose herself in the details she saw there, the story behind his scar, the sculpted nature of his muscles. Compelling was an understatement.

"So what do you suggest?" She asked carefully.

"There's only one option." The words were laced with displeasure. "You'll have to spend the night here."

"Spend the night," she repeated breathily. "Here. With you?"

"Not with me, no. But in my home, yes."

"I'm sure I'll be fine to drive."

"Will you?" Apparently, Thirio saw through her claim. "Then go ahead." He took a step backwards, yet his eyes remained on her face and for some reason, it almost felt to Lucinda as though he were touching her.

Rain began to fall, icy and hard. Lucinda shivered.

"I – you're right," she conceded after a beat. "Are you sure it's no trouble?"

"I didn't say that."

"Maybe the storm will clear quickly."

"Perhaps by morning."

"Perhaps?"

"Who knows?"

The prospect of being marooned in this incredible castle with this man for any longer than one night loomed before her. Anticipation hummed in her veins.